DEEP ROOTS

REALMWEAVER BOOK ONE

VANESSA ROADES

DEEP ROOTS

DEEP ROOTS
Copyright © 2023 Vanessa Roades

All rights reserved. No part of this book may be used or reproduced in any manner whatsoever without written permission of the author, except in the case of brief quotations in critical articles or reviews and certain other non-commercial uses permitted by copyright law.

This book is a work of fiction. Any resemblance to actual persons, living or dead, events, or locales is entirely coincidental.

First paperback edition: June 2023
ISBN-13: 9781739022907
Cover art and design by Shinirikaya

Cypress

DIANTHUS | Summer and Spring
Starmorrow - Cereus
Moonwarden - Kinthe
Former Starmorrow - Ashvaren

HEATHERWOL | Autumn
Sunmirren - Adamantine
Moonwarden - Sigyn
Former Sunmirren - Firewe

SILVERSHALE | Eclipsed
Sunmirren - Vyriseh
Former Moonwarden - Khidell
Former Sunmirren - Saezdrith

THE CRYSTAL GARDENS | Winter
Formerly THE GLASSWOOD
Sunmirren - Scintia
Former Starmorrow - Aurelius

HYACINTHUS | Former kingdom of Spring
Former Sunmirren - Nia

Gods & Goddesses

THE NELAERYN FEY AND ASPECTS

RELYN
Logic, justice, and nature

THE ARCHFEY
Vengeance, protection, and instinct

NELE
Life, birth, and death

THE WOVEN

More gods to be introduced

KARADENZA REALMWEAVER
Creator of humanity, magic, and the universe
Head of the pantheon

THE BLIND ADDER
Goddess of poisons, medicine, surgeons, and assassins
Patron of Ventaris

THE CARRION QUEEN
Goddess of predators and prey

CHIROSCUROI
God/dess of beginnings, endings, and crossroads

EOJHEST
God of night and secrets

FAOWIST
Goddess of day and knowledge

ILHAREL
God of snow and winter storms

THE IRON PHOENIX
Goddess of fire and destruction

MADAINN
God of seas, rivers, and sea monsters

THE MYTHMAKER
God of musicians, artists, and storytellers

PIQUE
Goddess of plants and insects

STAVENTA
Goddess of crafting and invention
Patron of Staventene

Karadenza Realmweaver and her Woven gods took root in a new universe. They kept their names from their far-flung galaxies. This time, old errors would be corrected. Old dreams would be realized.

When they had nearly finished the Tapestry, another goddess arrived, alone, trailing like a star: the Nelaeryn Fey. Despite her frailty, she frightened Karadenza, as Karadenza knew she was powerful beneath her injuries and was fleeing something. She wanted her own corner of the world. That was all.

But gods cannot settle for the small. None know that better than Karadenza, who so often destroyed worlds and left gods behind because they consumed more than they were due. So much power can never share a fragile world.

Mythos, published Age of Illumination 16

1

Eirjatal

Age of Shields 250
Cypress

When he finally reaches the gates of Silvershale, Eirjatal lets himself wonder—only for a moment—if he's been carrying Rhoheme's corpse this whole time.

The wind steals the sound of her breathing, if she's still breathing at all. The icy rain numbs her warmth against his back. Eirjatal's stubbornness in these muddy, dark woods cost them their supplies and precious time. He was determined to bring Rho to Silvershale's steep walls instead of bringing its elves to her.

He couldn't leave her. He doesn't know what creatures may have followed the scent of blood coming off of her and the panic coming off of him.

Silvershale spirals upwards, its trees so bare, white, and distant that it seems caught in a spider web. Lights pop along the tangle of bridges and staircases that make up what he can see of the city when so far beneath it—and when still locked out. Eyes gleam down at him, feline and uncanny.

Silvershale doesn't get visitors. The sharp peal of the wreath of bells over the doors must have shocked every elf inside.

Eirjatal adjusts Rhoheme on his back. Her cheek is pressed against his pointed ear, beneath where their horns interlock with all his shifting and all her slipping. Something too hot to be rain trickles down his neck. The black liquid from her mouth again, Eirjatal supposes, and then vows to not think on it again until he's inside.

"The Nelaeryn Fey is as much my maker as She is yours. Let me in!"

His voice chases itself through the metal trumpets installed up the tower city. Windows slam shut.

Fire spills into Eirjatal's palm, too eager, too easy, thanks to his frustration. The rain extinguishes it with a hiss, but his skin is still hot enough to warm Rho's fingers as he presses them to his chest.

Last thing she said to him was, "Worst plan you've ever had."

The metal doors drag inwards. Their patchwork hinges are beaten into the grey wood of the tilting trees. In his home kingdom, Dianthus, everything is a theatre of honeyed wealth and sentimental artistry, but here it's all practical, even the charmed phrases engraved on the doors. They express good health and fortune, warming the edges of his exhaustion as he passes them.

Perhaps there's also a spell to catch cruel intentions at the door—but most likely not. From what Eirjatal knows, Sunmirren Vyriseh happily meets her enemies when they're fully armed and thinking they've fooled her.

He steps out of the mud, onto the stone. He blinks away the silver rain as a bat swoops down; a woman steps from its silhouette.

"I heard the bells; no need to shout," she drawls.

She stares owlishly at the elves. Her hair's as wet and red as the contents of her wine glass. Her dress clings to her body with the svelte shine of a siren pulling itself onshore, and her tongue laps a trickle of rainwater from where it's settled in the corner of her mouth.

Agitation and anxiety catch up to Eirjatal's heels and sink in their teeth. They make him jump at the gates slamming shut and snap, "Get your Sunmirren."

Her hair sticks to her neck in swirls like veins. "Why did you take Dianthus's little tinkerer so far from home?"

"I can explain later. We have travelled a long way, and time is short." He remembers himself. "*Lady* Radiance."

Radiance continues to stare. Rho continues to die. She must see the bites in Rho's arms, the blood. The black has trickled its burning way to the top of his spine. Her nostrils flare. Rain makes the red in her glass splatter her fingers.

The vampire has more expendable eternity than the elves, and indulges in it as she says, lips pulling back over her fangs, "Shall we pretend you had no hand in this?"

"I didn't."

"Don't bother convincing *me*. There's always some boring drama with you Dianthus elves." She pirouettes and flicks a finger off her glass. "Come."

Eirjatal hesitates. Silvershale is painted so thoroughly by human folklore to look cruel that even he sometimes believes it. But it's one of the four Cypress kingdoms of elves. And it will help them.

Nelaeryn Fey watching, I hope it will.

That said, Silvershale elves are undeniably bizarre. As a vampire, Radiance wears a human body, and yet Eirjatal stands out as much as she does while they walk up the spiraling staircase. He's tanned compared to their sallow grey skin, and his hooked horns are mundane amongst this gallery of oddities: multiple sets of pinprick-light eyes flashing in the dark, tails whipping around corners, and a nude female elf who inspects them from her seat on the railing, fanged abrasions on her body gasping in the rain.

Eirjatal's mud-caked boots slip on the metal stairs; his stomach swoops at the height. Constellations of lanterns hang in improbable places between moonlit blue leaves. Climbing to the castle is like walking into the stars, so bright and silver he can practically feel the light spackle his cheeks.

At the top, Radiance sets her hand on a jagged metal structure and murmurs a phrase. Hand-written script illuminates and opens the door.

It's like a jewelry box inside, dim and velvety, with not so much rooms as short stairwells leading into pits and compartments that fit into what strange space the canopy allows. Bats chirp from channels in the ceiling. Radiance's pets, it seems, as between them hang tangles of fabric and bells.

The glowing queen of Silvershale stands from her table. Radiance takes such a long drink from her glass that her next order comes out breathless. "Put the girl on the sofa."

When Eirjatal sets Rho down, Vyriseh seems about to scratch him behind the ears—but he shouldn't have the time to register how she's looking at him. Eirjatal drops to a knee a moment too late.

Sunmirren Vyriseh's voice is smoky and kind. "Eirjatal Ga'vrynn. Not spending as much time on your knees after Dianthus's new king took you as his favourite, is that your problem?"

Eirjatal has never spoken to Vyriseh beyond briefing her on schedules and ensuring her apartment is to her standards when she visits Dianthus's palace. But he knows how others speak to her.

"Knowing his tastes," he says, "quite a bit more time, actually."

Thankfully, she laughs. "Stand. You already caught me undignified, so what's the difference?"

What are her standards for *undignified*? Her white hair is pulled into a ribbon-streaked bun, and her black gown brings out the yellow facets of her four eyes. He's dripping on her floor. She straightens his coat with two hands (rings inlaid with bristling crystals), swipes the thumb of her third hand across his mouth (lavender-grey skin coming back smeared with black ichor), and uses the fourth to tilt Rho's face towards her.

"Oh, dear. What did you two stumble upon in my forest?"

It wasn't in her forest. It wasn't in her kingdom, nor his, nor their goddess's. Eirjatal chokes on that confession. Rho is the only person he trusts with it.

As Vyriseh crouches next to Rho, he realizes she's wearing an opulent dressing gown. What time of day is it? Silvershale is always dim and blue. He and Rho spent so much time underwater.

Eirjatal hasn't truly *looked* at Rho since dragging her from the river, and even then, panic blurred everything. He'd slammed the water out of her lungs. Gave her air. Then sat back on his heels and felt the tether of black who-knows-what between his mouth and deep in her throat. He'd wiped it on his sleeve and now it's down the back of his neck and he can still taste it and she's still drowning in it. Fire curls to the surface of his skin, but he smothers it in his fists.

"There were bets on when you'd snap. I'm a little disappointed…so bloodless."

First Radiance, now Vyriseh. Elves are famously good at scandals, running the gamut from gory to glamorous, sadistic to salacious. He's been dethroned for the most outrageous display many times in the last two centuries, but Vyriseh is still pinning him with a mean smile.

Vyriseh swipes her finger inside Rho's mouth and it comes out black, ruining her ring. Her extra eyes shut, first with a clear eyelid, like a reptile, and a hum trails from her lips. Magic shimmers through the room. Eirjatal's own sorcery is quiet, controlled by flexing a muscle rather than reciting a spell—it's the same with most types but hers. Whatever spell she's using, she stops it mid-scale.

Vyriseh laughs. "Eirjatal Ga'vrynn. You've given me a corpse. I can't help you."

"You can. I need a way back to Dianthus, whether a carriage or your portal, and some vitaea to close the bites."

"And can you pay for that?"

She watches him unbutton his coat but doesn't offer a hand to receive anything. She's sometimes paid in information, sometimes in memories, sometimes in favours. He pulls out an object and unwraps it for her; the silk is soaked, but the necklace inside is untarnished.

Metal lilies hang from a heavy chain. Sapphire bleeds through needle-thin veins and colours the petals, flush and heavy. It's unabashedly Dianthus.

Sorcerers are rare in the four elf kingdoms of Cypress, and adoration of their work is even rarer. Rho would have raved for *days* about Vyriseh's expression. Emotion wrenches in his chest, simple in its urgency: he has to save Rho so he can tell her.

The Sunmirren clasps on the necklace. The lilies bloom under her stroking fingertips. "Were you always planning to pay me to help you home? And then Rhoheme had a spot of bad luck?"

"Essentially."

Eirjatal has tried to like her smile, *this* smile, the one that knows too much. He has tried to like how she compliments his staff and her generosity to his king. But he's relieved to have Rho between them, even if she can't put up much of a fight.

"What poisoned her came from the *humans'* world, and the humans' gods." Anger flashes in her yellow eyes. "You have how many centuries left, Eirjatal Ga'vrynn? You'll be spending them begging for the Nelaeryn Fey's forgiveness."

At least she doesn't add what truly hurts—their goddess may feel betrayed by Rho, too. The humans' pantheon, the Woven, have always been cruel to Her.

"But...one of their gods can resolve situations like these. A human's god, and a god's humans, and a temple, and all their...oh, it doesn't matter. Dianthus would *never* let you. Unless I underestimate Rhoheme's worth."

Worth? Rho's a part of Dianthus's new court. She rebuilt much of its castle, dismantling its dark legacy and feeding the roots of Dianthus's new start with her magic.

She's saved him more times than she knows. The only reason she's in this situation now is because she tried to save him one last time.

Vyriseh strokes the necklace, counting its value under her fingertips, holding her knowledge between her teeth. She wants an offer.

So much for the Fey forgiving him—he'll need *Rho* to forgive him for this one.

"Anything you want," he says. "If you can save her—"

"It involves a human priestess." Vyriseh's second set of eyes, smaller and flint-sharp, flick open, and he braces. "You won't like it."

"Of course I won't. Humans are bad enough, much less their gods. Name it."

Vyriseh smiles. She extends a hand to him, knuckles turned up for him to kiss. It's the hand with the black ichor coating her ring and smelling of a dark, wicked magic. "Confide in me what you two were *actually* doing in the human realm, and you have yourself a deal."

2

Irving

The sun of Cypress shines, as Faowist bids it.
The nature of Cypress grows, as Pique bids it.
Candles burn, rivers run, as the Iron Phoenix and Madainn bid it.
Too weak to make more than the elves, on the eve of Lightbringing, the
Nelaeryn Fey bargained with the Woven to help Her build our world.
Cypress has been warned.

Moonwarden Kinthe, sermon, Age of Shields 212

Two Weeks Later

In Dianthus, even the cheap seats come with champagne.

Irving Whitfore startles when a waitress passes them a glass, and the waitress seems equally surprised when Irving asks for two.

"Friend stepped out for a minute." Irving aimlessly gestures around themselves, leaning on the balcony. It overlooks the frothy Dianthus palace gardens, made of metal as frail as lace, where the lovebirds go to give Irving and their fellow lurkers few places to settle their eyes.

The *friend* could be any of the noble elves crowded at the palace for the opening night of Lightbringing. Or, considering they've been alone all night, they could simply be finagling for a way to forget the rest of it. Either way, Irving's fantastic at smiling like someone who needn't be questioned.

Well, back home in the human realm they are. Here, they always push their luck.

The elf waitress hovers a hand over another flute on her tray, expression pinched and ruby-encrusted bracelets clicking like dice. She's studying them.

Maybe she's puzzled by Irving being an Autumn elf on an island full of Summer—or she noticed their resemblance to the male elf headlining the event in the gardens below. Maybe it's because they're wearing the only glasses in Cypress.

Most likely the tang of human in their blood. Elves are hounds for that.

Irving flashes her the full force of that no-questions-needed smile.

As soon as she's gone, Irving sets the second flute on the rail. *Is* it champagne? Cypress wouldn't debase itself by getting imports from the human realm, Etreal. They'd probably be too scared to drink it if they did. The distinction gives Irving pause because there's more edge in the Cypress stuff.

...But right now, they need an edge. They throw the flute back. Bubbles fizz up their nose like the fireworks earlier tonight.

Irving's situated themselves so any elves peering up at the balcony only get an eyeful of gas lamp, yet Irving can still see their father in his bone-white robes gliding through the crowds below, every noble drawn into his orbit. Moonwarden Sigyn touches faces, hands, throats, in a trance from the prophecies he's breathing in like the incense fogging up Irving's balcony.

Irving can practically hear Sigyn's low murmur, like he's shushing you before the curtain rises, as he tells elves what the Cypress goddess, the Nelaeryn Fey, gave him of their futures.

Irving tries to blindly set aside their half-empty glass but knocks something on the way. They whip around to see Noah barely miss catching the flute before it catapults overboard.

The glass explodes into a shower of sparkle on a hydrangea-lined pathway. There are a few thrilled screams. Sigyn doesn't even pause. Irving and Noah lunge for the remaining glass—Irving's a split second faster, so they lift it to her and say, "Nelaeryn Fey's blessings for Lightbringing, my intrepid thief."

With theatrical disappointment, Noah scrapes her brown bangs between the short horns curling from her forehead. Her uniform's ruby-dotted cinch and layered ankle skirt out-dress Irving's pressed trousers and suspenders. Gold eyeliner spirals into feather-like designs on the shaved sides of her head, and metal cuffs glimmer around her plump wrists. Way less dramatic than the other faces Irving's seen tonight, but still ridiculous for a servant. She puts down a tray of small wooden boxes (safely on the floor) and, just as easily, shrugs off the attentive servant persona by slouching on the rail.

"Didn't expect you to want to meet *here*. No one gets into the palace gardens unless they work in a castle or a temple. You're not pretending that too, are you?"

"How *dare* you? I'm just a Hawk."

"Autumn spies aren't allowed either, and you know it. Double so for half-humans lying about being them." Noah plucks a room key from her skirt and slides it into their trouser pocket. "You could've lied your way into a better bed than an inn, I bet."

"Suggestions?"

"The Dawn Hall guest wing, where I could serve your room and *this* could be a lot easier." She takes one of the boxes, flicks it open to show the contents, and slips it into the bag at their feet. That tiny Heartswain flower, bloody red as its namesake, eases their tension loads more than the alcohol did.

Heartswain's use is simple. It conjures illusions of the user's desires. The value's simpler—wealthy humans love anything that comes from a romantic Cypress fairy tale.

The rest of Noah's side of their deal is in a trunk in Irving's inn room. Noah nudges a bigger box to them on the rail, and they press a hand over it so it doesn't go tumbling too.

Noah's right, even if she has no idea. They *could* have gotten a palace room, and they *are* here with permission—as Irving Isabren Whitfore, no fake identities. But they didn't want to stay with Sigyn in the Dianthus palace, the Dawn Hall, stumbling through Cypress etiquette while everyone made faces at the smell of human blood.

Irving's childhood as an Autumn palace brat is so distant that even at this party, they don't feel like what they are. The Moonwarden's kid.

But now that they've got Heartswain in hand, their purpose slots into place, the next steps clear: head back to the human city of Staventene, then touch base with the organization who booked their next week. Irving usually sells to estate parties to feed the city's economy of gossip, backstabbing, and hunger for revelry, but *this* exchange's way less certain. It's a private, generously-paying affair whose host's name Irving tried to argue (and peek at a few checkbooks) for. The House of Ciphers keeps their affiliations on a short leash.

Irving already has a portal ticket, a fountain pen made from Staventene gold. They need to get out of here cleanly—even if that requires a chat with their father.

To the bigger wooden box, Irving transfers heavy metal tokens wrapped in scraps of fabric. Noah flicks one open. Inside is a statuette of a woman aflame, her wind-whipped gown strung with chains to hang her off a rifle sling for luck. Revealing it feels like taking out a dagger at a dinner party.

Irving scans the gardens; Sigyn's vanished. "I shouldn't indulge you."

"And I shouldn't indulge Dianthus's heretical morons." The next's a token shaped like fire curling over a snapdragon. "It's what we do. Indulge people who don't know any better. What, are you getting tired of this?"

"No."

"You're what, twenty-four? That's when things start going downhill for the human half of you, right?"

Irving rolls their blue eyes. She'll have centuries more than them, but right now, she can't be much older than they are.

"These weirdos are seriously pushy about getting the Iron Phoenix's attention this year." Noah sets the box on her tray. "And these go for way more than the home crafts they usually make. You should've gotten them blessed in her temple."

"I don't mess with Woven god temples."

"I bet if you tried, the Cypress in you would exorcise itself."

"Don't I wish."

Their next words vanish when they feel a stare on the back of their neck.

Sigyn's scaling the balcony stairwell. His gold clockwork arm steadies him on the rail. For a flash, he's the high priest, gliding under the moonlight to read futures given to him by the Nelaeryn Fey. Then his interested look at Noah is very *oh, you're making friends.*

Irving says to Noah, "You should get back to work." They shoulder their bag.

Noah's gone still. Their father's higher in power than the three queens and one king of Cypress combined, and a mouthpiece for the goddess whose sacred gifts they're planning to sell off like cheap absinthe in the human realm—the realm of her enemies. Parsing Sigyn, their father, from Sigyn, the Moonwarden, is impossible.

Sigyn hovers a few meters away. "May I interrupt?"

Carrion Queen, just shoot me. Befuddlement unfolds on Noah's face. As Dawn Hall palace staff, she's probably never seen Sigyn up close, but she's seen plenty of Irving. They share a lanky, tall silhouette, pin-straight blonde hair, light brown skin smeared with pale marks across their faces and hands.

Before she can suspect her way to their most shameful secret, Irving says, "My turn for a festival prophecy, I guess. Have a good night," and ducks into Sigyn's shadow.

3

Irving

A Moonwarden has such powerful love for Cypress, for they have embraced the Nelaeryn Fey's love for Cypress. But I confess this; we have fear, too, for our maker is often powerfully afraid.

Moonwarden Sigyn, sermon, Age of Shields 196

"Is Staventene going to catch another plague? Or will the portal malfunction and tear me up on the way back to Etreal?" Irving asks while following Sigyn through the labyrinthine gardens, leaving the party behind. It's getting louder and lewder; Irving wonders if Sigyn extricated Irving in a rare moment of paternal instinct. "If it's about a bike accident, that already happened twice, so I can handle a third."

Sigyn seems confused, like he isn't the one who can tap into the future like it's a radio station. He's always a few steps away from the *now*.

Irving adds, "The automobiles. They're harder to drive than we thought."

Irving's joking, anyways; they paid three months' rent for an Etreal sorcerer's charm to keep their father from scrying on them.

"I only want to show you something."

Stray elves caught in private business or flirtation taper off (or scurry away with awkward gestures of respect at Sigyn). Dianthus's personal legends top the walls in fine metal latticework, studded with gems the same colour as the sea on the other side of the palace. The air's thick with the powdery smell of more flowers than is reasonable, filling in the lattice to muffle music and conversation.

The Dawn Hall's luxurious grounds are a mystery, but Irving's spent plenty of time in Dianthus's city. Usually making Noah travel to the city for their trades is a huge risk for her, especially since Dianthus used to put the rest of Cypress on edge with how hard they cracked down on any insult to the Nelaeryn Fey.

Dianthus switched kings five years ago, the same time Irving jumped ship for Etreal. Irving doubts things have loosened up. Cypress never wants to change, no matter how bloody or unreasonable it is. Same with the Fey.

Even thinking that around Sigyn feels risky.

Sigyn finds his destination in the twisting paths without any turnarounds. It's a secluded little grove with a low pool. The peonies surrounding it aren't the usual pastel rainbows; they're porcelain blue, inspecting the water with cocked heads, and Irving swears they're emitting light. The white walls of the pool are sculpted with moon phases. Mirrors spiral out from the center of the water, in metal frames so delicate that Irving at first thinks they're hovering.

Sigyn sits on the pool wall, white robes falling without a wrinkle, a gesture like a sigh. Irving scuffs their shin on the way down. Despite that, they sometimes wonder if it's *Sigyn* that the humans in Etreal see when they look at Irving. The elves see nothing but the human, and the humans see nothing but the fairy tale.

Great for work, at least.

Sigyn says, "This was made by Rhoheme Ges'ill, a Staventa sorceress."

So she's able to breathe life and unfathomable detail into metal, like the goddess herself. Elves with magic from the human Woven gods are so rare (and, consequently, infamous) that Irving has heard her name, but they've never met her.

Irving leans over the pool. The water's velvety black despite the full moon and glowing flowers. With his metal hand, Sigyn tilts the tiny mirrors at the base of the structure, and there's a hum at the connection, like fuzzy music playing in another room.

It's the sound of a particular sorcerer's magical signature meeting its twin. A stupid loneliness stretches awake in Irving. This Rhoheme elf made Sigyn's clockwork arm. Another person who knows why he needed it when Irving doesn't, another part of Sigyn's nearly three centuries of life that Irving doesn't get to learn about.

The mirrors adjust themselves until the top mirror fills with the reflection of the moon. Then, pale and touchable as honey, the reflection drips down the structure, mirrors tipping with its weight. Light draws through cracks on their faces to make illustrations.

A town with white constellations raining on it. Monsters crawling from the light. And two figures traveling to a castle of moonlight to save it all. An elf and a human woman, though the figures are too tiny to reveal *that* detail.

It's a real story, polished into a fable.

They used to love when Sigyn told them this story.

"This is you and mom."

"It was commissioned by Heatherwol as a gift for your mother. When Penelope left, Rhoheme and I supposed it would suit here. The new Starmorrow has a love of whimsy."

What Sigyn means, Irving guesses, is Heatherwol's *queen* commissioned it. Adamantine was always nice to their mother, even when she decided that Sigyn's family was better off as the Autumn castle's secret.

"Twenty-six years isn't long to make a new folktale, Sigyn. That's got to be breaking your record."

Sigyn understands Irving enough (barely, but enough) to know they're teasing, and also to know they're far from it when they add, "Lots about stars, not so much about humans."

"This is not meant to dismiss the difficulty of finding a place in Cypress, but to remind you there *is* one."

The sentiment drops in Irving's chest like Staventa's forging hammer. "I guess we were due an argument."

Something fades behind Sigyn's eyes, like he's assessing all the possible ends to the conversation. Too bad that anti-scry charm means he can't cheat anymore.

Irving gets ahead of him, gesturing at the mirrors. "We don't belong in Cypress myths, Sigyn. We're living people even if Cypress forgets it all the time." They hesitate. "All three of us are."

"Return to Heatherwol. Or elsewhere in Cypress, if you need your space, but you both must make plans to stay very soon."

Irving's about to retort about their life and their mother's career being built in Staventene, but—*must*? "Will mom be okay?"

"Penelope is fine."

"*You* using the present tense isn't any comfort. I know you like to keep your visions secret because of human gods eavesdropping or whatever, but you can at least tell me what this is about."

Irving waits for an answer, but Sigyn's gone three years without explaining how he lost half his arm and who knows what else.

The moonlight has reached the final mirror, one no bigger than a pocket watch. Sigyn and Penelope's story ends, impossibly, with a marriage that's still nauseatingly romantic despite the distance and visits where Penelope packs rowan charms to keep Cypress from enchanting her. Elves can't do that, but Etreal superstition dies hard.

"I am," Sigyn says, not looking at Irving or the pool or anything *here* and *now,* "uncertain of what these next few months will make of me. I would rather you near, while I know myself. Not for forever, but for long enough."

"Just say 'oh, cryptic shit' next time." Irving removes their glasses and rubs the sweat from Dianthus's sweltering night off their nose. He's only interested in them if it's about something catastrophic.

"I saved your life once by foreseeing it." Sigyn's tone has a brittle edge. "Do not doubt me."

Case in point. Irving queues up an excuse, but it evaporates when Sigyn flinches and clutches at his metal arm.

The clockwork seizes with a series of grinding clatters. The glow behind the sapphire panels gutters out, and the pool's mirrors tilt too quickly. Their light hangs in the air like thrown flour.

A second later, it's over. Sigyn smooths the tension from his mouth and relaxes the offending clockwork in his lap. The light patters into the pool like rain.

Sigyn glides through every movement, never doing anything as abrupt as even a sneeze. Seeing him flinch almost made him seem real.

"It's due for repairs." Lie—Irving doesn't need a Moonwarden's foresight to see that. "Will you speak to Penelope?"

"She'll listen to *you* more than she'll listen to me."

"Not about this."

"Fine, I'll tell her." They're not going to tell her. "I need to get back to my hotel and pack." Irving stands. "And don't use saving my life against me. It's weird."

"May I walk you?"

"You don't want to go back to the party?"

"Cereus and his inner circle," Sigyn says as he gets up, "celebrate Lightbringing like elves a third my age."

Irving snorts. "I can't imagine spending the summer here."

As Sigyn leads them out of the labyrinth, Irving's head is noisy with things unsaid. Sigyn's the longest-serving Moonwarden in a millennia, and that comes with a responsibility that kept him away from his family, and a belief in his own untouchable power that had him making that family in the first place. Being half-elf means being born into a cosmic custody battle between two jealous goddesses—the Nelaeryn Fey and Karadenza, the head deity of the Woven—but simultaneously being hated by them both. How Sigyn squares that with his lifetime devotion to the Fey is another mystery.

Half-elves come from the intoxicated dalliances in Etreal songs that make Irving's pointed ears burn. Not fantastical adventures to save Etreal towns from falling stars. If history didn't prove that to Sigyn and Penelope, then the elves who tried to kill her certainly did.

When they part, Sigyn says, "Please speak to your mother. I ask you to believe in me, though I know that is arrogant. Believe in how I constantly fail you, I suppose. In the power that keeps us apart. I think I am going to ruin something and I cannot have either of you suffer for it."

Irving can smuggle Heartswain out of Cypress for years, they can mingle with Etreal gentry, but they can't spit out a reply before their ancient father touches their shoulder in the same vacant way he did to the strangers in the garden, and turns up the street into a slat of moonlight.

Whenever Irving comes to Cypress, they're carrying some combo of three lives in their jacket.

The first is an Etreal ID card for Irving Whitfore. That human family name carries them out of the Etreal station and safely back to their Staventene apartment. They belong, against all odds.

The second is the Hawk. No name, only a wristwatch enchanted by a Mythmaker sorcerer to create the Heatherwol spy faction's tattoo. Used when Irving wants to slide from Staventene to Dianthus for Noah without Sigyn being told. Which is most of the time. Elves who aren't Hawks can never enter Etreal.

And the third's a formality. The identification is for Irving Isabren Whitfore Aphithea, embossed with a gold Heatherwol crest to approve their movements between realms. Penelope wanted it. Sigyn could make it happen. It made Adamantine nervous, because they're all better off if no one in Cypress knows Irving exists.

Which suits Irving fine—especially when they're moving a trunk full of Heartswain.

They lean their head back against the portal station wall, enchanted watch clipped on, Derby shoes on the trunk, flipping the fountain pen ticket to Staventene between their fingers. They're accompanied by the distant revelry, singing wildlife, and the station master in terse conversation with two elves (one's insistent on involving herself even if she's drunk). Every so often Irving checks on the small box with the single bloom in their bag.

Heartswain batches are nastily sensitive and codependent; they all react if something bad happens to only one of them. Heartswain manifests your deepest desires, but those dreams twist into something vicious at the first sign of fear.

The elf with a goblet of wine in her hand is watching Irving. She's leaning on a male, who's holding her up by the waist. Her black bangs part over short horns, and her dress is a tangle of gauzy layers like a butterfly fresh out of its cocoon. Not their style, but they're still envious of the very Cypresian skill it took to make that. Irving lifts a few fingers off their bag in half a wave.

"As a warning, tourists may have heard that Dianthus is into day drinking," the male says, right as the female slides out of his grip. He grabs her belt, but when she smacks him off he drops further into his conversation with the station master.

She heads straight for Irving. "You're not *leaving*, are you?"

Irving relaxes into the performative confidence that carries them through Etreal and closes their bag on the Heartswain. "Lightbringing isn't my thing. It'd definitely be no more fun with me there."

"Oh, I wouldn't be so sure. I'm Tavreah." She tips her head to the male with the station master. "We manage the Dawn Hall's staff. Eirjatal won't admit it, but we can always use more help. Why not? Meet some crown jewels, listen to some gossip?"

Their House of Ciphers job in Staventene already has them booked to eavesdrop. "Sorry. I'm not any good at pouring drinks."

"Please. I run the Dahlias of the palace." At Irving's blank expression, she supplies, "Whores. And the smell of that blood of yours…makes elves feel like hunters, you know that?"

Pushing off the desk, Eirjatal warns, "Tavreah."

Tavreah darts towards Irving as if to avoid him, but her skirt snags on Irving's trunk. She pitches forwards; Irving catches her around the shoulders, getting wine on their shirt for their trouble.

Once Eirjatal's heaved Tavreah off, she's helplessly giggling through an apology. His straight auburn hair is nearly to his waist like Sigyn's, so they must be around the same age. His horns curl forward from the base of his skull like a laurel crown, casting shadows over green eyes that look as if he hasn't slept in days, and a stern face that says he'd fight sleep off if it approached at an inconvenient time.

"Apologies for my partner," Eirjatal says. "We have manners to work on."

"No problem. Really. This is *exactly* why I'm leaving."

Irving unsticks their wine-soaked shirt from their chest. They're about to insist Tavreah and Eirjatal not mind them, when the weight of Eirjatal's stare settles on their bag.

Black smoke is curling out like a calligraphy swirl. The Heartswain. Soured by the wine that's spattered on the undone clasp of the bag and must be drenching the inside.

They shrug the bag behind their shoulder. Bitter dread hits the back of their mouth. The Heartswain's magic sniffs out an old fear on the closest person, embroidering dull pain in Irving's side—in the scarred space where one of their ribs should be.

Then black smoke shoots from the trunk of Heartswain to the ceiling. Tavreah screams as it expands into something as wide as the ceiling, something disjointed like a poorly-strung marionette, reeking like carrion and seawater. It drags itself over the hanging lights with insectile legs, bearing down on them—it's real enough to cast a shadow.

A gust of flame throws the trunk into the wall.

The fire sucks back into Eirjatal's hand with an audible hiss. He looks nearly as shaken as Irving feels when he walks over to the trunk and kicks its burnt side so hard his foot goes through. Bloody-red Heartswain spills all over the floor.

4

Irving

Heartswain revealed to Relyn the first elves' deepest desires, so She might know that, in this realm so precarious, we would not draw the eye nor ire of the gods who hated Her.
We follow Her laws to protect Her. To disobey is to doom Her.
There is always a piece of us planted in Cypress. There is always Heartswain ready to betray us as our ambition grows.

Moonwarden Khidell, sermon, Age of Shields 164

Irving's lucky, all things considered.

They're lucky there's no longer a war between the humans' gods, pressuring Cypress to act on its worst instincts. They're lucky they could live in Staventene for school, work, sanity. They're luckiest of all that Sigyn can have anything he wants, order around anyone he wants, *save* anyone he wants, as an added bonus for bleeding divinity.

All that luck weighs on Irving as they wait for the king's justice, hoping that Sigyn never, *ever* hears about this.

Tavreah, as hilarious as she found the situation, isn't here. Instead, a priestess takes post in the corner of the gazebo and Eirjatal goes through their things. Irving valiantly keeps their mouth shut.

Who knew it'd be Cypress that arrested them? Staventene has so much more to lose. Irving can use all the euphemisms they want, but Heartswain's a tool to gather secrets and weak points for rivalries among Staventene's elite. The interview with the society they're supposed to meet in an hour, the House of Ciphers, had felt like its own court proceeding.

But Irving would rather Staventene's laws. Noah assumes Irving is born and bred in Etreal for more reasons than their tidy accent. Human blood, no matter how small the sliver, doesn't easily escape Cypress.

Moths cloud around the gas lamps and lizards crawl over Irving's shoes. Eirjatal picks up a wristwatch from the pile. He reads aloud the tiny, senseless poem engraved on the back. As he puts it on and his reading activates the spell, Irving can't squash a cringe. A tattoo of a hawk talon appears inside his elbow, peeking over his metal bracer. He shoots Irving a taut smile before snapping the watch off. The tattoo gives way to tan skin and he places the watch on the low table between Irving's chair and a green divan.

"Sorcerer back home wrote that for you, I suppose?"

Of course they did. Cypress doesn't handle sorcery well. Because magic's given by Etreal's gods, Cypress sees those bloodlines as tainted. The elves used to blind and banish any they could get their hands on (Irving figures they'd have done worse if the Fey didn't get so bent out of shape by elves killing each other). And yet here's Eirjatal with the Iron Phoenix's fire magic and Rhoheme's work is in the Dawn Hall grounds.

"Or maybe it was you and this all gets more complicated. Mythmaker sorcery is notoriously slippery." Eirjatal gestures at the priestess. "Check, could you?"

She pulls a tiny blade from her half-moon hairpiece. It's metal with a delicate glass core. Irving jolts when the priestess slices their palm—in concert with two figures entering the gazebo.

The new Summer Starmorrow is laughing at something the elf behind him said like they've stumbled into a party, not a courtroom. Gold jewelry trails off Cereus's tunic and antelope horns, and his lean muscle and tousled black hair turn up the volume on his proud, musical swagger. He fixes his amused dark eyes on Irving as his companion comes up beside him.

Irving's blood slides into the glass core of the knife, but they hardly feel the sting. Any excuses, half-truths, and misdirections fade as they recognize the female with Starmorrow Cereus.

Sunmirren Vyriseh's the kind of gorgeous you want trapped in paintings and stories, something to admire but unable to see you in return. Her skin's gray-lavender of pressed lilacs. One pair of arms is draped in loops of white fabric, the other glittering with jewels like fine armour.

The priestess releases Irving's wrist. Speaking of Mythmaker sorcery—story goes that decades ago, Vyriseh sang an Etreal town into destroying itself.

Shit. They didn't expect *this* audience.

Vyriseh slides onto a bench. She pulls off her high heels and sets them beside her. She used to visit Heatherwol to talk business with Sigyn, but their mother always tucked Irving away.

"You've got good timing." Cereus relaxes into the low divan across the table from Irving, throwing an arm over its back. "I've been praised all night, I'm a *bit* drunk, and the rest of the night's booked with things way more interesting than this. So what did you almost get away with?"

Eirjatal says, "The staff I sent would have told you."

Vyriseh clicks her tongue. "Eirjatal assumes you've been ignoring him, Cereus. Your pet's terribly brash."

"I need a refresher," Cereus says, pushing his black waves between his horns. Then, like something's occurred to him, he snaps his fingers. "Half-human."

Annoyance twists in Irving's chest. Cereus clarifies, "You smell different. Kind of...earthy, like you're already rotting in that direction. You know that?"

"I bet the glasses tipped you off too."

Cereus grins back. His bottom canines are sharp and a touch too long.

While Eirjatal gives the abridged story, the priestess angles the blade into the gas lamp light. The glass throws beads of blood-stained colour across the floor and Cereus's face, whose veneer of drink and pleasure fades as Eirjatal goes on. Irving braces for the worst but their blood shines red and clean and normal.

Free of magic. Still takes them off-guard.

If they'd been here only a few years ago, the response would've been different—but back then, they didn't have the guts to steal from Cypress anyways.

Vyriseh is fixing her white hair. "I think exceptional thievery is worth congratulating."

Eirjatal says dryly, "I'm sure they were congratulated plenty in Staventene." He hands the watch to Cereus, who slips it on. Cereus seems genuinely rocked by the symbol that appears on his skin. He barks a bright laugh then tosses it to Vyriseh; one arm darts out to snatch it while the other three fuss with her bun.

Their casual manners put Irving on edge. Under the previous Starmorrow, Dianthus wasn't exactly known for due process. Maybe to Cereus, that means disinterested cruelty. Irving *can't* be convicted here. Cypress has one fear at the core of every rash decision: human ears hear the Fey's secrets and human mouths spill them to the Woven.

Irving *is* ferrying secrets, that's the stupidest part. But they're secrets that'll make Etreal debutantes eat each other for petty nonsense. Nothing Cypress has to worry about.

"So, what was the plan?" Cereus leans back. His tunic falls open over his chest, the thin gold chains clattering. "Honestly, this is the first time I've gotten to sit in *days*, so chew on your answer all you want. I've got Vyriseh around if I think you're lying."

Sigyn's untouchable. He'll make you untouchable, too, if you admit who you are. He could help Noah—

Or you can.

Irving says, "I sell Heartswain in Etreal."

Cereus furrows his brows, wrinkling his red eyeliner. "That's legal?"

"No." They let their nerves leak into their voice. "If this comes out, I'll be in their courts next."

"Who buys it?"

Vyriseh grins. "Who can *afford* it, I think, is the question the half-human cares about."

They risk eye contact with Cereus. "People whose secrets are made of money."

"They'll hate you if this gets out, huh?"

"I bet."

Eirjatal catches on. "You're being tried *here,* Whitfore. Heartswain is Dianthus's responsibility given by the Fey, and so it's Dianthus's responsibility to handle you."

"*I'm* not the Fey's," Irving says, sharper than planned. "So I don't think you want to tidy Etreal's mess for them."

"You betrayed part of the Nelaeryn Fey to the humans, a reality that, I'm sure, inspires no shame in you. Etreal wouldn't understand what you deserve for that *mess*." Eirjatal sets a graceful hand on the arm of Irving's chair and steps into their field of vision. The lamps paint the shadow of his horns over his eyes, and his voice is as controlled as a scalpel. "Your mind and your blood may belong to the Woven gods, but your fate belongs to us."

"It's the least we can do for you," Vyriseh chimes in. "We can claim you when the Nelaeryn Fey won't. She *especially* won't after this."

Cold crawls up the back of Irving's neck. It's an easy jab to give a half-elf, only made rusted and jagged from frequent use. *The Fey—none of her aspects, not Relyn or Nele or the Archfey—doesn't want you.*

"It's a *plant*," Irving argues. Eirjatal is still boxing them in. "And Etreal doesn't give half as much of a shit about Cypress as you think it does. The Woven are too busy messing with each other to take down the Fey, and if they wanted to, do you really think Cypress would still be here?"

Cereus sighs. "Please, don't get mouthy."

As edgy as Irving feels, they have the room where they want it. They pitched to Noah, *I'm the one with Etreal written all over me. They always want revenge on Etreal. They'll never trace it back to you.*

And what does revenge on Etreal mean under this new Starmorrow?

The king himself doesn't seem worried. "I've got a holiday to get back to."

"You aren't done here," Eirjatal snaps.

"But someone," Cereus says, propping his head on his hand, "agreed to dance with me."

Eirjatal shuts his eyes in exasperation before he straightens up. "You're a Starmorrow and quite flirtatious at that. I'm sure that list is very long, My Light."

"And I always keep you at the top, Eirj."

Vyriseh's gaze alights on Irving and her head tilts. "Surely you have *something* in your defence."

"Should I start before or after all the evidence was found in my luggage?"

Vyriseh laughs, the sound rough but musical. "Did you have help?"

Irving tries to channel the feeling of confidence that they wield against humans during the exact exchanges that are on trial. They'd managed a version of it when dealing with the House of Ciphers. *They're* the one made from a world that Etreal only knows from fairy tales and raw superstition. They're the one that runs the show.

They could get Noah dragged in—or pulled out.

"No."

"Thievery is not an easy task. The palace gardens do not have walls easily scalable or locks easily picked."

"I said no."

Eirjatal says, "I have no interest in teasing out information. Search them, Vyriseh."

Vyriseh gasps a curling Cypresian curse. "Cereus! Now he's ordering *me* about. How long of a leash do you give him?"

"Pretend it was my idea." But something's killed the king's casual ease.

"Oh, is this all I'm good for?" she sighs. When she gets to her feet, Irving realizes what Eirjatal means with cold shock.

Vyriseh kneels in front of them. She presses a hand to Irving's jaw, the other to their temple, and the others daintily hold a necklace of sapphire lilies against her chest. Her smaller set of eyes flick open. They're entirely yellow, without whites or pupils.

Vyriseh whispers through a smile, "You betrayed Her, even in your petty way, half-blood. Before, Dianthus's king would cut out your eyes and tongue and leave you to the mercy of the Etreal wilds."

Those are apparently her parting words, because next, she hums something soft and papery, the sound that moth wings look like they should make. Irving braces.

Even if they didn't expect Cypress to do it, getting caught wasn't a surprise. Every time they try to force something under their control in their life, they go too far.

But besides that—it's one thing to take advantage of Etreal's fascination with them, of being seen as less a person and more a dark enchanted night in a story. It's another to know that *Cypress* knows. That sick satisfaction must be the last emotion Vyriseh gets a taste of before her magic empties their mind entirely.

Her magic is the cold, exposed discomfort of an empty room. The gazebo, their own body, their emotions, are stripped down into objects, small and easy to examine. She sorts through them like they're a deck of cards.

Irving dully watches the suits slip by, one by one by one.

After some dreamy, liquidy amount of time, Vyriseh steps out of their head and everything floods back in—the end of that bitter, smoky curl of satisfaction at Cypress knowing what they did. The lamplight, the stinging cut in their hand, the heavily perfumed air sipped into lungs made shallow by anxiety. The aborted alarm of Vyriseh knowing everything, literally as easy as a song. Irving takes a breath for some defence of Noah—

Sigyn. She knows about Sigyn.

With bizarre affection, she brushes her thumb up the smear of pale skin between their eyebrows as she stands. "No one else of concern to us was involved."

Irving fights not to balk. Eirjatal raises an eyebrow at Vyriseh. "You're saying it ends here."

"Yes. Now!" Vyriseh lifts herself backwards onto the frame of Cereus's divan, crossing her bare ankles. "What to do, what to do? Dianthus must protect Heartswain, and here you are, outsmarted by a half-blood of all things." She sends a manic smile to Irving; she knows their opinion on exactly that.

She sets a hand on Cereus's shoulder. He glances at it, then unfolds himself from the divan. Irving lifts their chin, finding it easier to appear unaffected. If Vyriseh's going to keep quiet, then Noah's safe and Sigyn can be happily ignorant.

Hopefully.

Cereus asks, "Do you know many myths?"

Too many, after growing up with a Moonwarden for a father. "Not really."

"But enough to know that the Nelaeryn Fey's endured enough humans and gods taking things from Her. And what She's done about it." Cereus's voice goes oddly soft. "Blinding, you know. We're supposed to take something *that* important from you."

"If I could interject," Eirjatal says smoothly. "Rhoheme needs the help."

Cereus scans Irving like it was them who made the suggestion. "That'll ruin them."

"By our metrics, they're already ruined." As if he's heard a joke he doesn't find very funny, Eirjatal gives a dry smile. "If you don't feel comfortable returning them to Etreal, then remember that we have few uses for a half-blood, but even fewer for a half-blood blinded."

Cereus glances at Vyriseh, who nods. Cereus *is* the youngest of the four Cypress rulers, so maybe Vyriseh's mentoring him. That doesn't make Irving feel better about her knowing *everything.*

Cereus steps away. "Give them to Rhoheme, then."

The female who made the mirror statue and Sigyn's arm? Feeling unmoored, Irving begins to ask what this is about, but Vyriseh adds with a wink like she and Irving share a secret, "Oh, it'll suit you. Let's wrap this with a bow, shall we?" She pointedly taps a spot on her shoulder.

The spot mirrored on Cereus bears the metal clasp of his tunic. It's engraved with a curling peacock feather, raining sea water and shells. The previous king's was a mad-eyed eel.

Cereus ruffles his black hair. His smile's back on, but it's fitting all wrong. "I've got to get back. This wasted enough time."

"I'd rather your involvement," Eirjatal says.

"For what? You're the one with fire."

"Oh, do it for a dance, My Light."

Cereus's playful grin is apparently not an indication of him giving in, because Eirjatal huffs and unstraps one of his bracers. It bears the same metal sigil as Cereus's clasp, small enough to fit in his palm. When Cereus turns to the exit, Vyriseh catches him with a hand to the chest—hard enough that the impact's audible.

Irving eyes the metal, fighting not to squirm. A tendon lifts against Eirjatal's inner wrist. He sets his palm to the metal. The edges glow a vibrant red. "Drop your shirt down your back."

On instinct, Irving flicks their gaze to Vyriseh's. She's folded two arms on Cereus's shoulder, her chin propped atop them, patient and pleased as if she's watching someone unwrap an exceptionally genius gift she bought them. Why did she lie for them? Better question—why do they wait for her nod, her twirl of a finger, before standing and turning around?

Vyriseh says, "You've disobeyed Cypress, Irving Whitfore. If you return to the humans, we'd be remiss to let them think you got away with it completely."

Better you than Noah, they think, and swiftly after, *Sigyn could've handled it all himself.*

Irving takes a deep breath. They face the wall and unbutton half their shirt, then shrug it down their back; it'd be more humiliating if Cypress had even a whisper of modesty.

Eirjatal moves Irving's blonde hair in front of their shoulder. They lock their teeth together. Sharp heat radiates off the metal.

"You're going easy on me."

Eirjatal says, "Be thankful for what you are. If neither realm have any claim to you, then you have no loyalty to exploit." And he presses the burning metal between their shoulder blades.

5

Irving

The staff hate me or are so wary that their comportment only comes across that way, but I dislike proving that I am gentle.
I cannot imagine what it was like, locked in this palace with Ashvaren. Perhaps they find it as frightening to now be locked with his enemy.

Eirjatal Ga'vrynn to Sunmirren Adamantine, report, Age of Shields 245

"I know you're Sigyn's," Eirjatal admits out of nowhere.

A stab of alarm stops Irving on the stairs. Did he figure that out before or after he branded them like livestock?

Either way, he held onto it for all the time it took to go up six dizzying, suspended metal stairwells to the locked door they'll be spending their days in, to give Irving the key (with a butterfly wing bow, of course), and to instruct them to lock their way in and out and tell nobody what goes on in there.

Showing admirable restraint, Irving asks, "How?"

"Sigyn and I were close from before the Nelaeryn Fey called him. He let me see you as a child. Had you called for Sigyn's help, well." Eirjatal exhales sharply, some imitation of a laugh. "He can make a hurricane politely turn tail. The fact that you didn't tells me that you might have some honour."

Irving isn't sure what to make of Eirjatal knowing their father before he was a Moonwarden—and the resentful sting that comes with it—but they forge on. "I was caught. I'm not going to cheat my way out of a shitty hand once it's on the table."

"I won't tell anyone. You're aware I know, and that's all I need."

For what, leverage?

Then Eirjatal hesitates. It seems wrong, like a dragon mincing around a mouse trap. "Your arrest was about principle and divine ego. Your sentence is…the way you use the word, it's more *human* than that, do you understand?"

More human. More basic and vulnerable.

"What put you here does not make you a bad person. So I trust you to behave."

Irving fidgets. Their shirt unsticks from the seared skin between their shoulder blades. "If I'm so honourable, why not tell me straight away what's in that room?"

Eirjatal turns down the stairs. Irving follows through the elaborate shadows that the moonlight paints through the open lattice walls, dodging moths and one hungry chameleon. Irving thinks that's it, until Eirjatal shoots over his shoulder, "It's an infirmary. And her name is Johana."

Unhelpful. Mostly.

That's not a Cypresian name.

"The Autumn nobility stays on the fifth floor," Eirjatal adds. "Mind it."

Eirjatal drops Irving off at the staff building in a way that couldn't be less like how their mother left them at their first apartment in Staventene: abrupt, frigid as the Glasswood, and without giving Irving's question about their missing luggage more of an answer than, "You have a uniform now."

It's so late at night that Irving isn't sure if it's a stress or exhaustion headache raking its claws through their brain. But the common room's still alive and noisy.

A dozen staff members trade food and shots off serving trays Irving recognizes from the garden party, lounging in jewel-studded uniforms like they're pyjamas. The furniture's woods and metals are carved with the old Starmorrow's eel or other symbols from past rulers, but no matter the time they came from, they all make Irving feel young and confused and entirely out of place. In Etreal, twenty-four is when your adult life is picking up steam, but here, it's too young to have anything useful to say, and too old to bother worrying about.

Someone asks, "New hire?"

Irving starts to answer, but a familiar voice barrels over them. "New hire, my ass. Irving!"

Noah has hustled in from what must be an attached kitchen considering the tray of food she drops with a crash by a game board. Relief washes over Irving—even if Noah's greeting is a punch to their shoulder.

"I missed you," they breathe.

"You're delirious. What happened? Eirjatal called down for us to prepare a room, but I—why *you*? Are you cutting me out?"

From the sofa, a Summer female asks, "Mind introducing us?"

"Mara, you get your room back. They're moving in with me."

Irving lets Noah pull them by the wrist. She's the smallest familiar thing, but right now, that feels incredibly valuable.

That relief's stalled by the same elf—Mara—gasping, "What in all the Amber Crawl ripped you up?"

Noah spins them around. She swears. "You're bleeding."

"It's a burn," Irving says. "Palace's brand." They touch their collar; the fabric's stiff.

"Eirjatal?" Noah asks.

"Eirjatal."

"*Eirjatal?*" Mara exclaims.

"Then what did you do?" someone else asks.

"And what's it say about us that you're staying *here?*"

Eirjatal made the whole deal with Rhoheme sound so grim and secret, and Irving knows a little about keeping secrets. But the burn feels like the Carrion Queen's shot an arrow into their spine, *and* they're a little pissed that their only shirt is bloody, so they snap, "I'm stuck every day in some infirmary on the seventh floor. That's my sentence. Can anyone give a straight answer on what that's about?"

The staff trade confused glances over their gold wine and frothy pastries. Finally, Mara says, "There's no infirmary on the seventh floor."

"Come on." Noah steers them to the back of the hall. Like a well-paced script, when they're far enough away, Irving catches whispers from the staff that amount, more or less, to *half-human.*

Noah ushers a bristling Irving into one of the rooms and shuts the door. It's a double dorm like Irving had when they attended university in Staventene—their skin crawled at sharing space with a stranger, but now the room seems cozy. Sepia photographs spill like a waterfall from every inch of wall to the bedsheets.

Some are of the staff, ranging from artistic to silly—others are of huge insects that look like Pique made them on a dare—others are of the city. One's even of Tavreah, so at ease with the camera that she let it capture her doing her hair.

"I didn't know you took photos," Irving says.

"I didn't know you were a Feyspawn *idiot.* What happened?"

Irving sits on the bed when Noah's cleared enough space and explains their arrest.

Noah hangs up the last of her skirts and sighs. "Flukes have taken down smarter morons than you. I bet if Eirjatal wasn't there, you would've made it."

"The Heartswain reacted to him like—" They snap their fingers. "I've never seen it go so bad, so quickly."

"He always vanishes when someone brings out Heartswain. Story goes that the war cracked him or something." Noah tosses a shirt at Irving. "That's from an old roommate. It should fit."

It's a button-up, like most clothes in Dianthus. Luckily buttons help with getting a shirt over horns *and* with avoiding an injury.

"You look like shit, you know. We'll figure out the rest in the morning."

"No." Suddenly, everything piles up and tangles like fabric caught in a sewing machine. Eirjatal knowing about Sigyn, Vyriseh knowing *who knows what,* the cagey mystery of the infirmary, Cereus saying that that mystery will ruin them, fucking *half-human* this and *half-blood* that. "You've got to get me out of here."

"I do *not!* What've you ever done to get *me* out?"

"Started doing crime with you! And then taking the fall for you!"

"Well, I—you did?" She blinks. "Oh, Irving, you did."

"Eirjatal took all my stuff, including my Staventene key." Irving stands. The shirt fits them lengthwise, so it's way too big in the shoulders. They could tailor it if the palace has supplies, but screw it, the shirt only needs to take them to the station. "You've got to have something that I can use to jump to Heatherwol." Their mother might have left some Staventene knick-knack behind in the Autumn castle.

"Do you think I sashay off for a vacation whenever I like? I don't have anything."

What about their glasses? If everything from the lenses to the frame is made from purely Staventene materials, it'll carry them the right direction through the portal. They take the glasses off, but a Ventaris brand name on the arm laughs at them. "Something in the Dawn Hall, then?"

"You'll never make it through the portal without getting caught."

Irving runs a tan hand through their hair, wincing at a twinge from the burn. They could unscrew a lens from the frame, but Noah's right. Getting a key is only half the problem. "I have to. I have a job in Etreal. They'll think I ran out on them."

Noah folds her arms. "You signed on with screwy people again, didn't you."

Is the House of Ciphers screwy? They introduced themselves to Irving via an unmarked letter. They wanted to take them, a ton of Heartswain, and an entourage of elites out of the city, to put Heartswain's ability to pull out a rival's secrets and shames to the test. Irving still doesn't know the name of the Cipher member who found them in the first place.

"Maybe."

"And now it seems like you ran off with their money."

"And their intel."

"To Cypress. I bet no one expected that out of the rabbit."

Rabbit. Half-human.

What has long ears, is far from home, and will die by winter?

6

Irving

Every world Karadenza Realmweaver made was a test for each god beneath her to prove their worth in cleverness, creativity, and loyalty. If they failed her, when she left a world behind, the goddess of magic and life would not take them along.

Worship none or worship all. As long as you do not scorn them they do not care. It is not our love they are concerned with. It is Karadenza's.

Mythos, published Age of Illumination 16

Irving wakes to walls plastered with grainy black-and-white photographs of Dianthus's sea. The sound of it floods in a second later.

No chance of forgetting that this isn't their cramped Staventene bachelor, where they can kick shut the door without getting out of bed. *Definitely* not their suite in Heatherwol's palace, where staff tidied up at night like well-behaved ghosts.

But it's also not a dungeon.

Noah says, "Fey's broken horns, dude. Who were you in Etreal? A courtesan? Get up."

Irving rolls onto their back—and hisses from the burn. Noah wouldn't get vitaea because she didn't want to get in trouble with Eirjatal, so it's as raw as it was last night. Light from the outside gas lamps scatters stars on the floor and runs wet off the photographs. Noah's in her uniform, hands on her round hips, guarding a wicker basket on her bed.

Memories from yesterday tangle around Irving's insides. No, this isn't a dungeon, but without the relief of *not* being blinded, it seems a lot less harmless. Irving has no idea what time it is, or if the House of Ciphers is in the mood for a breach of contract lawsuit when Irving doesn't show up.

Noah tosses a uniform at their face and says, "Happy first day."

While Irving finger-combs their blonde hair, Noah gestures at the basket. "Eirjatal wants you to take this, so I bet it's for Johana." She drawls the name. Irving told her everything last night, too worked up to sleep and the burn too painful for them to respect Eirjatal's request to keep it secret. "There's a letter and some—I don't even know." Noah takes out a little canister of white spiders. She shakes it. "Maybe Johana takes these with tea."

An hour later, Irving sets down the basket of spiders, unlocks the infirmary door with the butterfly-wing key, and knocks.

For a while, nothing happens. Irving rocks their foot against the floor, worry prickling like static electricity under their skin. They made it past Sigyn's floor safely, but now they feel trapped between the infinite fall down the stairs and whatever's lurking in this room.

You've screwed over Cypress for two years straight. If you really need to get out of this, you can do it again.

The knob turns—they jolt. A flustered, weedy woman peeks through a scant inch of open door.

Human.

Apparently, Irving's not the only one trapped where they shouldn't be.

Johana's gaze ticks to the tray, then behind them, then to the pale patch of skin between their eyebrows, like she can't meet their eye. Even if she's the squirrely one, Irving feels like they did when fresh to Staventene, trying to get a job with absolutely no credentials.

They say in Etren, "I'm here to help? I have a note from Eirjatal."

"Oh. Oh! Then—sorry, come in. I'm so sorry."

They squeeze through since she doesn't bother opening the door any wider.

As soon as they're in, they realize she *couldn't*.

The infirmary—or what's been hastily turned into one—is like an old dollhouse, shaken up and left to gather dust. It's barely bigger than Noah and Irving's room. Chances are Johana was too distracted to immediately answer the door, but everything from open notebooks to herbs on a cutting board is in a state of half-progress so Irving can't figure out what she was working on. Honeycomb shelves are stuffed with alchemical equipment and jars of unidentifiable gore, and a desk in the back shoulders a huge terrarium of plants. A tray of surgical scalpels teeters on a tower of leather-back books. On a writing desk are the remnants of an altar; Irving recognizes the framework, but there's nothing votive left behind, like Johana tried to hide it.

And on the other side of a folding screen is the shadowy shape of a bed with someone in it.

After awkward pivoting on Irving's part and hasty rearranging on Johana's, Irving's set everything down and found a chair. Johana folds up into an origami square in a corner and buries her face in Eirjatal's note. She seems to be staying as far away from Irving as possible.

In here, the thick perfume of sea and flowers is shoved away by the musty smell of hot cobblestone streets and candlewax. But Irving can't see any candles. Or a street, for that matter, since all the curtains are drawn.

Why block out that sun and fresh air?

Before they can offer to crack a window, a massive snake slithers out from under an ottoman. Irving yanks their feet up onto the chair rung, but the snake twists up their leg anyway.

Johana jumps about as much as they do. "Oh, that's—Marie's nice. She's happy to see someone new. But I can take her away—"

"It's fine." Johana's nerves are putting them on edge, and the snake isn't helping. It's thicker around than their arm, white as ash, and tasting the air—and probably all the fear in it. There's a perfect black dart shape on its white head.

Marie eventually drops to the floor and disappears under a divan. Irving exhales in a gust.

"Now that I've seen everyone…" Tentative, Irving holds their hand out. "I'm Irving."

Johana's making a face that probably isn't too far off from how Irving looked at Marie. It's not *unfamiliar*, being feared, but Irving's carved enough of a home in Etreal that it hasn't happened in a while. They have no idea what to do about it.

But fear makes people obedient, so she takes their hand with the bizarre jerk of a marionette.

Her grip is weak. Her dark hair has fallen out of a fashionable wavy bob, and her dropped-waist dress under her oversized, mismatched jacket is so obviously from Etreal that it makes Irving long for their tailoring side-job in a Staventene theatre.

And her hands are smattered with burns and gouges. Something a Songbird addict shares with a priestess doing hard training.

A *specific* priestess. One who might keep a snake as a pet.

"You're from a Blind Adder temple."

Johana holds her hand to her chest, like self-consciously protecting a childhood toy. "Correct."

Irving brushes away a crawling sensation up their spine—it's so severe that for a second they wonder if the white spiders got loose. "Don't worry. I'm not like the elves here—I don't ascribe to anything." Which in Cypress means you're dangerous, and in Etreal means you live under the divine's radar and have a huge selection of religious swears. In both realms, it's your dumb, deliberately blind decision.

Johana picks at a nail. Scars aside, her hands are spotless. "Her name…echoes strangely, doesn't it?"

"In this room? I think it feels most at home."

The Blind Adder is the Woven goddess of medicines and poisons—or life and death, if someone's really desperate. Irving's not a praying person. Equal-opportunity heretic. But a point in the Blind Adder's favour is that she's in almost every god's good graces (except the Nelaeryn Fey's, of course). Her worship is quiet, her followers even-keel—if you ignore the ones keen on assassinations.

Despite Irving's own history with the goddess, she's part of why Irving trusted the House of Ciphers. The Blind Adder's iconography was woven into their own: her snake, but with wings and a key.

The temple's basic motto is give and take. Balance in life and death. Irving glances at the folding screen.

The case must be pretty bad if the elves dared involve a human Woven priestess.

Irving quickly uproots any seeds of interest. It's not their business how Johana got here. Their only concern is Johana knowing her craft enough to not kill them, and Sigyn never seeing through Irving's charm that blocks his scrying—or running into them in the halls.

"I'll need to run some tests on you. He"—Johana gestures at Eirjatal's letter—" says you don't have magic, but—other things, there could be other things."

"Right, I—"

"But before—you should see Rhoheme."

Marie slithers out from the divan to follow Johana, who moves, quiet as a will o' wisp, to the folding screen. Irving's stomach flips.

Johana drags aside the screen. "It's…as simple as this. The universe wants her to go, but the elves need her to stay, so—so we give *you* to it instead. Death isn't one big moment. Not really. It's a lot of little things. A breath that doesn't finish, or a vein that tears in the wrong spot, or a heartbeat that's too soft or too hard. The Blind Adder…breaks you in bits, to build her back up."

In the bed, light runs greasily off Rhoheme's long black hair and the rotten felt of her small antlers.

She's dead, Irving thinks. She died in this suffocating room with the deluded, death-fearing elves like something forgotten under the floorboards.

The amber skin on her chest and tattoo-covered arms peels back, giving way to ridges of a jagged *something* growing out of her—it's the greenish-grey of dead coral, but slick like glass. Along her jaw is the shadow of even more, pressing between her bone and skin.

The whole Dawn Hall sings with her magic in close proximity to itself, but it's dead silent in here.

"What happened?"

"Sirens. The venom, it—it paralyzes. Turns a victim into a part of the ocean floor, or the rocks, or a shipwreck, whatever the body is unlucky enough to cling to after they steal what they want…"

"There aren't sirens in Cypress." They're Madainn's thing, the Woven god of the sea.

"That worries me, because the only cure *is* a siren." Johana rubs her mouth. "I wish I could tell you more about…how it happened. About her. It would help the Adder forge the connection between you two if I could."

A phantom pain skitters down their arms and neck. It nestles in the scarred spot under where they're missing a rib.

"But they don't let me leave, so they don't let me learn."

Johana gives Irving a smile, and Irving has the sudden sense of helping someone at a riverside fill their pockets with rocks.

The morning consisted of Irving anxiety-cleaning with Johana measuring this and that, mumbling about properties that seemed too complex to fit in their blood. Occasionally she spiced it up by warning how expensive what they were handling was, with so much panic it was as if they were juggling the stuff.

Now that they're out of the makeshift infirmary, the Dawn Hall yawns, infinite and fanged. They have to go to the kitchens (and maybe detour for vitaea since Eirjatal told Johana to not give them any), but they don't feel keen on returning. Not because of Marie or the basilisk stomach twisting like delicate jellyfish in a jar or those creepy white spiders. Not even because of Rhoheme.

When Johana had sat them down and set up bleary incense to magically test the property of the blood, Irving had blurted, "I was a really sick kid."

She'd paused. Peered. "How?"

Why was easier to answer.

"If something weird comes up that you can't explain with the half-elf thing, it's probably that."

A dull sting from the phantom rib, announcing its starring role in the story Irving wasn't telling. Irving pushed, "I'm fine now."

Slipping the needle under their skin, Johana had murmured, "Maybe you have a bit of Adder's favour already, then."

Now, Irving heads downstairs. They shield their eyes against the midday sun. Every staircase is squished between the sounds of the sea on one side and the music of Lightbringing in the city on the other. The halls shimmer with rainbow butterflies (and the pixies chasing them). The world's back in focus after being obscured by shadows all morning, and it's dizzying.

Irving freezes on the landing when they hear Sigyn's voice.

Heatherwol's queen, Sunmirren Adamantine, replies as the two descend the stairs, "And this project must be dealt with *now?* Is Vyriseh on a deadline?"

"She has resources here that she does not in Silvershale."

"I hope this isn't an excuse to lock yourself away. Cereus is already put out by your timidity; if you hide, he'll break down the door."

Irving won't be able to make it around enough of the half-moon hall before their father reaches the landing, so they duck blindly into the nearest room. Shutting the door on Sigyn's soft laugh, they swallow their heart.

A minute passes. Sigyn and Adamantine's voices are too muffled to pick out words. *Vyriseh?* Sigyn would occasionally work with her (not telling his family what they were up to, as usual), but what project's serious enough to carry into Dianthus?

And would any part of it involve Vyriseh saying she knows where Irving is?

Irving backs away from the door—and bumps into something. They spin to grab it. It's a podium engraved with mythic poetry, and when it's steady, the gleaming varnish reflects the rest of the room.

It's either an art gallery or an armoury. Same thing in Dianthus. Hung on the walls of the long, narrow room are elaborate ship flags, bows, rapiers, arrows with useless, frilly fletching. The rug is embroidered with sprawling myths of the Fey and the sea. Guarding it all are two suits of armour.

They're not the heavy pot-and-kettle type that make up Staventene's automatons. They're lithe, with chainmail intricately woven to give the impression of shifting fish scales. Their silver helmets have the silhouette of the Nelaeryn Fey's double sets of horns, bottom left broken on each, and are stuffed with hyacinth and oleander that spill down the chests like gore. Light slices along their sea glass flails.

They lead the way to another pedestal at the top of the room. Whatever's inside is very shimmery, very intricate, and very much moving.

When they bring Heartswain to Etreal estates, Irving can't help ogling all the fancy nonsense nobility show off, so they cross the room. Inside a glass box is a structure made of intricate, tiny channels. Beads of crystal travel through it, being weighed and tipped by minuscule mechanisms. It's glass too, and so detailed that the tangled structure stands on tufts of flowers that glitter like Dianthus's white beaches.

Irving searches for where the beads begin—and finds that they come from the box itself, melting under the sun at the perfect center point.

They touch the glass. It's freezing and damp. Ice.

Alongside Autumn, Summer, and the Eclipsed, there's a Winter kingdom in Cypress, too. It's not so crazy to think that the Dianthus king snagged one of their art pieces, even if they haven't left their frozen undersea kingdom since before Irving was born. Even if Sigyn says they never will.

Irving recovers some sense. Eirjatal may do worse than burn them if they're discovered here, especially when their reputation goes no further than *heretic* and *sticky fingers*. They step away, and their reflection shatters across the structure.

But the reflection isn't of Irving.

It's of unfamiliar elves, and a sense of loss that plunges into Irving's chest and wrenches hard like it wants Irving's heart to replace its own.

Irving blinks and it's gone.

They turn out of there, the suits of armour watching them go.

7

The Blind Adder

The Blind Adder knew from the beginning that the first god to silence would be Chiroscuroi.

Chiroscuroi is in the middle of a shallow circular pool of honey-thick light, dancing in strange bursts. The Blind Adder steps right into the light.

The first odd thing is that Chiroscuroi doesn't notice.

The second is that Faowist is on the far right shore. Eojhest is on the left. The sun and the moon give the Adder the same wary look.

The third odd thing is that the pool begins to tremble.

The Adder doesn't spend much time here—the god of endings and beginnings is prone to fits and tattling—but she recognizes the tang of magic from rituals and worshipers floating around her. It's not *for* her, so it doesn't feel quite right, but that's better than it feeling *wrong*. It used to; no longer. Just another little way Karadenza tried to get them to not hate each other.

(Though the Adder thinks the Mother Goddess likes a bit of drama.)

Another step, and the Adder drops through the pool.

She falls into the stale human realm. It's a Staventene city street. Gold and amber. Dust that shimmers as automobiles trundle past. The road still smells faintly of horse. The temple ahead coaxes her with broad colonnades.

Inside, a ritual is indeed underway. From the ceiling hangs an enormous metal sun on chains, full of candles. A crowd is arranged in perfectly even lines, their bodies making pathways up to a stone statue of Chiroscuroi, who presides over the mortals with stern flamboyance.

The Adder has never cared for such things. She prefers symbols over totems, totems over paintings, paintings over statues. She prefers…less clarity.

Just as the Adder slips into a human guise, she is stopped at the door by a frail priestess, who asks for her name so she may add it to the ledger to be burned.

"Marie."

She steps into a line and watches the ritual. They all played games like this, centuries before the absent mother, Karadenza, got wise. Once, gods slithered through each other's temples, whispering lies in the ears of followers, damaging relics and votive objects and maybe even changing the course of worship for decades. The Carrion Queen once masqueraded as a High Priestess of Pique and made the goddess of plants' life a living hell—were there hells in that world, anyhow—transforming the temple into a parade of worshipers entranced by the rot and ruin she promised would bring a verdant spring.

But now, that's a little tacky.

The Blind Adder opens her hand to reveal a fluffy white mold. She blows it out over the crowd. It hangs in a haze for a moment and then descends, and the worshipers go with it, dropping harmlessly and witlessly to the floor.

She minces around them to the Chiroscuroi statue. The god is emanating from it. Much stronger than expected. They're shown with the head turned so both faces can be seen in profile from the front, with hands crossed, one flexed into a rune for *end,* the other for *beginning.* What world were those from? This world began with letters instead; Karadenza wanted to see how that would work, so she wove this tapestry with wheels and cobblestone roads and welded metal and the written word.

"Chiroscuroi." Chiroscuroi likes baubles and incense, but it would be rude to offer that if the Adder followed up with her plan. *That* would be tacky. "Chiroscuroi."

Nothing. And yet the presence of the god pulses out, so strong that it's like Ilharel's wintry winds against the Adder's face.

She steps closer. There, beneath the statue's chin on the *end* side, is a white knife. Buried so deeply that the hilt nearly vanishes, and is otherwise concealed by the hewn cowl.

She reaches for it—

"Don't," Faowist says.

"We can't figure out what it is," Eojhest says.

The Blind Adder obeys, sliding back into her true form to put the twin deities at ease. She does not touch, but still her hands—cut at the wrist with many floating hands reaching and wandering—drift closer so she can touch the edges of the magic emanating from the blade.

This is made of bone. A sea serpent's, if she had to wager, because Madainn seems to make those things solely to skin them for parts.

"Madainn has sealed Chiroscuroi?" the Blind Adder asks.

"It's from Madainn?" Eojhest minces closer, big dark arms holding himself protectively, ropes of wiry black braids falling off his broad shoulders and into his youthful face. "But it was—"

Faowist shoots him a glare. Her face may be stern, but the eye on the back of her head is flicking around nervously.

Eojhest, bless him, forges past his sister—he knows better than most about the importance of hierarchy among the Woven. Better than the Blind Adder, clearly, considering what she intended when walking in here. "The Iron Phoenix did this."

"What does that mean, Chiroscuroi is sealed?" Faowist clutches her golden logbook. In all those pages bursting with things she's seen, there's nothing quite like this. This world is Faowist and Eojhest's first, after all.

"You recall what happened to Ilharel during the Age of Beasts, when he shattered? We can be physical, ephemeral, power alone, dreams, so on, but those are fragments of us. Ilharel couldn't pull those fragments back together." Also a result of Madainn's mischief. Ilharel had to beg the Nelaeryn Fey for the power to fuse himself again, and winter is now more volatile than ever. "Madainn has locked some of Chiroscuroi's aspects in this statue. But others are still where they belong." Those others can still damage the Adder's plan, but are less aware of what's going on in the mortal plane. With this tricky spell, most of the snitch's eyes have been closed.

Not the Blind Adder's intended solution, but a solution nonetheless—which she will *not* tell Madainn, because he's insufferable, and her plans are safer if he doesn't know she was here in the first place.

Faowist's clever brain is still spinning and so is the sun-shaped eye. "Madainn and the Iron Phoenix must be working together again! Why would they want Chiroscuroi sealed away?"

"It's dusk and yet I see no moon," the Adder says. "You have duties to get to."

But as they step away, the Adder recognizes the quick look Faowist shares with Eojhest.

Chiroscuroi is not the only god who grovels at Karadenza's feet.

The torches flash. The twin gods vanish. The torches do not *stop* flashing, and a warm breeze of magic rolls over the Blind Adder.

She picks up a sconce with one of her many floating hands. "Phoenix."

The flame morphs into the orange, flickering face of a woman, blue glowing behind her grin, crackling hair twisting towards the ceiling.

"They'll warn Karadenza Realmweaver," the Adder says.

Her voice is like popping embers. "Mouthy, mouthy. What is it with these sky deities?"

"They watch. All they do is watch."

"Oh, I'll put a stop to that."

"Be secretive this time."

She rolls her white-hot eyes. "I will. And the way I'll silence you, Adder, will be the most secretive of all."

"Madainn ended the last world. I have tricked Karadenza more than once. Think hard about who you'd like to ally with in this game."

The Iron Phoenix surges out of the sconces. "How do *you* think you'll win this thing? Have you found a way to poison us?"

She blitzes out of the temple, every sconce exploding, her cackling in their crackling.

Her fire convalesces in the metal sun above. It burns bright as the congregation awakens, stumbling to their feet and turning up their faces to the corona, awe drawing their expressions into white emptiness. The Adder leaves.

She is not halfway down the block when the temple explodes. Fire erupts with the sharp curls of a whip, but it does little more than spray ash across the adjoining buildings. The Adder stands in the street among the bucking horses and rattling buggy tires and screams of passersby. The disaster leaves all the worshipers unscathed, so when the dust settles, they are the tallest things in the rubble.

The statue's head rolls down the steps towards the Adder. She stops it with her foot.

The blade has jostled out a little, but when she picks it up by the hilt, the head comes with it.

"Chiroscuroi. Are you in there?"

Their voices seep out. Saying nonsense. Hollow, trapped, rumbling around inside.

The Blind Adder tucks the head into her jacket and it vanishes. Madainn is a menace, but he can be useful when he puts his mind to it.

8

Eirjatal

I don't think we need the Hawks in Dianthus. Kinthe foresaw it, so Rho's automaton caught them in the halls. What were they going to manage with swords, anyways? The last king took two hundred years and a gun! More imprisoning will do nothing. How about the Hawks mingle with the rebels and see how they think, so Kinthe can teach them instead?

Starmorrow Cereus to Adamantine, letter, Age of Shields 248

Eirjatal supposes that scowling at his king isn't the best way for him to enter the banquet. But Cereus is like an excited dog when he's got his subjects' attention, and Eirjatal doesn't trust him to not jump on the wrong lap.

Across the Dawn Hall ballroom, a sun-bright Cereus extricates himself from his fawning civilian admirers. His torso and legs are bare except for shiny paint that curls around his toned calves, stomach, chest, up to his mouth kissed with gold and his smile that burns in Eirjatal's chest. Chains glittering with emeralds are drilled through his antelope horns, a more ostentatious crown than any human type Eirjatal's ever seen.

Cereus is gorgeous and infuriating. And meeting Eirjatal's glower with a cocky grin and a crook of his finger.

Eirjatal's sure he doesn't look pleased about obeying.

He dodges through sunburst headdresses and flower-embroidered skirts and one Autumn female with a flurry of metal falcons in her hair. To kick off Lightbringing (especially Dianthus's favourite part, when the Fey won part of the sun from Etreal's goddess of light), the Dawn Hall's thrown open the ballroom to anyone who can stagger in. The tables are piled high with food and drink in gratitude for each kingdom's unique harvest, and the crowds are dense in gratitude for each other.

Eirjatal would have *dreamed* for an occasion like this as a youth, even if everyone attending would have prayed to avoid bumping into the previous Starmorrow, Ashvaren.

But with managing Irving Whitfore, the daily anxiety over Rho, *and* with all the preparation for this evening, Eirjatal is on the brink of an apocalyptic migraine.

The music comes from elves whose business sense Eirjatal grudgingly admired when they, realizing they were being hired by the palace, tripled their booking price mid-sentence. Eclipsed guests roll through the crowd like smoke and diamonds. Autumn elves take most of the dance floor while Summer elves burn through the food and stare at each other as if they're dessert. No Winter elves to speak of—not here, not anywhere outside their kingdom these days. Eirjatal may as well be representing them on his own with a snowy fox sparrow brooch that pins shut his embroidered chiton, idly preening itself.

Cereus pulls Eirjatal by the hand into what would be, if Cereus was any other Starmorrow, an impenetrable sphere of intimidation. Instead, he's been kissing the cheeks of old and new friends all night—both nobility and citizens. He nearly does the same to Eirjatal, but at the last second pivots into an awkward press of their foreheads. He smells like smoke. Eirjatal's chest tightens.

Cereus says, "You look like you'll set someone's head on fire."

"If your guests keep pushing around my staff, I just might." Easing back, Eirjatal lifts his chin at Cereus's new chimera kitten (an awful gift from Vyriseh) as she prances around some cooing, cajoling Autumn elves. "And if Ringal pulls down a tablecloth, you're *all* going up in flames."

Cereus laughs. "Lucky me you weren't so cranky during the show." Thanks to some clever metal contraptions Rho created last month, Cereus and Tavreah had set themselves—and parts of the ballroom—on fire. It was an outrageous way to kick off Lightbringing and welcome Cypress at large to Dianthus, and it was made all the more elaborate (and, frankly, safe) by Eirjatal controlling the fire in the fringes.

The marble floors are carved with veins, meant to gather rain from the open ceiling and glitter in a massive portrait of the fierce Archfey when seen from the upper balconies. They're still flickering with fire, sweet with starter fluid.

Dianthus is still uncomfortable with him, but Cereus tries his damndest at every turn to prove Eirjatal's part of the palace now.

"Thanks again for helping out," Cereus says, squeezing Eirjatal's shoulder. Casual as a friend. "I felt damn near untouchable."

Then, because *friend* is a word neither of them can quite fit the other into, he cups Eirjatal's jaw and tilts his head up. Cereus takes in the shiny powder around his eyes, the four-strand braid pulling back his auburn hair, his constellation-shaped ear cuffs that cost him a day's wages and a charcoal portrait of the jeweler. "You look fantastic, Eirj."

Eirjatal pulls away, hoping it doesn't seem rude, but that hold turned the tightness of his chest into a vice. He's awful at conjuring compliments that don't sound loaded, so he says, "Tavreah wouldn't have let me come downstairs otherwise."

Rho wouldn't have either. The thought stings like a wasp bite. Tavreah likes her friends as handsome as the Dawn Hall's decor. Rho, meanwhile, compares dresses by how much they scream, "Don't fucking talk to me," and shoes by how much they add, "*Please.*"

Cereus's gaze flicks to something behind Eirjatal. "Ada and Sigyn are coming. Here's your chance to bolt."

"We get on fine," he retorts, though he does consider it for half a second.

Cereus bear-hugs Adamantine but doesn't touch Sigyn. No one touches Sigyn. Maybe Rho should have prayed for the Fey to make her a Moonwarden to get her privacy.

Adamantine has let her hair loose in a black cloud of soft curls, sprayed with silver paint like the night sky; Sigyn contrasts with waist-length blonde braids threaded with black. Their floor-length crimson robes stand out in the crowd of skin-baring fabrics—Adamantine's is framed with silver leaves, Sigyn's with fox fur.

Sigyn says, light humour in his voice, "Such lavish pageantry can only be expected from you, Starmorrow Cereus."

Adamantine smiles tautly. The shy Sunmirren had narrowly dodged Tavreah pulling her into a dance in front of everyone. "A harkening to the Iron Phoenix, less so."

Cereus shrugs. "I didn't mean *her*, I meant *fire*. That's what Lightbringing's about. Celebrating everything that makes up Cypress. Fire's part of the Fey's world too." He pointedly pats Eirjatal's shoulder.

Eirjatal had *told* Cereus and Tavreah, the two nutcases, that someone was going to think their display of fiery wings and threatening elegance was referring to the Iron Phoenix. As the last elf in Cypress with that Woven goddess's power, Eirjatal prays no one thinks he came up with the idea.

Adamantine says, "Moonwarden Kinthe notified me that there are still followers of hers in the city. Apparently they are increasingly agitated this year."

"And *they're* still a part of Cypress." Cereus's smile blunts his stubborn tone. "I want to let them know they're welcome in our celebrations."

Sigyn says, "This Lightbringing has similar circumstances to when the Iron Phoenix made her threat on Cypress in the Age of Beasts. Some minute details match the story; the constellations, for one..." He blinks at them like he's remembered he's being listened to. "The worshipers want something to happen, but haven't yet decided what: the Fey has foreseen little."

Adamantine says, "If any saw your display, it may be misconstrued as support."

That's one too many jabs; Cereus deflates.

"They wouldn't be here," Eirjatal says. "They distrust any rulers. It's Ashvaren's loyalists who pose the bigger risk." He flicks a hand to the guards lining the walls. Cereus had fought him on that. Being grilled at the door didn't exactly promote a trusting kingdom, and throwing elves on guard duty rather than letting them participate in their own religion was worse. "They think the palace still belongs to the late Starmorrow."

Adamantine returns, "And if the *loyalists* misconstrue the new palace's intent?"

"Broken horns, I get it." Cereus ruffles his short, wavy black hair. "I should worry more about getting stabbed in my sleep."

Eirjatal shuts his eyes to not roll them, and Adamantine's black-painted lips purse, but Sigyn says, "Fascinating, to turn to the Iron Phoenix. Their paranoia has lost a source, so they seek the comfort of something more frightening than their wildest nightmares."

Cereus was once Ashvaren's amiable ambassador, but when Ashvaren was assassinated, Adamantine and Vyriseh (after the Moonwardens' approval) ushered him onto the throne. They taught him everything since Dianthus has a shortage of nobility who don't think like Ashvaren.

There was yet another assassination attempt on Cereus three months ago. The Fey deals with murderers Herself—and one should hope it's Relyn, not the Archfey, who does it—but since they failed, the punishment was up to the Dawn Hall.

Tavreah wanted banishment to the Briarlords, who could whip anyone who'd forgotten the Fey's teachings into shape. Kinthe, walking Ashvaren's path, wanted them blinded, deafened, and dropped over the border into Etreal so the humans could deal with their Archfey's echo, the monster that comes from Cypress deaths in Etreal. Rhoheme said to put them to work rebuilding the city. Eirjatal backed her up.

Cereus entertained them for a while before admitting he was always going to ask Adamantine.

Adamantine smirks. "Alright, no politics. What do you make of Madainn's monsters in the Glasswood?"

The name of the Woven god rings against Eirjatal's ear like struck glass. The silver brooch-bird flutters its snowy wings, stirring to attention.

"Come on, that's still politics!"

"No, it's a world event. We discuss world events at parties. A punishment of our royalty."

Cereus shakes his head. "I think it was just another day with the Woven. At least *our* goddess has the manners to stay where she belongs. Up on a star and out of our heads. No offense, Sigyn."

"None taken."

Yet Sigyn is fixed on Eirjatal. Eirjatal refuses to react, even if the Moonwarden's stare is like a spider crawling up his temple. He feels…exposed without Rho to take half the attention for him. The name of the sea god sticks in the back of Eirjatal's throat like the ichor from Rho's lungs. He snags a glass from a passing tray so he can burn away the taste and has something to do with his hands.

Adamantine is referring to what drew him and Rho to the river in the first place. Winter's Sunmirren Scintia told *him* first. But the information unsteadies him as if he's learned it for the first time.

Adamantine asks, "What do you think they want?"

"Something Winter left behind in the war?" Cereus's top lip pulls in irritation. Like Ringal trying to intimidate a very scary dishrag. "You don't want to send in more Hawks to find what the bastards missed, do you?"

Sigyn says, "We understand searching the wreckage of Winter is a bit much to ask. But considering Madainn's previous…impact on Cypress, it is worth sending a campaign. Perhaps we could borrow someone like Eirjatal."

The little fires in the marble floor flicker to the rhythm of Eirjatal's pulse.

"Things change way too fast; I can't throw him out there, like, *good luck figuring out what humans want with us* this *decade*. You haven't been a Hawk in—what, thirty years?"

Eirjatal has been with Cereus through the bud and bloom of his rule—he can smell Cereus's anxiety as easily as he can smell a human's. It's infectious. Eirjatal is grinding his sharp, curved canines. Not so long ago, this would have made Eirjatal feel closer to him. Now, it's another tenuous gap, and Eirjatal doesn't know how to help him across without doing something stupid like finding all the answers for him, or kissing him until he forgets what there is to worry about. Of course, that last one's now off-limits.

Eirjatal's thoughts have slipped too much. His drink sets on fire.

Cereus and Adamantine keep speaking as Eirjatal narrows his world to the glass, the heat spasming in his grip, the pulse pounding against his skin. He keeps it off his face with two centuries' worth of practice. He supposes he should be flattered; Adamantine and Sigyn feel as if they can openly talk about Madainn's monsters around him. They wouldn't if they knew his last encounter with sirens.

The shadow that exploded from the trunk of Heartswain flutters behind his eyelids. Bit by bit, he leaches the heat back to his heart.

Cereus says, "You could ask *anyone* else. There's something about Dianthus that breeds Hawks."

"True. Rhoheme worked with us too." Adamantine brushes a curl off her forehead. "Is she attending tonight? I wanted to ask her about working in Heatherwol for the equinox…"

Cereus and Eirjatal share a glance. Cereus's eyebrows nudge together.

Eirjatal minutely shakes his head.

But she'll help, Cereus's expression pleads.

Eirjatal interjects, "Rho left with the other Spring elves, up-island to Hyacinthus's ruins for Lightbringing."

Adamantine's reply is aborted by Tavreah's near-scream of elation. She elbows Eirjatal into Sigyn and thrusts her goblet in the middle of the circle.

Tavreah cries, "To the Lightbringing and fucking over the Woven!"

Cereus knocks glasses with her; Eirjatal half-heartedly joins in and gets alcohol all over his sandals from how hard Tavreah smashes their cups together. Tavreah is always too much, but considering what topic she interrupted, Eirjatal thanks the Fey for her.

Tavreah's in her dress from the earlier fire show, a sultry black gown embedded with light-catching jewels so bright that it seems sewn with embers. Eirjatal has sworn off sex with both her and Cereus since concealing the truth about Rho and yet asking for intimacy feels cruel. However, it's profoundly unfair that looking at Tavreah all dolled up has nowhere near the effect on him that Cereus does.

"I want to dance," Tavreah announces. She points at everyone in the circle, starting with Adamantine: "You aren't nearly drunk enough." Sigyn: "I've seen the art, I don't want to see you dancing like the Fey." Eirjatal: "*You* are in serious stick-up-the-ass mode, I can tell. So that leaves me with…" She pivots to Cereus. Before she can quip, Cereus swoops her into his arms. Sigyn effortlessly plucks her glass and sets it on a passing servant's tray before it goes flying.

Cereus asks, spinning Tavreah around, "Something to say?"

"Nothing, my blinding, terrible Light!" Tavreah shrieks a laugh, clinging to him. Then, waving an arm at the sparkling crowd, she calls, "Vyriseh! Dance with us!"

A gauzy powder-blue dress complements Vyriseh's lavender-grey skin—and plenty of it, thanks to the plunge of the neckline, the open leg, and the fragile strings of diamond making up the hint of a belt. Up her arms wind live white begonias.

After sashaying to their circle, Vyriseh hooks an arm around Adamantine's. "Maybe with you, Ada dearest, people will stop staring at me like I crawled out of a cave."

Vyriseh tosses Eirjatal a private wink before dancing away with the Autumn Sunmirren. Over Tavreah's black ponytail, Cereus meets Eirjatal's gaze. His smile is boyish and hopeful, and he nods to the dance floor.

Tempting. The last thing Eirjatal wants is to be left alone with Sigyn. And being close to Cereus once made the whole world melt away.

But Eirjatal's too tired for Tavreah's antics, and too stressed out for Vyriseh's, and being so near to Cereus inspires feelings that are too frustrating to endure.

"I want hazard pay if you two set something else on fire."

Cereus's smile dims, but he rekindles it with all the sunshine of Dianthus. As he follows Vyriseh and Adamantine, he passes close enough for Eirjatal to be struck hard with the smell of smoke, and even harder by Tavreah's open hand missing his rear and getting his hip instead.

Sigyn watches them go with a mild smile. "I feel so old."

"You're not. You're only…"

Only what? Not included, not inviting, not a friend? Eirjatal sees why he married a human. Every elf is too afraid to relax with him.

Eirjatal included.

(Maybe Tavreah's the exception.)

They lapse into silence and the party traipses on. Elves, citizens and upper court alike, stare openly at Sigyn like he's the Nelaeryn Fey Herself, practically spilling their plates when giving him a gesture of respect across their chests. Kinthe, Dianthus's Moonwarden, commands obedience, not *reverence* like Sigyn does—perhaps because he's the longest-serving Moonwarden of the last millennium, or because seeing his face in person is far more arresting than a painting or poem will ever be.

Fey, do not make me talk to him. Even if You must let Ringal pull down an entire table.

Eirjatal says, "I should return to the kitchens, see how things are going."

"You should. Before, though, would you mind…"

Sigyn's eyebrows are drawn together, and there's an unfamiliar tightness around his mouth. He's pale beneath the discoloured smears of his skin.

"Are you alright?" Eirjatal asks.

"Perhaps not. Would you mind escorting me somewhere quiet, if the Dawn Hall can spare it…? My arm," he says, and Eirjatal notes how he's clutching the beautiful clockwork limb beneath the folds of his robes. "I think there's something wrong."

driver for its tiny pieces. Rho can't handle things being half-fixed, half-finished. Not projects, not books, not decisions. Arguing with her was exhausting.

Rho would have stuck with Eirjatal in that ballroom, fingers intertwined with his, handling all the small talk with enough charm that he didn't need to bother. Eirjatal and Rho would usually turn in early to his apartment, talk over one of the four scratched records he bought as a Hawk in Etreal, scatter the dregs of their conversation while they danced (well, more of a sway), and she would eventually fall asleep in her heels on his bed rather than walk to her tiny suite in the city. They would sleep back to back.

Rho spent as much time in the Dawn Hall as Eirjatal and Tavreah, yet refused Cereus's offer of an apartment. *"When Ashvaren's old court coups this place, I don't want my head on the gates I built."*

"I have painkillers." Eirjatal retrieves a canister of vitaea, and asks as he splits the roots from the panacea of a plant, "Is this trouble new?"

"Barely a couple weeks. Too young, yet, to tolerate." The mechanical arm's base is implanted above where his elbow once was, each notch and lock made with careful detail. "No disrespect to Rhoheme's work, of course. She did warn me her only exposure to prosthetics was a Staventene automaton manual you gave her. Besides this, it's been perfect."

Sigyn is studying the apartment. Eirjatal's bookshelves are well-used and better-dusted. Maps of both Etreal and Cypress are framed on the walls, decorated with delicate coded notations from the travellers he bought them from. A writing desk faces the balcony doors overlooking the labyrinth gardens; the globe on his Relyn altar casts a long shadow over precise stacks of sketchbooks.

A drawer is nudged open. Eirjatal wants to leave the vitaea to shut it, self-conscious. He caught Tavreah digging through it last week, searching for old pictures of Rho and them. She must have come back.

"Forty-six years ago," Sigyn says, head back against the brocades.

"Pardon?"

9

Eirjatal

Sigyn won't tell me how he lost his arm. It gets to me that his whole life is a locked safe—even to us! His oldest friends, if you can say he has those!—but he can sniff out everything about you and me.
The amputation's horrific, by the way. Like something chewed it off. But I don't think anything hurts him anymore.

Rhoheme Ges'ill to Eirjatal, letter, Age of Shields 147

Once in Eirjatal's apartments, Sigyn unlocks his arm and sets it on the coffee table. The way the mechanical fingers fall with the exact tension as a limp hand makes Eirjatal shudder.

Rho would be in hysterics. She'd let Eirjatal and Sigyn fumble around each other while she fussed with the mechanics, using a hairpin like a screw-

"When you last left Cypress." Cereus's question. "The Hawks were housed in the Heatherwol palace before the expedition; we had drinks, and it was the last time you did more than smirk at my jokes."

"Perhaps that says less about me and more about how you aren't very funny."

"I recall being quite interesting to you when we were young, working together on the road."

"I think I was simply amazed that an Aphithea was out of the library and in the sunlight."

A faint smile crosses Sigyn's face. *Aphithea* has gone the way of all elf bloodlines, more a cataloguing system than a family. "I was connecting what I knew to what I was learning. Mapping familiar constellations onto unfamiliar skies. You were sweet to listen to me."

"Why, out of everything, do you remember that?" Eirjatal asks. Because of their connection to Her prophetic powers, a Moonwarden's personal memories are finicky, fragile. Something Eirjatal and Sigyn have in common.

"I wanted to remember it, that's all."

Eirjatal crushes the vitaea with sharply fragrant peppermint and hates that he knows what Sigyn prefers in his tea.

Long before the portals were installed, Eirjatal and Sigyn fell into a friendship that felt immortal in the long supply caravan travels to the Winter kingdom. They were both *much* too far from their centennial to feel as superior as they did. Annoying to their older peers, but invaluable, too—they were the only ones with the gall to walk in human cities.

Imagine *that*. The Age of Beasts and its accompanying war brewing across Etreal, and these two idiots proudly exploring crowded human streets. Seeing how humans reacted if they wore the formal dress meant to impress the Winter Starmorrow like they'd stumbled out of a ritual, if they booked time at a brothel, if Eirjatal smiled with his Summer fangs and Sigyn spoke in riddles to maidens like some alluring folklore monster.

How incredible it was, to be instinctually feared, ferociously desired. Eirjatal's stories from that time make Cereus squirm.

Sigyn's stopped talking, but he can sink you down with him, wherever he wants you. Eirjatal can't imagine what it's like to have him tell your future. It must be like drowning in his quiet sea.

Eirjatal hears the faint music of gears and chains as the palace turns to chase the sun. Eirjatal pulls in a pitcher of rain water off the window sill, and pours it into a teapot that he's heated with his magic. Then Sigyn speaks up so suddenly that Eirjatal flinches.

"I arrived in Dianthus with a very dark feeling. Almost like a sickness. But I don't want to scry on every door and every elf." His grey eyes meet Eirjatal's green ones. "Something is wrong."

Lying outright to Sigyn is idiotic, even if the Woven are a blind spot to the Fey and Vyriseh has meticulously plucked Sigyn's mind, like petals from a flower, to prevent him from sleuthing his way into Rho's infirmary. "That news about the Glasswood has upset Kinthe and Cereus."

They don't know half of what happened. It's Eirjatal and Rho who know, thanks to Scintia sending him an urgent, classified letter. She wrote that Madainn was crawling up the Glasswood's shores, over the ruin of the Ineiren Fort that he once brought down with Eirjatal inside it.

He sets the teapot on the table. Sigyn grabs his hand.

The alarm of being touched by Sigyn overpowers his worry about the topic for a senseless second. His skin is unnaturally cool and terribly soft, much like when they worked together on the roads, as Sigyn would meticulously tend cuts and calluses to keep the hands of a scholar.

"She wants to tell me about you," Sigyn murmurs. "But She is finding you hard to understand. It is all shadowed to me. Only this..." He traces a finger across his palm and up the underside of his arm. "You are not finished bleeding."

Eirjatal recalls a night over two and a half centuries ago, standing watch at the fire, Sigyn holding both his hands with strange wonder and saying he would love to have magic.

It's Woven magic, Eirjatal had argued. *It's an offense.*

Still, how incredible that it is yours. Humans given that power by the goddess are divine. You stole that divinity from her. I'm envious. I'm so fragile.

The religious instinct in Eirjatal pushes him to confess it all, but he can't.

If Sigyn takes one look at Rhoheme and the Woven god they've let into the halls for her, he'll remember the Hawk reports of Madainn, and know why Eirjatal was involved. He'll want to help and it will all become too much, Madainn seeing them all, Madainn knowing them all, their fear and secrets gifting him a bloody feast to lord over the Fey.

This is for Eirjatal alone. He can't let anyone else get hurt.

He pulls away.

"Tensions between Cereus and I have returned. That's all."

"A lover's spat is *not* all."

"Maybe the Fey is a romantic, Sigyn." *Lovers.* Hardly. They were a red moon, so far away from Sigyn's precious waxing moon wife. They were friendly in bed and out of it, but never *lovers.* "Maybe it's not a spat to me, and my black cloud is so heavy that it darkens the whole palace."

Sigyn's face softens with sympathy, a sentimental pastoral portrait. "I could have warned you of this years before he broke your heart, my friend."

"I ended it with him."

"But is your heart not still broken?"

"You know I'm prone to dramatics."

Sigyn sets his hand in his lap. Despite himself, Eirjatal craves another brush of his skin, another memory from before the Ineiren Fort and before Sigyn left him in the snow. "You are still injured, and so you are still in pain. There is no shame in that."

"I'm managing. I've been managing for a long time."

"Not alone, I hope?"

If Madainn kills Rho, I will be alone with it. "No."

"I do not want to lose you more than I already have."

Cypress is built to let elves forget. After so many centuries alive, complex histories soften and simplify, like detailed paintings of leaves and fingertips melting into vague colour washes that invoke unconscious, animal feelings. Like trust. Affection. Eirjatal's memory is a crowded gallery warehouse with slashed canvases next to scenes rendered in such detail that they make him dizzy. He remembers Sigyn either with a fondness so immense that it seems impossible, or a hatred that spatters across scenes it has no right to.

When Sigyn first inherited the connection to the Nelaeryn Fey, he apparently couldn't remember who he was, what he wanted, what he'd done. But he recovered himself bit by bit, and on the way, learned how Eirjatal's memory became such a mess too.

Eirjatal *hates* the chance that Sigyn thinks he is shattered from the memories of the Age of Beasts and the Ineiren Fort falling around him. Of Sigyn leaving him behind, never to truly return.

Sigyn isn't the only elf to walk through fire re-forged.

But it's undeniable that only one of them was scorched.

10

Eirjatal

Sigyn invited us to meet his kid. You'd better come. I'm not going to be awkward around Penelope Whitfore alone. Also, the ambassador asked me again to build protections for those evocations Sunmirren Scintia gave Ashvaren. I can't. I hate this. Is this how you feel? Like you can't breathe with all the feeling inside you? It's brutal.
I can't believe Sigyn got laid.

Rhoheme to Eirjatal, message on a recording bird, Age of Shields 226

Eirjatal dearly wishes the Eclipsed spy had at least *one* eye for him to look at while they speak.

He worries that awkwardness is making him look even more on edge, more controlling than Vyriseh accused him of being when they both first put together this plan.

She's saying, this time from the mouths on her arms, "As of yet there's been nothing but tracks to follow through the Glasswood."

"Are you speaking to the humans at all? The other side of the mountains are riddled with temples to Ilharel, and I've heard that Madainn worship has been encroaching—"

"Yes," she says, this time from the fanged mouth peeking out between her long white bangs. "Obviously. They've given us nothing new; they aren't prophets like the Moonwardens."

"And Galistan? Scintia's soldier?"

"Still missing."

He's getting the sense this spy is tired of being needled, but unfortunately for her, there's too much on the line for him to not needle. Vyriseh's spies have been reliable in getting Johana her components to keep Rho stable (and once, a spellbook she forgot in the panicked exit from Ventaris). Perhaps she thought she could get away with a quick report if she caught him halfway through cleaning votive objects in Rho's workroom, but unfortunately for her, he wants to know everything. He only trusts himself to know everything.

"Are you sure you're the best one to send to the humans?" Eirjatal asks. "You're not exactly...subtle."

She lifts a hand, and he nearly expects her to shoot him a rude gesture before she twists a black ring, says flatly with the mouth on her neck, "*Petrichor*," and seamlessly transitions into a nondescript human woman.

"Ah."

The spy suddenly turns—and freezes Whitfore, who was passing in the hallway. Whitfore's paling face makes no mystery of their shock when the spy drops the spell and becomes the eyeless, mouth-covered Eclipsed elf once more.

"Thank you," Eirjatal says. "Please—"

"Keep you updated. Yes." She sweeps into the hall.

While Whitfore's still staring after her in alarm, Eirjatal says, "Come here."

Whitfore drags their feet. Eirjatal wipes cleaning solution off his hands with a rag.

The votive objects are the most activity Rho's workshop has seen in two weeks. They're for another ritual later in the month, about the ocean and streams, a reminder that water is not all Madainn's. Vases, bowls, hollow statuettes, and other vessels crowd the table, unearthed from Moonwarden Kinthe's collection and curated by Tavreah's stylish eye. The act of cleaning them is itself religious, considering how much value She places in organization and care.

Interpretations of Her three iterations dance in everything from rough stone to soft gold. Nele, the motherly watcher of newborns and the dying; the Archfey, the wild and wicked creature of vengeance and survival; and Relyn, the cunning wanderer.

Eirjatal offers a hand and after a moment of hesitation, Whitfore sets their bandaged arm in it.

"Noah's been helping you with this," Eirjatal says. The bandages, cold from the vitaea tincture beneath, are secured with Noah's dragonfly-tipped hairpins.

"Not the burn, though."

"I'd hope not."

The bandaging is sloppy—Noah does everything in a rush, from folding laundry to getting impatient, but Cereus likes her attitude. She tests the limits of the new rule, and Cereus is eager to prove that there's nothing to fear.

Eirjatal unwinds the linen. He frowns; beneath the black staining of vitaea, there's no bruising, no cuts. With enough innovation, the different species of vitaea can cure nearly anything, but Woven influence dulls their magic. When Eirjatal was in Whitfore's position, he was riddled with evidence of Johana's magic for days.

Eirjatal asks, "What have you told Noah?"

"If *either* Johana or Noah learn too much, they'll leave Cypress via the bottom of the Avinreach." Whitfore pulls their arm away and leans against Rho's worktable. "Noah doesn't know it's Rhoheme or that Johana's a human priestess. But if she figures it out on her own, that's your fault for not locking *me* in that infirmary."

"You're faring better than I was."

Eirjatal visits Rho when Whitfore has gone to bed or is out for dinner, and though she never stirs, she seems to not be getting worse. Whitfore's bizarre appearance in Dianthus seems more and more like a clever ploy by the Nelaeryn Fey, as much as Eirjatal loathes the idea that She knows what he let happen to Rho. "Do you worship their Blind Adder?"

"No."

That answer came fast. "You're full of surprises, then."

How strange it is to see Sigyn's child grown up. Whitfore is the spitting image of their father—blonde hair, amber skin, nose objectively too long for their face. They have their father's build, lanky and steered by the shoulders. Eyes not so blue and not so grey but plenty cold. But while Whitfore is like sharp hoarfrost, Sigyn is slick black ice. They hold themselves differently. Someone like Sigyn is all about how they hold themselves.

It still puzzles Eirjatal that Sigyn's half-blood lived in the Heatherwol palace for nearly two decades, and yet information about them is scarce. Moonwardens are typically private. Kinthe has hardly left the Dawn Hall in her near-century of service, a statue for prayer rather than an elf with wants or friends. The Nelaeryn Fey had another life before Cypress, and asking questions about that isn't proper. Neither, then, is speculating on the personal lives of Her chosen vessels.

Only the nobility have intimate access to the Moonwardens, and somehow, so did Eirjatal and Rho. Rho earned his trust via her time in Heatherwol's Hawks. They held the secret of Sigyn's Etreal family—a secret that, perhaps, no nobility wanted to examine because the implication was too grim.

Back then, the Winter elves were, one by one, falling into a dead sleep by what Cypress helplessly called a curse. The Eclipsed Moonwarden, Khidell, was captured and killed in Ventaris, his magic unable to pass on. Elves with Woven magic were exiled or systematically disillusioned from the whole affair of a bloodline (certainly not helped by Eirjatal's own mother burning herself to death in public after Ashvaren ordered her exile). For reasons that the Fey *still* has not explained to even Sigyn, it was becoming nearly impossible to conceive a child, and besides, elves aren't famous for their instinct to care for useless, ugly things.

Then years of fear and suspicion about half-bloods diluted into this: the elves were dwindling, and Sigyn presented a glimmer of resilience where no one wanted to see it.

Rho said that if anyone could make a sexually-depraved fluke look like the Fey's will, it was Sigyn—but Cypress would sooner denounce *him* before seeing half-bloods as a sign of Cypress's recovery.

Eirjatal can't help but ask, "Do you not subscribe to the Fey at all?"

"That's considered a pretty rude question in most circles."

That gently taunting cadence—that's the Sigyn he knew. "Around here, there's the belief that an elf without the Fey is not an elf at all."

"Around here, none of you believe I'm an elf anyways."

"And? Neither do you. But you know you look like one. You would not have been in those estates otherwise."

Their shoulders stiffen. But they lilt, "Curious about them?"

"I was alive when the stories they told about elves were true. Villages spun tales that became tangled epics by the time they reached cities. I'd like to think I inspired some on my own." *As did your father.* "But I was never right at their ear like you."

"Are you encouraging me?"

Eirjatal scoffs. "I *am* impressed. Cypress can use all the advantages we can get."

"You had me fooled, with burning me and all that." Whitfore asks, "Why did you ask about the Fey?"

"Because you are from Her. Something in both of us belongs in Cypress. Where do you think that piece of you should go, if not to Her?"

"Honestly, if the Fey actually wanted me, she shouldn't've opened negotiations by telling me all the reasons she didn't." Whitfore pulls their blonde hair behind a shoulder, wincing. "I don't waste time worrying about it."

Unbelievably, it's sympathy that pushes up in Eirjatal. Half-blood children put the Nelaeryn Fey in the precarious position of owning something that belongs in part to the Woven, and the Woven in the enviable position of having claim over something the Fey cherishes. Sigyn is either fantastically selfish or thinks he has so much sway over the Fey that he can push Her into challenging gods much stronger, older, and allied than She is.

Before Eirjatal can reply, a sound like twisting rusted metal shakes through the table. Eirjatal snags a tipping vase before it hits the ground.

"Stay."

He sweeps down the hall, but draws short at the top of the stairwell—something heavy crashes against the metal walls, making them vibrate. Both he and his magic don't like being surprised.

He doesn't get the chance to brace. He clutches blindly at the rail as the bottom stair explodes.

A sea-glass morningstar is pulled from the stairs, raining splinters, and around the corner lumbers one of the armoury's sentries. The metal joints groan, and oleanders and dirt spill from its empty face onto the rug.

From behind him, Whitfore—who apparently can't keep out of anything—hisses, "Since when is that *alive?*"

"It's Rho's," he snaps. "And I said *stay.*"

The automaton seems to be searching, blind, through the hollow cavern of its helmet for whoever woke it up. Eirjatal sees no one else. Of course not. Any thief would have darted or is already taken care of in the armoury.

Eirjatal takes a careful step down the stairs, trying to not alarm it or himself. It towers two feet taller than him, twice as broad. Its joints make an angry, shivering sound that he can feel in his teeth. A plate bears Ashvaren's eel crest. Beautiful enough to be Rho's, cold enough to be the old Starmorrow's.

Rho gave her sentries a failsafe, but he can't remember for the life of him what this one's is.

Is it a spoken command? It can't be as simple as "stop." Not some physical switch; it won't let me get that close. It has to be spoken then, but knowing her, it's a damn riddle. Why didn't she ever tell me?

Eirjatal glances around it. It slowly pivots to keep him in its sights. Behind it, the wall of Vyriseh's unoccupied room is crushed. Beyond that is the door to the armoury, ripped off its hinges, and a shadow flickering around the curve of the hall.

And a guard, coming up the other staircase, with much the same idea as Eirjatal, but far too fast.

Eirjatal has barely gathered enough breath to speak before it strikes. Faster than its grinding joints made it seem capable of. Its weapon hitting the corner of the wall clangs like a gong, yet cruelly doesn't cover the sound of morningstar hitting skull, body hitting floor.

A torrent of heat races up his back and down his arms—he throws a hand out so he doesn't burn his own face off. He incinerates the sentry's helmet and all the flowers within it.

But it isn't alive, so it doesn't react to the fire and doesn't hesitate in lunging for him. He ducks and nearly loses his footing in the ash and twisted pieces of helmet, and crashes shoulder-first into the wall.

His back is to the body. Its presence seems as immense, as immediate, as the sentry, pressing in behind him.

Eirjatal Ga'vrynn, you pathetic bastard. You know death.

The grinding sound again, so loud that he can hardly hear himself think. The hall narrows. Ice slips across the back of his neck, freezing every instinct in his body.

Whitfore cries out.

Eirjatal startles out of the way.

The glass edge of the morningstar clangs off his decorative bracer. Heat sparks in his veins and burns away the phantom ice.

Back then, in the Ineiren Fort, his fire froze under his skin.

Back then, calf-deep in snow, with no escape under the will of gods that didn't belong to him, fire did so little.

Now, it melts the suit of armour and whatever metal heart Rho gave it into a twisted statue.

Eirjatal stills. He lets the fire starve, curling hungrily into every corner of the hollow armour, rather than snuffing it out himself. He isn't sure he could if he tried. He's shaking. The sentry melts into itself like paint dripping down a canvas.

Rhoheme will be furious.

Whitfore minces around what must be the guard's body, back of their hand pressed to their mouth.

"Find..." The word drains him of air. He swallows and manages, "Find someone—" *to help? To check on him? Maybe he's alive. I should know his name.*

Unable to find the rest of the phrase, Eirjatal ducks beneath the armoury's destroyed doorframe.

Curiously, the other sentry didn't even make it to the door before collapsing in a heap of metal and dirt. At the head of the hall, Scintia's evocation still stands, tidy and sure, on its pedestal.

Eirjatal circles the structure, hunting for fingerprints, for a crack, anything—throwing all his attention into it. But it's flawless as always, patiently dripping beads through the levers and scales, as complex and purposeful as capillaries. A mystery to Scintia herself, who made it, much less to everyone else.

Then why did Rho's security react? He turns to the collapsed one and risks touching its pauldron. Nothing. The room no longer hums with Rho's magic.

Whitfore's suddenly behind him. "Someone's coming up—"

A gust of fire hits the floor between them. Whitfore leaps back. For a flicker, their shout from the stairwell rises in his head like a tide and brings his pulse with it. He remembers the sound of glass striking bone. Worse sounds than that have played an endless call-and-response in his nightmares, but it's been a long time since he's been scared like this.

Eirjatal closes his fingers around the residual, comforting burn. Drags in a long breath. There's little use in telling his heart that it's over.

"I'll speak to them. Stay here. I mean it."

11

Irving

We have heard of your exploits with the estate of Anya Zarina and the curious nature of your existence in Staventene. We extend an invitation to discuss your resources and our use for them. Our primary concern is transparency within the elite of Etreal, the aid of which you are uniquely positioned to provide.

House of Ciphers to Irving, self-destructing letter, Age of Shields 250

"They really hate you, rabbit," Noah says, tearing a breakfast bun in half.

Irving takes the offered pastry with a groan. What they saw earlier makes the bread and honey taste like ash. The red dawn barely breaks on the horizon, the night having been full of interrogations and Eirjatal telling the same story a million times over. Noah was lured in by the chaos. Now, she and Irving sit at the end of the hall while the nobility discuss in the armoury.

"Tavreah was putting your sun goddess to shame, breathing down your neck like that. Feist, or whatever her name is."

"Faowist," they correct blandly. "And of course. I'm apparently the only criminal this palace knows exists."

"Say it was a thief. Think it could've been Johana?"

"She's too afraid to crack a window."

"But she's got the run of the Dawn Hall during the night. Well, the three hours where the Dawn Hall bothers to sleep."

"Eirjatal locks her in." Irving leaves out that they're the one with the key. They glance at the guards keeping either of them from booking it down the stairwell, then whisper, "…Okay, honestly. It wasn't you?"

"No! You be honest. It wasn't you?"

"Nope."

"Someone's trying to steal our thunder," Noah mumbles into her food.

"Why would anyone even want those things?"

According to Noah, there are five of them, one for each kingdom of Cypress—even the defunct Spring kingdom that Ashvaren dissolved. They were made by Scintia and given to Ashvaren to protect, a job he took so seriously that he even risked using Rhoheme and her power from Staventa, the Woven goddess of crafting, to do it.

Noah brushes crumbs off her skirt. "Maybe elves could smash them and sell off the pieces as bits of Scintia's magic? Everyone's so superstitious about her, especially since Winter got cursed…you could make up any story about what'll happen if you put it in your stocking, and elves would fall for it."

"Speaking of…selling. Sorry, by the way."

"What? Why?"

"Our whole thing's pretty much gone up in flames. I don't know if you needed it, but—"

"We weren't gonna ride off into the sunset together as kingpins. I'll figure it out. I mean, I'm the one who still has an actual job." Noah huffs. "You didn't say anything to Cereus. That's loads better than an apology."

"It's not like outing you would've helped me."

"I'm…" Noah's fringe tumbles into her round face. "I worked here under Ashvaren. Even the staff pushed each other into the mud for the chance to look the cleanest, you know?" Her expression eases into a smirk. "But I'm pissed. I wanted out of this palace and now I'm right back on the slow track. Thanks a lot."

"Yeah, but—"

A new voice joins in. "You two aren't eavesdropping, I hope?"

Noah yanks Irving to their feet and all but shoves them into bowing. Sunmirren Vyriseh sashays the rest of the way down the hall and taps a dagger-nailed finger under both their chins to straighten them up. She says, "Just between us, there was no gossip worth hearing. I escaped as soon as I could."

"Do you need something, Sunmirren?" Noah's tone is floaty and kind, which is so unlike her it nearly makes Irving laugh.

But Vyriseh brightens. "I do, actually! I need help fixing up my room. In all the chaos, it seems the Dawn Hall forgot about me."

Her yellow gaze settles on Irving. Their stomach sinks, and not only because they'll keel over if they have to go another hour without sleep. Noah's incredulousness wafts off her in waves but Irving sees no choice besides, "I could help."

"Oh, divine! You," she points at Noah, "grab some bins. And a mop. I wasn't warned about all the blood. No one expects the Sunmirren of Silvershale to be squeamish."

The attack happened so close to Vyriseh's door that blood reached her room. It's not apparent at first, as the wall it's sprayed on is scorched black.

A frozen wave of silk and sparkle spills across the floor. The apartment reeks of melted metal and charred fabric. Irving steps over an armoire's broken leg, carved into a humanoid, seaweed-wrapped calf.

The memory pushes in—the glass-studded Morningstar, the arc of it as heavy as a smithing hammer but quick as a whip, and the elf's skull giving in like a plaster stage mask.

In Staventene, the estate drama was all lover's quarrels and illegitimate children and banal corporate evil. But this... Who was going after Scintia's creation? Why?

Leave it. It's the Fey's problem now, if she even cares.

As Irving sorts through debris and ruined clothes, Vyriseh's gaze hovers, icy, on the back of their neck. Most of her dresses are Dianthus's style, with real flowers and feather-light embroidery and swaths of exposed skin. When Vyriseh came to Heatherwol, she would shop the local markets and bring tons of Silvershale presents. Luckily she never gave Adamantine anything as high-maintenance as the chimera kitten she gifted Cereus.

Vyriseh came to Heatherwol, but more often, Sigyn left for Silvershale to stand in for Vyriseh's lack of Moonwarden. Her previous one, Khidell, was studied, tortured, and killed by a Ventaris academy a few decades before Irving was born—one of the many reasons Cypress nurses a specific grudge towards Ventaris, a city of ambition and academics.

But maybe it was more than religious duty that called Sigyn out there. Adamantine did mention Sigyn and Vyriseh having a project together.

Who knows. Maybe he's just cheating.

Irving lifts a black gown with a burned-through bodice. Its seashell detailing has mostly turned to white ash. They start to set it in a trash pile—and Vyriseh whimpers.

"I want that one fixed. A seamstress made it especially for me." Clearly; it has two sets of sleeves. "I haven't even worn it yet."

The fabric crumbles in Irving's fingers like wet paper, but even so they note the fine material and the artsy waste of time that is Cypresian stitching. Even the thread that seals the hem is shaped like ferns. "She'd be flattered to have a repeat customer."

"The damage would reveal our trouble in paradise, wouldn't it? Though…" Vyriseh approaches and trails her fingers along the burned bodice. "Could I ask you to help?"

"I'm sure Eirjatal can point you to one of the maids."

Vyriseh tilts her head, a loop of silvery hair falling on her high cheekbone. "Aren't you a tailor back home?"

A flash of alarm freezes them.

"You work in a theatre. When not in Staventene estates, of course. Surely something so ostentatious is not beyond your skills."

"How do you know that?" Despite themselves, there's an edge to their tone.

"I was curious," Vyriseh says, like she can't be expected to be anything else. She touches their wrist. "Radiance was in Staventene. I asked her to look around, learn a little."

Irving's grip tightens on the ruined fabric, the boning biting back. They expect sniffing around from Sigyn, not from the queen of a kingdom they've never stepped into. "You were curious about what I did with Heartswain, then?"

Irving knows about Radiance from Sigyn. Since Khidell died outside Cypress, his Nelaeryn Fey-given magic couldn't pass on to the next chosen elf in Silvershale. It makes sense that Vyriseh replaced her Moonwarden with a companion that could rip out a few throats—or slip away in bat form if she was caught.

Cypress hated her choice. However, Irving's getting the feeling that no one tells Vyriseh *no*. She and Sigyn aren't so different in that respect.

"Did you know the people you worked for are looking for you?"

"Are you lying?"

Vyriseh folds up her dress against Irving's chest; it makes Irving aware that their heart is hammering. "Why would I lie?"

"To scare me after finding out who I was selling Heartswain to."

"Oh, Irving. No. I'm Eclipsed. We're the original thieves of Heartswain," she says with a light laugh. "We stole it from the Nelaeryn Fey and ate it with such greed that eventually we became our nightmares. Frankly, I admire the gall. There's Cypress in you yet." She sweeps to the unharmed vanity and opens a jewelry box. "I don't want your fear."

She hands over a folded note. The broken wax seal is imprinted with an interlocked winged snake and key. Irving's pulse stutters.

The House of Ciphers.

It's addressed to a name Irving doesn't recognize and they'd bet is fake. Irving skims, unnerved by the weight of Vyriseh's stare, and catches, 'traced back to the exposure of Anya Zarina's fraud schemes' and 'ill-advised to hire a practiced liar' and 'perhaps Etreal gossip catches a higher price with Feyspawn' and 'easy enough. End the gentleman's agreement to let them sell and find what else they've spread that they shouldn't have. Ventaris laws are shaped around protecting its elites from Cypress, after all.'

Their balance swings. They flip the sheet for more words, but there's nothing. They can only gasp, "Radiance would make a good spy."

"I suppose you understood all that better than I did."

They're four days late to the appointment with the House of Ciphers. Of course someone got suspicious. Of course they've got eyes like Faowist, seeing everything at once.

And it's not like Irving was very good at keeping the information they gathered to themselves—they had to store what they were going to resell somewhere out of their own head. The Ciphers probably broke into their damn apartment.

Cypress can use all the advantages we can get, Eirjatal had said. Of course it looked like they were doing this for Cypress.

"Now, now." Vyriseh takes the dress and sets it aside. One of her hands squeezes Irving's shoulder and they feel like shattered glass. "Not being able to defend your livelihood and reputation…that's the true punishment and Cereus can't even take credit for it." She laughs behind her hand. "But you agree you owe me quite a lot, don't you?"

"Owe you?"

Vyriseh counts on her fingers. "I lied for you and your accomplice, directly before the Starmorrow. I risked Radiance in Staventene, so close to these Ciphers who come from Ventaris, who I have much reason to fear. I've given you a piece of home, and let you prepare for your downfall before you go free. And, well…"

She lets the last one hang.

"Whoa, whoa," they say, panicked enough that they nearly slip into the familiar language of Etren. "I am paying you back. What about—"

"The dresses? They can repay the lie that let the little serving girl go free, and ensure I don't let it slip in the future."

"I didn't ask for this." They snap the letter in the air. Even Noah would balk at their tone, but this is Cypress. They don't feel inclined to respect anyone.

Vyriseh plucks away the letter and folds it into quarters. Her second set of eyes flick open, as unnerving as Marie's. "I have a simple request that will clear the debts. Are you much of a religious person, Irving Whitfore?"

"No."

"But you know what Etreal elites know," she tucks the letter into their breast pocket, "and they know quite a lot about their gods. You see, the Autumn Moonwarden and I, well…you're not the only meddler in the family. While you and your dear mother live in Etreal, he chases down its legends with me." She turns on a heel and swipes a book off her bed. "What scares him so much about asking you? You two have so little time as it is."

Vyriseh hands them the book. "This is from that little Priestess. She tried to help, but there's nothing that writing can tell me that experience cannot relay much, much better. Tell me and your father stories of your world that will never be ours, and I'll consider it all repaid."

This is way too close to what they want, so close she must have read it in their mind: a chance to learn about what Sigyn's always up to. By the way she's smirking, she must know she's playing all the right notes.

But Irving can't do it as themselves. Here, Staventene, their stupid hubris with the Ciphers—they never really do anything as themselves. And that other person is cocky without concern.

So they say, "If he knows I'm involved, he's going to stop me. Throw in a disguising enchantment for free, and I'll help."

12

Eirjatal

Only Scintia and one other survived the Evertide that night. They stayed for Relyn. They fought like the Archfey. I have seen them, and I say that they sleep guarded by Nele. She only shows herself to the newborn and to the dying, and I think, at once, they are both.

Sunmirren Firewe's notes on the fall of the Ineiren Fort, Age of Beasts 4

Blood drips out of Eirjatal's fist into the waves.

Eirjatal needs to focus on the water and the blood and the begging but he can't. When the moonlight tips off the tides, he can see the pallor of Rho's face in it.

Logical Adamantine decided they couldn't puzzle out what happened if they were tired, so Eirjatal had gone to his apartment, and laid on his sofa perfectly still, and pressed his hand to his heart every time it sped up to a panicked race without permission. Eventually, it pulled him to the seashore.

He shakes his hand, blood flecking off his fingertips. Rho was the only one bit in that river, but he was slashed—the sirens know his scent. Madainn has lived in his dreams, in the back of his neck, for centuries. He knows Madainn. He knows Madainn's minions, those whose pulses beat with the god's heart.

He knows how to anger them, clearly.

If only he knew how to *summon* them.

The water is abnormally quiet.

Eventually, he bites open a vitaea flower bud with a fang, presses the petals like stitches along the cut, and wraps his hand in a scrap of linen.

You are not finished bleeding.

Sigyn had traced this exact cut in his hand.

He'd also threatened more damage with that steady vertical line up his inner arm to his elbow. Four centuries ago, Nele wept a river in the Glasswood after an elf killed himself, and that river still runs, tempting in the otherwise barren tundra, but packed with enough salt to dry you out like game. It's never happened again. But a cut like that…

Eirjatal stuffs his hands in his pockets and keeps walking. It's like stepping off a high platform into the dark, abandoning the shore like this.

Halfway up the beach, he spots Cereus's silhouette flashing in the puddles of gas lamp light, hanging ivy making blurry shadows on his face. Eirjatal meets him on the stone pathway leading to the Dawn Hall.

"Eirj!" Cereus touches Eirjatal's arm, reconsiders, and pulls back. "I couldn't find you inside, then saw you off the balcony and—what are you doing out here?"

"Do you need me for something?"

Cereus's gaze flicks to the ocean behind them. Whatever he thinks is going on, it can't be anything flattering—but the truth isn't any better.

Finally, Cereus says, "Do you want to contribute to the funeral offerings? Also, if you know a contact I can tell before the city…Tavreah couldn't find anyone."

Words fall, hollow, from his mouth. "Did you notify the rest of the staff?"

"Only when I couldn't find you. I'm sorry if you wanted to do it yourself."

Cereus is too empathetic to convincingly play stupid; he knows Eirjatal disappeared because he wasn't up for it. Not now, and not then.

Eirjatal knew everything about everyone in the Ineiren Fort. Names, histories, homes. He knew what they looked like when they were dead or (worse, much worse,) dying. When he was brought back to Dianthus, somehow all the details vanished. As if their canvas in his memory was locked away and he still can't get the door open, but it's there, he knows it is. Scintia reported everything for him instead.

"When is the funeral?"

"Morning, first thing. I'll be in town to help organize. It's kind of a…" Cereus's smile comes in more crooked and soft-eyed than usual. "Tavreah said it was a damper on Lightbringing, but right now Nele's closer to Cypress than ever. It's going to be gorgeous."

He falls in step with Eirjatal. Eirjatal takes care to keep Cereus on his side without the injured hand, but allows himself their brushing shoulders. This compassionate, defiantly optimistic Cereus is his favourite.

"Kinthe wanted us to all talk *before* starting any funeral stuff. But what can we say that's more important than the city knowing someone's gone back to Nele?"

"To her credit," which he is loath to give, "this was a near-miss theft on one of the last remaining pieces of Scintia."

"But Kinthe and Sigyn scryed on all the wards and said there won't be any more suspicious stuff. Sigyn even said that the Fey doesn't want us to take Scintia's evocations out."

"Why on earth?"

Cereus furrows his black eyebrows. "Rho didn't tell any of us the solutions, so the Fey doesn't know them, and She doesn't want to learn them?"

"Damn, he never changes."

"Ada suggested guards because maybe it's us *doing* something that'll stop whoever it was from trying again, but," and here his voice transforms into the vulnerable surety of the ambassador who defended Eirjatal and Rho from Ashvaren time and time again, "I don't want anyone close to the wards. Are they *all* like the Summer ones?"

"Knowing Ashvaren and Rho, yes."

It's not as if Rho filled their shared apartment with death traps, but she was more interested in innovation than practicality. While she was remaking the labyrinth, he had to sidle around butcher paper full of maps and notes spread on the floor, and he talked her down from automatic gates and sphinx-like riddles to lead you into secret nooks (though she did tease him that she worked *one* in, if he could ever find it).

The light diffuses through the leaves, casting green and blue shadows on Cereus's inconveniently beautiful face. A wave of black hair has fallen over the subtle point of his ear.

"Eirj, I don't think anyone was stealing *anything*. I think it was Rho."

The alarm from that statement overpowers any thoughts of handsomeness. "In what way?"

"You've seen how Sigyn's arm is bothering him. And the Dawn Hall…every part of it that she made…there's something off, right? It sounds different. And now this."

"You think the magic is failing without her?"

"We have no idea how her magic works. Rho said that her family never made anything they didn't destroy, so we don't know what happens to their inventions when… Does yours work differently from hers? The gardens kept burning after Yrena died."

"That's how real fire behaves, so that doesn't explain much."

The implications of that story—of his mother immolating herself decades ago—unravel like a spool of barbed wire. Is Rho losing her grip on her magic? Or is she tightening her hold on it until it chokes?

Cereus sighs, running his hands through his hair. "I wish there was a way to ask her what happened. With that creepy priestess that Vyriseh brought…"

The cold wave of a memory strikes Eirjatal. In Etreal as a Hawk, they would spread rumours amongst each other about the Woven. *The Bladelord sharpens his sword in the ears of rulers and sycophants until all they hear is the ring of gold and set off to war. Eojhest's the most moral of them all, but apparently he can't even remember to guard his own nights—in case you think humans are at their worst during the day under his sister.*

They say Blind Adder priestesses can speak to the dead. Only for a second. But it's enough for what they need.

Cereus asks, "You're alright?"

"Will you forgive me something?"

"What is it?"

"The Blind Adder. I need a ritual."

Cereus relaxes, like he was expecting some horrible confession. Then with a firm hand behind his shoulder, he leads Eirjatal to the castle. "I'm not Ashvaren. I want you to do whatever you can to save her."

13

Irving

If you live honorably, do not fear death. With someone to beg your quality at your bedside, the Blind Adder will consider saving you. If you live dishonorably, and there is style, notoriety, and ardent cruelty to that dishonorableness...do not fear death. The Blind Adder is a goddess who has overseen millions of bland, quiet ends, and bland, quiet people, and she loves nothing more than a surprise.

The Four Lives of Sybil Viran, published Age of Illumination 31

Vyriseh isn't very careful with her books.

Sitting in bed, Irving frowns at the frayed nubs of pages. A whole chapter's been ripped out. Not a loss; living in Staventene has taught them more than this book can cover, at least in breadth if not depth. But that proves Vyriseh's point. She wants to hear it from the mouth of someone who's lived in it.

They flip to the table of contents to see what's missing, working around their light source (a couple blue starlight pixies striking poses like the illustrations).

On the Banquet that Laid the Tapestry. Story goes that right before the planet's opening night, all the Woven gods had dinner to brainstorm the final touches. Each of their chalices contributed. The most innocent was Eojhest's. The god of night gave a toast so enthusiastic that his sloshing wine made the red dawn. Some of them set their chalices around the Tapestry, with stories warped by time about what would happen if mortals recovered one.

Irving wouldn't be surprised if there's some stupid Cypress conspiracy that the Woven schemed to poison the Fey during the banquet she wasn't even invited to. Maybe chasing down those conspiracies is part of the Moonwarden job.

"Sorry. Theatre's closed," Irving whispers to the pixies as they close the book. They set it and their folded glasses on their bedside table. Noah's been dead asleep since they got back, but Irving's still thinking of the scattered reflections they saw in the evocation and the blood sprayed on Vyriseh's armoire.

The pixies try to get their drawings back, but the pages are too heavy. It takes three to get the cover open. Then it's a matter of scrabbling at the pages to turn them, their soft blue light smearing over the ink—

And the symbol of a winged snake and key.

Irving pushes up on an elbow. There on the publisher's page, between the tiny feet of the pixies, is the symbol of the House of Ciphers.

They have the feeling that someone's following them through a crowded street.

A knock on the door practically shoots them out of bed.

Noah doesn't stir. The pixies scatter into the bedsheets. Irving waits, not sure they didn't dream the sound, until it happens again.

On the other side is Eirjatal.

"I need your assistance."

Irving unlocks the infirmary door. They would have rather knocked to wake Johana up, but—

Johana jumps away from Rhoheme's bedside, so fast that Irving jolts too. The priestess drops a jar and it explodes on the floor. Of *course* it's the jar of spiders.

"It's just me. Holy shit."

"I only thought—I'm sorry."

Johana presses a hand to her heart like Irving and Eirjatal came in pointing pistols at her. Careful not to step on any spiders, Irving sidles around Vyriseh's dress, piled on a desk like a billowing fog amidst what they salvaged from her armoire for spare fabric.

White spiders skitter everywhere, like snow tossed by the wind, but when Johana folds onto the floor, their paths redirect so they all dance into her palms. Amidst the glass are the yellow cosmos Irving brought her yesterday, hoping to liven up *this* room, not the spiders'.

While Irving tidies the glass, Johana tips the spiders into Rhoheme's mouth. Marie appears out of nowhere and slithers across their feet.

Eirjatal asks, "You can let me speak to Rhoheme, Priestess?"

It's the first time Irving's ever heard Johana say "No."

They'd wager it's the first time she's ever said it to Eirjatal, considering how he double-takes. Johana seems equally shocked.

"Is there a reason why?" His Etren is jagged, thickly-accented, unlike Sigyn's.

Johana lifts a hand to her shoulder, then freezes, like she realized Marie isn't there. "The ritual…it's risky. It doesn't—this isn't routine. If it was, I'd be—I'd *love* for you to speak to her. But summoning her into Irving…"

Irving interjects, "Sorry?"

Eirjatal makes an unfamiliar gesture that, despite the language barrier, definitely means *shut up*, staring down Johana in a way that explains the perfect behaviour of the staff. Johana chews on what Irving assumes to be the lengthy processes, prayers, and theologies that she murmurs to Irving all the time, but she settles on, "It's *difficult*."

Irving says, "Please explain *summoning*. And *into*."

"We'd...we'd exchange your consciousness with Rhoheme's. She'd take your body. Only for a moment." She's already caving.

Eirjatal says, "Priestess. If you fail to prove your use, you do not go home, you understand?"

That one *no* was all Johana could muster. She skitters to her wall of equipment like a whipped dog.

Irving's indignation must be written all over their face, because when they turn to Eirjatal, he says in Cypresian, "We know the end of this argument."

Ice slides under their skin. Eirjatal can easily tip Sigyn off. Their relationship's paper-thin as it is. Irving doesn't need to go shearing holes in it.

Eirjatal continues, "You react better to the magic than I did. It's impressive; you're resilient. I'm surprised you aren't enjoying the notoriety more, given what your last job was."

"I only like it when I'm paid for it."

"No, if you're anything like your father, I think you enjoy being a bit of a myth, too."

"Well, if you're sweet-talking me into it." They'd placed some distance between the Eirjatal in the workroom and the Eirjatal who burned Dianthus's sigil into their back. Naive.

Johana's fussing from corner to corner, pulling down seemingly random jars, opening and closing drawers, darting like a minnow hiding under rocks. For how apparently integral Irving is to Rhoheme, Johana doesn't like them knowing much about the rituals, so all Irving thinks of to do is collect a couple chairs from the crooked stacks.

Eirjatal's pulled aside the screen to see Rhoheme and it's frozen him.

Eirjatal traces her ragged wounds, where Irving and Johana have broken out and shaved down the stone that grows from her bones. Irving feels like they should sense the touch, considering how much of them is running through Rhoheme's veins.

Irving moves beside Johana in the far corner of the room. She's failing to open a cork on a vial of black tincture, so Irving takes it from her.

They ask, voice low, "Do you know the House of Ciphers?"

Johana freezes, but they aren't sure if it's from the question or them taking the vial away. She murmurs, "They work closely with my temple. They have many publications like that—atypical interpretations, questions..." She taps out a black, powdery something into another jar; it's so fine that a thin cloud of dust curls out of the neck. "I don't, well, I didn't get where I am from accepting what I was told. They're good for questions. They ask you to question things. Why?"

"If they work with your temple, you must be from Ventaris."

Johana perpetually looks like someone's holding her worst secrets over her head, but Irving senses a new layer to her edginess. Maybe it's got nothing to do with the Ciphers. Maybe she's afraid of Irving, as much an elf as any to Johana, knowing she's from Ventaris. That's all.

Ventaris. It's bizarre that whoever brought her in for Rhoheme found help there, in the city that gave Cypress so much grief.

"I know the Ciphers too."

Eirjatal cuts in, "Whitfore, come here."

Johana turns away, so they approach Eirjatal. The spiders have resurfaced, black with the ichor they eat out of Rhoheme's lungs, and they scatter among the sheets like poppy seeds. Eirjatal is smearing something between his thumb and forefinger. It's flaky, the grey-green of what grows out of Rho's skin.

But there, on Rho's arm, is a ridge of gold.

It's as polished and bright as the gold all over the labyrinth gardens, the Dawn Hall, the destroyed armoury. They say, surprised to find themselves a bit breathless, "It's never been like that before."

"Has anything else changed with her since you've joined us?"

They shake their head. They aren't sure, really. Every improvement with Rhoheme is swallowed back up in a day, like the tide pulling in.

Once they're both seated, Johana ties a waxed cord tightly around Irving's wrist. She ties the other end around Rhoheme's. Eirjatal, pushing back Rhoheme's hair from her forehead, asks, "Is that all?"

Johana takes the poultice she prepared and smears it along two creases in Irving's palm, then Rhoheme's. With rare steadiness, she says, "Rituals are simple, because the Adder isn't only for the rich. Whether they live or not…isn't decided by what they have." The light flicks off a snake fang—that she pierces into Irving's palm. They flinch with a curse.

Eirjatal's gaze tracks her. He inhales through his teeth, tasting the air and the mortal scent of her. Her fear. Irving can smell that too, if they let themselves focus. *Some think it's predatory*, Sigyn explained to them with self-conscious candour, *and others call it defensive, like a deer sensing a wolf. I suppose it depends how it's used.*

Eirjatal flinches for Rhoheme when the fang goes through her palm with much more resistance. No blood rises around the fang.

Irving's stomach flips at the idea of her taking control of their body—a complete stranger. With the Blind Adder at the helm.

Marie lies half on Johana and half on the back of Irving's chair, Johana touching the black dart on her head. Irving shuts their eyes. Tries to relax. They've never seen Johana involve Marie, like a tether for comfort, and they've also never felt so sure with the snake so close.

Johana says, "She won't be…exactly how she was before. She's been whittled down to…she's small, small enough to travel between you. She can only feel one thing at a time."

Irving thinks she's warning Eirjatal, but when they crack open an eye, they find Johana looking at them.

They've dealt with other people's desires via Heartswain for years, with people's emotions boiled down into mindless instinct, trying to pull Irving into the fray. They can handle this. They nod.

Johana pulls on a thread of magic like tying off a stitch, Marie curls up to rest her head against the base of Johana's throat, and it begins.

The rise of the Blind Adder under their skin is too eager. Too familiar. Like she's emerging from somewhere *inside* Irving. She's known as an external god, sitting at bedsides or dealing in cards and dice—so Johana's rituals never stop being unnerving, forcing Irving to roll out their shoulders and take a deep breath of the stagnant air to find their own skin.

But this time, something else has found it first.

Irving's heart shoots into their throat from the sudden crowding. The feeling of their clothes, the velvet chair, their braid pulling tightly behind their ears, the bite of fang in their hand, are plucked away one by one and replaced with a heartbeat like a fist slamming against a door.

They're underwater.

Bubbles sear their nose. Tight clothes constrict their lungs. Boots weigh them down, but not as much as the pain, ripping through their arm and down their side, into the unnervingly empty place beneath their rib cage.

Irving tips hard against the bed. They can blearily see the cot and feel Eirjatal grabbing their arm to steady them, but *Rho* is drowning, brackish water heaving into her lungs, and an acrid poison crawling through her veins like it's alive.

Eirjatal hisses, "Let her *through*, Aphithea."

Maybe it's the Cypresian name they left behind, or it's how they feel like weak threads tangled together, or maybe it's Rhoheme surging towards the sound of *that voice, his voice.* But Irving is slashed away, and Rhoheme finds herself freefalling in a body she doesn't belong to.

14

21: Forty-three Winter elves succumbed to complete catatonia. Recollections of onset are incoherent, though scant patterns originate from Sunmirren Scintia's dreams.

98: Dianthus's Relyn prayer tree rots when touched, but has not died. Situation unresolved.

186: Another nest of dead Briarlords found on perimeter search. This has finally inspired camaraderie amongst the camps.

Hawk records selected by Khidell for Sunmirren Vyriseh's investigation. Footnote: *If the goddess is prophetic, perhaps, too, is the realm.*

The world is too bright.

Rhoheme remembers black water, a pain ripping her in half. Moments ago, a heartbeat ago. But here she is in the light, everything searing and sparkling—

Air trapped inside her lungs burns and boils. She anchors herself to Eirjatal, coughing. Black venom sprays white shore—white sheets. She's drowning. She's drowning. Panic roars in her ears and her nails dig into Eirjatal's skin as if, could she crawl into his body instead, she would live.

"Rho. Don't come back to me like this—you didn't die. I saved you."

A rattling inhale surges through her chest. Rho gasps, "Not yet, you haven't," and the voice isn't hers. It's hardly this body's, choked as it is with river water and poison.

Eirjatal presses something into her palm, and she empties of pain. The light softens.

Fox sparrow.

The little bird picks at its feathers, and though it's made of metal and emerald inlays the colours of his eyes, it feels *soft*. Her magic hums. The most alive thing about her, still shimmering, still singing.

She wasn't drowning. No. She was tracking this tiny bird in the dark, all the way to where it pressed against Eirjatal's heart. She found it over and over.

"I knew you survived," she whispers. "Because of this."

A tickle on her nose cuts through the haze. She realizes she has control, she can breathe, and so she does, while blood drips off her face and onto the sheets.

This isn't her face.

The hand holding the fox sparrow is light brown with fine bones casting shadows as it moves—as she moves—like how light swims off scales.

And the body under the sheets is hers.

A painting of herself. Something she'd return to the artist, demanding what parasitic shadow they saw crawling under her skin and how to erase it.

Eirjatal thumbs the blood off her—off *whose?*—nose and mouth, blocking her view of herself. He whispers, "I'm so sorry," and his tone splinters. "There's a priestess—"

"Of the Blind Adder. I know." She isn't sure how.

His expression breaks in the way he's only ever let her see. So she's real enough. "I appealed to Relyn and Nele. I explained all I could. I'm sorry that the Blind Adder," he says with a flinch, "is the one keeping you."

There's a fang in her hand. This hand. And a cord linking this body to *her* body, dripping with a sweet-smelling substance that soaks gradually down the cord.

Don't bring me back.

Not yet.

"Rhoheme, what happened at the river?"

Rho's out of sync with this magicless body. It has hollow places. Not like a real body at all. Gouged-out wounds, bleeding bits of a goddess that isn't hers.

"Why did the sirens attack you?"

She clutches the pin so tightly that she can feel the feathers carving grooves. But it tethers her here more than this body does. It's what she knows. Metal, gears, *her* magic, *her* mind.

Sirens.

Sirens.

Scintia sent a note to Eirjatal. Madainn was looking for something in the Glasswood. That was the first surprise, and the second was that she had always had soldiers out there keeping an eye on it, in a way that reminded Rho too much of Eirjatal's paranoia. Scintia insisted Dianthus would be scoured next. Cypress had stolen something the god needed. Rho thought Scintia was delirious. Madainn lived in her and Eirjatal's veins, after all. Scintia told *him*, not the nobility, and that was as obvious a warning as a rattler on a snake.

What Madainn wanted, Eirjatal said, was either so immense that he had to know if he should alert the Moonwardens (*as if* he'd let someone else handle Madainn; he and Scintia were the same), or so small that he could safely give it to Madainn himself.

Rho built gold spears for the sirens, to buy a ritual that would connect them to Madainn. But she wondered, on those long nights when the sirens kept them under the river, waiting for the words of a god, what Eirjatal would offer his nightmare.

"I thought if they kept the offerings, they wouldn't care if we tried to run. But it was too late. Madainn was coming."

"It worked?"

"I overheard the sirens saying that we were liars. We had what Madainn wanted and would trick him out of it. If the sirens didn't kill us themselves, Madainn would have asked for one of us as an offering. I know it."

There's a spiral of emotion beyond her reach; she can't feel what it's made of, but she knows if it gets to her she'll damn near explode.

"You scared me," she says. "I know you—you'd die for this new Dianthus, and you'd die before you let Madainn claim Cypress again, but all that sounds like to me, Eirjatal, is that you'd rather die, so how was I supposed to trust you?"

Eirjatal murmurs, "You were right to stop us. To stop me."

"Always a step ahead of you."

"Always, Rho." His gaze ticks to her face, then back to *this* face. "I have to ask you something else."

"I have to *go*," she says, and it's so bizarre, like she needs to run for a coffee date, that she laughs—but it's not her laugh so it freaks her out all over again. She slaps a hand over this mouth.

"Go where?"

I can't remember. "I have to."

"One more moment. The ward for Summer's evocation from Scintia. Two automatons with hyacinths and oleander and—"

"And morningstars. He always wanted so much."

"Including your silence. I know, Rhoheme." He breathes her name like poetry. She has always loved Eirjatal's armoured exterior, and how it gives way to someone no one but her will ever know, because he doesn't know who's in there, either. She has always loved his ruthless mind, and always wanted to stop it from eating him from the inside. But he isn't made to be fixed. She figures he doesn't think so either, though he's never said as much.

He tilts up her head; she snaps back into the room. "Can you remember what happened to it last night?"

Rho clutches at this chest. *There*—that emotion, those ribbons, they strike her like when Eirjatal brought her a radio from his Hawk travels and she broke it open and it burned her fingers in bright red stripes.

It hurts. It hurt.

She was in the dark, and someone broke her magic.

She whips her head around and finds the priestess. This is who has been tending to her. She doesn't recognize her at all.

But the white snake on her shoulder…

That nameless feeling presses closer, wrapping up tight, knifing down her throat. Maybe it's a scream.

"The wards, Rhoheme."

I have to get back. I have to get back.

Morningstars and morning prayers. Space and time and a world forgotten. Free creatures, free flight, dawn again in the Dawn Hall, and—

She says, "I don't want you to. Not yet. I'll tell you when. Not yet."

"What are you talking about?"

"*Shhh.* I'm trying to remember." She presses a fist to this face. "I kept the solutions in my head so he couldn't kill me for them. Vyriseh…he hired her to pull them out so he could get rid of me. Vyriseh lied for me." It's like trying to see her thoughts through moving water. Ashvaren, Vyriseh—Cereus always at her side and weathering the worst of Ashvaren's cruelty before he helped her safely out of her contract. "I could feel the fox sparrow. I feel them all. The wards—they woke up, and it was like someone broke me open, trying to take something out. I'm hurting Sigyn, aren't I? I killed someone?"

"Not you—"

"Yes, me. I was all over this palace and Ashvaren had to deal with it, he had to deal with *me*. A sorcerer in his home. Spring in his home. He couldn't kill all of us. And we made it ours. A new Dianthus, Eirjatal, we decided on that. We'd help it grow deep roots."

The priestess says, "The ritual will end soon."

Rhoheme looks at her.

At the snake.

Her magic is in every piece of the palace that belongs to it—walls and trinkets, wards and windows, labyrinth gates, Sigyn's arm. The Summer ward is dull and damaged, and she recalls the sink of her glass in a skull, and the snake sliding over the corpse.

She leaps to her feet, unsteady—this body is taller than her own—and though she takes a breath when looking at the priestess, she forgets why because she's remembered her own corpse.

Ruined. Weak. Poison blackens the veins and shale and cruel gold break out of her skin. She balls a fist and the soaked cord strains against the tendons, pushes the fang in until it stings.

Eirjatal says, "I will tell you to your face that I'm sorry."

"Focus on that, and leave Madainn to me. I don't have a lot of time. Don't save me yet."

She tries to smile. Instinct pulls her back to the snake. She meets the priestess's eye. Whoever's body this is, they smell human fear like she could.

And then Irving startles awake.

They heave a gasp and find their lungs miraculously empty, their body no longer underwater. They don't remember falling, but Eirjatal catches them over the cot. His hands are painfully hot.

Eirjatal hisses, "How dare you?"

Johana is holding the cord and Irving's thread scissors. The brackish poultice has nearly soaked through the entire thing. Marie is hissing, the sound thin and blurred. Irving is shaking hard enough that Eirjatal moves around the cot and steadies them.

And focuses on their eyes for too long, like trying to find Rhoheme.

They remember the Adder stretching and finding a comfortable space in them again like someone coming home after a long trip.

Irving jerks away. "She's gone. Don't."

Eirjatal stands. He fires one last loathsome glower at Johana before whirling from the room.

Johana tends to Irving, all the while stroking Marie. She hands Irving a glass that's murky with her best attempt at mixing in vitaea. They drink it all despite the texture. Johana babbles, "It's not so much up to us, you know, as it's up to her and the goddess; it's *them*. I try to remember that."

Their head is spinning. But it's when Johana sets Marie's comforting weight against their shoulders that a memory clicks into place.

"It's you."

"Well—no. I suppose it's *my* magic, but with something complex like this, something that dips into the domains of other gods that wanted to kill her, it—"

"*No*." They set a hand on Marie's scales and insist, "It's you who's after the evocations."

Johana's eyes are enormous and terrified. But Irving can't stop. A laugh bubbles up. "Maybe your temple? Maybe the Ciphers? Not only you, not if you knew you'd be stuck in this room. And you *failed*. Even better."

The only murmur Johana has in her defence is, "Don't be so sure I failed."

15

Rhoheme

Rho wakes up.

She has three cards in her hand, fanned out to show their illustrations. Her chin is on a fist. She's at a table, and there's a circle of face-down cards all gleaming like the points of a star.

Rho asks, "Is this why I wanted to come back so badly?"

"Well, you *are* losing," the Blind Adder says.

The Blind Adder first proposed a different game, but Rho negotiated for this one. It wasn't some Etreal thing, precisely picked by the goddess so kings and peasants alike would know the rules when they were least capable of learning new strategies.

This is a Cypress game. The goddess jested when they began that Rho would have to teach her how to play.

The goal's to get rid of your opponents' cards while lying about your own.

In her hand is *The Kelpie, The Scout,* and *The Nightmare.* This half of the Heartswain pair shows the Eclipsed transforming into monsters. A shitty set. It's dangerous to have *The Kelpie* near anything mortal, and *The Nightmare* is useless when it's alone.

The Blind Adder also holds three cards in her porcelain white hand, so it *looks* fair, but there are three others face-down on the table at her elbow. She's connected to Rho by fine gold threads, so thin that Rho can only see them when she shifts in the exact right way, like spider webs.

"How was that possible?" Rho tries to gather the dregs of being in whoever's body that was—the warmth of Dianthus; the pressure of Eirjatal's hand; the musical hum of the palace's mechanics—but they're slipping away like the logic of a dream.

The Blind Adder observes her cards like an artist returning to her half-finished work. "It worked because my priestess asked."

The goddess's skin is so white that the blueish atrium light colours it like a canvas, same with half of her long, pin-straight hair; the other half is midnight black. Eyes flat, flat, flat, like onyx marbles. Her hands are cut at the wrist, hovering a few inches away from where her suit's sleeve ends, with a rotating set slotting into place, all different colours and ages. She adds, tilting the cards so they jut at equal angles, "And there was already room for us in that body."

A new set of hands slides into place. The same thin, light brown hands of the body Rho was in.

Rho sets her cards down. "I need a second. I need to…" She stands.

Her sentries waking up, stabbing deeper than her skin, muscle, bone.

The fox sparrow, broken but alive.

The give in Eirjatal's expression when he saw her behind the stranger's face.

She holds the bits of memories, like promising puzzle pieces while scanning the rest of the pile for a match. She'll recognize it as soon as she sees it. "Can we take a break?"

The Adder tilts her head. "That's only fair. I expect the transition was a little difficult. Let's pause."

Rho's heart stops beating.

Her sense of the Dawn Hall snaps away. It's always too distant to pin down—like a heartbeat too, or the reminder to breathe—but now that it's gone, she knows it.

Pause.

Hah.

Rho takes a step from the table. The Adder moves with her. The goddess says, "I couldn't help but overhear. Were you implying to him that you can still sense your magic?"

Lying here is useless, but the gods aren't used to having to pry for the truth, either. "It didn't seem worth mentioning to you."

"Why not? It would have been *quite* the advantage."

At that, a new card slides from the star and into Rho's fan on the table. The Blind Adder invites her with a gesture of that weird carousel of hands. Rho peeks at the new card.

The Dream. Heartswain's second half. She fights to keep a straight face, annoyed with her own eagerness. As if her survival can be designed by a game of cards.

They've been playing for a while, even if the passage of time is watery and inconsistent here. She's tried to remember her friends' strategies. Tavreah favoured pretty cards, Eirjatal thought too hard until he was strategizing for a game no one was playing, and Rho couldn't lie to people she trusted. Cereus never stopped smiling. He almost always won.

Rho strolls out of the atrium. The Heartswain cards *have* to be a joke—she's further from the Nelaeryn Fey than ever.

The atrium exit spills into nothingness except for a bridge of disconnected glass stairs, bobbing like lily pads on water. She takes a careful step. She wears light, lacy slippers and a diaphanous dress the colour and shape of streaky clouds—not what she arrived in, that's for sure. She's a gift and she has no idea who (or what) she's wrapped up for.

But she knows what she's looking for.

The stair holds her weight.

She stomps down the rest. Still the threads link to the Adder, teasing her with how tethered she is here. Her nails dig into her palms. She's being watched—she didn't grow up with suffocating paranoia of the Woven only to get to their domain and not be careful. But she's as alone as she'll ever get, so she opens the floodgates of her memories and tallies them all.

It was his fault.

It was my fault.

It's so much both of our faults that it doesn't matter anymore. We're fighting together. As always.

She swipes at a couple rogue tears and continues down the spiral, each stair dipping with her weight.

For now, her dying's on pause. Thank Nele, or the Adder, or none of them. She pushes her thoughts towards where she wants to be, and the world unfolds like an envelope to admit her.

Her breath catches. She's on top of a waterfall.

Rapids rage around her hips but don't push her over the edge. Good thing, that, because there's a monster at the bottom.

It's as long as one of the Dawn Hall's levels, some skin-crawling mixture of a crab with its hard shell and pincers, and a centipede with its low, snaking body and twisting way of moving. It moves in agitated circles in the pool. She can hear the chittering and the movement of a hundred joints even over the roar of the water. It's partially transparent, like she's only seeing a ghost.

Eirjatal has tried to describe it to her a dozen times, but he insisted for all the clarity of his memory, he could never get it right, like trying to recite every lyric of a song. You thought you were flowing to the right words, right up until you got to it. Rho scratches her arms. Madainn's strange pet.

So where's Madainn?

She's only seen winks of other gods, heard half-notes of their voices.

The Blind Adder keeps Rho away from them, as if—

"They'll find a use for you, if you aren't careful," the goddess says from beside Rho. It's a strange sensation, to be frightened without a beating heart. She feels assured almost instantly.

"You don't want him for revenge, I hope."

"No. Whether I win your card game or not, it won't matter if Madainn still does what he wants to Dianthus."

The tail of the Adder's long, black coat floats in the water, not sodden, not damaged. "Some of the other gods will want you. More than any other mortal I dared spend time with."

"Because I'm like a favourite toy they want to take from the Fey. How are *you* any different?"

Beneath them, the monstrous ghostly serpent twists upon itself, hunting something Rho can't see; the rumble of every joint plays up her spine like piano keys. The Adder says eventually, "You're also a toy they'd rather be broken than not in their possession."

Rho grits her teeth. She can't wander around here playing cards. She *knows* the Adder overheard her swearing she would take care of Madainn. So she says, "Fine," and into her hand appear her four cards.

She feigns thinking—she has to appear serious, after all. *Be Cereus, confident in every losing hand.* She picks *The Scout* and *The Kelpie*, and offers them out face-down. "I sacrifice these two cards. In exchange for a favour from you. We can play like that, right? The prize is something outside the game, so the wagers can be too?"

The Adder smiles with white, white lips. She has her own cards, all six of them in her hand this time. The hand that holds them is the scarred one of the priestess with the snake.

There's something about that snake, but she can't…

The Adder asks, "*Can* you sacrifice those cards?"

"Yes. One is *The Thread.* The piece of magic the Fey unraveled to acquiesce your Karadenza. You can say I'm lying—and you gain them if you're right, or you lose your highest-ranked card if you're wrong. Both our goddesses took risks."

"That's a very lucky card."

"You said that sensing my magic from here *is* a good advantage."

She holds the Adder's flat gaze, keeping everything but her determination off her face. It isn't hard; maybe all she needed to start playing dangerously was a reminder. She wants to hear that mechanical hum, the bees, the conversation of the palace again. She wants Eirjatal to apologize to her face, and then she wants to hug him.

The Adder considers her cards. She considers so long that Rho is reminded that despite the priestess, despite the fortune of walking in a realm with gods rather than being six feet under, the Blind Adder doesn't want her to survive.

And then the Adder closes her fan of cards. *The Kelpie* and *The Scout* vanish.

"What do you want?"

"I want to know where Staventa is. The goddess who gave me my magic. I want to build something."

16

Irving

Staventene responded to the years that needed industry with industry. Grey Eves responded to the years that needed battalions with battalions. But Ventaris does not answer, it asks; and so Ventaris will create a new century that needs wonder, education, and curiosity both ardently academic and fantastically frivolous.

Ventaris memorandum, Age of Shields 199

Irving's mother, Penelope, met Sigyn by essentially breaking into Cypress with little more than her horse and a demand that the elves' fabled Moonwardens help her fix her town from the starlight that fell on it. It was gutsy, stupid, and totally un-Whitfore of her—at least until she redefined the family name.

So it's the Whitfore in Irving that tells Johana, "I don't get how you're doing this, but I want in."

Noah, leaning against the infirmary wall behind Irving, grumbles, "Buy her dinner first."

Irving figured their explanation about Noah's previous involvement with the Heartswain thefts would put Johana at ease, but that theory failed. Johana's white-knuckling her chair like she's on a Ferris wheel that's stalled at the top. Marie coils circles around her shoulders, somehow shooting disparaging glares at Irving and Noah.

Johana squeaks, "How I'm doing it?"

Irving props their elbows on their knees to force their feet to stop tapping. A headache builds pressure behind their eyes. "I'm the one with your key."

"Oh, well that's—same concept as what…as when you switched places with Rhoheme. Just…Marie and I. Not for long."

Noah's double-take breaks her staring contest with Marie. "Wait. You were a snake?" She squints. "…A snake was *you?*"

Johana flicks a hand at Noah like she's swatting a fly, but her anxious tone drains any dismissiveness from the gesture. "Marie's my tether. It's not so hard, we're already connected…"

"She's your what?"

Irving explains; Johana looks like she'll chew her own hand off if she has to answer any more questions. Besides, speaking eases their own frantic energy like a pressure valve. "Etreal thing. Sorcerers get their magic tied to an object, like a staff or a token or something. You know how Eirjatal—sets things on fire sometimes?" they ask, thinking of him nearly burning them when they surprised him. "It's to stop that. But they don't usually tether to living things. It kind of defeats the purpose."

"It requires a lot of trust—from the temple, and the Blind Adder, and Karadenza. And a flawless record." Johana sets a protective hand on Marie. Irving notes the black dart on Marie's head again. Maybe it's to alert others that she's no simple snake. If anywhere would take advantage of that knowledge, though, it'd be Ventaris.

Why have a living tether instead of a ring or a staff? What if Marie dies? *Can* Marie die, if Johana doesn't?

Irving leans back in their chair. "I guess the trust a priestess needs to get *that* is the same trust she needs to steal from Cypress."

Johana shrugs like a twitched marionette.

Despite the jumpy leg and the eager, tangled thoughts, Irving still feels the drag of the ritual. Their breath is wheezy, like that river silt's caught in their lungs—something Noah's definitely noticed since she keeps shooting them alarmed looks. Well, the looks are either about the wheezing *or* the whole situation. After Johana confessed, they had to wake up Noah. They couldn't have this discussion without her.

"So your temple asked you to do this? Or was it the House of Ciphers?" Irving asks, thinking of the Cipher emblem in Johana's book.

Johana squeaks, "Both."

"Why? The Adder keeps out of the Fey's business."

Johana brushes her scarred fingers on Marie's head. "I don't know. *Honestly*. Why they offered me to the elves, what's so important about the creations…I didn't mean for anyone to get hurt. A-after what happened to that guard, I'm going to stop. I'm not even *taking* them. They gave me a tool, made to…I guess it captures a bit of their magic, since it's so much like the magic of your clerics, and then Karadenza priestesses can read what's—" Johana coughs over the end of that sentence like she's swallowed it wrong. "It may not even work."

"Yeah, I remember Ventaris's whole deal with trying to crack our magic," Noah retorts.

Irving barely stops themselves from rolling their eyes. In Staventene, Ventaris killing Silvershale's previous Moonwarden, Khidell, is practically forgotten, only living in university libraries. Here, it's a scab Cypress can't stop picking at.

"Please," Johana blurts, jolting so Marie has to whip her tail around her arm for balance. "You're not going to fix anything by exposing me. You're going to risk Rhoheme, because *no one* will replace me, and..."

"Okay, whoa." Irving leans on their knees, trying to ignore their brain sloshing in their skull from the change in posture. They're talking with their hands now, full of fizzling energy. "I already said I want to help."

This is a chance to get their foot in the door before it slams shut on them. They'd be stupid not to lunge for it. They're as trapped as Johana in the webbing of the Dawn Hall.

They say, "It was a job for the House of Ciphers that got me here."

"Got you *arrested*," Noah corrects.

"On a fluke."

Johana glances between them. Marie settles her chin on the priestess's fingers, like a dog dropping its head in its master's lap. Irving has a belated shot of guilt about how she's backed into a corner. For a split second, they see what they look like: Sigyn or something like him. Quiet trouble but still trouble. *I'll help you, but who knows what I'll ask for as thanks.*

"Rhoheme's onto you. And if Marie's caught out of this room, no one's going to listen to how important she is to your magic before she gets squashed. Johana, the House of Ciphers already trusted me once." Irving chooses to ignore the vitriol in the letters Radiance recovered. "I've got no alliance to Cypress. I can help."

Noah exclaims, "You're not getting your brain put in a snake!"

"Agreed. No snakes involved."

With a switch to cutting Cypresian, Noah snaps, "What's wrong with you? Rhoheme's last—sentry *thing* killed someone. Rhoheme herself was pretty much unhinged. The Dawn Hall will do worse than burn you if you're caught."

They aren't so limber at hopping between languages. "I'll be fine. The castle's distracted."

"You didn't even tell me you worked with people in *Ventaris*."

"Does it matter?"

"*Fey watching,* the fact that you have to ask…" She narrows her eyes at Marie. "Besides. This is all way too creepy."

Noah's words weave a dim thread of logic through their blaze of excitement. But they want to cry out, *I need another shot.*

I help them, and they'll trust me again. I need to get home—I need something there for me, or it's not really home anyways.

Maybe the ritual made their edges all brittle and bare, but the thoughts surge, urgent. They're *not* another elf slinking into the city to make trouble or tales. But Eirjatal was convinced that's what they are and the letters betrayed that the House of Ciphers suspected it too.

So when Johana starts, "They won't let an elf—" Irving throws in the words like they're lit fireworks, "I used to be a sorcerer for the Blind Adder."

Noah's stare burns into their temple but they focus on Johana—whose face regains some colour. The priestess asks, "What?"

"It wasn't tethered to anything. I told you I was sick for most of my life. I know *you,*" they say to Noah, "have seen my scar. I got rid of the magic when I moved to Staventene."

"With surgery?" Noah says slowly. "How'd that even happen?"

"Let's say it's been helpful with Heartswain. If something goes bad, I know what's coming out to scare me."

Johana murmurs, "Who would remove your magic?" like Irving said someone robbed them blind. But her tone is sympathetic, no longer so cornered. The change burns—but they remind themselves *this* is the reaction they were banking on.

Johana asks, "Would you take it back? A temple could help. It wouldn't hurt."

Fuck no. "Sure."

They let the confession hang. They aren't sure what they want with it. It sounds like a desperate last bid—*I'm like you!*—but it seems so brittle in comparison to everything else that's different.

But Johana does what she wants with it. Something that unlocks the fortress doors of her doubt and lets her ask, "Did you mean it…that I'm putting Marie at risk?"

There's this yawning pit of sadness in her dark eyes, like all she wants is for Irving to say no.

And for a moment they nearly do, guilty about backing her into a corner. With Heartswain, they've seen people come face to face with their deepest desires and their furious fears, watching them play out with a horror that understands it's fake, but a hopelessness always terrified for the moment it turns real.

But it helps nothing to lie. They hold the power here, and they aren't sure they don't want it. "You won't have to anymore."

"Okay," Johana whispers. "I have…in the city, I have a contact. Envai Farrow. Speak to her. But please, begin as if I…*I* asked *you*. I wasn't trapped by you, I was only trapped *here,* in this room. Will you?"

"Of course."

"I have to get home. No one can get hurt. Not me, or you, or Rhoheme. No one." Her voice firms up. "And if Envai says no—"

"I don't say a *word,*" they say. "And if you decide you don't trust me, well. You can make it look like an accident."

Noah kicks their chair. But Johana's smile is terribly sad.

17

Irving

One surprise they didn't advertise: the theatre has an actual elf on the payroll. A glance of that is worth the price of admission.
Maybe it's on purpose, because there's nothing else enchanting about that farce of a theatre.

Staventene arts magazine article, Age of Shields 249

First thing the next morning, Irving finds the perfect excuse to slip into the city without Eirjatal's suspicion. They need fabric and thread for Vyriseh's nearly-finished dress. Noah, meanwhile, was tasked by Cereus to trawl the grounds for photographs.

The themes of Lightbringing shift every few nights, but the days are for the pillars of food, artistry, and good company. The streets have exploded with art and offerings and tourists. Autumn, Eclipsed, even Briarlords—

elves from mixed-heritage wilderness clans who are lured to excitement like vamps to bloodshed. Stalls and wanderers barter anything from creatures to accessories, gems, clothing, locks of hair, savoury secrets.

Despite themselves, the theatre tailor in Irving is giddy about Dianthus's styles. Chains of smashed shells and cracked pearls, hourglass earrings filled with coloured sand, body paints, silks, piercings, live flowers glued to skin. Decorated strangers offer themselves up to Noah's camera. Not so dissimilarly to how they look at Irving, some are wary of its otherworldliness—others, enthralled. Human tech dips in and out of Cypress, but apparently Ashvaren would have none of it. To engage with human ideas was to submit to human ideals.

As Irving keeps an eye out for Envai Farrow, Noah snaps some shots of a statue that watches over the thoroughfare. The blown glass and gold depicts Relyn putting a chisel to one of her four horns. She traded the horn to the Woven for bits of their magic. Faowist lent her the sun (but on a different schedule than Etreal), Madainn lent her rivers and rain, the Carrion Queen lent her hunger and hunting, so on—all for a scrap of horn that guaranteed them a favour once she recovered all her power. Karadenza, of course, didn't join in.

There are no Woven statues. Lightbringing's about self-sacrifice, not alliances.

Elves figure the Nelaeryn Fey abandoned a universe, since she found the Woven while injured and on the run.

Karadenza ends worlds when they don't go her way and picks which gods to pack up with her to the next one. True to her full title—Karadenza Realmweaver. But the Fey won't say if she was always alone or where she came from, besides stray stories she'll feed her Moonwardens. Sigyn finds scraps of them in dreams or his own memories. When Irving was little, in the few times Sigyn remembered his kid, it seemed like Sigyn was the one remaking the world. Bedtime stories became legends, not the other way around.

Sigyn wanted them to bring their mother here. But Irving can't think of a single reason she would be safer in Cypress than in Etreal.

A longing for Staventene comes out of nowhere, stronger than they've dared feel so far.

It doesn't seem right that what they built in Staventene is *over*. They know they can hit the ground running, but here in Cypress, they're stuck in free-fall.

"That looks like your girl," Noah says.

Irving rips their gaze away from the Briarlords. Noah's craning on tiptoe to see over the crowd, so Irving leans down to follow her pointing finger. Johana said dyed red hair, and that particular silhouette is bright as Heartswain.

They pack up the camera. They sidle around three Briarlords who are watching various monsters being presented for a chariot race. Irving knows from living in the Heatherwol palace that trying to govern the Briarlords is hopeless, but now they see why Adamantine insisted on trying. These ones each hold glittering chains that lead up to the necks of three human women.

They're facing away and dressed in the bramble-embroidered finery of the Briarlords. Irving *knows* they're human, or at least their Cypress blood does, bubbling with a strange ferocity. The city is full of Briarlords. Explains why no one reacted to the smell of Irving.

Everything within Irving stills as one human turns, and Irving can see her eyes are stitched shut.

The Briarlord presses something to her mouth. Candy, Irving figures as she smiles with relief, like a pet that knows no better.

That blood of yours... makes elves feel like hunters, you know that?

They jog after Noah to a booth on a garden path. The redhead female manning it snaps shut her book—a tawdry romance, by the cover—and hops off her counter of aquariums to greet them.

Irving says, "Envai Farrow, right?"

She scrutinizes them like they're pinned to a board. "Who's asking?"

Irving hands over the bundle of silk Johana gave them. Envai flicks it open with a knuckle. Like to block Irving from seeing her reaction to the contents, she sweeps her curtain of wavy, half-shaved hair over one shoulder; it's a brilliant red that screams rare pigments and expensive upkeep. Earrings line her pointed ears. She's too pale to be Autumn but she has no horns, and Irving wonders about that for all of a split second before they hate themselves for thinking in the cold, caste terms of an elf. Besides, since she's with the Ciphers, maybe she's a human with a glamour and she doesn't know the distinction between the bloodlines.

Envai takes out Johana's necklace. She twists the thin chain around her fingers in a cat's cradle, squinting at the pearly teardrop vial, corked with jagged quartz. The shadows it casts on her face move independently from the vial's sway, like a film projected against a wall.

Envai huffs. She tucks the necklace into her back pocket.

Then she yanks Irving by the shoulders over the counter.

Irving's hips bash into the wood but that isn't half as shocking as Envai suffocating them in a hug. She cries to the crowded street, "Oh, wow! I can't tell you how happy I am to see you!" Her voice drops to a hiss. "Who the fuck are you?"

They're so startled by her violent tone, the clove smell of her hair, and being grabbed, that they practically squeak, "Irving?"

"Irving! And a new friend! Come in, let's catch up, I'm sure no one will mind if I step away for a tick." She drags Irving and Noah around the counter. She snaps down four rolled-up tarps to enclose every side of the booth.

Irving trades an incredulous glance with Noah. *Master of disguise,* they mouth, ears burning.

Envai digs out a music box from under the counter and cranks it. Carvings of the Woven god of art and stories march along the edges, and as a shivering tune plays, runes engraved between the tiny Mythmakers glow. It's charmed by Mythmaker sorcerers, like their watch with the Hawk tattoo and whatever disguise spell they'll get from Vyriseh. It takes a full verse

(Envai holding up a finger as she loudly rattles off niceties) before Irving's ears pop.

"Now no one can listen in." Envai settles against the counter, rounding on Irving. "Before you catch me up…take your hair down?"

Envai looks so curious that they pull their blonde hair free of its low, messy knot. She nods knowingly. "Irving Whitfore, obviously. Saw you hosting at a Staventene estate once. You wouldn't recognize me; I prefer glamours."

"How I wear my hair's the least recognizable thing about me."

"Got me. The name put it together. You're just cuter with your hair down." She grins. "You've oiled Staventene's gears with a lot of information over the years. Weren't you supposed to be fucking off with the higher-ups? I was so jealous. *Spoiled upstart*, I thought."

"I—"

"Got arrested," Noah chimes in.

"Oh? Lucky me. Do tell." Envai gestures like an emcee pulling the first act on stage.

Irving explains it all, framing the guard's death and Marie's narrow escape as the push for Johana to ask for Irving because of their history with the Ciphers. They mention the disguising spell (though not that they technically don't have it yet). While they speak, Envai tilts her head like she's trying to solve one of those illusions that's a vase one way, faces another. Irving gives her a touch too much information.

By the end, Envai's shaking her head. "I guess a new Starmorrow doesn't fix everything."

Noah interjects, "Do all rabbits become turncoats, then?"

Irving retorts, "I'm only a criminal on one side of the border."

But she's fixed on Envai. Envai's expression blooms into something prettily delighted.

"Good nose, Feyspawn! We aren't *all* turncoats. There's only lots of opportunity for it. Etreal's obsessed with us, and Cypress learned it's gauche to be too mean to us. Thanks to your new lush on the throne, by the by."

Irving takes in Envai anew. They've never met another half-elf. She doesn't seem at all embarrassed about Noah calling her out; instead, she fires Irving a wink.

"This one's got some revenge fantasy on Cypress," Noah says, jabbing a thumb at Irving, "but I'd guess you have Ventaris's interests in mind."

"It's not like *you're* making any use of Scintia's evocations."

"You can't know how to use them."

"We have a better idea than Cypress does."

Irving asks, "How? Dianthus hasn't taken in humans since before those things were made." And even then, they couldn't exactly wander palaces and ask questions. Too busy being enslaved or killed for sport.

"When the Sunmirrens dragged out Ashvaren's corpse, the court they cut free had lots to say. Some fairy tales hit better in desperate times. Best, when the teller's pissed, think their realm turned on them, and think the evocations aren't about Cypress at all."

Noah explains to Irving, "Ashvaren suspected that Scintia was tainted by Madainn too, 'cause of the Winter curse and the Fort."

Envai gives an open-palmed shrug. "And yet he kept her toys."

In wards built by someone he thought was already doomed because of her Woven magic.

Noah blows her fringe out of her face. "I don't know what's up with you two. Are you that eager to become echoes?"

Before they can stop themselves, they fire Noah a glare.

When elves say they're physically made of Cypress, it's never so obvious as when they die. A Moonwarden dying outside of Cypress, like Khidell, can't pass on their power, and anyone with elf blood dying outside of Cypress is destined to wake right back up as a ghoul, euphemistically called an Archfey's echo. They destroy anything they can, and usually, that's humans.

Half-elves, though—rumour goes that the broken, sharp shards of Etreal in them cut through that connection to Cypress even if their hands are buried in her soil from birth to death. *Rabbit* is kid stuff to Irving now, but this mention carves into them with something cold.

But Envai scoffs. "I'll do it right in this city if I can manage. Some of you act like it's still the centuries where Cypress could do whatever it wanted to Etreal. What've you got now? A kingdom without a Moonwarden, Winter elves cursed, Spring turned into dust, everyone else dying out and too romantic about the past to troubleshoot it? This era's payback, if you ask me, and Irving and I are perfect to do it." Envai has curved, sharp bottom incisors; they turn her crinkle-eyed grin wicked. "Anyways. If Jo's trapped, it's probably best to get help."

Irving shakes off a bit of defensiveness—Noah's never thrown them being half-human in their face. "I don't care what's in those things or what Ventaris is doing with them. I only need the promise that if I help, I get to speak to the Ciphers."

Envai gestures indulgently at herself. "You already are. I respect the Ciphers dropping you the instant it looked like you flaked. But I also respect you having the dignity to not *entirely* crawl back to us. As far as re-hiring interviews go, this one doesn't suck."

"Irving," Noah warns, "she's agreeing too easily."

"Ventaris," they return. "Overconfident."

"And I'm not scared of you," Envai says.

"And if I get caught, you'll be long gone, eh?"

"Of course."

"With Johana alongside?"

Envai shrugs, smiling in a way that's sussed out that the lack of answer makes Irving uncomfortable. *It's fine,* they reassure themselves. *You don't want the power here.*

Irving extends their hand for Envai to shake.

Noah sticks in hers, too.

"You need someone to watch your back," she mutters.

18

Irving

Elvish offspring have no right to the property or wealth of the parent. Family names are categories to keep them organized within 'kingdoms.' A child may never learn of their parent's death. Wealth is either cycled back into the society, hidden, or given to companions. It betrays a cynical disinterest in teaching or nourishing, and a reluctance to give up comfort to ensure the future, as if they don't feel deserving of it.

Ventaris Academy notes on Khidell, Age of Shields 200

"Seriously? You're not just *asking* for trouble. You've tracked her down at a bar and bought her a drink she doesn't like."

Noah's eyebrows are high enough to vanish under her fringe as she stares at Irving's reflection in the mirror—well, the reflection that Irving's trying on. Standing in a Dawn Hall staff office, they itch at the ribbon around their wrist, embroidered with a spell, trying to make sense of where their movements end and this body begins.

She was the first person they thought of. Leila, their boss at the theatre in Staventene. She's got a head full of wavy brown hair and a heavyset seriousness from Staventene's rough, industrious living. Opposite of Irving.

Mainly because she's human, which Noah clearly doesn't care for.

And, apparently, neither do Irving's nerves. They didn't expect the twist of discomfort when seeing themselves like this, but here it is. It's not about Leila's femininity; her body may be female like Irving's, a fact they've never shied from in how they dress, but it's different in the ways that matter. Irving imitates her posture from nights skating around her backstage, fixing seams and digging out shoes from under wardrobes with breaths to spare before costume change. They fold in, she stands straight.

They feel like a plaster cast of a person, all dull colours and crumbling edges.

"Pick an elf, Irving, seriously."

"I can put the hair over the ears, look."

"We're more than ears and horns, dummy. But you really do need both. Don't you know any elves you can turn into?"

"Only elves who are already in Dianthus."

"There has to be someone." Noah slips the ribbon off their wrist. Like with the watch charmed to make the Hawk tattoo, the illusion vanishes. It doesn't melt or shimmer. It's simply gone from one breath to the next, leaving them with a brief feeling of falling.

Noah continues, "You didn't live in Staventene your whole life. No way. Not even Fain's Shadow," she says, referring to the town right outside Cypress, rife with blinded rebel elves and half-blood children discarded on the beaches. "Or else you wouldn't've been able to get inside Dianthus to meet me. So?"

No harm in offering up a little, right? Irving says, "I was in Heatherwol. For a bit."

Noah twirls the ribbon on her finger. "Was the elf parent there?"

"Yeah. It wasn't anything special. I got out as soon as I could." They take the ribbon back, searching their memories for someone who wouldn't be recognized here—not by the guards, and definitely not by Sigyn or Vyriseh when Irving has to work with them. That flips their stomach all over again. It's like they woke up fragile today, unhelped by handing over the dress to Vyriseh, half-expecting her to root around in their head again and find their new lofty dreams of traitorous idiocy.

Noah's staring at them too hard, expression sour.

"What?"

"Nothing. You remember you smell human, right? You can't hide at *all* looking like your Staventene friend, and the point is to attract *no attention.*"

"I think you should use this, Noah. You have no out if they catch you."

Noah shakes her head so hard that her brown forelock dusts her brows. "No way. Etreal technology's one thing, but a Mythmaker charm?"

"It's from Vyriseh."

"Who got it from the Mythmaker. Besides," she scoffs, "I was fine robbing this castle for years."

Irving ties the ribbon back on. The memory they summon's missing some pieces, but immediately, blinking back at them is an elf female. She has a delicate, papery flare of orange leaves on her brow and shoulders since they remember her in autumn the clearest. They were so jealous of those leaves.

She's a maid who took care of them for over a decade. It wasn't easy to find an elf willing to help *and* to keep their mouth shut about Irving's existence.

"Brush the bangs over the leaves—yeah, perfect!"

Their memory of the female is hazy, but at least they remember the cadence of her voice. Vyriseh said the spell couldn't make things up whole cloth, and so every detail that they don't know is replaced with bits of Irving. Irving remembers those hazel eyes because of how often they watched them for any sign of violence or wariness, but her long, pointed ears are entirely Irving's, as is the length of her hands, and they're definitely in the narrow, pointed jaw and skinny collarbones. They can feel the scabbing burn on their back, but the tracks on their arms from Johana's needles are gone.

But they really don't look that different.

Annoyance surges in them. The gap to Leila required a skyship to cross it, but this? They aren't so far away from Cypress as even Envai, who only had the important pieces of the Fey that humans throw on paintings and poems to signal otherness at a glance.

Irving's got *Moonwarden* blood in their veins. They're so much like Sigyn that they can't understand how Noah hasn't put it together other than the sheer impossibility of it. If the gods weren't always in a pissing contest, if the Fey didn't need to be handled like glass, they wouldn't be torn between the Nelaeryn Fey and Karadenza. They would be the Fey's.

Why did she let them exist, like *this*, just to deny them?

Why did Sigyn?

Noah pats their arm. The thoughts go up in smoke. "Let's test it out."

The pair leave the part broom closet, part office—each floor has these, a spot for staff members to trade tasks and grab emergency equipment. There's a wall of tiny lights with labels for rooms and workers to show who's where, each room equipped with a speaker.

Irving's a little unsteady on their feet. There are tons of stories where people don't realize they've been transformed until they scream at their mirror—how stupid are they? *Everything* feels crooked. They've put their glasses in their pocket and their face feels naked, vision sliced by the obtrusive shadow of the female's nose. Their gait doesn't suit her body.

They tour the floor. Mara waves, negotiating shifts with another servant. Tavreah seems more interested in making sure Noah can do photos tomorrow. Noah nods politely to the guards stationed on every floor.

"Poor bastards. They'd rather be anywhere else. Tonight's all about

Eojhest's stars and stuff, and starlight makes the Eclipsed crazy; that's always fun to join."

Irving asks, not realizing the question was in their mouth until it spills out, "Does it bother you, what I am?"

"A reckless dumbass?"

"A half-elf."

Noah looks away. Does she remember what she said to Envai? Or is it all so *normal* to her, like calling herself Summer or Rhoheme Spring? "I mean, the Fey and Karadenza are gonna fight one day, that's for sure. But it won't be in my lifetime. So who cares? You're not the enemy yet."

"What am I, then?"

She folds her arms, fingers pressing into her plump forearm. "An excuse."

"For?"

"Irving, out of everyone who should've committed that shit to memory, it's *you.*" She taps on the shoulder of the guard at the bottom of the stairwell, getting him to move out of the way. He double-takes at Irving and so Noah only continues speaking once they're around the next corner. "I don't interrogate you about me being Cypresian, do I? Considering what *other* stuff you get up to, I think I have a reason to."

"It's not about you."

"It's about everyone, right?"

"It's about the Fey." And Sigyn, as tightly as those two are bound. They're getting itchy with irritation at her, so they change the topic. "I'd interrogate you about more interesting things. I don't know anything about you."

"Feeling's mutual. I know you were in Staventene and were a university drop-out."

Universities have no patience for people who stop being sorcerers. "Why do you want to leave Dianthus? Won't you be leaving family behind?"

"Behind—?" They're at the door to the library, where she showed them an evocation earlier. The door's locked. "Eirjatal took these keys. Time to use my old skills again."

"Noah, do you?"

"No."

"No one?"

"I have sisters." She brightens. "See, there's your fact. I have two sisters. All the same mother. That's a serious rarity in Cypress."

"Won't they miss you?"

She stares like they've accidentally glamoured on a third arm. "They don't even know where I am." Something softens whatever retort she seemed geared up to give. "That happens here, you know? Blood's thin, no matter who you are. Time waters it down. You either pick a family of friends, or you end up alone. But it's a fun fact, huh? Three kids. Weird."

How old is she? How many years past twenty-four did it take for that connection to be more water than blood? "Sure. Weird."

"I'll miss Cypress, though."

"What?"

"What?"

"This whole time, when you said you wanted to leave Dianthus, you meant *Cypress*?"

They get a rare Noah hesitation in exchange. "Yeah? What, you're really going to talk up Staventene all the time and then give me *that* face?"

"Etreal's not easy."

"You think I can't handle it?"

They hardly can. Why does she think they're fighting so hard for the Ciphers? "No, but you could go anywhere in Cypress. The camera—elves love art, and you have a skill no one else has. You could help Cypress get over this fear of Etreal tech a bit."

"You're not the only person who doesn't feel like they belong."

"You *do* belong."

"Cypress thinks that being in the same room as an idea they don't like means believing in that idea. It's why we're still so weird about elves like Eirjatal. And you." She sighs. "You always made Staventene sound so interesting. I want to *learn* from people."

"Where would you go?"

Noah mumbles, "I dunno. Where you are, I guess."

"We really are friends!"

"Shut up." Noah jingles her key ring, like to distract them from the conversation. "I've got Eirjatal to distract. How about you talk Johana into making a little something to get these guards out of the way?"

19

Irving

Regulation 2: All enchantments invented by the sorcerer must be tested and approved by an Academy authority.
Regulation 16: All transformation enchantments must follow the regulations outlined in 16.a to 16.n.
Regulation 31: All sorcerers must participate in a five-year-long inquest and traineeship, including surveillance and magically-invasive mental examinations, to classify the sorcerer's intentions, politics, and morality.

Rulebook on Mythmaker sorcery, updated Age of Shields 243

Irving stares down Rhoheme's tower of a ward puzzle and contemplatively bites on that Autumn female's thumbnail.

"What d'you think happens if you get it wrong?" Noah asks.

"I'm trying to think positive."

"How much room does that take up in your head? I'm not seeing a whole lotta solving."

"At least backseat drive *helpfully*."

It took them long enough to pick a ward. Eirjatal had been lurking, at least until Tavreah pulled him away to the ritual site, insisting the guards could handle it and he wasn't going to waste good sleep or prayer on something Kinthe and Sigyn were sure wouldn't happen.

Of course that's what their scrys told them. Johana was going to quit. Now Irving's on it; the future's shifted. And Irving, thanks to their old charm from Ventaris, creates a scrying blind spot for themselves and everything around them.

Twisting metal ivy and quartz-winged bats sing faintly with the turn of gears, leading to the ceiling where they flare into a silver canopy. While dusting it months ago, Noah found a hidden beetle and its tracks as thin as thread that Irving's meant to guide through the tangle of metal to unlock the grate over Scintia's icy evocation.

It's a puzzle of making a pathway without any wrong moves. The chandelier light swims on the fur of the bats so they look like they're breathing and on the purple-tinted glass bodies of two massive panthers at the tower's base.

The first evocation belonged to Dianthus, and this one apparently belongs to Silvershale.

Whatever that means. Not their problem.

Noah arrives at their shoulder, hugging a wine bottle (the room's less of a wine cellar and more of an adoring exhibition hall for the drink). Irving slides a bat away then unfurls a metal vine into the allotted space, giving the beetle an inch to scoot upwards. They hit another tangled crossroad.

Noah throws back her head. "This is gonna take all night."

"Bright side, nothing's come alive and strangled me yet."

"Or taken a bite out of your leg."

She produces a corkscrew from her apron and gets to work on the bottle.

Despite both their casual veneers, Irving knows they're both wary. Tonight's the night of Lightbringing that's about the Fey bargaining for Eojhest's moon, so the palace is weirdly empty of nobility and even some of the staff. This hall's even quieter because of the herb concoction from Johana that Noah slipped off-hours into the drinks of the guards, knowing they'd take their toasts as their pithy replacement for actually participating in the rituals in the labyrinthine garden below.

Johana padded her explanation with way too many mumbles about how she doesn't know elf physiology for Irving to feel comfortable with their pace on the puzzle.

The path of the beetle catches a touch. Thankfully their panicked slide of a vine doesn't activate anything, and they're a step closer.

The cork flies across the room with a *bang* that nearly takes Irving's heart with it. They swear; Noah stares at them, wide-eyed and guilty, until a smile cracks her face.

"Hand it over."

She does. It's oddly syrupy and floats with actual sprouting seeds of *something,* growing bright green despite drowning in a dark wine cellar. When they've got a mouthful, she unhelpfully says, "Oh, yeah, don't swallow those seeds or this night'll get a lot more fucking weird." She adds, ducking to peer at the evocation behind the metal grate, "I still think we should've asked Rhoheme how to solve this."

"I felt too much rage coming off of her," Irving says with a shudder. "She wouldn't tell me anything if I asked."

And why should she? From how she interacted with Eirjatal, Irving would think it'd take a lot more than saying *I'm the one literally keeping you out of the ground* to convince her to ease up on what she saw as hers.

And there's that thing she thought when possessing them. *Morningstars and morning prayers. Space and time and a world forgotten. Free creatures, free flight, dawn again in the Dawn Hall.*

The whole exchange has blurred like a dream, but they understood that part as useful. The rest was muddled with Cypress paranoia that doesn't belong to them.

"Besides," they say, feeling a mite defensive, "I know what I'm doing."

"It reminds me of how the Autumn Moonwarden does his"—Noah makes a wiggly hand movement—"stuff."

"It does, eh?"

"'Eh?'" she imitates in a high tone. "It's freaky hearing your words in that voice." She takes the bottle back from Irving and swigs it. "Kinthe's got this room full of hanging glass, but he only ever brings a box of glass pieces. He's hardly left his room since the festival's kicked off. He's usually a loner, but never like this. He's scrying so much that I get a headache from dusting in there."

At best it's got to do with his project with Vyriseh. At worst, that cryptic bullshit he told Irving before they parted for good at the gardens.

Then Noah gets a familiarly arch expression on her face. She likes to tell them things they don't know—or that she thinks they don't know. "It really does look like his scrying, you know. Did you know it was Sigyn who first scryed on Ashvaren's death?"

Irving cuts a glance at her. "Isn't it against the Fey to scry on a death?"

"Not if you search *around* the death. Rumour is that Sigyn knew there would be an assassination, some kind of upheaval, and there was no way Ashvaren was letting go of the throne without being blown off it. Ashvaren called him a liar but the staff sure learned how that scry bent him outta shape."

Irving says, "From how Rhoheme and Eirjatal talked about the wards, she hated doing them for Ashvaren."

"She hated *him* and definitely didn't make a secret out of it. I mean, he took down her kingdom, so fair's fair."

Dawn again...

"Using a symbol of his eventual death would get the point across, you think?"

"All we've got to work with." Her quizzical gaze lingers a second too long, and they can guess what she's wondering. Why do they know the pattern at all?

Sigyn can transfer his visions with a touch. So when Irving was a kid, he'd give them little things that wouldn't mess with their head, like upcoming palace hires, how a scary book would end, sketches of people they'd eventually meet (freaky to meet someone in Staventene and realize they've seen them already). Not for long, though. Those disappeared at the same time Sigyn did.

They only found out from an overheard argument between their parents that Sigyn had started scrying on when, exactly, his human family would crumble.

In other words, when Irving would kick it.

Why pick that wound, if you'd use it to hurt me too?

After they learned *that's* what Sigyn was puzzling out, they were haunted by that pattern of shifting glass, especially before they got the courage to get their rib removed and the Adder's magic pulled out with it.

They force a few pieces. Snap the beetle up into an empty place, breaking the pattern that feels horribly natural under their hands even if they've never done the spell.

With mechanized ease, the thorny metal ivy whips around their wrist.

Irving yelps a curse. The thorns plunge through their sleeve and skin. The metal doesn't ease up—even with Noah persuasively swearing at it—so they're both forced to watch while the silver is slowly threaded with blood. It courses into the structure until the ward's satisfied and the ivy snakes away.

The beetle, the bats, and ivy clang back to their starting positions. And there's a loud *crunch* from inside as the structure shifts down. It's crushing the evocation. They have limited tries.

"Lesson learned," they mutter.

Noah kicks a panther. "You think it took that girl's blood, or yours?"

"Think *positive,*" they remind her, pushing up their sleeve to see the female's skin riddled with punctures. They flex their hand to stretch out the pain.

Fine. Sigyn's a part of this, too. What else is a surprise?

Now that they know the pattern, they get back to where they stopped in a fraction of the time. Noah's generous with handing over the syrupy wine.

"When this is done," she says, "we take those seeds with us and have a hell of a night."

"Deal."

Endings, endings, endings. They move piece after piece after piece. Death, like Johana said, isn't one event, it's a million tiny things going wrong.

Penelope once admitted, "Your father told me that on our wedding night, he knew when I'd leave."

Her point was clear—how can he enjoy stuff when he knows when it's going to vanish? He's constantly living in the death of things.

Shouldn't he have known to try to fix things with Irving before they left, too? Or was fighting that inevitability not worth it?

To reach the top of the puzzle, they climb on the back of a panther. Noah holds their leg. The ward's metal branches spread across the ceiling like silver veins.

One more click and a tunnel opens in the ward. Irving hooks their fingers under the beetle to help it over the sharp ledge. The pathway swallows their hand up to the wrist, then up to the forearm. It's warm, like a living thing.

And then the beetle slots into a depression. The grate locking in the evocation shudders open. They release a startled laugh. The beetle bursts out the top of the ward, free of the tracks, free of the maze. It whirs with metal wings into the branches on the ceiling, vanishing safely into the silver.

Noah takes the vial from Johana out of her apron. "How does this thing work? Ugh—*charmed* things, seriously, I never know what they'll do if I touch them wrong..."

This evocation's a complex mess of coils. Noah appears to get the vial working, if the glow means anything. She tucks the necklace into her blouse.

Irving says, "Grab the bottle and we'll get out of here before the guards get on our asses."

Noah raises her eyebrows. "Drop that spell. I let you look like *her* when messing with the guards' drinks, but I'm not walking around with a stranger. *Definitely* not looking like I'm going to get high with a stranger."

"Are you saying you're fine with people thinking *we* get high together?"

"Don't be weird."

"Noah, that's so sweet."

"It's just less suspicious if *we're*—"

"Because people think we're friends—"

They both freeze at a metallic creaking.

Noah gives them a stare like it's from *them*—and they yank her by the wrist out of the way of a panther, sprung to jolting, mechanical life.

Irving snags the wine off the table and they both race for the hallway. Irving drops the spell in their panic and they barely catch their much-longer stride. They'd be apt to trip otherwise.

The glass paws of the two panthers pound behind them. A glance thrown over Irving's shoulder proves that they're somehow nimble and feather-light, all their joints precisely carved to lunge without resistance, and they're effortlessly gaining.

At the base of the stairs, Irving heads for the next flight, but Noah shoves them the other direction. "Out! We need to get outside!"

"That's like four floors down!"

"Who's the intrepid thief here?" Noah cries with another shove. She scratches at the wall at the base of the stairwell until she finds an embedded grate and yanks it out—a panther barrels into it. The automaton's chest sprays glass chips, and its inner gears spin like a panicked heartbeat.

It gives the grating another go. The top busts from the wall.

Inside the panther, Irving spies a thin thread of red swirling through the skull—their blood.

"It's tracking me."

"Yeah, exactly what everyone else in this plan was hoping for." Noah darts around the corner. They're never going to make it to the staff apartments without getting trapped. They only drugged two floors of guards, and the ones below them right now are doubtlessly hearing this.

So where are they?

It again tries its hand at the grate, buckling the metal. Noah's gone. It's not like they *want* to get caught, but why in the Crawl is no one reacting? Surely the Dawn Hall isn't *that* sedate on ritual nights.

The grate gives in with a puff of plaster and yelp of metal. Irving dodges away, but they can't catch their footing before one of the clockwork beasts catches *them*.

Their back hits the bottom stair, head narrowly missing the metal edge. The wine bottle rolls across the blonde wood. Shockwaves from the burn and the weight of the glass panther on their chest explode stars in front of their eyes.

Irving clamps their hands over its snapping jaws. They're not very strong as it is, and this thing is like having the weight of an ornate Heatherwol orrery fall on them; their arms are instantly shaking from the pressure of pushing back. Between their fingers, the blood it took swirls, bright red, flat, empty of magic. There were times when their blood used to smoke and spark, another symbol of how Etreal was pulling them away.

"You think it took that girl's blood, or yours?"

Theirs, clearly. That handmaiden hadn't even pricked herself on a needle around them.

But they know someone else's blood. They've spent far too much time with someone else's.

Irving grits out the ribbon's spell from between their teeth. The feeling of looking down off a long fall fizzes in them, and when they take the next form, they throw their faith in with it.

The change in shape slips their grip on the panther and it lunges, sinking its fangs into their hand. Blood seeps into the tracks. Thick, black, sludgy blood, all the magic in it dimmed, all the life in it rotten.

The black spreads through its head, painting over the gold, the teeth all the while piercing further into Irving's hand—Rhoheme's hand.

The panther releases and hops back, unnervingly agile. Irving pulls themselves up, unable to take their eyes off the sentry, but in their periphery they see grey-green shale pressing against their shirtsleeves.

The panther surveys the hall like Irving isn't even there. Its heart whirs with Irving's actual blood.

Vyriseh handed them this ratty little ribbon for practically nothing, and *this* is the kind of illusion it can pull off? No wonder Mythmaker sorcerers in Etreal are surveilled to the Amber Crawl and back.

The wine bottle flies out of nowhere and collides with the panther's head, spraying glass and wine everywhere. Noah wrenches Irving to their feet, eyes round as Marie's.

"Don't look like *her*!" she cries, right as the second panther bounds down the steps.

And finally, elf footsteps coming too.

They hurtle around the corner together. Irving can't lie to the enchantment about how they know Rhoheme is dying, so everything hurts even besides the beating the panther put on them, weighing them down. Noah ushers them through a nondescript door and they land in a similar office to the one where they tried on disguises. Noah shoves aside a desk with a typewriter.

Irving dispels Rhoheme's appearance. They think of the approaching footsteps, the dead guard on the stairs from the Summer ward.

You did what you had to, and that's it.

Noah drags open a slat in the wall and Irving doesn't need her to pull them through this time.

It's a tight fit for them both, with the ticking gears and hissing pipes snagging their clothes and hair. It's sweltering and only lit by the occasional panel of latticework wall, but Noah confidently moves along.

She explains, "For palace repairs. No one remembers how to navigate them besides Rho."

"And you?"

"I was working here," she hisses, flinching when Irving untangles her sleeve from a spinning gear, "under Ashvaren. And stealing for *you.*" Noah squints at them in the dim. "Are you smiling?"

"Am I?"

"You miss your Staventene friends, don't you?"

"Noah," they say, "no one else would *ever* do this with me."

She rolls her eyes. But she fishes for their hand, and they give it to her as she leads them through the walls. "We'll spill out in the woods. But her panthers are gonna know where we went if you're sticking to that shape. So be ready to run."

20

Eirjatal

Relyn, Nele, and the Archfey. Logic and faith, life and love, and vengeance and survival. I dream of Them all. Do They appear according to what Cypress needs or to the Moonwarden themselves? Once, Relyn was my closest companion. But now the Archfey is warning me. Of what? I will investigate.

Khidell's journal, recovered Age of Shields 203

"Something's wrong with Sigyn."

A breathless Cereus has interrupted Eirjatal, mid-prayer with Relyn. Eirjatal lifts his head from where the concentrated beam of moonlight was washing his face.

"Why does that involve me?"

"*He* said it did."

Cereus has always been rather reasonable with his religious priorities.

Whatever is going on with the Moonwarden is apparently more important than prayer, even prayer in apology about Eirjatal's mind always being so stuck on Madainn.

Cereus leads Eirjatal to Sigyn, against the labyrinth gates. He's struggling to get his clockwork arm detached.

Eirjatal moves away Sigyn's shaking hand and unlocks the arm. The process comes easy. He remembers some from Sigyn unlocking it in his apartment, some from watching Rho endlessly fiddle with blueprints. It feels inherently wrong to brace a hand on Sigyn's shoulder; he isn't supposed to be touched, but he also isn't supposed to be in pain. He seems more real than ever.

"Thank you," Sigyn says once the arm is removed, and then the gems along its back shatter, one after another.

Hidden mechanics inside the arm pull all out of order, flexing the metal unnaturally in Eirjatal's hands and emanating a horrible tinny screech. Sigyn hisses through his teeth, clutching the base still embedded in his arm. A thin trickle of blood soaks through Sigyn's sleeve.

There's a screech and a *bang* overhead; Eirjatal whirls to see the metal top of the nearest labyrinth wall collapsing as if crushed by an invisible hand. It breaks in two to the accompaniment of Sigyn cursing, low and bitterly ironic.

Eirjatal stands. "Get Tavreah to watch Sigyn and send guards in to flank the palace."

Cereus takes his shoulder. "What's—"

"Rho." Eirjatal's already turned to the Dawn Hall.

"What do you mean, Rho?"

"All this is her magic, isn't it?" He's willing to bet on what's distressing her.

As Eirjatal follows his memory of Rho's butcher-paper drawings of the labyrinth (hoping she was kidding about riddle-locked passageways), the metal whines and wails. Rivets ricochet in the dirt. Rho's moonlit structure of mirrors and water crashes down; elves worshipping the moon around it leap back in alarm. Whenever he lets his mind stray off which turn to take and the war between checking on Rho or the wards first, the blood in Sigyn's sleeve pours behind his eyes.

Everything snaps back to clarity as around the outer edge of the palace bounds an enormous glass beast, throwing rainbow facets of light. One of the panthers from the Eclipsed ward.

The panther will have the scent of whoever it couldn't catch.

Adrenaline flares up his chest, into his wrists, but he wrestles his power down. He should be with Rho. But if this caused her fury, then he'll follow it for her.

Don't save me yet.

A break in the tropics that flank the beach shows him that eyeless Eclipsed spy, skirt hitched up so she can run on the sand after the panther too.

He calls her back. "Check on the priestess and Rhoheme. Ensure it's not her—" Seizing? Possessing the castle? He has no idea, but she doesn't question him as she darts to the Dawn Hall.

He takes the next blind corner—and nearly trips over the panther as it collapses near a pool in a fantastic spray of mud and moss. The automaton's inner gears catch and whirr with the same tinny tone as Sigyn's arm. The vibrating tension of the metal draws hairline cracks in the violet glass.

He catches his breath and approaches, while bats swoop from the canopy, snapping at tiny embers floating off him.

The surface of the pool breaks with the shape of a siren tail.

He staggers back. The tail sways up again, an orange muscled marvel with fins like tattered masts—and then another, turquoise and smaller but still striking the rocks with enough force that the panther is jostled a few inches into the pool. Water soaks his sandals. They're fighting. A long, webbed hand tries to snag the cracked skull of the panther before it's ripped back under the water.

Ice trickles down the back of his neck, yet fire flashes in his palms.

This is his chance. He can boil the water, so quickly that neither realizes in their frenzy before they're dizzy and dying. Then pull one out, or both, cut open their throats and the pouches of venom and end all of this *now*. Face Madainn's next move with Rho.

Or perhaps they'll kill each other for him.

Fixated and shaking, he tries to get a picture beyond the blurring tangle of scales and claws and fangs beneath the surface.

When the sirens claw at it again, the panther snags in the rocks so its crystal cracks with as simple a sound as a wine glass snapping from its stem. His heart kicks. It's like leaving Rho behind in the dirt.

He lets his power funnel freely; chased by adrenaline, by fear, by fury, it rips to the surface of his skin. A wall of steam erupts around the sirens' hisses of surprise, and he takes the chance to wrench the panther off the rocks. The glass melts.

A clawed hand snags his wrist.

He's pulled into the thickening mist right before she lets go with a cry of pain. He underestimated how huge they are, how fast she can lift herself onto the rocks above him like a snake about to strike. She snarls down at him, skin pink from the heat. Gills beneath her ribcage flare with a reeking rattle. Her hair is the texture of seaweed and black as rot, stuck to her sunken cheeks.

Burn her. Sink his fingers in her throat, and boil whatever muck it is that runs in a siren's veins.

Burn her. He can't move.

She whirls around—her smaller, turquoise rival is lunging for the shore. Without her black eyes on him, the fog of his fear parts enough to allow a jet of flame to roll off his palm. She ducks beneath the water to avoid it. A wave heaves over the rocks and soaks him, icy.

Cut her open and end all of this.

He pours magic into the mossy rocks. The steam billows, thick as syrup in his lungs.

"*Stop*," one of the voices cries—so thin and shocked he nearly does. He waves away the mist to see the two sirens in such a tangle that he doesn't know who spoke. The orange one holds her rival against her, hand so large that her thumb's claw is in her gills and her other fingers are in her eye socket. The sirens twitch and thrash as one mass.

The orange one says, "That's *mine,* not yours. Mine. Unless you'd like to join it." She's panting from the heat. "*Fire.* Phoenix. Your blood shines too, doesn't it?"

Slowly so it doesn't hurt him, he pulls the magic back. They all struggle to breathe, but bit by bit the mist thins.

"Aren't you sweet," she purrs, cradling the head of the smaller siren under her chin like a prized bauble. Her prey is pinning Eirjatal with the sort of panic that's desperate for help from anyone.

He burns off the panther's mighty glass head. Moonlight trickles off the tiny teeth and the threads of silver in the working jaw. He almost expects it to bleed.

"Don't you want it?" he asks the larger siren. "Take it. Then get out of here."

The gills on her neck flare. He tosses the head into the water.

It sinks fast; she dives faster. Her massive tail swings above the surface like the mast of a sinking ship. Both Eirjatal and the smaller siren don't dare move, waiting for her to resurface, but the water eventually goes still.

"Come closer," he says.

She sinks up to her chin in the water; her black hair spreads along the surface, shining with faint rainbows like an oil spill.

He sets a threatening hand on the rocks again.

"I could swim back to sea," she whispers.

"But you won't. You want this. Madainn made you a collector." He drags the panther further up the rocks. When she follows it, he tenses; he hasn't missed that she's looking at *him* the way the orange siren looked at the glass head. But she doesn't seem so big with the water concealing the snaking length of her tail and torso. Her mouth is tipped open with her tongue rolling, soft and black and watery, around her rows of tiny fangs. Her cheeks are satiny and membranous; he knows her jaw can open grotesquely wide.

She stops, not close enough for him to grab her.

He starts carving through the chest of the panther and the flood of magic releases some of the panicked pressure in his muscles. "Do you have a name?"

"None you can say, Feyspawn."

"Some find mine hard to say as well."

One hand reaches up to rub the eye that the other siren scratched. *That's a very real thing to do,* he thinks, feeling delirious. "What is it?"

"Eirjatal." The name comes from him as if pulled by hook and line. Offering his name up to Madainn again, like the god will recognize it. He still can't catch his breath.

"There was a man who called me Corsair."

"Before the drowning, I presume?"

She smiles.

"Here." He offers out the mass of glass he's freed. It's heavy, a clumsy job, but her eyes fix on the powerful gears settled inside it like a heart.

"Why, Eirjatal?"

"A welcome to Dianthus."

She powers forwards—far too close, far too quickly, perhaps only two thrusts with her tail and she is close enough to grab it from his hand with awe. "I want more than this," she says. "I have never tasted Feyspawn blood."

It's as much a cue as any. He swings a shard of glass at her with his other hand.

The glass shreds scales then cuts smoothly through flesh, but she's wrenched around, grabbed his arm, and her jaw is endless like the maw of a snake, black and black and black, and she bites.

She recoils with a screech—her teeth have clashed on his metal bracer. He stabs again, and the glass pierces through her cheek, at an upwards angle so it embeds in the roof of her mouth.

She closes her clawed hands on his throat, not quite squeezing, and they freeze there for a breath, either one with the final move if they risk the other's to take it.

Don't, he hears, over and over, *don't. Don't let go, don't give up, don't listen, it's only a siren. That's all. Kill her.*

Blood pools on his hand. It's such a fluorescent red that it's almost orange.

There is such violent fury in her eyes, such purpose. Madainn's monsters in the Ineiren Fort were hungry or lost or mindlessly obeying orders and still they killed a kingdom. Corsair's going to remember him.

He wrenches the glass out of her jaw. She tries to claw his throat anyway, but a rock whistles through the dark and hits the water. In its ripples, Corsair has vanished with her prize.

Cereus drops beside Eirjatal. "Was that a fucking siren?" He reaches for Eirjatal's arm then jerks back. "She—"

"The bracer." His laugh is shallow, shaky. "She couldn't…"

The peacock feather on the metal bracer is chipped in the half-moon of her teeth. Violet venom streams down the metal and stains his sleeve; it must release like a snake's. *Venom. What Johana needs. Diluted, but…*

Cereus turns his arm. The leather straps are bit clean through, and his blood runs bright.

21

Irving

Only when The Queen's Carriage was towed into Brenwardin did we find her crew: clinging to the bottom of the boat, bones now chalky barnacles, hair and nails varnished wood exactly like the Carriage. They were at Madainn's door and I guess he answered.

Brenwardin coastguard report, Age of Beasts 2

When Tavreah kicks open the door of their room, Irving's thankful they and Noah had already changed out of their muddy clothing at top speed.

Noah shoves the glass vial into her drawer with a conspicuous crash. Tavreah snaps at Irving, livid as a swarm of Avinian imps, "Get over here like the Amber Crawl's on your rabbit heels."

Tavreah drags them by the collar like a misbehaving dog. Their imagination spills a tangle of possibilities: Johana's escaped. Rhoheme's dying for good. They've been caught and the Dawn Hall's taking Johana down with them.

Instead, the problem's Eirjatal.

In the infirmary, Eirjatal, at one of the desks, bends over his gory arm. A white sheet beneath it is stained red. Cereus paces from wall to wall. Huddled as far away from the king as possible is Johana, like one of Pique's leaf sprites watching an errant ember. Marie is twisting herself into knots on the counter, hissing up a storm. The tension makes the infirmary seem like it'll burst at the seams when Irving and Tavreah cram themselves inside.

Guess no one's looking too closely into the theft tonight.

Tavreah slams the door, crowing, "Bit by a siren. A *siren!* What are Madainn's parasites doing this deep in Cypress?" She whirls on Johana and switches to strained Etren. "If you've sent out prayers for help because *your* goddess is *useless—*"

Johana seems about to scramble onto the counter with Marie. Cereus pivots off his pacing to wrap a strong arm around Tavreah's shoulder. He says in Cypresian, "We have Vyriseh and her people on it. They'll be fine; Silvershale's dealt with worse."

Irving slips out of the way, but the lack of space knocks them into Eirjatal's desk.

Eirjatal hisses, voice caught up with gravel, "Why is it that your father can't foresee anything *halfway useful?*"

The half-moon of gouges in the underside of his arm are almost...foamy. Irving realizes that's because of the sticky moss growing from the wound.

Johana leads Irving by the sleeve to the back corner. She can't even meet Irving's eyes on a good day, so feeling her boney frame against them spikes their adrenaline. She whispers, "The vial?"

"Got it."

"Pass it on as soon as possible." She sucks in a shuddering breath, gathering up Marie. Irving notices that her hands shimmer with spider webs.

That's a move Adder worshipers make to protect themselves if they think someone's breathing down their neck. Especially with the intention to kill them.

Johana pulls her sleeves over her hands. "I'll need your help."

"With?"

She brings down the rum bottle with the white spiders, then snatches some thread scissors. "Stop the venom from spreading to his heart. Please. And if you...I know she's not with you anymore, but... Give me your hand?"

They do and immediately regret it. She flicks the scissors first around her little finger, then theirs, giving them matching cuts like rings. She holds both the cuts to the black dart on Marie's head until the snake slithers up Irving's shoulders.

"What—"

"Trust me," Johana begs, shoving the bottle of spiders into their hands and scurrying away.

They trust what little they know about the Woven too, and they're pretty sure that was a callback to how during the Age of Beasts, the Blind Adder gave Pique a handful of severed fingers off her collection so those sorcerers could borrow a bit of Pique's power.

She didn't. Did she?

The cut's already closed.

Irving opens the bottle once they're sitting at Eirjatal's desk. Marie is still hissing, now right in Irving's ear; Tavreah bares her teeth and her Summer fangs right back.

Eirjatal asks, "Could you keep enough of the venom to save Rho?"

Johana quails as Tavreah and Cereus suddenly focus on her.

If she *did* save Rhoheme, where would that leave Irving? Would Cereus send Irving back to Etreal with the Cipher's letter hanging over their heads? Or would he think the risk of all they've learned here was too high?

"Priestess. Yes or no?" Eirjatal's pupils are shot wide. Mossy wood breaks through his skin with serious speed. Blood bubbles and streams all over the cloth. Irving ducks their head and gets back to the spiders.

"This is hardly enough for you. Rho—she likely needs more components than venom, like bone, tissue, and—" Even when Johana's expression firms up, her voice is still as frail as Heatherwol's perpetual autumn leaves. "But—but I can try."

"Of course she says that," Tavreah snarls. "She knows what happens to her if she's no use."

Johana may not understand Cypresian, but Tavreah's tone said it all. Johana repeats, "Maybe not today, but I *will* save them *both*. I am bound to it."

Irving shakes ten snow-white spiders into their palm. *Ten.* They tip their handful onto Eirjatal's torn arm. "Try not to think about it."

Eirjatal sneers. The spiders (they count again) skitter into the wound, their white legs effortless in the slippery blood, off to swallow up the toxins and die. His blood has a coppery sheen to it.

Johana says, "Don't let them get lost in him. They might get swept away. And it's live venom, so they'll die quicker, and—"

"*Priestess,*" Eirjatal snaps.

Irving steadies Eirjatal's arm as the infirmary fades into the familiar sounds of every other day here: Johana clanging and clattering her way through her equipment, the faint ticking of the palace's machinery, the book pages rustling from the window Irving insists on keeping open. Marie's stopped hissing; she presses against Irving, the black dart on her head pointed at Eirjatal, whose breathing is slowing.

Tavreah moans behind her hand as more material breaks out of Eirjatal's arm. Boat nails, like his skin is the mossy wood rotting on a wreck.

Four spiders, now black, skitter out. Irving brushes them aside.

"Irving, don't lose them," Johana says, voice high.

Tavreah says, "Oh, Fey watching, they'll eat a hole in his heart!"

Cereus retorts, "What? No. Could they?"

Irving worries the inside of their cheek. That ring Johana cut…

But the whole point of Adder rituals is that anyone can do the simple stuff. Anyone can learn her tricks, from easing a headache to sewing shut a bullet wound. The line between magic and science is blurring. You don't need to be born with her power, and you don't need to be obedient to her, to use it.

You don't need to belong to the Adder.

They hope.

Irving trails their fingers down his arm to the open wound, the way they've seen Johana do to Rhoheme. Leading the way, sort of. The strength of Eirjatal's pulse nearly makes them yank their hand away—they feel like they can sense everything inside him.

Johana warns, "Irving," and when they respond, "I've got it," they're surprised that it's the truth.

Six more spiders, black and swollen, crawl out of the bites. As they hover their fingers above Eirjatal's arm, the spiders dance a confused pirouette, unsure where Irving wants them to go.

They can't deny the rush.

It worked. For once, I actually made it work.

Johana's folding the cloth soaked with Eirjatal's blood, into and out of perfect quarters. Every time she opens the cloth, the blood and venom are split onto opposite corners. She's human, but she holds all their hearts in her hand.

Once she's catching no more venom, Johana unwinds her spool of twine. She ties Irving's hand to Eirjatal's, and Rhoheme's to them both. Irving recognizes her pattern as Karadenza's weaving of the world in Illumination Age art, lotus-shaped knots and loops.

And then Cereus puts in a hand, so suddenly that Johana winds the twine twice around his wrist before turning off autopilot.

"Let me help. Please." Cereus and his gold jewelry are fantastically out of place in this wrecked room, like a king in a ransacked castle. "I'm your

Starmorrow. I have to keep you safe."

Eirjatal glowers at the king; veins have burst in his eyes, feverishly bright around the green. "Indeed, you are the Starmorrow. No one needs you hurt."

"No, come on. I'm—" Cereus hesitates, then narrows his eyes at Eirjatal. "I'm ordering you, actually. Let me."

"*No*. These three and I are already tainted."

Tavreah yanks Cereus's hand away from the desk, scrubbing it with her sleeve like he stuck it in mud. Johana frenetically finishes tying.

Eirjatal turns his back on Cereus, glowering at Irving instead. He mutters, "I trapped her with Madainn, so if the sirens kill me too, well. Suiting. Johana."

The priestess murmurs incantations in old, warped Etren, poetry of webs and wanderers. Simple rhymes anyone could remember, but it's a sorceress's power that gets the web glowing like Eojhest's stars on their strings.

She paints the twine with a mix of venom and tincture. It's simple, but when it soaks into the twine, magic hits Irving like a kick in the chest.

Eirjatal crushes Irving's hand; it feels like they're fighting to stay anchored to the table, to the room, to gravity. The tangle of twine is taut between them, but after a few infinite beats, it begins to dip and move.

There are ghostly hands, dozens of them, hooking commanding fists and dainty fingers into the twine, helping the tincture along. The magic does the same to their insides—before, it was like the Adder was pushing them into a corner of themselves to make room for Rhoheme, but now it's like they're being pulled out of their own skin.

It's familiar.

The infirmary slips away. They're as much a part of the ritual as the thread, the herbs, the venom. A memory takes the place of all the missing sensation. They rediscover themselves on a stone table in a cultist tent. Something had gone wrong. The cultists took the rib and left, Woven through and through.

Rhoheme is sitting next to them. She crosses her legs, smoothing the wrinkles in the starch of her suit. Her eyes are flat black.

And then she's the Blind Adder, exactly the way she appeared that night, modern and sleek. "I promise I never toyed with the Fey's bloodlines, even back when it was in style. That magic's from your mother."

They turned their face into their arm and the shallow, cold puddle of blood beneath it, and there she sat, as patient as a priestess in her own temple, her tiny smile maybe only a trick of the light.

"I didn't ask for you."

"No, I suppose you were doing the opposite." She had an unplaceable accent that Irving hasn't heard since, even in the melting pot of Staventene. An accent from the realm she was a part of before Karadenza adopted her, probably. "Chiroscuroi cultists? Clever, though ghastly. They want anything Cypresian they can get, and I suppose a rib is a good prize. Why not get a tether?"

Why bother? By leaving Cypress they'd left the Fey before she could leave them, and by leaving the Blind Adder they'd left Karadenza, too.

They'd smiled, the expression heavy enough to melt right off their face. The room filled with the faint *tick* of blood dripping off the table. "I don't think I've got the time to explain."

"I won't let anything happen to you. I wouldn't want to miss the end." She'd folded her long, bone-white hands over her knee. The hands were floating an inch or two away from neatly cut wrists. No bone or blood inside, like she was made of marble and time had broken her pieces away.

The infirmary explodes back into clarity. Johana's fingers are wound in the tangle of twine, while the phantom tugs follow along, like she's playing a complex song with them on piano keys—Eirjatal is braced on the table, blood in his grit teeth, but the nails and wood are gone from his gashed arm.

Breathless, Johana says, "I can't—I can't find her. Let me try again. Let me—"

The Blind Adder had released their shoulder, then nodded, satisfied.

She said, "I've gotten tired of helping those who destroy themselves. Sometimes it's too sad. Sometimes death is best. Where do you fall?"

"Depends. Did it work?"

A series of floating hands slid into place like Ferris wheel seats, one after the other. "Chiroscuroi is a god of divergence. You followed the path you wanted."

"So yes?"

Irving's own hands took their place at the end of her marble wrists. "Yes. But I so like my collection."

The infirmary floods back. Irving blearily lets Johana rip the ritual away. With it comes a feeling of lightness, but not wholeness. For the first time they feel blamed for it.

Eirjatal stands. He sways, but Cereus steadies him. His arm is still open, blood threaded with something clear. His mouth and nose are bleeding.

Johana whispers, "I'm sorry. I couldn't—"

Rhoheme. They were trying to save Rhoheme. Irving's dizzy, nauseated. There's blood on their chin.

Eirjatal's hands set on fire and Johana scrambles behind Irving's chair.

She babbles, "I needed more. There was hardly enough for you. The books say—venom, yes, but organs, there's a kind of magic in the—"

Eirjatal whispers, "I'm not angry. You did what you could." He massages a thumb into his palm. Fire blazes up to his elbows.

Irving sets their head on the edge of the cot as Eirjatal and Johana discuss his next steps. Marie slides across their back, the weight keeping them in the room.

Back then in Staventene, they lived—obviously. But the Blind Adder's slipped into their lives countless times since then. Johana. The House of Ciphers. Every time Heartswain chose to remind them of that moment.

Before she left, Irving asked her, "Who prayed for you to save me?"

"I didn't get his name. Beautiful arm, though." She peered down at them with flat eyes. "Ah. Now I see why you didn't choose a tether. Do you think he and the Fey accepted your apology?"

22

Eirjatal

Humans have a preoccupation with love and how we misunderstand it.
How could we understand? We have red, waxing, new, waning, crescent—
they have one gnarled love for everything.
Brides are willing and brides are stolen. Passion is sweet and poisoned.
One can only achieve a facsimile of life without romance. But it is also the
way of madness. Imagine murder out of love...they do. By their definition,
love is not something the Fey has ever felt.

Spring huntress after escape from Ventaris, notes, Age of Illumination 116

Once Cereus helps him into the elevator, Eirjatal leans his head against the juddering wall, feeling like shattered glass, unable to fit all his sharp bits back together.

Rho insisted she go with him to the river—she saw in him the same fear that got him bit today. And that lost him his chance to save her.

The only time this haunting truly feels hopeless is when it hurts other people.

Don't save me yet.

The elevator is humming, humming; it sets his nerves on edge.

Right as the doors start shutting, Cereus sticks his foot out to jam them. Ringal barrels in, chasing a bumblebee; Cereus picks Ringal up and waves her prey out the doors. While the elevator descends, Cereus buries his face between the chimera's featherless wings. Eirjatal had his reservations when Vyriseh gave Cereus the kitten, as if Rho was a dead pet to replace, but perhaps Vyriseh gave him somewhere to turn his affections when Eirjatal froze him out.

In Eirjatal's apartment, Cereus gets him to the sofa and Ringal chases the edges of his coat, so the decision is silently made to get Eirjatal out of it. Ringal promptly attacks the fabric and gets tangled in it.

"Finally a worthy opponent, huh?" Cereus asks, rubbing her belly until she latches onto his hand instead. Eirjatal smiles but his eyelids slip shut, heavy. Fey's horns, *everything* hurts. Blood dries on his clothes and his face, reeking of metal. The faint humming of the room presses on him, like he's underwater, and his hearing goes tinny.

His arm is oddly numb. He can still see it on Johana's desk and those white spiders skittering through his blood. White spiders, like little curls of snow.

An exhausted weight pulls his eyes shut, and the snow spills across the desk, fills the floor, and pushes down the walls with great howls of wind.

Even if he always remembers Sigyn alone leaving him in the snow, logically, he knows Sigyn brought most of his caravan with him. Sigyn hugged him furiously before he left with that Carrion Queen priestess, like he thought he could break off some piece of Eirjatal and take it with him.

(Well, maybe he did. The part that could sew skin shut after it was sliced open.)

He only held Rho's hand, because she was so sure the sirens would drown them the instant their heads were submerged in the river. He said he'd go first and squeeze her hand if something went wrong—or, he'd teased, perhaps the sirens would be so efficient that it'd go limp right away.

When he opens his eyes, Cereus is gone, but this is *Cereus*—he didn't leave without a goodbye. Eirjatal keeps himself awake by prodding Ringal's paws until she's whipped herself into such a frenzy that he has to carefully extricate her from the fabric.

"Eirj. Are you cold?"

His jaw aches, like his teeth were chattering. "I'm alright."

Cereus takes Eirjatal's hand and starts cleaning off the sticky, drying blood with a damp cloth. It's a dishtowel. Eirjatal can't be bothered to mention it.

Cereus's wavy hair has fallen into a messy tousle on his forehead, and without thinking, Eirjatal fixes it behind Cereus's horns. He presses his fingers to the warm skin behind Cereus's ear. He can feel Cereus's pulse—or maybe that's his own, tripping back to its proper pace.

Cereus whispers, "If I ask to help you with something, can you please listen to me?" He sets the bloody cloth aside (far from Ringal) and gently sweeps Eirjatal's hair off his temple. "Can you please let me *help* you?"

"We were using a thief for a reason."

"I mean...before that. All the time. You're always helping *me*. I want to return the favour. You do everything alone."

He studies the shape of Cereus's mouth. He doesn't want to have this inane conversation. He wants to kiss him.

And why not? some bitter, lonely thing seethes. *I can't do this. I can't lay awake thinking about Madainn beneath the palace and whatever was growing from my arm and how Rho is broken under so much worse.*

"No one is going to be like Rho to you. It's probably good some stuff's for you and her and no one else. But I don't want you to think it *has* to be that way."

Cereus looks at his hands as if buying himself a moment to think. Eirjatal has seen him face down a broken kingdom and a court that didn't trust he could fix anything, and yet *here* he hesitates.

"There's so much of you that you hide away, like Rho's the only person who can handle it. Or worse, like *you* are."

"Is there a reason this is coming up now?"

"Did you and Rho commune with Madainn? What happened to her?"

It takes Eirjatal a breath and half a retort before he realizes Cereus didn't say what he'd been preparing for: *Why didn't you tell me?*

Before the ritual, he'd said Madainn's name to Cereus. "That was our business."

"You don't have to trust me with everything. And like I said, I don't need what you and Rho had, because you two have gone through everything together. But I want to know what stops you from feeling that, you know, feeling like you can make space for me. I want to fix that, because you have more of me than you even know, Eirjatal."

The waters were already high from Corsair, the ritual, Rho, but now Eirjatal feels like it's boiling. "There are parts of me you don't deserve to make yourself love."

"Do you really think that? Even love as a friend?"

"Anything."

His head is killing him. He presses heat out of his palms with his thumbs. Is this a confession? What happened to casual, easy?

The anxieties hit like waves. Most mornings, they roll harmless and low on the beach. Some mornings, he stands in the surf. Others, he's drowning in it. Repetitive and old but still powerful, no matter from how far away he sees them coming. If Rho becomes another wave—she's better than the trenches his mind has eroded for centuries.

"The sirens, all of this... You're worrying me. I know what you've..." He searches for the next words in another corner of the room before focusing on Eirjatal again. "I followed you for Ashvaren, remember? I know what you used to do. About Madainn. All the travelling and the worrying, but—"

Eirjatal pushes to his feet. The light-headedness nearly pulls him back down. Cereus catches his elbow but can't help letting him go even as he says, "Eirj, please?"

He wants to retort something, but the thoughts can't order themselves into something sensible. The waters have surged, and to the Amber Crawl with words. It suddenly seems like labour to breathe at all.

"I don't want to know that stuff because of what Ashvaren made me do. I want to know because you trusted me enough to tell me."

Eirjatal presses a hand to his mouth. If two centuries have given him anything in the way of defences against this fear, it's that he can see it coming from a mile away. He needs Cereus to leave, but stronger than that crashes in the need to do something about all of this.

He failed Rho again. He lost her again. Vyriseh's spies haven't even found Galistan, Scintia's soldier, in the Glasswood wastes. This could all be over in moments, and he could be none the wiser, too terrified of sirens and protecting the useless smallness of his life. He doesn't understand—Rho's cryptic message, the failed ritual, the automatons waking up, the horrible ringing in the walls, the unnerving calmness of Dianthus.

He swallows what air he can, pivots, and crashes into Cereus who's suddenly come up behind him. "I need you to send Scintia a letter."

Cereus's voice quiets, like when he was first coaxing Ringal from her crate when Vyriseh gifted her. "I don't think that's a good idea."

He can't design his demand in a way that will keep Cereus none the wiser. Scintia understands this better than Vyriseh, than Cereus, than anyone ever could. She saw it. She can tell him what to do. Make him feel less mad. She knows him.

And that is exactly why Cereus is hesitating.

So he tries to correct it. "Never mind. I'll find Vyriseh."

"For what?"

"Fey watching, does it fucking matter?" he snaps. "You think I'm deluded anyways."

"Eirj, take a breath, okay? Scintia doesn't answer anything we send."

"She answers me. She will this time."

"You're...Come here." Cereus steers him back a few steps and it's the first time he's had cause to notice how much stronger and taller Cereus is than him. He's put firmly back on the sofa. Ringal's backed into a corner, her wings flat on her back; she's picked up what Cereus seemingly hasn't.

"Scintia will sort this out. If you can get—an invitation, something—I don't want to write to her. I need to speak to her."

"I'll do that. Official letterhead through the Hawks and everything. What's this about?"

He says the only thing left in his arsenal, "It's between us."

No irritation crosses Cereus's face. He truly is a better person than Eirjatal gives him credit for. Rho has less patience. "Okay. I know things are weird right now, so I don't expect things to really change yet. But I'm starting to get the sense that if you keep holding all this, it's going to crush you. It's been ages, Eirj."

"You sound like Sigyn," he scoffs. "He and Vyriseh have offered, you know, to fix this. Years back. She may be able to with her magic."

"Why haven't you?"

Because I can do it myself, he nearly snaps, then it hits him that he hasn't managed to in two centuries. It's cyclical, it's not always at its worst—*this* is not its worst—but it does seem like it's forever.

"I don't know."

Cereus sets a hand on the side of Eirjatal's neck. "I don't mean *fix it*. I don't mean changing at all. I mean letting me help you."

What does this all look like to you?

Something impossible, clearly, for the next thing he says is a soft, "Do you want me to go?"

"Please."

23

Irving

The Academy slammed their doors after telling us to turn our ire where we pleased. The sky, the earth, no one would hear us. The Woven never listen, and Ventaris is the most godly place in the world. And so the idea trickled through the Hawks like poison: turn our ire upon their city, and burn every human who drank from Moonwarden Khidell's torn-open throat.

Hawk after attempt to retrieve Khidell, interview, Age of Beasts 200

There are two things Irving didn't bargain on when they took Vyriseh's offer to let them in on her and Sigyn's work.

One, that they'd feel so horrible on the day it happened that they genuinely considered negotiating with a Sunmirren and a Moonwarden for a rain check.

And two, that Vyriseh would bring them (as Leila) and Sigyn into the long black halls of a Ventaris tower.

They know that's where they are, even if the world's filtered through a headache. Besides the Ventaris iconography and the countless displays of dragon parts, it *feels* different. They hate that it feels different, like the Nelaeryn Fey tethers part of them to Cypress and they're tripped up by the tug of her jealous claws. Etreal should feel *right.*

Irving couldn't figure out what Vyriseh's portal key was as it passed from hand to hand to hand to slot, but it was made of the same shiny obsidian glass as the door she's opening now. They're flanked by obsidian statues of serpentine dragons, Ventaris's symbol, including a bull-faced Dvrasken Dauntless and an insectile Gilded Diver from Kava.

Vyriseh waves them into a hexagonal room. Irving collapses into one of the chairs that frame a black, equally-hexagonal table, and their blood rushes back to their head.

If they had their magic back—if they knew how to use it—maybe they could heal themselves. But even if the spiders thought differently than the priestess who checked their blood on the glass knife, they know they're empty.

Sigyn sits across from Irving. As always, he's brought his scrying tools with him, a teakwood box hardly bigger than a paperback, and sets it safely on his lap. As Vyriseh meanders to her seat, she touches the back of Irving's head. The faint hum of her magic meeting itself shimmers against their skull.

On the walls are melting portraits and watery landscapes, reminiscent of the space between consciousness and sleep. Tiny glass sculptures of more dragons and bat-winged, horned Aphrodin sit in little alcoves.

Engraved straight into the table surface is a map of Etreal's mainland with a peek at the continent of Kyphae at Irving's elbow and a smattering of Bechegran's Isles at Sigyn's. Vyriseh stands between them at the westmost Glasswood. Cloudy blots of silvery paint make forests and metropolises like Staventene and Grey Eves are rendered in three-dimensional, minuscule castles. When Vyriseh turns on the electric chandelier, they gleam with tiny internal lights—but Cypress remains a shrouded mystery.

Irving asks, "Why Ventaris?"

"Why?" Vyriseh studies Irving long enough that they realize they should shift out of their very-Irving posture of elbows on the map. They fold their hands in their lap.

Vyriseh continues, "What choice did they have but to lend me a sliver of a tower, after torturing my Moonwarden Khidell and selling his death throe confessions like romantic chapbooks? We were even for the pain after the massacre we gave them, and we are now even for the advantage Khidell gave to them."

Irving didn't miss all those sealed doors in the hall. What else is here? Does she only get this room? Maybe Vyriseh's not allowed to stray, like a girl taking a dangerous forest road at night.

Vyriseh claps both sets of hands. "Let's start."

"Wait." Sigyn's Etren is more polished than Irving's and they thank the enchantment for giving them Leila's accent. "Can you assure her, Vyriseh, that she will not leave with too much heard, too much to say?"

Unlike Johana.

"I can't promise she won't ask questions she needn't ask, or we won't answer in ways we needn't answer. But I'm not worried. No elf nor human will believe that Ventaris lets me walk here."

To Irving, Sigyn says, "Sunmirren Vyriseh has put you in a difficult position. I know how Cypress and Etreal tilt the truth until it reflects the image they wish, especially in regards to each other, so I understand your fear. Would you like to leave?"

Irving goes cold and still. They're sent back to when they finally admitted they wanted to leave Heatherwol. *"If you do leave, I hope it is to find yourself. I hope it is to find faith. Something needs to shield you, if not me."*

And he kept that promise, even if he had to bargain with a goddess that wasn't his to do it.

Sigyn adds, "I have a human partner and a half-blood child. It is not in my interests or instincts to be unsympathetic to you."

"Why are you here, then?" they ask without thinking. "Where are they?"

"Our lives are very different. The Fey keeps me from them."

You were a Moonwarden when you met Penelope. You knew the Fey would.

Vyriseh interjects, "He's so very serious. I apologize. Besides, I'll be freeing her from her Briarlord captors regardless, as we discussed." She squeezes Sigyn's shoulder.

Irving's mother is the only person they've seen touch Sigyn. Not even Adamantine. So Vyriseh doing it makes them feel...they don't know *what* they feel, but they hook their heels in the chair rungs to not squirm.

They're seeing one of Sigyn's walls fall, one that they had to scale like a stranger.

They say, "I'll stay. I'll help."

Vyriseh pulls a painting from the wall then sets it on the map. It's a horizontal scene, divided by vertical slats representing the Woven. The art makes their delicate head swim, with its simplistic, smudges of subdued colour instead of Cypress's precise lines and bright inks, and in each of their hands...

"The Chalices."

"Do you know them well?"

"I'm not supposed to trust elves with these things."

"Don't fret, dear. Do you really think I want to know more about the Woven than I must, for my realm's safety?" Vyriseh taps the Adder, a ghost as pale and watery as the real Adder was when observing Irving on that bloody cot, years ago. "Start here. We're in Ventaris, after all."

The Adder holds two Chalices instead. One drips black liquid off the rim, the other silver. The Chalices were given to each of the Woven gods at the feast that started the Tapestry. Etreal celebrations to mark the new year imitate the Woven's, and Irving can hardly remember the last one except for waking up somewhere they didn't belong. "One cup lets you heal anything or raise the dead—and the other lets you kill with a touch."

Vyriseh smiles wryly. "And what of finding it? Hasn't Etreal tried? Hasn't Ventaris?"

"Cultists have, apparently. No luck."

Vyriseh taps a finger on Faowist. The goddess of the sun holds her goblet protectively with her dark hands. "And hers?"

"Impossible to recover," Sigyn says. "She fashioned the cup into her logbook where she records all Etreal events. Not even the other Woven can get her to part with it."

Irving can't believe themselves, but they're actually irritated. They're supposed to be the one who knows things about Etreal. Even if it's useless fairy tales.

Vyriseh points out the Carrion Queen, draped with dizzying red viscera and black pelts. "And?"

Irving steps quicker. "Shattered into slivers that she fired into a dozen animals across Etreal."

Sigyn says, "The animals became immortal, and to strike their heart would make you their master."

"It's actually to *free* the arrow from their heart."

"Oh? A reversal for the goddess of predators."

"A lot more impossible, too. How to get to an animal's heart without killing it? Much less the right animal."

They're speaking too much like themselves. Still, Sigyn smiles across the table at them. Even with their irritation, they realize that there are no expectations here. No history or vague mess of a future.

And yet what they really want to ask—*did your human wife teach you all this?*—sticks in their throat. "How do you know this?"

Amusement flits across Vyriseh's face. "We have personal experience with the Carrion Queen. Have you ever heard of the Packmothers? The Age of Beasts?"

"No and yes."

Vyriseh steeples her fingers. "Ah! It will humble you to know that you're speaking with one of the heroes who ended that war with the gods."

"You—?"

"Him." Vyriseh smirks.

Sigyn does little more than resettle his hands beneath his chin and slide his gaze to Vyriseh. Irving asks, tone sharp, "What does that mean?"

Vyriseh's dangling bait over Irving's head, and damn them, but they're lunging for it. "This was over two centuries ago. A war where gods knew that only divine beasts could take down divine beasts, and that they had much to protect after Madainn made the world his experiment. Cypress, too, was caught in his tide, so to speak."

"The Carrion Queen," Sigyn adds gently, "negotiated for our protection by creating beasts with the Nelaeryn Fey. I was their keeper, and so took the title of their victory, although it was a Carrion Queen cultist who first brought them to me."

Irving stares at their father, dumbstruck, wondering if last night's ritual totally unhinged them. They always knew Sigyn had countless lives before them, but this?

Sigyn isn't modest, isn't even proud, only observing the painting like it's a contract he's about to sign. It's always this. It's always this careless boredom about his own weird, unbelievable power—no wonder he never told Irving. No wonder he doesn't ever bother with Irving, because what's a half-blood, ex-sorcerer kid next to legends like *that?*

Vyriseh asks, "And what of hers?"

Karadenza, at the center of the painting, her might reflected a thousand times over by shards of mirrors surrounding her like a sunburst crown. Even in the simple painting, her eyes blaze, brighter than the Iron Phoenix's fire, deeper than Madainn's seas.

"It's not real. None of it is," Irving says, all too excited. "Karadenza's too protective over her worlds. She wouldn't let them scatter all this power around for humans to take."

Vyriseh leans an arm on the table. "And yet humans have still hunted for any bit of power they can take."

She steeples one set of hands, while the other trawls over the map. There are pegs scattered around the landscape and she offers a few to Irving.

"Show me every corner you've even heard a *whisper* of these Chalice searches. Any rumour, any news article, any murmur. I remember, dear, you had a little affiliation before you came to Cypress?"

Anya Zarina—whose secrets made the Ciphers drop them—boasted at her party Irving attended that she was funding a new archeological dig in Grey Eves for a piece of Karadenza's Chalice. A century-old automaton was found buried with the bodies of unlucky explorers and Anya couldn't help telling the exclusive lead to anyone who listened. It's all rumours, all fairy tales.

But Vyriseh seems absolutely sure that they know it *all*, to the point that when they take a breath to resist, her second set of eyes flash open and she reminds, "Or I can always look by myself. Humans' minds are easy to navigate."

Sigyn tilts his clockwork hand to the painting; it doesn't seem to be moving so well. "As I understand, this was a fete for the final stitches on the realm. A realm the Fey was a part of, but all this magic unfolded without Her knowing."

"Yeah?"

Vyriseh rolls one of the pegs across the table; it bumps into Staventene's miniature castle. "It's a world so near ours, girl, with myths that can shake their realm but leave *us* sprawling. Our goddess may not know, so we must know *for Her.* There is security in knowing."

"Humans do not loathe her like elves are taught to loathe the Woven. You pity Her. Which is kind in its own way." Sigyn seems almost concerned. "Do you think She has a right to at least know?"

Irving asks, "Does she want to know, or do you?"

"It's difficult to explain, but our emotions are not so different."

They dig their nails into their palm. Sigyn connects himself so easily with a goddess who threw them aside. And here he is, messing with gods again, and for what?

But it's also the most they've learned about Sigyn in ages. Maybe if they play nice, dig up all the murmuring from the Ciphers about this nonsense, they'll at least earn the story of what happened to his arm.

"Fine," they say. "The last mission to seek out Karadenza's was in Grey Eves."

24

Eirjatal

Do we need to wonder over a motive for his assassination? It's the same reason an animal would rather chew off its own paw than die in a trap. Cypress is weakening, but Ashvaren's death is not a reason why.

Dianthus political chapbook, Age of Shields 245

Eirjatal's sketchbook is propped on a knee as he draws room after room with charcoal. Slats of sun cut across the blonde balcony, so bright and sharp that they seem able to slice his hands. Parrots chatter in the tropical forests that crowd the shores and packs of sprites colour the beach like fireworks. He should be mapping his home and its light, but he's mapping the Ineiren Fort.

Eirjatal narrows his world into strokes of black. Some amorphous anxiety flits at the edges of his mind, like snatches of conversation he half-hears, shadows dodging out of sight.

Eirjatal details chandeliers the shape and size of longboats, scraping away the black with his nail to light the candles. The tangles of a steel tree, untouched while the throne was broken down for weaponry. The windows framed in heavy frost from the cold consuming the body heat of so many elves crammed into the fortress. Sunmirren Scintia—only a citizen at the time, younger than Cereus is now—would breathe against those windows and write military plans in the fog.

Eirjatal slept, shivering and stiff, with blankets over his head like an elfling. The blankets were stitched with thick feathers that smelled of carrion and whose stems scratched his face. There were times he was trapped awake, either from the cold or terror about which of Madainn's monstrosities would come crawling out of the Evertide next, and he'd hear Scintia drifting through the halls, barefoot, whispering about brutal ends.

Occasionally, he followed her to that frosted metal tree and they prayed to the Archfey together. Scintia would help him to his feet afterwards and was always surprised. "Your hands. They're still warm." She'd press her own palms to her throat, like she could steal that warmth. Every time.

Now, like with each drawing before, Eirjatal scuffs the charcoal with the side of his hand. Smears the rooms until they're full of dust, rubble, the torrent of paralyzing, icy seawater that punched out the windows with Scintia's frozen fingerprints. Madainn razed the Ineiren Fort in a war between the Woven, a war that wasn't even the Fey's. The Age of Beasts.

For a flash, Eirjatal nearly tears up the drawing. He wants to rip away the memories threatening to solidify. Drag them down with the fortress and dare the shadows to push in. He knows they can do worse than fitful sleep; the cowards are out of practice.

Early in their friendship, Rho made a tiny steel model of the prayer room based on his drawings. If drawing the Fort helped, she said, then maybe seeing it would help too. Even if he needed to destroy it. He kept it, and she added rooms, building the Fort in its entirety and clearly loving the intricate detail work, until sometimes he would draw for her rather than himself.

No matter how deeply he'd fallen, he always knew Rho would be patiently waiting with a hand extended over the edge. That was a far better guarantee than any prayer.

Over the last couple days, Vyriseh took it upon herself to search the city and surrounding tropics for possible thieves. Apparently, she found something even better.

Vyriseh takes Cereus, Kinthe, and Eirjatal to a rundown temple on the road to Spring's crushed kingdom, Hyacinthus. Cereus and Vyriseh are trading increasingly absurd ideas about revitalizing it, Ringal sitting on his shoulders and batting at her glittering hairpins, when they enter and all stop dead.

Three elves kneel on the broken stone before Vyriseh's guards. Subduing them must have been a feat, as blood spatters their nondescript clothing, but they're thoroughly defanged by words written in deep purple across their faces. A Mythmaker charm looks to have stolen their consciousness.

Vyriseh flings out her four arms. Her lipstick is the same shade as the writing. "Ashvaren loyalists! Scheming during *Lightbringing*!"

A statue claims the back wall of the temple. Relyn wears a dress made of glass hammered right into the clay, the Archfey roars with fangs like Summer's, and, seated at Their feet, Nele cradles a child and skull. All of Her ears and eyes are chiselled away. The loyalists hid their actions from Her but apparently still wanted Her presence.

Kinthe steps towards them, but Vyriseh neatly slides into her path to take a blade from an Eclipsed guard.

"One peek into their heads told me they were planning on plunging this," she presses the tip to Cereus's clavicle, "into our beloved Starmorrow tomorrow night."

Magic sears Eirjatal's hands. Cereus hefts Ringal into his arms, paling.

Vyriseh asks, "What shall we do?"

Kinthe is quickest. "The typical banishment won't suffice."

Perhaps Cereus knew Vyriseh wasn't going to show him anything good and that's why he brought the chimera; he's clutching her like a lifeline. "They didn't even attack me!"

"Would you have rather had this conversation while bleeding out?" Kinthe's tension runs through the temple like a discordant note but doesn't show on the Moonwarden's face. "The Nelaeryn Fey elevated you, and they've directly scorned Her."

"Hurting them won't fix anything." Ringal is squirming. After Cereus sets her down, he stays crouching on the level of the rebels, absently touching where Vyriseh pressed the dagger. "It'd give them more reason to hate me. It'd make me like him. I want to hear what they have to say."

He's a touch breathless, like his words are racing ahead of his body. It's leagues better than his wobbling disinterest in Whitfore's trial, and it's not enough.

Eirjatal says tightly, "They would've killed you, Cereus. We have been lenient before, and still this happens, over and over. They don't want you to listen."

Kinthe adds, "They don't believe you'll ever do *more* than listen."

Ringal chases a butterfly around Nele's foot. The three loyalists sway to unheard music, sweat on their bloody brows.

Cereus murmurs, "Of course they don't. The Dawn Hall's lost its fangs."

Kinthe puffs up. Eirjatal fights the instinct to put himself between them. "And why not prove we still have claws? We've had our half-decade of proving you are not Ashvaren. Don't let them think you can be taken advantage of."

Cereus darts a glance to Vyriseh but she's inspecting the dagger. "We got Ashvaren's allies out of the Dawn Hall but they're still in the city. I know." Now he looks to Eirjatal. Whatever he sees on Eirjatal's face makes him frantically continue, "But there're too many bruises in Dianthus for me to go, you know...throwing my weight around."

"I hardly think branding your thieves is out of line," Eirjatal says.

"They're gonna have that brand forever, Eirj. *My* brand."

While Cereus is picking his words like they're stepping stones across a rough river, Kinthe is that river: inevitable, icy. "Thieves are the least of it. Iron Phoenix worshipers have multiplied under you."

Eirjatal scoffs. "What of the Starmorrow who made the Phoenix seem a preferable alternative?"

"I only think *this* Starmorrow appears too permissive when it comes to her." Kinthe's sneer is pointed. "And all the Woven."

Eirjatal figures if Vyriseh didn't do the sales work, Kinthe never would have allowed Johana in the palace at all. Kinthe isn't afraid of her like Cereus or Tavreah, but she loathes Johana, precisely the way she was trained to under Ashvaren. Ashvaren would kill Johana for the gall, and dump Rho over the border for the risk.

Eirjatal snaps, "Hold your tongue. You speak for the Fey, not for Ashvaren, no matter how he saw himself as a god above Her."

He's hardly finished before Kinthe sets her hand on the bare back of his neck. Whatever fire that has been building since this morning is drenched with icy water, so suddenly that he chokes.

Vyriseh sweeps in. She quickly de-escalates, but Eirjatal is too foggy from Kinthe cutting off his magic with her own to hear her.

"How about you two discuss somewhere less...electrified?"

Suddenly Vyriseh's got her hand in Eirjatal's, pulling him to the loyalists, and Cereus, Kinthe, and Ringal are outside the entryway.

She bursts into giggles. "The way Cereus looked at you! He wants you to save him from everything, you know." Redirecting to the kneeling elves, Vyriseh sobers. "If Cereus had his way, he'd invite his assassins over for dinner and give them the best knives."

Eirjatal flexes his hands. They're freezing. "And Kinthe's hissing in his ear."

"She's always hated me, too, but luckily, Saezdrith protected me even after she passed me the throne. I'm extending that protection to you and Rhoheme."

Vyriseh already has by holding his and Rho's secret, by sourcing Johana's components, by searching the borders of Cypress for sirens and the Glasswood for more information.

Don't save me yet.

Eirjatal shakes it off.

Vyriseh kneels in front of a female and orders him to do the same with the crook of a finger. The temple is overgrown, soft with moss and summer canna lilies, thriving despite its abandonment.

Vyriseh says, "You, Rhoheme, and I are best to teach Cereus where to draw the lines in this new Cypress. We know what's in our own heads, how the magic affects us...who is or isn't whispering in our ears. Only we know who can't be trusted and what must happen to them."

Vyriseh pulls out a hairpin and offers it to him. It's a long amber needle, shining like glass around a core of flame.

"What will you do?"

He's always admired Cereus's heart. As the ambassador, Cereus mingled in the city, using Tavreah's brothel as a rebel hub, learning elves' stories, their wants, their fears, and nudging Ashvaren this way and that to help them. He helped Rho escape the Dawn Hall after Ashvaren roped her into making the wards and wanted her for more. He visited Eirjatal in the dungeons, hopelessly optimistic.

But that isn't enough to protect Cypress.

Eirjatal couldn't kill that siren. He can do this. He *has* to be able to do this.

He takes the hairpin. "Release her."

Vyriseh smears a thumb over the spell. The female wakes with a sharp gasp and her wide eyes find him.

"Cereus's firestarter," she whispers.

Eirjatal expects her to sneer at him, but her face is wan with fear. He tips his head to the broken altar. "You've been concealing your actions from Her. You don't believe you act for Her, then?"

Her jaw is tight—until Vyriseh hums a few notes, and the words spill like they've been knocked out of her, "We must change Cypress. So when She returns, everything is the way it's supposed to be."

Vyriseh waves off the explanation, but it hooks into Eirjatal. He'd always thought of Ashvaren's loyalists as clinging to the Fey's skirts, more desperate than newborns crying for Nele, deathly terrified of humans, of the Woven, of elves like him and Vyriseh and Rho.

"Acting beyond Her laws is to protect Her, then. You don't trust Her to act first?"

Vyriseh replies, "Of course they don't, Eirjatal. The Fey often forgets about saving us."

The Age of Beasts, the Ineiren Fort, Winter's curse, the Packmother massacre in Heatherwol. Missing Briarlords. Sigyn's arm hacked off and that secret kept close. Khidell's torture splashed across countless pages in Ventaris. A dead Eclipsed Moonwarden, a lost Winter one, a Spring one giving up her power to Kinthe before being banished to Etreal. Ashvaren forcing Hyacinthus to its knees and beheading it anyways. Ashvaren's guards closing a Moonwarden's glass collar around Eirjatal's neck and pressing a needle into his ear.

Madainn, hunting something in Dianthus.

The female has found the pin he's holding. Instead of making an attempt at escape, she tilts her head up, as if presenting him with her eyes.

"Oh, dear." Vyriseh sighs. "I used magic on her, so she thinks she deserves it."

"Do you?"

The female's breath comes in shaky bursts. She's clenching her jaw, like speaking to them is enough to be a betrayal. Vyriseh sings a bar, and the female grits out, "Yes. They're crawling through me. They're—"

"Vyriseh, please."

The Sunmirren mimes locking her lips. The spell drops and the female does too, clutching her head.

"This," Eirjatal shows her the needle, "is not because of the Woven. This is because of *you*. Trying to kill the king She chose—do you understand?"

She whimpers, nails burying into her black hair. Each use of Vyriseh's spell seems to break her down a little further.

She's frail and shuddering in his hands, but he woke her up to give her a chance to fight. He wasn't given one. Ashvaren collared him to choke out his magic, starved him for weeks, and had two guards holding him like vices.

Ashvaren didn't give him a chance. However, his magic did. It burst through that frail collar, killing the guards, and made even Ashvaren hesitate about swiping his head from his shoulders.

That was the first time he felt it was his. Wild and wicked, but his alone. No Woven would save him like that. Apparently, the Fey wouldn't either.

The female folds in his arms. Corsair had strength and conviction when they fought. This elf has nothing.

He pushes the needle into her eye with too little force. He makes himself watch the sink of the amber into the brown of her iris, the stream of blood in her lashes. Not deep enough to kill her. She's bracing her hands on his chest; if she jostles him, this will be so much worse.

He also, he has to admit, gave her a chance to fight so he could watch that, too. See her bend, when she wanted the same of Cereus, of Eirjatal, of Rhoheme, of the new Dianthus. He bends her until she snaps.

She lies on the floor, whimpering, wailing, after he steps away. Vyriseh pets her hair then whispers another lilting spell. Her mouth curls uselessly around silence.

Vyriseh takes the amber pin from him. The female's cheek is faintly burnt where he was holding her.

"Thank you, Eirjatal." She leans into his field of vision, her expression soft, but for that strange second set of eyes, which flicked open at some point and is taking him in like a keen-eyed owl. "I will handle the others."

Her work is efficient, passionless. She doesn't remove her spells before stabbing out the eyes of the two kneeling elves. She replaces the bloody pin in her hair.

Eirjatal asks, "Won't you deafen them?"

"They're going over the border, firestarter. So many Woven whispers there." She smirks. "Let them stay afraid."

While the guards gather up the rebels, one approaches Vyriseh instead. She says, "Sunmirren. There has been news from Sunmirren Scintia."

A stab of alarm jerks Eirjatal to attention. The guard turns to him instead.

"She accepts your request to see her."

25

Eirjatal

Who is Cypress after the war? Are we right to abandon Relyn's tenets that kept us interconnected, letting Ashvaren poison his realm with his paranoia? Elves over the border, humans dead in our lands. Are we right to be afraid of ourselves? The cultists, the rage, the despair, the eventual assassination. Who is Cypress after the war?

Firewe to Sunmirren Saezdrith, letter, Age of Shields 49

Rucking up Eirjatal's sleeve, Tavreah pulls a disgusted face at his (entirely bandaged) injury. "I don't understand," she mutters, jabbing his palm with two dagger-sharp fingernails, "why you didn't burn her to a cinder."

He knows all too well. But Vyriseh gave him a gift with those loyalists. He's broken open access to that part of himself once more, the part that isn't so afraid of justice.

They're on the palace's beach, where a scattering of bonfires burst with different colours thanks to the votive materials elves throw in them. Some competition ended tonight, but Eirjatal hasn't been paying attention—very obviously, apparently, since Tavreah and Cereus baited him into joining the court's betting pool and spent what they won off him on intoxicants.

The Dawn Hall is quite good at ignoring problems rather than wallowing in them. It's getting harder for him.

Especially tonight. He's lucky he's moved on from offering blood, or else Tavreah would certainly have something to say about a cut in his hand. Instead, he offered something else, in case Corsair is still interested in greed.

Tavreah says, "Is there no vitaea on this? Relyn weeps for how ugly this scar will be. You already have this monstrosity." She points at his inner elbow, where Rho removed his Hawk tattoo, leaving mottled skin behind. "You're going to let Scintia see you like this?"

"The priestess suggested I not use it. She doesn't know how it reacts with her tincture."

"And you trust her?"

"More than I trust you? When it comes to medicine, unfortunately yes."

Tavreah mimes smacking him, but slows at the last second to merely pat his jaw. On his periphery, he spots a feminine silhouette weaving their way along the treeline towards them, fantastically drunk.

Tavreah pulls his attention back to her. "Anyways, I wanted you for something."

"Is it quick?" He'll have to check back on the trap he set for Corsair.

She rolls her eyes, untangling her black hair from the sheaf of necklaces and silk scarves that serve as her shirt. "Maybe I'll make it anything *but.* I've seen so little of you. I'm worried about Rho too, but do you trust that priestess or not? Do you trust Vyri or *not*?"

Everyone has been tiptoeing around the topic, but Tavreah only knows how to kick open doors and make a ruckus. When he started working in the Dawn Hall, she was the first to drag him out of his room and push him into the palace's particular carnal affinities.

Past Tavreah's shoulder, that figure leans into a tree. There's something strange about the silhouette besides the unsteadiness and how Dianthus is not one to let anyone wander unaccompanied.

"If you don't, you *need* to tell Cereus. He's relying on you being sure about Rho. Why do you keep—?" Tavreah turns. "Oh. Stop staring, you ass, you're going to embarrass her." She winds their fingers together. "Okay, okay, I need your help making an Eclipsed girl jealous."

"Does she have a name? I don't want to put in effort if she doesn't have a name."

Tavreah grins wickedly. "Perhaps she does. She has many mouths to whisper it."

He thinks of the female spy telling him they knew nothing more of Galistan, and in Silvershale's fine rain when he first brought Rho to Vyriseh, fanged mouths open along her back. He lets Tavreah pull him a step—but stops when that stranger slumps to a knee. She's alone. Besides that, something's off, like she's been cut out of paper and stitched into the scene.

Tavreah gives another tug. "Kiss me, then her."

"I think she's one of mine."

"Then she shouldn't be drinking in the first place."

He pulls Tavreah in, kisses her hard, her lipstick smearing across his mouth. He heats up his hand against her ribs, enough for her to fold into his shoulder with a giggle and for a reddened handprint to show up. "There. No mistaking it."

He and Tavreah have only ever been on-and-off together, mostly on nights when they were both too out of sorts to find someone better, but it oddly relaxes him. Like touching someone alive pushes away the lingering bite of the twine and skitter of the spiders under his skin.

Tavreah thumbs the lipstick off his mouth and smears it along the shell of her hip. "Better."

"You've been busy, Lady of the Dahlias."

"I may be swept away at any moment, so she should stop giving me all those coy smiles and make a move." She whirls back to the beach, gauzy wrap-around skirt flaring out. She flaps a hand at him. "Enjoy babysitting."

He reaches the stranger and crouches next to her. Something is odd in her smell; not human, but still tangibly wrong. Her leg is twisted beneath her and she's hissing in pain. He doesn't touch her, suddenly aware of how easy it was to scald Tavreah. "Is there someone I can take you to?"

Her dress is not gauzy like Dianthus', or lace and leather like Heatherwol's, but the wet, rubbery texture of seaweed. It clings to her back in such a way that looks like bones are pushing out of place.

Until he's suddenly sure they are, and her hiss is swallowed up by an airy laugh.

"You," she gasps, the effort of turning her head to him throwing her on an elbow. "I wanted *you*, blood in the water."

The face is human, pale-skinned and lovely, but he sees the siren in the emptiness of her eyes. Like he could drop pebbles in them and never hear them hit the back of her skull.

"Corsair."

It worked, but he didn't expect *this.*

She tumbles on her back and pulls him down with her. She smells of the sour sea and blood, like she stole her human skin off a shipwreck. She's as heavy and solid as the automatons marching out of Staventene, and when he tries to pull away, he learns she's as strong as them too.

Tangled around her arm is what he left a mile upshore: a chain anklet dripping with empty inlays for gems that Rho was going to give Tavreah for Lightbringing. She scrapped it but charmed it to change from silver to gold to black depending on what jewelry it's next to.

He sends a furtive glance around to be sure they're still alone. Her heels dig into the sand. She's presenting herself as little more than a weak, writhing menace, doing all but ripping open the dress (which, he sees now, grows out of her skin) and presenting her beating heart for him to carve out.

He heaves her to her feet. She fights like a hooked fish thrown onto a boat, nearly yanking him off his feet. She wails, "I'm no use to you dead."

He snaps, "Stop whining. What do you want?"

"Pretty things. Pretty things," she cries, like she hates the words as she says them. "Spears and glass and little hearts. I'll do what you want, Feyspawn, for that."

Predictable. The glass panther was the first hit and he made the fish an addict. "Hold on to this spell a little longer and I'll help you. I want something from you. We can make a deal, just be quiet."

She's transforming under his hands. The notches of her spine press like clam shells against the thin human skin, her lungs labour as they push higher into her throat, and Fey's broken horns, she *wails.*

Blood in the water. Blood in the water.

He can't burn her without risking ruining her for Johana, and he can't exactly claw her apart. His weapons are stored upshore.

The Dawn Hall is thankfully empty except for the guards and Radiance's whispering bats swooping in unnaturally rigid patterns along the ceiling. He whistles; Vyriseh gave them a tune so the bats, trained to track the patrols of guards and rounds of staff and where elves are *supposed* to be, won't alert Radiance. The bats then perch in the latticework walls and on statues, watching him pass.

The elevator carries them up, humming madly from the anklet. As Corsair's dress melts into her scales, he notices the cut in her cheek from him, and a different white scar across her throat. It's much older and made of three lines, like claws. It stretches beneath where her human ears are shrivelling like autumn leaves.

"I don't want to die with you," she whispers.

"We're almost there."

She collapses on the threshold of his apartment, dragging him to his knees with her. Her legs are fusing with sticky tendrils of skin.

You blinded one of your own. You did it without mercy. You can kill a monster.

And the walls of fear slam up around him.

He knows himself. He can't cut open an emissary of Madainn, especially not here, a place he trusts to feel safe. He won't survive hurting Corsair, much less the day after, the night after, the rest of his life.

He runs the bath.

In the middle of wrangling her into the tub, she's a full siren again. Her claws scrape his back as he heaves her in. In her struggle to fit, her massive fin up smacks the overhead torch and sprinkles the floor with lantern oil. Her hair makes a shroud around her face under the water.

There's a knock on the door.

A curse flies out of his mouth, but whatever panic burst in him abates when he hears Vyriseh saying, "Do you need a hand?"

I've killed before, he thinks as he stands and lets her in.

Vyriseh's feet are bare, her ankles coated in sand. She explains as she grabs a drafting compass off his desk and heads for the bathroom, "Radiance is one of the bats. Makes her feel safer than being stared at all the time by elves, you know. She saw something interesting."

Vyriseh folds two of her arms and points him towards the tub. She presses the compass in his hand as he passes. He feels like little more than a soldier, a spy, again, and tries to turn that into armour. He could kill anything Madainn sent over the border of the Glasswood. He's travelled in Ventaris, the city with a temple or sigil on every corner. He was on the campaign to retrieve Khidell from the Academies—that turned into a massacre of whatever humans were in the way once they wouldn't relinquish the Moonwarden.

He killed his own kin for following orders, and cut out the eyes of others for fearing the Dianthus he's letting evolve with inaction.

And he can't do it. Something isn't connecting mind to body, intent to heart.

What is this? What is happening to you?

What has been happening to you?

Corsair's eyes are brighter. With a pleased purr, she folds her arms on the side of the tub and props her sharp little chin atop. "You want something. I smell *want* better than anything. Besides," she hisses, "fear."

Gods feel through their creations, their worshipers, and he will certainly feel her die.

Something in him knows that that fear is so small compared to what will happen if he doesn't do it, but logic keeps slipping away, like trying to grasp ink in water.

Vyriseh says his name, slow, with a tinge of music to it.

He meets her eyes. All four are open.

"I can't," he says. He holds out the compass. Releasing himself of that comes as a physical relief, a gasp of clean air after suffocation, the sharp release of his magic after burning up inside.

Vyriseh snatches the compass. Corsair hisses and her jaw unhinges, gills flaring, tilting her head this way and that on her long neck, and in all that he sees nothing but an animal making a last bid at seeming stronger than it is.

"Since when are you so sentimental?" Vyriseh takes Corsair by the hair. Her large webbed hands scrape pointlessly against Vyriseh. "When will you get this chance again?"

He has nothing in his defence. Maybe she knows this because Vyriseh buries the drafting compass into Corsair's throat.

Corsair vaults herself over the edge of the tub with the last of her strength. Thankfully, instinct forces Eirjatal to duck in, bracing her around the shoulders so she can't overwhelm Vyriseh. The smell of her so close, his body being pulled towards the water, her blood jetting on his face, lights up a terror in him—he drops her and she slumps into the tub, twin burns sizzling on her shoulders. She's clumsy, filling the tub with bright, bright blood.

Eirjatal tries to swallow down the panic, but it storms up inside him.

The room suddenly seems to have weight and pressure and anger all directed at him.

At Vyriseh, he snaps, "You are dealing with things you don't understand."

"You're not exactly clear-eyed on the matter of Madainn either, darling."

"I've dealt with him for centuries, and—"

"Have you?" she asks. "Is Ashvaren right about Madainn crawling into your body after all? Or have you only been in a very long dream?"

"I didn't *invent* that he's interested in Dianthus," he hisses. But suddenly he isn't sure. He recalls everything Cereus rehashed from his time watching Eirjatal for Ashvaren, when Madainn drove him mad without doing anything at all.

Scintia wouldn't imagine it. Scintia isn't as broken as he is, is she?

Vyriseh pulls the chain on the plug. Swirling blood leaves streaks in the basin. Corsair's fathomless black eyes are open.

Vyriseh asks him where to find pins to tie up her hair. Then she returns from his bedchamber with her hair in a bun, jewelry discarded, nearly spilling out of one of his robes. She's still wearing her high heels. She's brought cooking knives and passes one to him.

He tries to take it but they both note his shaking hand. Vyriseh presses her fingers to his forehead and a few lilting bars later, his hands are steady again. Whatever corked his lungs eases up.

She sighs. "I'm sorry for what I said. If you can't do these things, then I already told you, didn't I? Rhoheme and I are like you. We know Dianthus better than anyone else. We can make these decisions. And when she comes back, everything will be much easier."

Despite her spell to calm his anxiety, he still jumps when Vyriseh sets all her weight into the knife and cracks it through Corsair's chest. He breathes through his mouth to stave off any nausea.

"I expect with this," Vyriseh says, tipping into the tub to get a better angle with one set of hands on the knife and the other balancing her on the tub, "Johana will have enough material to screw up a few times. Are you alright? You're pale."

"You're vivisecting someone in my bathtub."

"Some*thing,* Eirjatal Ga'vrynn. And this stays our secret. Imagine if Cereus knew you were doing this? He'd have more concerns than some paranoias you displayed a decade ago."

He's focusing on breathing, but that snaps him out of it. How does she know about that?

She continues. "Cereus can't know what Scintia told you. Neither of us want to push him into such an awful position…having to decide things that will make him feel in his heart that he's like Ashvaren…how cruel of us!"

He confesses, "Rho told me not to save her."

"What?"

"Yet. Not to save her *yet*. I got in contact with her through a ritual, and that's what she left me with." Saying it is a relief. "Johana said she was pushing back."

Vyriseh's eyes narrow. "She's hovering somewhere far from Nele, isn't she? Can you blame her for being confused? Well, we have an entire corpse to drag her out with this time. Souls are not so strong."

In the corner of his eye swims Corsair's turquoise tail, her black hair spilling like ink, that horrible orange blood only getting deeper in hue. He can't touch her. He's never been in this position, but that seems like a certain rule. *Don't touch her and Madainn won't know it was you.*

He runs his hands through his hair, heart rate picking back up.

"And if Madainn comes? What is there left to do? Sacrifice myself?"

"I have ideas. I have been a queen for a very long time. I know you're worried. You're leaving to see Scintia tomorrow, aren't you? And the Moonwardens are coming too? Stressful, isn't it?"

No wonder she and Sigyn work together; they can both read each other's minds and feel very clever about it.

"It doesn't matter. You need to see Scintia, get all the remaining information you can, and I'll handle the last couple details. When you come back, we will wake her."

"What do I do? Wait?"

"Try to forget. You have to learn how one day, after all."

Eirjatal cleans the bathroom and then takes the longest shower of his life in Tavreah's Dawn Hall apartment.

He heats the water with magic—in part to purge the anxiety and in part to burn off the feeling of Corsair's insides—so when he comes out, steam chokes up the bathroom. He doesn't know where to go. Certainly not back to his room; his gorge rises at the thought. Tavreah will ask questions if he stays in her room, but at least she won't care about the truth if he makes an amusing lie. He has a passing thought of drifting to the staff apartments and checking over everyone's morale and seeing what he can do to help, doing *some* good, but that vanishes when he finds Cereus in Tavreah's bedroom.

Cereus is going through her vanity. He double-takes at Eirjatal and his braided wet hair. "Was Tavreah in there with you?"

"No? Are you looking for her?"

"She said she had something to show me in the city. Last I saw, someone pushed her in the ocean."

"I think she has a date," Eirjatal says, thinking of the female she wanted him to make jealous. Still, that was an hour ago, and Tavreah has gotten bored in less time.

Cereus groans. He snags a pair of emerald ear cuffs from a jewelry box. "These are her apology." He turns for the door, then stops and swivels back on a heel. "You wanna come with? I was going to find some friends from before…" He makes a vague hand gesture, indicating the castle and his role with it. "But they get weird when it's just me. You'd show them that they can treat me like they used to. You've never taken an order from me in your life."

Eirjatal hesitates.

"Come on," he says, blasting Eirjatal full force with a grin. "I miss you."

The prospect of being with Cereus is nearly frightening. Not because of Cereus himself, but because Eirjatal isn't sure how his own feelings will shift, moment to moment.

But he's not going back to that apartment, beating with Madainn's heart.

On their way out, Cereus hooks one of the cuffs to Eirjatal's ear.

26

Eirjatal

Sigyn received the Nelaeryn Fey's agreement that Cereus should take the Dianthus throne. I see why She supports him, despite his youth. He loves these kingdoms in a way Ashvaren never could. As such, I advise we bar Moonwarden Kinthe from asking the Fey for confirmation. She made the oath to never lie about her visions under a Starmorrow who is now dead. She must learn again that Sigyn has final say.

Adamantine's letter to Vyriseh, Age of Shields 245

Rho used to call Cereus a "fucking glorified tourist."

She was bitter that his ambassador job let him move without restrictions all over Cypress, even to the destroyed and forbidden Hyacinthus, which Rho only knew as a youth. Honestly, Eirjatal was bitter too. Dianthus's inner conflict closed its people off to so much, and even when Eirjatal got permission to leave, he couldn't help being pulled back.

Cereus was magnetic. He seemed determined to make you smile if you passed him—and knew that his own smile was often enough to do the job. He was willing to be friends with absolutely anybody, whether their interaction started with a bought drink or a scathing insult about how cushy it was to be Ashvaren's pet. He was still too spoiled to take part in the citizens' hardship, but he *asked* about it, which was more than the other noble classes back then.

The new king had a narrow set of skills, all of them focused on people. He had very little mind for paperwork and fine print. When Eirjatal was hired, he was ostensibly a staff manager, but he took on the worst of the records reorganizing for Cereus's sake.

Cereus is the same male now as he was during his years as Ashvaren's ambassador; he plays the attendants of the brothel like a fiddle.

They found Tavreah hosting the main hall event. She used to run the establishment before transferring to the palace.

She's carrying a decorated gold pitcher. Both employees and clients place offerings within, small pieces shaved off something they are thankful to the Fey for providing them. Tavreah keeps a ritual blade in her silk belt, because the most common offering is blood.

One female trims a lock from her corkscrew curls, spiralling out like a storm cloud and gleaming every colour from the jewelry around her. Another cuts a neat gash upon her rather impressive, milk-white cleavage. A male accepts a kiss on his knuckles from two beautiful consorts and smears the lipstick print on the metal; Tavreah teases him for being cheeky. Another takes a folded sheet from their pocket and reads aloud the most syrupy, overblown poem Eirjatal has ever heard, then drops it in the pitcher while announcing, "Praise be to the Fey for evolving my talent so that I now recognize what drivel I used to write."

It's all playful, joyful, and honest.

Tavreah dances the pitcher over to Cereus and Eirjatal at their table with other elves who've stayed a careful distance away from them. Glasses slow on their way to mouths and forks are set down in a rainfall of clatters. Everyone wants to know what a king will praise. But Cereus gestures for Eirjatal to go first.

The pitcher is shimmery with red on its lip and throat. He thinks of the streaks of blood in his bathtub. The *crack* of Vyriseh's weight on the knife on Corsair's—*the siren's*—sternum.

Stay here.

He could cut his hand.

I am grateful the Fey kept me alive comes to his mind like a rehearsal, regardless of how sharp tonight has been. He has long tried to encase the phrase in amber, so even if he doesn't truly believe it, it won't fall to pieces.

But Tavreah doesn't offer him the dagger. His blood, of course, isn't pure.

So instead he snaps a flame to life at the tips of his thumb and forefinger. A few elves jump; chairs scrape. He burns a black rim along the throat of the pitcher.

He is grateful to be alive with *this*, to have survived so much with it. It may be the only reason he has.

When Tavreah moves on, Cereus waves her off, throwing a bright smile that's clearly for the enjoyment of the whole room.

Cereus says, "What's already in there is what I'm thankful for. I want my people grateful to be here, happy to be as they are."

Eirjatal smothers a smile into his hand. Tavreah loudly accuses Cereus of sentimentality, but Eirjatal knows he's genuine. When she turns away to continue the offerings, Cereus squeezes Eirjatal's hand on the table.

The rest of the room leaves Eirjatal with a bittersweet feeling. The distraction has settled his anxiety into a soft thrum, and perhaps it's that quietness that allows the truth to bubble up.

This unending crawling under his skin isn't only because of Rho, or even because of Scintia's letter. It's everything. The assassination attempt, the religious weakening, and the shadow that dogs everyone in Cypress. Perhaps their city will be the next to be hacked at with tragedy.

Eirjatal has so little control over everything. The kick in his heart at Cereus's proximity is yet another vulnerability.

After Tavreah has led the room in a prayer song, one that gets raucous and rowdy at the end as they thank the Fey for hot nights and the hunger and means to hunt pleasure, Cereus pulls Eirjatal to his feet.

Eirjatal tells himself that their closeness is safe. It's always been safe—that was the point. He fills in the space of his worrying with the firm contours of Cereus's body against his.

Though he lost the ear cuff at some point, Cereus's jewelry is still ostentatious; he's wearing a ridiculous nose ring that twists through his septum and both nostrils and clicks faintly as he talks, and his earrings are hung with glass-encased beetle wings. He folds his arms behind Eirjatal's neck, anchoring them closely.

"I should've asked Vyriseh for a spell to look different."

Elves are still openly gawking at them. "Or you should have thanked the Fey for something boring, instead of showing off your silver tongue."

He rolls his eyes. "I was being honest."

"Please; you like being a showman. Unfortunately for you, I'm not so enchanted by your smile anymore."

Cereus grins. "Which one?"

"That one, though a touch less smug."

He keeps grinning.

This situation is all too familiar: Cereus recruiting Eirjatal into pretending he's only a minor celebrity in the city; this undemanding closeness; Eirjatal putting up a good show that he's not trying to forget anything.

Behind Eirjatal's back, something in this arrangement shifted in the last couple months. It's no longer so easy. But he wants it just as badly.

Cereus's thumb skims the back of Eirjatal's ear as he says quietly, "You don't have to say anything to this. But I can't stop thinking of what you told me the other night. *There's parts of me you shouldn't make yourself love,* right? What *part*?"

Eirjatal hesitates. "The part of me that desperately wants to lie to that."

"I don't mean to interrupt…" It's Tavreah, smirking at them. She opens a small velvet-lined box. Inside is a red Heartswain, roots still carefully attached like pale capillaries. "I think you could both stand to be a bit more honest with each other."

She leaves, stealing her ear cuff from Eirjatal on the way. Eirjatal notes that prostitutes are handing out the flowers around the room. Thank the Fey for what you have, and be unabashed in showing off what more that you want.

Cereus asks, "Do you want to leave?"

Worry whirrs inside of him, delighted to play along.

Corsair will drown him later. Why do her job for her?

Eirjatal takes the bloody bloom and touches it against Cereus's lips. Cereus's breath is hot on his fingers. "Perhaps this is all a ploy, like Whitfore's estates. They want to know if the new king craves war."

Cereus smirks. He uses his tongue to slip the Heartswain into the back of his cheek, and something about that simple movement makes Eirjatal's skin prickle. He focuses on that instead of the magic now popping into red illusions in his periphery.

Hillsides and waterfalls spill up the walls. Strangers, translucent, dart through. Jewelry flirts across brows. Elves kiss and converse while phantoms of themselves dance inside their skin, urging a touch more daring.

"Before I was king, I saw a lot of damage in the city that the rest of the court didn't," Cereus whispers right at his ear. "But I knew where the people planted their hopes, too. I only helped. *They* made the hard decision to put something into the dirt, thinking it may die."

This is what Cereus is good at. Cereus is like he was. If something goes wrong, Cereus will break.

Eirjatal replies, voice quieter than he wants, "You are a good king, Cereus. Honestly."

"Better because I have you."

"And Tavreah."

"Tavreah, Kinthe, *Rhoheme*." Cereus kisses his ear. "And you. More than ever these days, I know how much I need you."

Of course he's thinking of desires, when the whole room is filling up with them.

It occurs to Eirjatal how tightly he's being held, like Cereus thinks he's going to slip away.

Cereus asks, "If it was just you, just me, just this room—just tonight—what would you want?"

Eirjatal laughs softly, but what an invitation. "I'd want you."

"We're in agreement then."

"Unfortunately I can't quite imagine this into being a private room."

"Well, luckily I own a castle. So…"

Maybe this is the only way to be honest with Cereus in a way that won't hurt him.

The instant he gives himself permission, it's impossible to resist pulling Cereus down to kiss him. He knots his fingers in Cereus's hair for good measure. And clearly it's persuasive.

Cereus coaxes his mouth open with no concern for the crowd or the attention he's likely drawing, even in a ballroom full of magic. Then Cereus eases the Heartswain, still somehow dry and cold like a brittle piece of glass, onto Eirjatal's tongue.

His entire body tenses.

But he makes himself let it happen.

Cereus leads Eirjatal to the door. Desires flirt in his periphery, those that belong to him and those that don't. Proud ships with open masts, the racket of the wind in their sails cracking across his ears. Water washing over his shoes, leaving a salt stain in the leather. For a flash, there's Corsair, sitting in her human guise at a table, plucking a glass from a baffled elf female's hand and taking a sip; the wine falls through her neck and spatters the table. His desires look a lot like his fears.

And then they're out in the cool night air. Cereus backs him by the hips into the patio rail, the gentleness in that contrasted by the unwavering intent of the next kiss. It's an embrace that pulses down Eirjatal's entire body, fitting them together like they were deluded to ever be apart.

He is trying every trick he used on Eirjatal patiently one at a time years ago, like he wasn't a king, like he wasn't entitled to anything he wanted. Cereus cards his fingers through his hair, twisting his fist in it to expose his throat, and the next kiss is more a chain of half-caught breaths and bites. Cereus fumbles at the fastening of his shirt, until impossibly another sweltering mouth takes the bait and skates down on his collar.

Eirjatal's eyes flutter open. His vision is full of Cereus's gold-smeared cheek and so many red-lined illusions. Hands and every tattoo Cereus has hidden under his clothes.

Well.

And he thought Cereus was desperate to impress him.

He whispers, "This is embarrassing."

Cereus snickers. He pulls him out of the cloud of half-made illusions. The two spill onto the road, heading up the walk to the palace.

Eirjatal tongues the Heartswain, still in the back of his cheek. He's burning, but not in the usual way. It's a warmth that reaches inwards, not outwards.

There are footsteps behind them. He turns; Tavreah, maybe? An admirer of the Starmorrow, hoping to make a final plea to be included?

Eirjatal freezes.

Rho. She's standing in the street, watching him with eyes half-lidded like a judging cat. Her gaze flicks to their hands. He drops Cereus's without thinking.

She isn't real. He knows that. But his heart doesn't. It stammers and kicks, drinking up all that heat and overfilling.

"Eirj," Cereus cautions.

Rho says, more mouthing it than truly speaking, "You should bite that flower already. You're halfway there. You don't think it'd feel good to show him what's in here," she taps her forehead, "for once?"

He closes his eyes. He wants his wanting to be as simple as only here, only now, only Cereus. It's as simple as he's ever wanted his wanting to be, and so it obliges.

Eirjatal's under the ice.

By following the gauzy light through the ice, he found which way was up, but it cost him too much air to do it. Whatever pulled him down has died in the water; the freezing river fills his nose with clotted, thick blood.

Shadows suffuse over the surface; someone's walking above. He slams a fist against the surface, but the black is pushing in. Whoever's above kneels down, head tilted to take in his shape.

Scintia, so pale and still that as soon as he's found her, she fades into the silhouette of the trees and white sky above.

He jolts up in bed.

Air stabs against his ribs and he lets it all go in a gust. Equally as desperately, he inhales with a rattling, half-choked wheeze. He grasps for the headboard, anything to keep himself up.

Cereus rubs his back. He jolts away. It takes ages for him to catch his breath.

Alive again, awake again, and—he glances around the bed—nothing aflame again. *Thank you, Nele.* It's the aspect for the dying, so maybe he shouldn't use it, but that's the name instinct gives him. *I'm sorry you had to watch over me.*

"What was that dream?" Cereus asks, rubbing the sleep out of his eyes. "I thought you were having a fit."

"A memory."

Or maybe none of that happened. It's been so long, his imagination has spun so many tales, and he was one of the few survivors. If he wants to remember what happened, he has to read his own reports, but he doesn't like seeing himself from back then.

"Why did She make the Ineiren there?" Eirjatal whispers, laying back down. He feels like he's sprinted a mile; his hairline is cool with sweat. "Madainn could see it from his temple windows. And Dianthus. We're surrounded by him."

"No, we aren't. That's the Lightbringing, Eirj. The island's Hers. The water's Hers."

"It's all borrowed."

"Maybe. Whatever happens, it'll be way after we're gone, I bet."

Eirjatal snaps, "How fortunate we are. Only two kingdoms collapsed in our lifetimes."

Cereus sits up and moves towards the far end of the bed, ducking around the alcove of curtains and unlit candles. Eirjatal jolts at the sound of the loud, metal crank.

Another Rho invention. In the ceiling, panels the shapes of rose petals twist and fold into themselves like a blooming garden, pouring away from the center of the room and gathering into sculptures of roses in the walls and corners. Cereus's apartments are on the very top of the Dawn Hall, and so the roof opens to the star-filled sky and the silhouette of the statue of Relyn that crests the whole building. She's a wave of gold, rising to meet the black sky above them. Not Rho's, not that. That one is ancient.

Cereus knows something that stresses him in moments like these are closed walls, heavy ceilings. Honestly, that wasn't worrying him this time, but he sees the gesture for the kindness it is.

As Cereus lays back beside him, Eirjatal watches the sky and presses a hand over his heart, trying to cloak the stammering thing like how they brought Ringal into the Dawn Hall with her crate covered by a blanket.

"The water's Hers," Cereus repeats. "That sky, that moon, the ones we see—all Hers. You're Hers, and She'll always remember that."

Eirjatal turns his head and Cereus lets him kiss him first. It's soft, hardly more than a brush, and Cereus says against his lips, "And I'm yours. For as long as you need me."

That's certainly doing nothing to help Eirjatal's pulse. He pulls Cereus down to him, casting a hand down his smooth back and all the shadows of tattoos. "I'm anxious about seeing Scintia. I'm sorry."

Cereus fixes some of Eirjatal's hair around his horns. "Do you want to tell me about it?"

"That doesn't offend you?"

"What? That you use me?" Cereus grins. "No. You think I don't have stuff *I'm* trying not to think about?"

"What a match."

"Hey, *I'm* the one who said I loved you."

Eirjatal scoffs, rubbing his face.

"Sorry. I meant that to be funny."

He thinks of Sigyn's words, from what feels like ages ago—*is your heart not still broken?*

"You'll be safe tomorrow, Eirjatal."

"I won't. But thank you for saying so."

"Fine. Maybe something will happen, and it'll be shitty. Maybe. But then you'll come back to Dianthus and be safe again. You always have home." Cereus fits them together, loose and tangled, skin warm in contrast to the night above and the last of the nightmare. "And I know you hate talking about that with me, but I had to tell you."

With me.

There's a ritual where elves sleep together—literally or figuratively—under the moon phase they claim, with the dirt against their skin. Then the Fey will let them know if one partner is lying, to either themselves or to the other. If this isn't the right moon for them.

The word *love* is so easy in comparison.

27

Rhoheme

Rho walks into a room—or courtyard—or vaulting temple—whatever it chooses to be in the second between her thinking about looking up and her eyes actually doing it.

It decides on a stone tower.

Tangled, stringy plants hang upside down from window sills carved at senseless points. The tower reaches up so high that it fades into a blurry shadow. She swears.

She's lost. She's fucking lost in some divine fever dream.

And her heart is beating again.

Lost, hah. There's hardly anything else to lose. She climbs the window-sills.

When Rho started wandering, she didn't mind how every turn tumbled into some bizarre pocket of the realm's imagination. It was a relief to put as much space as possible between her and that card game with the Adder, even if she keeps catching glimpses of those golden tethers between them.

Besides, she likes moving.

Ready to leave was her default setting. Eirjatal's, too. Having a ruler whose whims decided if you were allowed to live or not would do that to an elf.

When Ashvaren kicked it, Eirjatal had finished packing travel bags for both of them before she even registered the news.

"We're going. This will collapse, and I'd rather not be caught under it."

"Going where?"

"Where do you *want* to go? Heatherwol has no choice but to allow us entry, and I'm certain Silvershale will play the neutral party—"

"Staventene." If Ashvaren could die, then anything could happen.

Grand, wheezing automatons strode streets lit with buzzing electricity. Some businesses blasted music to lure customers, so loud that you only knew where it was coming from by whose lights were guttering out. Rho pressed her face to a printing press window and watched the heavy machines create such delicate illustrations on such fragile paper. Airships rolled overhead like fat sleepy dragons. Using the last of his Hawk subtlety, Eirjatal found her a pistol and a crank-up radio, but he wasn't so keen on stealing her a car engine.

Rho didn't belong and the air made her cough and she and Eirjatal clung together with hoods up and hands clasped so they didn't get lost in the tidal wave of humans and automatons and monsters. Rho marvelled over how they *made* it all. Probably thanks to magicians like her who were taught to fiddle with cacophonies until they were harmonies. It was a city of a thousand beating mechanical hearts. A city of impossible possibilities.

Then Adamantine and Vyriseh put her in the Dawn Hall. Rho wanted to rip the whole place down, bursting with ideas from all she'd seen and refusing to take instruction ever again.

So fine. Rho likes walking and she likes thinking and now she'll learn to like climbing.

She climbs until the air is hot and full—and smells like metal. She hooks her fingers on the next sill and heaves herself up.

She's in a sweltering forge.

Carts the size of houses trundle like plough animals to either side of her, carrying so much coal that they teeter on their turns. The air shimmers with heat. Overhead swing the low moons of red-hot vats. The only lights are the glowing liquid that those vats empty into molds, and the rows upon rows of swords displayed against a stone wall to cool. They drip metal like they've already met blood on a battlefield.

Somewhere, a hammer strikes like thunder.

Rho scurries to a track with unmoving carts and crouches on the filthy ground to peek around a wheel. She told the Blind Adder she wanted to see Staventa—but not because she wanted a peek at the goddess. She wanted to forge something to help her against Madainn. But all these tools are bigger than she is.

She crawls on all fours between the carts towards the wall of cooling swords. The sweltering air stuffs her head with cotton. Her skin itches with heat. Her lungs aren't doing too bad—probably because the dirt granules are the size of apples. When the carts on the other track drive by, her hair lifts from the gust and the ground trembles like she's in the Dawn Hall's faulty elevator.

At the sword display, the dripping metal forms a silver and gold pool in a trough. Rho frowns at the blades.

Being so unoriginal bugs her, but she needs to start somewhere.

Rho shuts her eyes and thinks really hard about the swords shrinking down to her size. Really, *really* hard.

Opens her eyes. Nothing changed. She scowls.

Maybe she can snag one of the gems inset in the pommels. Is it too ambitious to get Madainn's monster from the waterfall to eat it, then explode it from inside? Besides all that—how is it fair that she's maybe-dead and in another world that operates on imagination and chewing gum, and she's still *sweating* like crazy?

Or maybe...

In the middle sword's hilt is a hole holding a glowing, shifting sphere, suspended on wires so taut that it seems to float. It'd comfortably sit in a palm if the sword was elf-size, but right now it's the size of Rho's head. Her blood's pulled to it, the way it is to her creations, to the very walls of the Dawn Hall. Everything here sings to her, but that sphere's a chorus.

Rho climbs onto the edge of the trough. When she reaches, she can barely touch the sharp point of the sword. She pushes her magic into it.

Power hits her like a freezing stormfront, nearly throwing her off her feet. It's *pure*. There's no pollution in this steel. Not a fleck of rust or some other mineral that's snuck in. It shines like a midnight lake, even when she melts a channel down the center of it. The hilt pours like water.

The sphere tumbles out. She catches it, bracing for the weight to knock her back—but it's as light as paper.

It's made up of interlocking, encircling rings. They twist in the direction of her hand, no matter where she places it.

In it she sees chains, garrotes, shackles.

Shrink, she thinks, and this one shrinks after all.

She dunks her hand into the trough of molten gold and silver. She can handle burning materials with little trouble. Another piece of her magic she discovered by accident. It helps with Eirjatal, since his skin can get as hot as a boiling pot. Rho wraps a rope of it through one of the rings and ties it around her waist, arranging the heaps of gauzy white dress to conceal the golden glow.

She jumps a mile when Staventa booms, "So you've found your way to my cage, elf?"

Between one cart and the next, Rho sees her. The goddess is as tall as the Dawn Hall even when seated. Whatever she's hammering spits sparks and illuminates her shadowy form in firework splashes.

Rho and Eirjatal studied the Woven gods that gave them their magic—*together,* since the whole process felt like taking a plunge off a cliff. Rho did it more for his sake, really. Eirjatal's, the Iron Phoenix, is a chaotic narcissist who has a terrible influence on Dianthus even without getting into the mess she made of his bloodline. Meanwhile, Staventa made the statues that stand in the sea, the Chariots, who guide sailors home and guard against Madainn's next attempt to crawl out. She lives in the mountains behind Staventene, having helped build the city centuries ago.

And she keeps out of the Woven's usual bullshit. So say the Etreal books, but Rho doesn't believe it—if Staventa really minds her own business, then why does Rho have her magic?

"Dangerous business they want you for, little toymaker," Staventa says, voice stretching with the effort of her work. Red sparks the size of bats take wing through the pitch-black forge.

Rho's minuscule at Staventa's feet; that fact nearly makes her cower again before she bites down on the fear.

"I am not a damned toymaker."

Staventa lifts the glaive she's made and turns it, so the red glow fills her shadowy form with colour. Her skin's as dark as copper stone, eyes glowing silver. She's older than the Adder—if goddesses can be old at all—with deep lines in her face like a carefully repaired vase. Long steel-grey braids are piled atop her head.

Staventa says, "I thought that if the Blind Adder wanted the dying kind to be our heroes, she'd look a little further than something like you." She tsks. "I need no heroes."

The word *dying* coming from an unsafe mouth in an unsafe place topples Rho over the edge. On the infirmary bed, she looked exactly the way Ashvaren warned. *One day, your magic will eat you alive.* This goddess gave Rho's ancestors a curse that wouldn't die no matter who they had children with or what rituals to the Nelaeryn Fey they did. And now she calls Rhoheme, after all she's gone through to hone and *honour* her magic, *the dying kind?*

And seriously—*toymaker?*

"I'm *Rhoheme*!" Her voice hardly overtakes the thundering, rolling carts, and it's rattling about as much. "And heroes for what?"

Eirjatal would tell her to flatter the vices of the god she's up against. Not like that worked when they dealt with the sirens.

Staventa puts the glaive on a pedestal with the care of setting a child in a cradle. "Rumours and whimsy and bedtime stories for gods. That's all this is." It sounds like the irony's so bitter she can taste it. "Madainn, I expect to do this. The Phoenix always flies in his wake. But the Blind Adder…"

"Why do you think I've got anything to do with the Blind Adder?"

She waves a hand over the glaive. Rho feels a familiar sparkle in her palms as sorcery carves tiny whorls into the glaive. That's the same way Rho decorated Sigyn's arm. "You're folded into your creations, and they're folded into you, even if you're too far to tell. They know your heart better than even you. And similarly, she's folded into you; you're folded into her."

Like we were taught to fear. Shit, Eirjatal, what have you done? "Can you give me a straight answer?"

"Why should I, when you don't believe what I am?"

"You think that because I'm not afraid of you?" Of course she's afraid. She's balling her fists to force them to stop shaking. "I've been here awhile. I can't waste all my time bowing."

Staventa's laugh is as rough and warm as the brick walls. "Honesty is what you wish? Then my honest answer is that you should turn back, go home."

Rho says, hating the shape of the word, "I'm dying."

"Then stop yourself from dying first." The designs she chisels out of the glaive curl in the air like burning paper. "I agree with Madainn on this only—I do not want Karadenza to know you're here."

Rho's ahead of most of Cypress when it comes to the right things to be afraid of, but still that name sends a shiver down her spine.

Rho inches along the tracks and still Staventa doesn't even glance at her. Maybe Staventa can't see at all. The vicious contrast between the black forge and the bright metal blurs Rho's vision. She wouldn't put it past the Woven to have the goddess named the Blind Adder not actually be the blind one. Their naming scheme is already a mess. "How would Karadenza find out?"

"Have you stumbled upon Karadenza in your scurrying?"

"I haven't seen *anyone* here besides you, the Adder, and Madainn—well, Madainn's monsters."

Staventa's mouth quirks, the fading heat-glow of the glaive flicking off a dimple. "*Here*? You are nowhere. I am in the rock, Madainn is in the sea, the Blind Adder is at the bottom of a poisoned glass and the root of a fang. Karadenza is nothing you can touch. Karadenza is like your Nelaeryn Fey."

"So she's everywhere?"

Staventa hums with amusement; the sound is a physical thing. "She is in realms far away. But she slips through when there is something interesting to hear. Like all of this..." She curls her lip. "Next time, she'll leave Madainn behind, and he can make his *own* lonely world of water and mischief and monsters."

"Well, you're in luck, if you hate all this hero business so much. I'm fighting for none of you."

"Oh? Then the Adder is keeping secrets from you as well."

"I'm only here because one of her priestesses is helping me."

"Priestesses all over Etreal are healing. Have you seen any other victims here?"

Is she playing card games with them?

Does this have anything to do with how she got bit?

Dread strikes Rho like a blow to the stomach. Staventa is talking too much. She's got to be trying to trick her. Rho turns back to the black pit. She got what she came for.

And she pauses. Voice sharp but small, she asks, "Why did you mess with the Fey? Why do I have your magic?"

She holds her breath. Rho's fought for her magic with no help from

Staventa *or* the Fey, so why does she care?

But she waits anyways.

Staventa says, "*Mess with*, pah! *Have*; that's wrong too. Elf, do you notice the difference between my name and the Blind Adder's? Pique's? The Carrion Queen's? I am not from the same universe as them. I have seen Karadenza Realmweaver collect and then discard many gods from our pantheons for ruining her creations. I have heard Karadenza belittle *my* quality when I am as capable of forging solar systems as she is. Then the Nelaeryn Fey arrived, a perfect rival for Karadenza, if only she didn't come to us so injured.

"I pitied her for that. With my magic, I gave her a gift," Staventa says, "because Karadenza will ensure that this is the last world she'll ever have."

Staventa's gaze settles on Rho. It's like another strike of her hammer, its weight shaking in Rho's spine. "Craft your own door out, little toymaker."

Rho says, "I will."

But Staventa stands suddenly with the sound of a mountain splitting. Without thinking, Rho runs.

A gleaming sphere seals around her. She slaps her hands against the walls. Coils of electric-sharp gold curl around the bubble. The forge floods with water that hisses on impact with the heat.

Staventa warns, "Madainn. Leave the mortal."

Rho thought Staventa was scary before, but at that tone, her insides melt into liquid.

"Oh, enough, Staventa," a masculine voice drawls. "I know all you have to do when sealed here is to yammer, but don't gossip about me behind my back and not expect me to turn."

Madainn appears at Staventa's size, crouching on a knee to pick up the bubble. Rho's first thought is that he's so much like the sirens, from the up-tilted black eyes to the nearly regal ruff of gills around his throat—and then her second thought is that this is the god who sent her here and killed off a part of Eirjatal and she didn't realize how much she wanted revenge.

28

Irving

You invite me to rally troops to recover what is left of Khidell in Ventaris. And why? He is unworthy of his title after so long in Etreal; it has been drained with as little dignity as an infected wound.
The Fey has divested Herself of him, so Cypress must, too. Perhaps the trap of Ventaris will close on your Hawks and the humans will have all the secrets they have ever hungered for. Perhaps I will close the trap first.

Letter from Starmorrow Ashvaren to Adamantine, Age of Shields 200

As soon as they enter the library, Noah slaps her hands over her ears. "Ugh, what is that *noise?*"

Irving—disguised as the Autumn female again—and Noah flip shut the bouquet-shaped locks on the heavy doors. There are no lizards or tropical birds. Not even the insects that perpetually crawl around the Dawn Hall.

That droning tone makes Irving uncomfortable, like how standing too close to a staticky phonograph itches the insides of their ears. Maybe the animals can't stand it.

The hall was deserted, even though Irving was prepped for guards with a twist of herbs and matches in their pocket (materials they lend to the thieves who pass through her temple, Johana explained, completely devoid of nerves or irony), and it took way too long for Noah to get the right pitch on the whistle that makes the bats trust their presence.

Since Eirjatal's out of the castle with the Moonwardens somewhere, Noah had to steal the library keys right out of his apartment, much better than having to take them off his belt. The security is not violent, but it *is* weird.

When Noah tries to follow them into the stacks, she does it with all the grace of a drunk.

"Are you okay?"

"It's that fucking song," she mumbles.

Vyriseh, they realize, right as Noah goes entirely still.

They wave a hand in front of her face. Her dark eyes are vacant. They feel fine besides the grating start of a headache, but that's nothing new these days.

Noah drops; they barely catch her. She's staring up at nothing. Is it meant to incapacitate anyone? Or only people with mischief on their minds? Then why not *them*?

Irving sets her down as gently as they can and starts hunting down the source of that music through the books, curios, and art.

There. Half-concealed on a high shelf between some plants is a music box, topped with a spinning, seated violinist who's giving Irving a coy little wink. Their first idea is to jam the mechanism with something, but they can't even see a gear and the violinist is deceptively sturdy.

They read the inscription on the bottom. Usually Mythmaker spells are gibberish, their meaning only really mattering to the person who cast it, but this one chides them with *Lie still and dream of the truth. See you in the morning.* A faint hum rises beneath the music from Irving's illusion meeting its match.

They hurry for the door then drop the thing into an empty vase in the arms of a statue, halfway down the hall away from the door. It chugs along at the bottom, tinny and odd and hopefully not about to cause more trouble out here.

When Irving's returned, Noah's sitting, rubbing her head.

They help her up. She slaps off their help and then their shoulder, but loses the verve halfway through so it's more like she wipes her palm on them. "Thanks."

"Of course." They crack their knuckles to snap out some of the nerves. "Let's block the door, just in case."

As they push a heavy writing desk into place, Noah asks, "Why didn't *you* go catatonic?"

"I'm wearing an enchantment from Vyriseh, and no one else could've set that trap. Maybe she sculpted it to ignore her own magic, for people they know are innocent? I'm guessing they're keeping that thing going for a while."

"Not convinced."

Noah leads them to the ward. This one's a shiny sphere at Irving's waist-height with the evocation trapped in its belly behind in paper-thin gold, sculpted into such accurate cloud shapes that when Irving brushes them, they half-expect their finger to pierce right through the fluff.

The bulk is patterned with star charts and planetary maps, all engraved in ridiculous detail, down to the fine illustrations of what Cypress sees in the constellations.

Noah says, "I picked this one because of you, Heatherwol. You better know what you're doing."

"I'll try. I was never much of an astronomy kid."

"I keep wondering what kind of kid you *were.* Here or Heatherwol or whichever. You're totally lying, and I really don't care for being lied to, and I think your father—"

She slaps a hand over her mouth.

"That music box was a truth charm too." They're unable to help the smirk. At least her terminal fear of honesty saved both their asses from an awkward conversation.

Her eyes narrow and she points at the ward.

Irving digs the female's longer nails into the hair-thin grooves. A few of the planets wiggle the tiniest bit, but don't give.

"I think there are pieces that should extend or open or something. We need to find the switch."

Noah extends her arms to the entire library. "We're in a room of switches."

"Book?"

"Book."

"There've got to be a couple thousand."

"Constellations? Planets? Rho didn't make the solutions impossible. The design's a clue." Irving follows her through the eight-foot-high rosewood shelves, until they reach one engraved with tiny planets. "One of these."

"Okay, there are a couple *hundred*."

"Think positive," Noah says, adopting their cadence. Then she snaps her fingers. "The shelf lights that can turn on once the skylight's not enough. Notice how the books are sorted by size first?" She points, and Irving notes how some shelves are taller or shorter, so the books arranged inside all form a perfect line, with the exact same allowance of space between the tops of the books and the shelves. Under each shelf is a line of tiny unlit electric bulbs. "It's so the lights don't burn the paper or catch on dusters when we clean."

All Rho's inventions so far have a physical component, they're not entirely magic. That's how Staventa's magic works. It's an enhancement, a manipulation of materials, not the ability to make things whole cloth. Staventene would have settled itself on the moon by now if it worked that way.

Noah continues, "I bet if it *is* a book, the mechanism runs along the lights, so it's out of place, unnoticeable, and the maids wouldn't accidentally trip it while cleaning."

"Genius, Noah."

"Only genius if it works. But thanks. I want you to compliment me more. No one ever does." She turns away very quickly.

Noah takes one bookshelf and Irving takes another, both skimming their hands underneath the shelves while they practically run from end to end.

Irving bumps into a book titled *Vitaea*, nudged a little out of place. That wouldn't mean anything if the library wasn't kept so immaculately. They tilt it.

The ward clicks to life.

It stretches nearly to the skylight, with dozens of planets, stars, and streaks of galaxies suspended on thin spokes and anchors. It's entirely made of gold, with some planets tinted copper, blue, or violet. The side of the Tapestry that not even Etreal's explored yet is carefully blank, like Rhoheme was waiting for the day they learned more. The whole thing ticks like a clock, planets drifting ever-so-slightly. Irving's seen a lot of planetariums, living in the Heatherwol palace where they're used for everything from mobiles to sundials, but this is one of the most detailed they've ever seen.

"It's gorgeous," Irving breathes.

"Too bad it'll try to kill us."

"Anything look particularly deadly on it?"

Noah takes a circuit around it; the way it bloomed enclosed the ward, so Irving can only spot some watery slats of ice through the gold. "Not that I can see."

"So...am I overconfident, or is the premise pretty easy?"

"The last one was easy too. Get the beetle all the way to the top. And so was the one before—don't get your head lopped off your shoulders."

"We probably have to arrange them correctly for a certain date. You'd know better than me. What events mattered to her?"

"I don't know. She was a loner. I wanted to talk to her, she was really smart and not afraid of any of that Etreal stuff and—" Noah swallows down whatever other truth was compelling itself out of her. "And she's been alive for two centuries; she probably had a lot going on."

Morningstars and morning prayers. Space and time and a world forgotten. Free creatures, free flight, dawn again in the Dawn Hall.

They find the Tapestry, slowly ticking around. Their reflection swims in the battered gold. It's tiny next to all the other planets and the sharp-edged stars. It's bizarre that still nearly half of the planet isn't mapped—all because the Evertide, Madainn's domain, blocks the way. Technically, Cypress sticks out the closest to it. Especially the island with Dianthus and what was left of the Spring kingdom.

It's labelled *Hyacinthus,* a name Irving's never even heard before. It's engraved with a delicate hand, framed with bees and its namesake. Rhoheme was Spring; they remember that vaguely.

Space and time and a world forgotten.

"When did Ashvaren destroy Hyacinthus?" Irving asks.

Noah quirks her eyebrows, then it dawns on her. "It's definitely the best we've got." She ducks into the shelves and, a few minutes later, comes back with a couple astronomy books.

Noah remembers the day it happened and Irving knows, generally, how to navigate the books and the charts. It's quiet and slow work, but Irving keeps looking over either shoulder—at the ward and at the door. But luck might, again, be on their side.

Eventually, they've got a pretty good guess. Noah doesn't remember the time it happened, so they decide on a generic midnight, giving each other raised eyebrows and shrugged shoulders. History books aren't any help either, and the fact that none of them offer much information besides an icy recitation of the events, preluded with Ashvaren's motives of uniting the island, gives more credence to Irving's idea that Rhoheme would throw Ashvaren's ignorance in his face.

So, with breaths held, the two of them spin the planets.

The sun and moon offer no resistance; the Tapestry itself is equally simple. They both keep their moves careful and precise, every new planet causing Irving to subconsciously grind their teeth, until Irving, on tiptoe, rotates the last planet into place. The *click* of it locking in is tiny, but Noah and Irving stare at each other like it was gunshot.

And then the core opens like the ribcage of some massive creature, and the evocation awaits.

Noah says, "No way."

"Yes way."

They try to give her a high five, but she only asks, "What are you doing?"

They put their hand down. "Staventene thing. Were you always so enthusiastic behind the scenes with the Heartswain?"

"No one to celebrate with, Irving. It's a lot more fun with you." This time, she doesn't cover her mouth.

Irving leans in. This evocation's made of ice like all the others, and so detailed that it nearly makes them dizzy when they try to focus on it; they lift their glasses to their forehead. It's a part of a palace. A long stone bridge, dotted with statues and torches, links two cliff sides, and the tops of the structure disappear into the shadows inside the ward.

Noah asks, "Is that Heatherwol's palace?"

"Yeah, actually. They pretend it's totally normal to walk in the wind to get to your bathroom to your bedroom."

"How do *you* know?"

They're distracted from an excuse and from taking the vial out of their shirt when a flash of blonde shatters across the ice. A cold feeling pulls hard at the top of their spine like they're about to pass out, and a dark shadow bleeds along the bridge.

Sigyn. In broken, blurry miniature, sliding from plane of ice to plane of ice. His hair is shoulder-length, sides unshaved, and he's in a black doublet and he has both his arms.

Noah says, "That's your father, isn't it? Um, I mean—"

A soft gasp cuts the quiet of the room.

Irving whirls around. A priestess, arms loaded with books, staring at them. She must have come out of some back room.

Then sweeping for the door.

"Fuck," Noah hisses. She jolts up—and the main column of the ward twists in on the evocation. It cracks in bright-white spider webs.

Irving throws all their weight into it to stop it. Noah does too, but she's staring under Irving's arm as the Priestess tries to pull the desk away from the door.

"Irving, we have to stop her. She saw me."

Something about Sigyn is inches away, if they can get the spell fast enough. "This is why I wanted *you* to take the disguise!"

Noah grumbles something back, but it's chewed up by her grit teeth as she braces her back against the ward. Even with both their efforts, it's barely stopped. Irving bites the chain of the vial and tugs it out of their shirt, crouches to brace their back against the moving panel, and fumbles the vial out against the evocation. The glass surface is exploding with fissures.

Footsteps on the other side of the door. The priestess calls something, but she certainly throws in the Cypresian word for *guards*. Irving's heart is high in their throat.

Noah gasps, "I'm going to stop her."

"No, you're not—"

"Yes!" Noah tries to duck out, but without thinking, Irving grabs her shoulder. Not hard. They both freeze.

Noah hisses, "This one's done."

She shoulders away from them. Instantly, the side she was holding back snaps shut, forcing Irving to duck out of the way and spraying them with shards of ice.

With whatever story of Sigyn they just lost.

They catch their breath. The vial falls against their shirt, their lap covered in sprinkles of finely wrecked ice.

Noah is hurrying through the aisles. Irving doesn't remember getting up, but they intercept her, duck around her, and spin the priestess around so they've got her pinned against the desk.

It's the priestess who cut their hand in the trial. She's no threat, but the guards banging on the other side of the door are—her information most *certainly* is.

So they transform into her.

Next, they turn into Mara, Eirjatal, Cereus, cycling so quickly that their head spins. Then Tavreah, Leila, their mother, and finally Noah, all yet another fake appearance and fake person.

The desk wrenches out of place as the guards barrel through the door. Irving's attempt at intimidation slips as they grasp onto the priestess for dear life, both of them losing their balance.

The priestess tears free and vanishes between the guards and down the hall. At least she'll have no idea who to say she saw doing it, but that doesn't matter quite suddenly as a guard heaves Irving up by the arm.

They're so dizzy from their quick-change that it takes a second for them to realize that they look like themselves, the spell's concentration having slipped in the chaos. The guard's hand is wrapped around their arm, right beneath the spell. If they're taken in, all of that's for nothing—at least Noah will be safe, if they make a good case for themselves imitating her—

The guard shouts and Irving pedals backwards out of their slackened grip. Noah tears by them right as the other guard cries out too. She pulls them to the door.

They throw a glance back. Marie, white as snow, biting over and over and over into the elves until they drop to the floor.

They're in the hall, then down the stairs, then onto the grounds once more. It takes them until they're deep in the tropics before they stop and catch their breaths. Irving's wheezing, lungs on fire, but too afraid to drop off their feet in case the chase isn't over.

Noah pants, "You...dick!"

"I *fixed* it. We were all hidden in the planets, anyways. I—"

"Sure, great, but shit, Irving, that was seriously close. Did you even get it?"

Their mouth is wrapped around a despondent *no,* but then they grasp the vial and find that it's faintly glowing.

Why is Sigyn involved in *everything* and for all he wants Irving to be included in Cypress, he doesn't tell Irving *anything?*

They ask, "Can I pass this off to Envai?"

"If you can dare part with it," she grumbles. Noah runs her hands through her hair, still flushed from the sprint. Then she says, "I'm going to leave with you."

For some reason, every mean thing she's ever said to them bursts through their head. Still, they say, "I know."

"Seriously." Her expression slips into something more vulnerable. "No way around it."

"I want you to come with."

"Good." She frowns at them. "That...that *is* your father, right?"

Noah knows the worst of them. They want to deny it. "Yeah."

"Great. *Great.*" She shakes her head, smiling faintly. "It's not like you can surprise me any more after that."

29

Eirjatal

These are worse than the dreams in the Fort, because I wake and I am no longer there, but I feel there.
Why save me? Ashvaren will throw me in the dungeons again. I've killed my kin now, and not indirectly the way I used to fret over. Why save me? You tempt me with the illusion that I will be protected forever. You forgive me, but can the Fey?

Eirjatal to Sunmirren Scintia, letter, undated

That morning, Sigyn had lent Eirjatal his fox-fur robe and a leather overcoat for their journey to the Crystal Gardens. Cereus was, rather predictably, distracted by the slim fit of the coat and was determined to make him late. Despite Cereus's best efforts, he could not eliminate *all* of Eirjatal's tension.

Eirjatal, Sigyn, and Kinthe's escort from the portal is a single Winter elf. Eirjatal would think they roused her from sleep if her white hair wasn't in immaculate knots and braids. The monochromatic light doesn't disguise the grey veins spiralling out from her fogged-over eyes. Her face is rough with hoarfrost.

It's a blessing in itself to be here. Eirjatal crushes the magic in his hands with steady pulses. *You may be the only non-noble to see this.* After the Ineiren Fort was destroyed, the Fey made the Crystal Gardens for the Winter survivors, though apparently, Scintia has never let go of the insistence that it was *her*. Some accounts confirm this. No one discusses it anymore.

They follow the Winter female. Sigyn's in his floor-length wolf-fur coat with shoulders squared, entirely relaxed; Eirjatal can tell, because everyone's faces are wreathed in steam except his. He doesn't have his clockwork arm. He's flanked by Adamantine's Hawks as they carry Scintia's Eclipsed and Summer evocations. No one would let Eirjatal see Scintia alone, so they supposed bringing the Moonwardens would be a good excuse to make the most of Scintia's rare invitation.

Before leaving, Kinthe again wanted them to try to crack more wards to move them all over, and Sigyn dug in his heels—Scintia hadn't asked for them. They weren't *supposed* to open any. Eirjatal cannot be bothered at this point.

Scant light leaks through the ice walls from the ocean outside. What odd torture. Her previous kingdom was destroyed by Madainn, and yet her new home is under the sea.

Sigyn draws level with Eirjatal and Kinthe. "I have not seen Sunmirren Scintia since before my child left for Etreal."

Always counting time by his precious humans, until one day he'll be counting around the day they died. Eirjatal asks, "What of her then?"

"She was safe. That is often the most one can say about Scintia."

Kinthe mutters, "I pray one day we can say she's sane."

Yawning open before them is a massive frozen cavern of white seawater, hundreds of miles off Dianthus's island and several hundred more beneath. The walls have grown in on themselves with spiky, bristling patches, the slow and steady product of breath and the Winter elves' minuscule amounts of body heat.

Eirjatal can feel eyes on him but struggles to spot the actual elves amidst the ice acting like mirrors. His heart is deafening—they'll all hear it. His breath is coming so fast that it makes a dense, cottony cloud.

This isn't a place for the living. This certainly isn't a place for a firestarter.

The Winter elves he once fought for are like a gallery of statues. The only hint of their movement is how the watery light shifts off their frosted skin. A female affixes a string like spider silk in her loom, tousled creation trailing on the floor; a male engraves something in a tablet like an ancient scribe. It's like walking through a Cypress city after a grand death, with portraits and statues lining every street, mere pale and yearning representations of the dead when they were alive.

This is not the worst of it. He knows most of them are frozen over completely, good as dead, hidden away.

He used to dine with these elves. He was trained by some on swordsmanship, and taught others to draw and speak their enemy's language in exchange, the little bit he could offer. They delighted in his magic—as a weapon, as a party trick, as a bit of bold excitement that got the females in bed with him. In the mornings they prayed, in the evenings they honoured the Fey in the purest way they could, by finding joy in their bloated corpse of a circumstance, in that frozen, wicked fort on its frozen, wicked seashore.

They're led to the smashed side of a wooden ship. It's trapped in the seawall, caught forever in a violent careen between a storm and sinking.

Fear hooks into the back of his neck. Eirjatal's jaw twinges; it's clenched.

Shining sculptures of ice lead their way through the dark ship to the deck. Even Kinthe slows her gait to stare. Teacups with matching kettles and saucers, floral designs rendered in engravings. Heaps of clothing that seem spun from starlight. Chaises, bureaus, and cradles fused to the floor. Scissors and cutlery and hair accessories.

And objects Eirjatal recognizes from his time with Rhoheme in Staventene. Long-nosed muskets and slick bayonets, gutted remains of vehicles, motion picture cameras with their films burst out across the deck, made of such fine ice that they're completely translucent.

Splashing up the undersea dome is an apocalyptic wave of ice, suspended with the anticipation and brittle quiet of a held breath, threatening to crush the deck.

And beneath it, Scintia sits on her white throne. Her pale hair and skirts emerge from the ice like her whole world grew from her. When she realizes who's come to see her, she smiles, and the spell breaks.

She's tiny. Fragile as glass.

Cereus said the last time he saw her was after his coronation. Cereus had to introduce himself, a tiny young king, a speck of candlelight in Ashvaren's thunderous, pitch-black storm. In Cereus's retelling of the story, Scintia had smiled with odd pity and said, "Make something new of Summer, for it will never make what it wishes of you."

That sounded like both a threat and assurance, depending on how Eirjatal tilted his head.

The entourage bows. Eirjatal's clumsy in his shakiness—it doubles upon seeing her. She burns onto the back of his eyelids.

Scintia's liquidy, rhapsodic voice is stern. "Don't bow. I *invited* you."

Eirjatal hears everyone get up around him. The Winter female gathers the evocations from the Hawks and lays them at Scintia's feet.

Scintia says, "Those were Ashvaren's."

Eirjatal plants a hand on the deck. The frost melts beneath it. *Get up,* he tells himself, but the thought is distant.

Kinthe makes a small clicking noise before she speaks, like her tongue was frozen to the roof of her mouth. "Sunmirren Scintia, they are currently under threat—"

Scintia sighs, like a breeze along the brush. "Don't *bow*."

It takes an extra moment for Eirjatal to realize she's referring to him. There's some inaccessible distance between his mind and muscle. He's too warm, like he'll melt right through the floor, or bring the ocean crashing down over their heads.

He asked for this. He needs information from her. He can't bend to this amorphous fear again.

Sigyn offers his hand. It's less impossible to make the distance between the floor and that, so Eirjatal takes it, Sigyn helps him up, and then the Moonwarden steps away as if he's done something so inconsequential as straighten a book upon a shelf. Scintia's studying Eirjatal as if she's trying to remember if she's read this particular book or not.

She says, "Eirjatal Ga'vrynn. You asked for me."

He drops his head again. How does she remember him? If she asks why he called for her, what will he say? "It is my honour to see you again."

"We both survived again, which is an honour in itself." Then, she suddenly adds, "I don't want these things." She draws into her throne like her guard is holding a rat. "I would not have given Ashvaren something harmless."

Kinthe clears her throat. "Pardon me, My Light. What do you mean?"

"I would only give a viper to one who could handle a viper."

"Cereus is capable."

Scintia veers into impatience, almost whiny. "I said *viper,* not sword. *I* can handle neither." Seeming bored with the topic, she adjusts in her throne. Her skirt falls around her legs like fine snowdrifts, but the back of it is impossible to discern from the throne itself. Eirjatal wonders if she can stand or if this is where her portrait will stay, a legacy for a beautiful queen that no one visits. She makes her own offerings.

Kinthe lets loose a tiny sigh. This is hardly a frustration for Kinthe alone. While Scintia can apparently recreate an entire car engine out of ice, she's disinterested in the other kingdoms, treating them to nearly a century of sending letters back unopened and damaging her portals like an angry child. Eirjatal supposes that next to losing your entire kingdom to Madainn, little else matters.

Sigyn steps in, giving Kinthe a little nod. "It is Lightbringing. If you would grace us with your presence for dinner, we have brought many things to share within the season with you. And of course, whenever you and Eirjatal would like to have your discussion, you are free to."

What does Sigyn think this is about?

Scintia brightens up like—well, like she's been told she's getting gifts. So the words out of her mouth are all the more jarring. "Sigyn, your wife has gone home!"

He smiles softly. "I am aware."

With a chorus of squeaks and cracks from her hair and dress breaking out of the throne, Scintia leans forwards and says, cloying, "You worry, but please don't. You are the red moon. The Nelaeryn Fey has decreed it. You will be with Penelope Whitfore when she dies. You have mourned your soul and blood before, but not like you will. Never before and never since."

Eirjatal winds his hands behind his back, pressing the warmth out of his fingers.

Sigyn's expression doesn't falter, but not in the usual way—it's as if he's nailed it on. "Thank you, Scintia."

"You're welcome. Now, I want your gifts, but not those. They are not for me anymore. They belong to someone else."

"What makes you so sure of this, my Light?"

She points at Eirjatal. "They're for him to destroy."

Kinthe's stare is like a shove between his shoulder blades.

"May I ask why?"

Scintia draws her foot up, slipping an ice heel on the throne, like she wants to curl into a ball. "No, Sigyn Aphithea, of the Packmothers, of the bloody, echoing halls. *No.*"

Too fast, Sigyn snaps, "You are referring to the Moonwarden now, Scintia."

"You are injured?"

Eirjatal jumps; Sigyn's appeared out of nowhere. They're all bedding down and Eirjatal was undressing the siren bite in a corner of the ship's belly; a candle flame from a fingertip showed him only yellowed bruises. The priestess was worth the trust after all.

"Rho's automaton. It meant business."

"May I have a word? Privately."

Will he pry on why Eirjatal contacted Scintia? Sigyn is the last person he wants to deal with. Sigyn *was* the last person he saw in sunlight before he was shut up in the Ineiren Fort for months. Times like these, the Moonwarden and the Ineiren Fort are the shadows that stretch under his feet instead of his own.

But maybe Sigyn will have insights on the day. Even the even-tempered Moonwarden had agreed with Kinthe that it was a failure. And they didn't even know the worst of it. Scintia wouldn't explain what she'd meant by Eirjatal destroying the evocations and offered nothing on the situation in the Glasswood when he got her alone. The Moonwardens located Winter elves who were awake enough to care and led them through molasses-slow Lightbringing prayers, while Scintia sat with Eirjatal in total silence, running frost-covered fingers over the edge of his hair and dodging questions.

"You're warm," she'd said, like it was a surprise all over again.

Sigyn leads Eirjatal into the main undersea chamber. Now that everything is dark, lit only by orbs full of glowing fungi likely donated by Silvershale, Winter elves begin to stir.

Eirjatal doesn't begrudge any of them for fleeing to Heatherwol and Silvershale and Hyacinthus when they had the chance. He's only ashamed that he failed them and quailed more at putting down a single siren than blinding a fellow Summer elf.

Eirjatal asks, "Are there any new theories about this?"

"No. Ever since she returned from the Ineiren Fort, she has been hidden from the Fey. Vyriseh and Adamantine have followed the example of the Sunmirrens before them, sending campaigns to investigate, but they have come to nothing."

Poor girl. She and Eirjatal were fighting for the same broken castle. They were the last defence, and they fell. But Scintia continued falling to this curse.

He recognizes a dramatic interpretation of the lethargy that cost him cumulative decades of disassociation, listlessness, fear of everyday terrors and exhaustions of existing. Not to mention the time in prison.

Who did Scintia have to help her? She didn't even have the motivation of her people to drag herself through it, once they all fell asleep. At least Eirjatal had Rho.

And Rho is now dying because she helped him one last time.

Don't save me yet.

Vyriseh is right in that they're the only ones he can trust.

So why is she stopping him from waking Rho—

Sigyn says, stare fixed on Eirjatal, "I would like to spend more time with you."

Has Eirjatal lost so much sleep that the hallucinations have circled around from unnerving to terrifying? "What?"

"We used to see the world together."

Yearning for the days before responsibility and royalty is Cereus's habit, not Sigyn's. Cereus brings buffers, friends he trusts, to the city—Tavreah for dancing, Rho for breweries and art installations, Eirjatal for temples and museums and music halls. All three of them agreed privately that it was pointless. He wants to make friends like before he was king, or even like before he was the rebellious ambassador who could free your loved ones from Ashvaren's clutches.

"I wasn't aware you missed it."

"Oh, not exactly. But I miss you." Sigyn smiles; it's like watching one of Noah's photographs reveal itself on paper.

Winter is waking up, elves shifting with icy crackles. Eirjatal wonders if Sigyn simply can't see the Crystal Gardens at all, if he's that far away from Cypress, yet somehow still focusing on Eirjatal so intensely.

"What is this about?"

Sigyn says with rare unsteadiness, "I have known for all this time that we hurt each other. It was before the Nelaeryn Fey chose me."

"Yes...?"

"And you have always kept your feelings from me, so I cannot feel them for you. I want to. Tell me. I want to make it right, for these days, I am...urgent to recover what I have lost."

"You can't make it right, Sigyn. I've become this, like you've—"

"The Fey would not subject you to this forever. There is a reason I am still in your life. There is a reason you are still in mine."

"Sigyn, we're in public. This isn't the time."

Sigyn's clawing for something, only coming up with a fistful of thin words, uncaring or perhaps entirely unseeing the world around them in his effort to find something better.

"I had you as a friend. There is a part of me that remembers that, like instinct."

"We are not the same—"

"I need to feel something while I can, Eirjatal. I am forgetting again. I cannot sleep and my history drains from me, my love for Adamantine, and my family, my wife...I..."

He's looking at Eirjatal like there's nothing else. Sigyn was once so graceless like this, when he was the elf Scintia apparently thought she saw.

Eirjatal asks, "Why would you remember me more than you remember them?"

Sigyn steps closer. Eirjatal feels his breath on his face and notes how the patches of pale skin have spread, incrementally, over his life, so they've entirely bleached out around his left eye and both cheekbones and the notch in the base of his throat.

"Because you have always found a way to hurt me."

Eirjatal snaps, "Are you afraid of losing me or losing yourself?"

A flash of uncertainty cracks Sigyn's face. Eirjatal fights a shudder. It's as if he's seeing the gore of the true Sigyn underneath the one that's closed around him like a chrysalis.

Of the Packmothers, of the bloody, echoing halls.

Eirjatal jerks back. "You resurfaced when you met your wife, didn't you? Yet here you are again. You're doomed to sink like this for Her, Sigyn. I can't be the one to give you the sword this time. Perhaps it's best to stop fighting it at all."

30

Eirjatal

He's looking for something, and perhaps it's what we took from him, because there's a part of him in us both. A flutter of his heart, a gleam of his stare, it's inside of us. He's looking for something. He will rip it from us. He will rip it from Dianthus, after scouring the Glasswood. Will you stop him?

Scintia to Eirjatal, letter, Age of Shields 250

Scintia is pacing, barefoot, outside his room.

Eirjatal sits up, clutching the rough feather-filled blankets to trap the dregs of warmth. She's murmuring looping, soft prayers. Kinthe should help her. It'll do Scintia good to pray with a Moonwarden for once.

His room is stone, with snow piled against the walls and ice dripping off the empty painting frames, their art taken to fill the fireplaces. Kinthe and Sigyn are gone. Instead, anonymous bodies intertwine for heat under heaps of blankets and furs. A hand slips off his waist as he gets up; someone he doesn't recognize, asleep, presses that hand to their chest to warm it in his absence. His breath comes out in clouds.

He's in the Ineiren Fort.

Scintia paces.

Eirjatal sidles through the bodies. The mingling of freezing air and warm skin fogs up the few windows. It's so quiet that he can hear Scintia's pacing (the shush of skirt, the tacky click of her heels unsticking from the floor) despite the wooden door and the shifting of fabric and hitches of breath from a few elves getting more creative in staving off the cold and the dread of tomorrow. Perhaps this is where he picked up his bad habits.

When he exits, Scintia is gliding away. He follows.

Throughout the Fort, she keeps a hall ahead of him no matter how quickly he runs after her. He'll turn a corner only to see her vanishing around the next. She keeps her patient, dreamy pace regardless.

With squeaks and crackles, ice crawls over the walls.

He enters the room with the metal tree that they'd prayed under—of course that's where her consciousness pulled her—and Scintia's cold hands wrench him around a corner and pull him to the floor with her.

She's breathing hard like she's been sprinting, but in true Winter elf fashion, it creates no fog. She puts a finger to her pale lips.

Although she tries to jerk him back, Eirjatal peers around the corner. The Fort's fallen away into grey rubble, and beyond, the Glasswood shimmers—gloomy, ephemeral—a wall of white trees, so packed with frost that Eirjatal sees the reflection of his auburn hair as bright as fire.

And through the trees march a bizarre parade of monstrous horse-like kelpies, sloshing muddy water in their footsteps that immediately freezes, and sirens darting between them on their imitation of human legs and wrapping their long hair around themselves like blankets. An enormous creature like a dripping Archfey echo, cloak made of kelp and fishing net, holds something in its arms.

The Ineiren Fort was overlooked by the Maw, the mountains that hid the Glasswood from Etreal. It was named for the jagged ridge shaped like the screaming body of something ancient, writhing on its back. Myths said it reflected one of the Archfey's battles with Chiroscuroi, god of crossroads, where She revealed the extent of Her monstrous self. One of the eyes shone cerulean, a gem, perhaps, that no one had ever dared try to reach for fear of incurring Her anger.

That eye is what this creature of Madainn holds.

The procession is scattered throughout the trees, reflections and obstacles breaking them into fragments, but still Eirjatal sees a male Winter elf being dragged behind the last of the water horses, his bloody face bright in the white landscape. Galistan, Scintia's devoted soldier who Vyriseh's spies were seeking.

Whatever they wanted, they retrieved, and Eirjatal has no doubt who will praise them.

"Galistan defended it. We thought it was ours. The watching eye of the Archfey. It was never ours."

"It isn't Madainn's. Scintia, what is it?"

Scintia's so delicate, curling up like she wants to be shielded by him. "I do not know. But they will find the next one in Dianthus."

"When? How can we prepare?"

"Do not let Sigyn know what is in the evocations. He can open them, but you cannot let him."

Hardly helpful, but he wonders if that's somehow the answer to both questions.

Eirjatal glances back around the corner. The procession has passed, leaving only a deep trench in the snow where Galistan was dragged. If it weren't for that, he would think this is his dream she's stepped into. The Fort tastes like fear.

But, he supposes, they both lived the same nightmare.

Scintia says, "Ashvaren was never meant to solve them. He was only meant to protect them if someone else solved them first." Her voice is shivering like she's on the brink of tears. "But he looked. They made him wilder, worse; covetous, craven. These are not our secrets. They are Etreal's secrets, so we have a chance to stop them from dooming us."

"Dooming us to what?"

"Ashvaren knew all the stories."

"To what, Scintia?" He wants to shake her.

"Each of the rulers knows their own; they are the ones who gave them to me. But what they mean, that is what no one understands."

Scintia looks above him. Then the skittering starts.

It shakes free snow and clatters the painting frames against the stone. Hundreds of sharp, insectile feet crawl up the Fort and onto the parapets. The sound shudders against his skin, curious about getting in. Bizarrely, his fear stays at a comfortable distance, like it's merely watching him from the other end of the room.

Madainn's monster crosses the roof and back down the other wall. The windows all blacken with the shadow of it, but then it passes, and light streams in anew.

Scintia whispers, "Sigyn can't know."

She pulls him by the hand into the dark passages of the Ineiren Fort. Now she runs full-tilt, stumbling over her skirt, her nails sawing into his wrist. She was always so stoic. Her desperation broke through only when she prayed, but even then, there was love in it, like she knew the Fey would come eventually. This, this is the fear he wishes he could act on, full abject horror, shameless.

They plunge into the black—and fall through the other side onto a stormy, snowy cliff.

Scintia is in her armour, frosted-over silver metal and fur, sapphire glaive in her gloved fist. The roaring wind whips her hair like a white flag. Eirjatal's hands are bare to better burn, his own leather armour wet with melted snow from the heat coming off of him.

Scintia yells over the wind, "He is coming back, Eirjatal. We were lucky that he still speaks to us."

He's breathing heavily. He recalls this cliff and this night, but his body knows it, his body was always ready to come here. "I can't do anything about it," he begs, feeling mad. "I tried. We tried. What was I planning, to negotiate with the Woven? I'm not a god, Scintia."

"What of Cereus?"

"He can't do anything. Saying that makes me a poor loyalist and a terrible lover"—the word catches, nearly stolen by the wind—"but he's so terrified of being Ashvaren, and worse than that, terrified of any choice that asks him to be."

"You sought Madainn."

He's trying to breathe but the armour is too tight, the air too icy. "I always do. It nearly killed Rho. I nearly killed her. She told me he's hers, now, but he's only ever been mine. It's safer that way."

Scintia's long, furred ears flick, listening. Eirjatal blinks into the snow, white sticking to his eyelashes, and sees a shadow bleeding along the white horizon. He knows that shape. His body has long been waiting for it, and it falls into its role like a well-rehearsed actor: blind, scrabbling for the way out.

"Are you afraid, Eirjatal?"

She's glowering into the wind, fingers wrapped tightly around her glaive. They're alone up here, except for what's coming. That is a relief and he clings to it. He doesn't have to see everyone die again.

"I don't want to give this pain to anyone," he admits.

"Are you afraid of him?"

The shadow solidifies, that creature pulling itself out of the icy ocean of the Evertide. Its many legs stab into the shore to pull itself through the ice and snow, and the earth shivers beneath his feet. He can't breathe.

"Are you afraid of them all?"

She's hollering now. The wind rages around them, tearing at his hair, extinguishing the fire from his fists. The sheets of snow tear apart and for a flash he can see the black-green sheen of its armour, the skeletal segments of its legs. Snow turns to ice against his cheeks and his mouth is frozen shut.

Scintia just screams, her heartbeat loud under the wind like something he can find and take as his own.

He remembers the fall of the Ineiren Fort. He remembers all the deaths as the world itself warred around them, how small he felt, how large the grief. He remembers knowing for the first time that he was a pawn in a world that hated him, and he held every scrap of fear until it became something like revenge, something covetous. The gods couldn't empty him. The world mattered to him. Cypress mattered so much to him.

The wind dies, the light dies, and Scintia grasps for him in the pitch dark of that night, the Fort around them, the worst of it gone, the dead around them like a neglected garden. She holds his face, lavender eyes wild and bright.

"I cannot save us. I cannot do this again. I am so afraid and I held it all until it trapped me." Tears freeze on her cheeks. Her voice is small and shattered. "But you are still free. You have to save us, Eirjatal Ga'vrynn. Do not fight. This cannot start another fight. I cannot save us, so you have to. Will you? Please?"

Eirjatal wakes, Scintia beside him.

He's on the deck of the undersea ship, amidst the ice creations—or what's left of them. He pushes himself up, wrist-deep in cold water, taking in the sculptures he's melted. Scintia is unconscious, but she's holding his waist too tightly to be dead. He extracts her with some difficulty and lowers her to the deck with shaking arms.

I cannot save us, so you have to.

The emotion that batters through his startled, confused heart is pity. This is how she feels beneath the silence. Like he felt in the Fort when he knew they were going to lose everything.

For how long has she refused help? She even let him know first that Madainn had come. Why does she feel like he's the only one she can trust?

The answer comes easily. It's why he can't trust anyone. It's safer to keep all of this to himself, to stop anyone from locking themselves away like Scintia.

Not even Rho can carry it all. And now with Scintia's pleas in his ears, he realizes he can't carry it much longer either.

Scintia's dress is half-melted from his fire. Her back is exposed, betraying her pale thinness. He checks her pulse and it thrums far too slowly.

Footsteps. Sigyn is approaching, first slowly, then briskly once he sees Scintia.

Sigyn, like Scintia, came to him to find his way back. What do they see that he doesn't?

But her voice cuts through his thoughts. *Sigyn can't know*.

"What's happened?" He crouches next to Scintia. "Nele…"

Sigyn won't touch her, so Eirjatal carefully turns her over. Frost grows on her cheeks and forehead, seals her eyes, freezes shut the seam of her lips.

"The Winter curse," Sigyn says hollowly. "She's gone."

31

Irving

Found someone interesting the other night. A half-elf in a Staventene estate. They had this magic that took things right out of people's heads. Anything you could dream of walked around like spectres.
And most importantly, they didn't seem to give a shit about any of it, except the cost. Reach out if you're curious. I can get a name.

Envai to the House of Ciphers, self-destructing letter, Age of Shields 250

The morning after getting the Autumn evocation, Irving shoots awake with the key on how to crack it.

They'd been stressing over it all night, long after Noah went to sleep and Irving had to stare into the dark. Could a Karadenza cursebreaker do it, or would they shatter the story entirely? Or a Mythmaker sorcerer—their whole thing is stories and illusions. But what can Irving do, ask Vyriseh for another favour and hope she's willing to look the other way again?

They dreamt of handing the vial to Envai. She set it in the back of her teeth like an unpracticed human using Heartswain (too easy to accidentally bite it and come face to face with something you hate and equally hates you).

"Hopefully," she'd said with a wink, "Vyriseh won't attack Ventaris for *this* one."

"It's not Khidell. It doesn't matter that much."

"You really *don't* know your father."

And then she wasn't Envai anymore, but a white-haired Cypress queen. Pale lavender eyes, long ears tufted with fur, dress made of ice. A storybook version of Scintia. They've never seen her before.

She touched their nose, finger ice-cold. Said, "Careful. The Blind Adder is listening."

She pushed them out of the dream.

What power did Ventaris have access to that Cypress did, too?

Khidell. Moonwardens.

Irving digs under their bed for the vial until the lights snap on.

"Irving!" Noah hisses.

They cover their eyes against the brightness. They scoop the vial from the toe of their loafer and slip it secretly into their pocket. "What're you—?"

"They caught Johana."

Ice slides down their spine. "What?"

"I'm on breakfast this morning but went early to let her know about," she wiggles her hand in a gesture that must mean the evocation, "but there were guards. They've got Marie. I had to pretend I got turned around but—they know."

Now?

Sigyn and Kinthe can return at any instant, but for now, Irving's got access to Kinthe's room of glass. This chance is never coming back.

Noah says, "What if Vyriseh gets her to talk? What if she talks anyways? Fey's broken horns, you fed her that line about taking the fall for her, right?"

"Do you *want* me to?"

"No!" Noah folds her arms over her soft stomach. "Seriously? You think between her and you, I'd pick *her?*"

Irving would pick Noah, too. Still, that doesn't mean they'd abandon Johana.

But the part of them that worried about the vial all night, the part that risked that priestess for this story, the part of them so *furious all the time* at Sigyn, says, "Johana's fine. They can't hurt her or else they'll lose Rhoheme."

Noah's shoulders draw up. "Not like she was gonna leave Dianthus intact, anyways."

That truth settles on them, comfortable as a guillotine.

"I'll make myself look like Tavreah or something and see what's going on."

"You're nuts."

"Why did you tell me if you don't want me to do anything?"

"I don't know. You're the one who does stuff. I wanted…someone to do something."

Irving's telling themselves the whole walk through the palace to divert to the infirmary. To at least give Johana the assurance that Irving's not going to break a promise.

But then they walk into Kinthe's scrying room and, set on a table like an offering in the forest of hanging glass pearls, is Sigyn's scrying box.

Did he forget it? Is he back already?

Johana's got mutually assured destruction to hold over the Dawn Hall. She doesn't need them. Not right now.

Irving unlocks the teakwood lid and opens it. The black velvet lining is smoky through the thin glass tokens that are perfectly arranged to allot a half-inch of free space right in the middle. Each token has a symbol scratched in. Sigyn said they were something the Fey gave him, maybe letters from her old world, but they're only scribbles to Irving.

They kind of hate it. They're kind of scared of it. It's like the Fey herself is in that glass, daring them to tempt fate once again.

They pushed her away by leaving for Etreal. They asked for her back by cutting out their magic. They mocked her for trying with the Heartswain and the evocations.

Who cares, when she's been keeping their family from them?

They slide one glass piece into the free space, teeth clenched like they're changing one of the stage lightbulbs in Staventene. The breaker's off. They're going to be fine. But the imagining of it going wrong is enough to brace them for pain.

They slide a few more, like the Eclipsed ward, like Sigyn keeping his own life at arm's length.

Life, beginnings. Then, fearing that the vial holds something worse than they expected, the scry pattern for death.

The symbols start to glow with icy white light. The vial joins in.

It's faint. Usually there are floating flakes of light that peel from the pieces. Maybe this magic's like Rhoheme's or Vyriseh's—it exists without the caster, waiting to be used.

The moonlight streams in the window, pooling around their feet. The moon is bright, full, like an eye, heavy with power, sending a shudder down Irving's spine.

White light rebounds amongst the hanging glass pieces, the vial. Vyriseh's voice joins in.

"You know, you may be the last person in Cypress who cares to know this story. Let me tell you of the bloodbath in Heatherwol's palace."

32

Vyriseh

Age of Shields 1

I was frightened and awed at being in the same auditorium as Ashvaren. I could only *imagine* how Sigyn Aphithea felt, pinned under his glower.

Ah, Sigyn Aphithea. Back then, Scintia…he was so young when he won us the war, then made a terrible mistake. He fell in love.

Let me set the stage a little better. You can start the recording here instead, if you…oh? Well, if it's all golden, let me get on with it!

The Age of Beasts was at its worst. The moment right after the dust settles, when the dead are being counted. Ashvaren was a rare sight. If you saw him out of his burrow and you weren't nobility…my dear, he'd likely be the last thing you'd ever see.

I was only a little fledgling, barely fifteen! I was raised by monsters, but Ashvaren's presence in the Summons was enough to give me vertigo. Luckily, I was protected by the other four rulers (Spring! *Spring's* Sunmirren was there. Do you remember Nia? I wonder where she is in Etreal...).

My dear Saezdrith had told me, "You will learn more about Cypress in this conversation than any book." Ah...something like that. She was always more of a poet than me. Not all things can be taught, I suppose.

Ashvaren asked, "Do your grounds feel stranger for the creature's presence, Firewe?"

The Autumn Sunmirren did not look up from the court files. If it bothered her that one of her own was on trial, she didn't show it. Funny, because she certainly enjoyed pointing him out when he was the hero.

But no wonder. We all wanted to get one over on Ashvaren. Saezdrith was the only one with the guts to admit it. How awful, when the ones you hate keep saving you.

Firewe said, "I don't believe their goddess sees through its eyes, but I will accommodate those who do."

Ashvaren heard the slight. He always heard slights. "Why *wouldn't* she be spying?"

Saezdrith loudly addressed the auditorium. "*She*? Karadenza or the Carrion Queen? Its mother is a priestess of the goddess of predators. I wonder if his skin broke when the bitch sunk her teeth in."

Sigyn idly fixed a pin in his hair.

I whispered a little tune. Papery illusions danced along the railing, looking down over Heatherwol's Summons. The eyes on Saezdrith's chest and arms watched as the sketch of a human woman bit Sigyn's long, beautiful neck. Saezdrith petted my hair and I was pleased.

"Let us suppose, Aphithea," Ashvaren said, eyes bright like the manic stare of an owl, "that you win this case. You cannot stay in Cypress with it."

Saezdrith interjected, "As if you know he'll keep it." From her I learned to always consider the most unexpected option.

Firewe said, "Why come to the Summons at all if not to keep it?" She was always quietly *knowing* like a feline. She made you feel like a fool, but a fool she loved for reasons you couldn't solve.

Sigyn's gaze flicked up to our balcony. "I'm fortunate that the Nelaeryn Fey granted me a child, especially when they are so rare. I'm only here to free that child."

"Don't act as if your depravity involved the Fey," Ashvaren sneered.

"She gave me the weaponry to end the Age of Beasts. It would not be more strenuous to give me a bloodline."

"The Age of Beasts," Ashvaren said, fingers curling around the rail like he imagined it was Sigyn's throat, "will not end as long as you mix the queen of those beasts with Cypress."

"The Packmothers were from an alliance between Relyn and Carrion Queen. If I was enchanted or a traitor, I would not have brought you such useful weapons."

"What would the Woven gain by allying with the Fey to fight their own?"

He thought the beasts intended to eat Cypress from the inside, didn't he? I'll admit, that scared me. I was already terribly afraid of being far from Silvershale for the first time.

"Would you like an answer or merely to listen to yourself ask?" Sigyn didn't break eye contact. "I *do* have answers. As you all have warned me, speaking with a Woven cultist does give one a better understanding of their gods than Cypress."

Ashvaren sighed. It's a sound I'm sure you remember. A warning, like the groan of something falling. He flicked a hand and one of the priestesses struck Sigyn across the face with the pommel of the dagger they used to test him for traitor magic.

I jumped. My illusion became Sigyn being struck again, again, again.

Can you *imagine* our famed Moonwarden being hit like a dog? What if I sing it right here on the table? No? Oh, Scintia.

Sigyn said through his teeth, "The Carrion Queen is the goddess of monsters. Madainn stole her gifts to create everything that has ruined Cypress and Etreal during this war. She was offended, and the Fey was too vulnerable to defend Herself without an ally—"

Another strike, hard enough that he staggered.

Sigyn touched his mouth. The priestess stepped back. Firewe shifted, likely realizing what I did—Ashvaren had whispered to her staff.

There, I learned that half the fun of power is having people who challenge you on it. What's the point without doubt to intimidate or flatter until it breaks?

Should I be embarrassed to tell you this? No, of course not. Are you even really hearing me, lovely?

What will happen to this story?

Will it sleep forever with you?

Anyhow.

Saezdrith told them to simmer down. She acted dismissive, but she gave me my interest in humans, pinning their mysteries to boards like butterflies, so I know she was invested. A curiosity she was covered in eyes, not ears! "Let's begin in earnest. Who is first to speak?"

Guards emerged with the first witness.

Saezdrith brightened. My illusion fumbled into her smile, then I snuffed it altogether. (A detail I'll tell no one but you!) "Your soldier, Ashvaren? I'm surprised they found enough shards to sweep together!"

Ashvaren scoffed, "It'll be our doom, trusting a Woven-cursed," as Eirjatal Ga'vrynn stood across from Sigyn.

His eyes were feverish, bright veins spiralling across his cheeks, from the vitaea treatments to cure his encroaching snow-blindness. It gave him the appearance of a corpse, unhelped by the stretch of his skin along sharp bones and the hard shadows his horns cast over his eyes. Perhaps being constantly surveilled in Dianthus's 'refugee' houses did not encourage a steady stomach. He wore his soldier's uniform. He was fired the instant the rescue troops dragged him from the Ineiren wreckage, so perhaps he was reminding his Starmorrow of all he'd done.

Am I right that you saved Eirjatal from exile after he murdered two of Ashvaren's court? Hm. Odd use of your time, love.

Sigyn said, so quietly it's a miracle I caught it and a guarantee I'll never forget it, "I am blessed to see you safe, my friend."

Eirjatal didn't look at him.

Saezdrith whispered in my ear, "Ga'vrynn's words will be a spell, but he doesn't have your magic. The best stories and songs come from what, Vyri?"

"Truth!"

"But you and he can push and pull the details, guide their attention, make a rabbit have a wolf's shadow, or a wolf hide in bright light." She held my hand. "And if you think the story should look *differently*... whisper it to me, and I'll show you how it's done."

Now, now! Don't worry. This case was fascinating, but what did it have to do with me? We were fighting over an elf who rose above his station, and, honestly, rose to the wrong occasion with that human cultist. (That was crass, please don't record that.) Laws about half-humans weren't yet decided, as they were so rare—rarer, still, for an elf to take advantage of the recovery situation to keep one and his human paramour within Cypress walls.

It didn't scare me like it scared Ashvaren. Even back then, the Eclipsed used humans for study, so Saezdrith and I did not think of them like the rest of you did. We understood that on the Tapestry, it was *us* who didn't belong. The *elves* who were the ghouls.

But we had to be better for the Fey.

Sigyn had to be better for the Fey.

So I only listened.

Eirjatal's hands stayed in the pockets of his robes. Nervous that we would see them shaking, I thought, and then I made another melody, elongating the shadows: *it's because he's hiding something*.

He spoke. Sigyn's supply caravans were used to trouble, but a few years in, the Age of Beasts stirred along with the war that would give it its name.

The Glasswood job became vital. After all, the Ineiren Fort backs onto the white sea of the Evertide. Everyone knows that's where Madainn makes his kingdom. Well, everyone but the Nelaeryn Fey, apparently.

(Could you cut that, too?)

In the depths of the war, their carriages were stuck in the snow inside Aurelius's territory. Lost and trapped, they must have felt, with Madainn's creatures hunting the woods, and humans hunting even closer—those woods became home to those who honoured the creatures instead of fearing them—but one day a human woman appeared at the border.

She brought five baby beasts—"Like wolves," Eirjatal said, "but from the Amber Crawl. It was impossible to not see that." So he *could* sing after all.

The human said the Nelaeryn Fey and the Carrion Queen had made the creatures together for Cypress's defence.

"Sigyn volunteered to speak to her. I tried to stop him, but he was taken with her. The monsters were taken with him, as well. His was likely the first beating heart they'd ever heard."

Firewe asked, "Was it clear she was an acolyte and not simply a human sent by the Carrion Queen?"

Eirjatal closed his eyes, like summoning the image, and when they opened he squinted against the lantern light. "She smelled of pelts. Acolytes always smell like their gods. We know our enemies on the road.

"Sigyn invited her into Cypress. Trusted her on instinct, he said—indeed, it must have been *some* instinct, and he's lucky that cultists have a way with animals."

Sigyn watched him with sympathy.

"He became single-minded on raising the beasts and delivering them to the warfronts. I wanted nothing to do with it. None of us did. They were not the Fey's. Neither was his infatuation with the cultist."

Sigyn asked, "What is her name, Eirjatal?"

Eirjatal cringed at the torchlight. "What does it matter?"

"We've called her the cultist or the Carrion Queen's—I see the colouring there." The shadow and light and song. "You would be presented to us very differently if we referred to you not by your name but by *haunted*."

They already called him that in the noble circles.

When Eirjatal didn't budge, Sigyn said, "Her name is Esme." He turned to the gallery of rulers. "May I speak again?"

Firewe gave the accommodating gesture before Ashvaren could.

"I see no difference here from what I've seen travelling for years with elves in Etreal. Believe that I'm enchanted if you wish, but also believe that I've kept my mouth shut about humans being stolen from cities, then discarded with their own half-blood to contend with, by my own friends."

Sigyn stepped closer to Eirjatal. "I'm surprised that it took me saying I'm in love with her for something so…structured and serious to be called."

"It's not that you love her, or think you do." The torches flared. They threatened to catch on the tapestries. He swore, whipping a hand from his pocket, and I jumped as all the lights guttered out. Ashvaren drew slightly from his seat. "It's *your* neck to bring her into your bed, but you brought these beasts to Cypress before you admitted where they came from. You had the Carrion Queen see the city. We are all forfeit."

"It's natural for us, at this time, to be wary of the Woven."

"Oh, shut it. I could excuse your effort to do something right in a time when rightness felt impossible. But this? I don't understand you, protecting this creature with the eyes of the Carrion Queen. They say it's only an echo in there."

Sigyn's lips parted, but it took him another second to speak. "What is it? She has the eyes of the Carrion Queen, or," he tilts his head to the gallery, "she belongs to nothing and is already dead? None of us truly know what half-bloods are like. We only act out of fear."

Saezdrith perked up. "Perhaps this is a chance to let us study!"

Eirjatal retorted, "If we keep the child, we keep the Carrion Queen. How is this up for discussion? It should die." He shook his head slightly. "What does the Carrion Queen have waiting for you, Sigyn? What did she promise you?"

"I'm not sure," Sigyn said. "I, at least, am more courageous than all of you, for I'm willing to see."

A chill descended. Ashvaren lifted a hand and said, "You may leave, Ga'vrynn."

Eirjatal whirled like he may have choice words for his king. His eyes glowed in their spider webs of veins and bruises. But a priestess set a hand on his shoulder and led him to the door, much like Sigyn once led the Packmother monsters through our halls.

Sigyn called, "You are changed, but so is the Glasswood. Don't take destruction for failure."

Eirjatal ducked out of the priestess's hands and made for the door. Back to us, he snarled, "I'll kill it myself if you're all so scared of it. Sigyn is not worth all the fuss he thinks he is."

He had no idea then, did he?

In the next hour, the child was killed.

Yes, by Eirjatal Ga'vrynn. Not because he wanted to, but because the rulers were afraid. Eirjatal was already forfeit. He'd seen too much, his blood dooming him from birth. Eirjatal would shoulder every eye, every bit of hate, of the Woven.

Sigyn insisted he had no idea where Esme had gone.

What a time, Scintia! The gods were using Etreal for fuel and food and fickle chess pieces. Etreal was realizing that they were not special, they were not wanted, and Karadenza had destroyed her previous worlds for less trouble.

And whatever they did to Etreal, eventually, Cypress would feel too.

But our night wasn't over. I'll tell you what happened to Esme and our beloved Moonwarden.

Doesn't it make you wonder—how could we have ever forgiven him?

33

Vyriseh

Saezdrith sent me into the halls of Heatherwol's palace to spy.

When I could keep my mouth shut, I was a quiet little thing—oh, it's easy to guess what creature she nicknamed me, isn't it?—and Saezdrith used my curiosity as an excuse for her own. She was most curious about Ashvaren. I had a flute in my coat in case I'd have to coax a guard to sleep or (in my wildest imaginings) coax Ashvaren to spill all his secrets.

The reason why I was sent out doesn't matter. What I *found* does.

Sigyn.

Saezdrith was bored with the case, so I hesitated. What if I stalled for too long and Saezdrith finished her nightcap with Ashvaren before I could enter his room (neither of us have ever known a Summer elf who would turn down a drink)?

But Sigyn was speaking the language of Etreal...and a woman spoke back.

They were on one of the outdoor, mountainside bridges that connect the wings of the palace, so I tucked myself into a statue alcove. I couldn't see them, but voices carried well out there, and I preferred to be hidden; I hoped my white hair didn't glow in the dim. The woman didn't smell human at all.

"If you know how to find me," the woman whispered, "you must also know how to stop me."

Saezdrith taught me Etren, so this felt like a secret only *I* could find.

Sigyn said to Esme, for of course it was Esme, "Don't do this. I can take you out of Cypress."

"You'd make me leave without even a body to bury?"

Some bizarre sound made my teeth ache and blurred their voices and my breathing. It was like nothing I'd heard before or since...Scintia, imagine the distant thrum of a city or wildlife, but it was the *sound* that was alive, and it was swallowing the space around it, and it was so, so close.

Esme said, "Go to your rooms. I'll smell you on the door and leave you be."

The sound filled the bridge like smoke. It vibrated violently against my heart. It was like the start of a spell that was too big and cruel for me.

Esme asked, "The necklace I gave you. Do you have it now?"

He sounded baffled. "It's with my belongings."

"When this is over, give it back to me."

A dead child, and she asked after a bauble?

"If you're leaving me, I'm not giving away the only token of you—"

"*Please*, my heart." I was surprised by—frightened by—the urgency. "Save who you'd like and raise the alarm if you must, but *give me that necklace*. You hurt me so much already."

I imagine that they were staring down at the end of their silly relationship and what they'd dreamed their lives would be—staring down at it like it was a thing wheezing for air and bleeding on their shoes. And all she wanted was this *necklace*.

Sigyn whispered, "Alright."

"Stay out of our way." And the sound approached me like a storm whose thunder I could touch.

I still consider it a miracle from the Fey that she didn't find me. She was statuesque, with more presence than I've ever seen a human have…perhaps she *was* the goddess of predators. So impressive was Esme, that she seemed commanding even alongside the bloodthirsty monster that she led.

The Packmother was as Eirjatal said. A wolf from the Amber Crawl, taller than her at the shoulder, a head that swung with a fixed, milky gaze as its massive muscles rolled, fur made of shifting brimstone slats with lava-like glowing beneath. The paws would have crushed my ribs with a nudge, and the jaws could swallow me whole.

Worst was the noise. Like it ate up the world around it without even opening its mouth.

Many of us had heard of the beasts Sigyn brought to Cypress, but it was only the soldiers who saw them. To me, even today, the Packmothers felt like the Archfey's. Ready to ruin anything at the simple command of their mistress. Like us.

Sigyn stopped Esme and kissed her. It was a drawn-out kiss that made me embarrassed, not because it was particularly salacious, but because it wrote out emotions that didn't belong to an audience. I thought, *This is the end of the story*.

But as we know, Sigyn adores a rewrite.

He went one way, she and the Packmother went another.

I wanted to see what Esme planned. And yet, I needed to warn Saezdrith. I feared then what I sometimes fear now.

If they have to choose, Cypress will not save the Eclipsed queen. I wanted to change that. I wanted to be a Sunmirren whose allies would go to the ends of the earth to save her.

But I was sure Saezdrith would tell me to gather the notes for a song.

So I followed.

And carnage was a step ahead of me.

I'm sure someone else wrote the details better—one of the many dignitaries who was targeted by Esme, one of the few who survived. I only walked through the wreckage as she tried to kill every elf in the palace.

Esme pulled guests from rooms and spilled curiosities all over the floor. She slit throats with her own hands. She opened doors and let her Packmother break in and kept walking without a flinch at the sounds that skittered out of the rooms. She strolled like a woman in a dream. At odd turns and twists, she would meet with another of the five beasts, all alight with blood and adoration for her.

Perhaps she had her monsters ignore the scent of children. Because sometimes I was close enough to feel them race past me for better prey.

How could Sigyn have ever loved her? Surely he knew she was capable of something like this. Surely his attempts to reach her heart were met with hollow rings. Surely he knew he was a traitor. Wasn't he afraid?

But we misunderstand elves. Of course he was afraid. We are all terrified of Etreal. Her command could kill his people. But her command could also protect him.

Regardless, who could blame her?

She had saved us—her goddess did, too—and we destroyed something so small and precious. We couldn't even allow our heroine a *baby* that would die in a *blink*.

She was a mother wolf, after all, and this was how she protected what was hers.

You understand the amazement I felt, don't you, Scintia?

At seeing so many of us die?

At the quiet? At the shame? You watch it now within your own kingdom. It's fascinating. A few times I couldn't help crouching by the dying, watching how they grasped for anything, until finally they only grasped for breath, and then lastly, for me.

Eventually, I found Sigyn and followed him into an atrium. I expected more carnage inside, but there were only the two of us, so he found me.

Sigyn pulled me in by the arm, but he was gentle. "You're Sunmirren Saezdrith's student, aren't you?"

I nodded. His robes were bloody, but his hands were not. Looking back, maybe I wasn't as confident as I thought, because I wanted to hug him, even if he did betray the Fey. He glanced to the door; the beasts were approaching.

"Hide," he said. "Saezdrith is clever. You will both be alright." He opened a cabinet and shoved aside its contents so I could fit. He shut the door on me.

Esme entered not long after. There was only one Packmother again—I could tell by the sound of it. The rest must have still been in the halls. Not all the beasts would live, but locked in that cabinet, I thought there was no way they couldn't.

"I couldn't find Firewe or Eirjatal. Why," she asked coolly, "did you know how to save their lives, but not our child's?"

"I don't know," he begged. It was the first and last time I'd hear him desperate. Perhaps I knew its rarity, for I inched open the door, and found something rarer. He was on his knees at her feet, hands clasped behind his neck in supplication.

"Do you have the necklace?"

He took a jagged black pendant from his neck. Esme pressed her hand against her own matching piece.

"Tell me what it is."

"Please give it over. It isn't sentimental, Sigyn."

"Esme," he begged from the floor, "you owe me this."

"I found it in Etreal. I never should have, and I shouldn't have kept it."

"Why?"

"It's Karadenza's."

The name of my nightmares, said so easily.

Sigyn tensed. "What does that mean?"

"Karadenza destroyed her own Chalice so no mortal could ever find it.

The Carrion Queen hid them across Etreal to protect them. But when I found this piece...I shattered it in two, so no one could truly claim it."

"And no one would look in Cypress." He turned the piece in his hand. It was like dull pottery, nothing so legendary. "What does it do?"

"She wants me to hide them, until she says it's time for us to put them all together." Esme crouched in front of him and touched his arm. "Sigyn, please. I'm sorry I didn't tell you earlier."

"What does it do?" he repeated.

"Only one can do nothing. But all of them will make a world." She laughed shallowly, more like a whimper. "Not a pocket like the Amber Crawl, but a *complete* realm like Karadenza's. It sounds incredible, doesn't it? Exactly what people would fight over during a war that seems this impossible. This world needs defending more than another needs discovering."

"If you want it so badly, then take me with it."

"No."

"What do you think you've done to me, Esme? They'll ruin me. They'll be too afraid to hunt you so they'll turn on me." He exhaled sharply. "And they're right to."

After a moment, she asked, "Will I get out safely?"

"Not without me," he said. "You injured the Autumn Moonwarden, but didn't kill her. Perhaps if I leave—Moonwardens' powers can't cross the border, so perhaps if I'm in Etreal—"

"And if the powers become yours anyways?"

Instead of replying, he stood and grabbed her hand. As they pushed open the door, Sigyn glanced back to my cupboard. The sound of thunder faded with them. And then I sat alone in the quiet for a very, very long time. In the dark, the deaths I'd seen lost their fascination and crawled under my skin instead.

Sigyn and Esme escaped. Two of the Packmothers were slain in Heatherwol's halls. And the Autumn Moonwarden died too soon.

And that's all I have for you. Karadenza's Chalice piece was in Cypress for months without us—or him—realizing what it was. A foolish token from a lover, they must have assumed. A pendant, dirty and old and strange.

Oh? What happened to it?

This is why I love you, Scintia. You know how closely I listen.

I have no reason to believe Sigyn ever gave his piece up.

Esme's? As far as I understand, it's hidden in an underground tower in the city of Ventaris. An old one they used as a war room. But I don't think that's the last we'll ever see of it.

Who do you think deserves a new world, Scintia, my sweet, empty-headed darling?

The humans? Or the elves, who never belonged in this one?

34

Irving

Something stays with me from those interviews with the elf.
At the end of all things, he said, it will not be the Humans against the
Elves. It will be the Elves against the Gods.

Notes from a Karadenza priest on Khidell, Age of Shields 202

Irving rocks back on their heels out of the vision.

I have no reason to believe Sigyn ever gave his piece up.

The phrase rings, stinging and brittle. Whatever searing fury they've always stoked about Sigyn is replaced by a quiet, patient cold. It has questions. About way more things than can fit in their head. Too many things they want to know and too many things they wish they didn't.

But Irving has always hit the ground on their feet. Only because they know how to start running immediately after.

They know where to go next.

So early before the dawn, the Dianthus portal master is receptive to any conversation, and so Irving makes it into the tunnel by using Vyriseh's enchantment to transform into the Briarlord who had the human pets. She didn't recognize the key they handed her.

That key, a tiny winged figurine of the Aphrodin, bites their palm when they emerge into the silent Ventaris tower basement. They stole it when slinking out of that Ventaris tower behind Vyriseh and Sigyn. They wanted a way to hop out of Dianthus, but they never expected it'd be for this.

With a shimmer of the enchanted ribbon, they take on the appearance of Vyriseh herself.

You've acted before, they assure themselves, trying to get their bearings within Vyriseh's body. *Well, sometimes. When they shove you on-stage if someone's sick. And this time there's no script.*

They follow the hall. Vyriseh's form is a headache to get a handle on; they quickly give up on the second set of arms and fold them behind her, and it's not like Irving's short, but Vyriseh's over six foot, so they bang their head once on a sconce and narrowly avoid doing it again twice more. They're lucky they have so much distance to practice before they reach the map room.

They need to erase all the help they unknowingly gave.

They try the door. Locked. And not with a physical key. A little inscription glows on the edge of the door.

No way Karadenza's fragments are real. They try to wrap their head around it, but they keep getting snagged—Sigyn had a piece.

But he got rid of it. Two hundred years have passed since then; whatever motivation made him keep it must have dulled over the years.

Well, he was willing to risk his kids twice, so clearly he doesn't learn.

They shove the thought away. It burns furiously on the way down; they focus on the door before it overwhelms them. Clearly it unlocks with a spell—

"Sunmirren," says a masculine voice behind them.

Irving freezes. They figured the tower wouldn't be entirely deserted—hence the disguise—but they still swear under their breath.

They force their shoulders to relax in Vyriseh's way, and turn.

A human man has approached from a branch in the hall. As he bows, an illusion washes off him.

The nondescript human morphs into an Eclipsed elf, his silvery hair tied up in such meticulous braids and knots that Irving can only guess at his age. When he straightens and the gas lamps light up his face, it's faintly lined, and even if they've shaken off as much Cypress tradition as they can, Irving's intimidated. Adamantine is the oldest elf they personally know and she may as well be a student in comparison.

Vyriseh is more…presence before words. So Irving walks to him before he can walk to her. His skin is more grey than lavender, papery and sunless. A scaly tail like a rat's curls around his shoes. Scars rope around his neck and chisel up his face, a rarity for elves because of how vitaea's prescribed for the tiniest nick. Vyriseh has specialty spies like Adamantine has her Hawks, so he's probably one of those.

There are a few words emblazoned on the back of his hand, ribbed slightly by his fine bones, but they seem like gibberish. It reminds them of the enchantment written into the ribbon they're wearing—and of the writing on the map room door.

They take a stupid leap of faith. "Good morning. I would like to check up on my—my maps, here." They almost want him to refuse.

He dips his head. "How fortuitous that you arrive now. Unannounced."

He seems almost…accusatory? Irving gives their best *oh, you know* smile.

"There have been interesting turns with your guests, my Light. I insist you familiarize yourself with them, first."

"And I insist on the maps."

But he's giving them such a significant glower that Irving feels cornered. They shouldn't push either way; they want to keep their mouth shut as much as possible so they can avoid tripping themselves up.

Shit.

They follow him down the hall, keeping a few steps to his side so he'll be less likely to notice Irving's questionable control of her far-too-many limbs, or their hesitation on where to go. To make matters worse, he tries to start a conversation.

"How is Dianthus faring, in the fifth year of new rulership?"

"Oh," they say. "Oh, well…" *You know this.* "Calmer. Cereus is lenient. Reluctant to…" They think of what Vyriseh said when handing them the ruined dresses and inviting them into this very plot, "admit trouble in paradise."

"I remember him as a boy. He marvelled over all, including me—if he ever gave any indication that he had it in him to become king, I would have been more flattered."

He's staring at them. They remind themselves that even if Vyriseh's no Cereus, she invites ease in her own way. But Irving doesn't like his expression. Like he's challenging Vyriseh to tell him to shut up. They can't imagine why.

"Is something amiss, my Light?" he asks, and it's a touch mocking.

"No. No, only impatient." Irving smiles.

Something about this elf tugs at Irving's memory, though they know they've never met him. He brushes his fingers along the dark walls like he may lose his way. He better not.

Eventually, they reach a door. The elf presses the writing on the back of his hand to a black glass panel and it inches open.

Irving acts like they always meant to take the first step, channeling Vyriseh's fluid confidence, and push the door.

And promptly freeze.

There's a long, dizzying hall, and Irving can't say much for the cages in their periphery, but the ones right in front of them hold corpses.

They stumble in another step, and another, and rest a hand on the wall to steady themselves and this towering body. Did she know? Is this a surprise?

Maybe yes; the blood is fresh enough to reek of human.

They get their answer when they look at the elf. He's already fixated on them, and he doesn't seem surprised by the pallor Irving feels cooling Vyriseh's face. It's like he gave a dog a command and is waiting for it to stumble its stupid way into obeying.

"What is this?" Irving asks.

There it is—that challenging glower. He says with the slightest lilt, "I was impatient."

The humans weren't stabbed or poisoned and left to die. There's blood splashed all over the floor, clothing torn open with an animal messiness to it. The light from the hall flashes over the face of the woman nearest.

Anya Zarina, the Grey Eves heiress Irving mentioned having started a search for Karadenza's Chalice.

The next person's face seems like it was mauled, featureless with gore. There's a pin on their nondescript lapel and Irving knows it before the elf opens the door further, bringing in more light. The winged snake and key.

Shit, shit, shit.

Irving says the only thing they can manage that doesn't sound too pissed or terrified, "They had more use."

"I apologize. Does this disappoint you?"

Irving steps out and sucks in the cool air of the hall, but the smell's stuck in their skull. They focus on their disguising enchantment over and over, so it doesn't waver from their pin-balling thoughts.

"They proved they weren't so willing to speak, even under pressure, as I was." The last part's dripping with acid. He tilts his head to invite Vyriseh away, as if the matter is closed. "Ventaris is strong even without its high walls and school and sorcerers."

As I was?

"They never...revealed anything? Even once you—" They scramble for a word, throat tight with nausea. "Once you threatened them?"

"They've hunted for the Chalices for so long that it's ingrained in them to stay quiet, like a poison inoculation. But I tire of being the curse under their city, Sunmirren; forgive me."

His scarred, vacant face creases with a self-pitying smile, and it hits Irving where they recognize him from.

Not his face but the feel of him. The sense of time and air getting thicker around him, the vacancy, the way he picks over his words and looks to them a moment too early. It's like Sigyn.

It's how Moonwardens who've held their power for too long act.

"Khidell," Irving breathes.

"Rare, it is, to hear my name from you, my Light."

"I'm sorry for that," Irving says without thinking.

Pretending to be Vyriseh in front of the Dawn Hall staff, who know so little about her, would be one thing. But her Moonwarden of decades?

"Thank you for the...update, but I've changed my mind. The Chalice. Let me see it." After what he said, Irving's more confident that it's here.

Khidell's face darkens before they've even finished the sentence. He proceeds down the hall. The tail tries to twist around his ankle but flicks away at the last moment.

It's only because of Khidell that Irving's mother knew Moonwardens existed and why she went to Cypress to petition one for help to save her town. They've seen copies of the records in Staventene, sitting pretty in the bookshelves of the elites, Khidell's death a mere footnote on pages demarcated with sketches of his bones.

Judging by the scars, the torture did happen, but then why do Cypress and Etreal think he's dead? Why does Vyriseh keep using Sigyn as her Moonwarden?

The halls are full of classically Ventaris displays of dragon bones, teeth, tapestries of polished skins. Khidell unlocks a different door with the same spell as before. Simple, but Irving figures it can be simple when it's hidden in a tower underneath a city Cypress is terrified of and the key belongs to an elf everyone thinks is dead.

This room's empty except for a statue. It's a marble rendition of the Carrion Queen and the Blind Adder trading snakes and spiders, animals that belong to both realms, but gifted by the Carrion Queen to the Adder after some nonsensical historical favour. Their platform's piled with gore and offal. The goddess reminds Irving of Vyriseh's recollection of Esme.

Irving figures something in them should sense it, either the pointless superstition of the human or the terror of the elf, but it's only their eyes that locate the Chalice piece. It rests in the Carrion Queen's hands, held out to the Adder.

It's like dull pottery, like Vyriseh said. And there are two pieces. Sigyn gave Vyriseh his half.

The massacre, running from Cypress to avoid his powers, the disregard for history repeating with Irving's neck on the line. Esme's warnings, abandoned for the endless hunger of Cypress.

Is this who Sigyn is?

"My Light," Khidell says calmly. He's drawn even with them. Irving can't tear their gaze from the fragment.

Nothing snaps down on Vyriseh's lavender hand when they reach out. The fragments catch them off-guard with their weight, like picking up a full glass that should be empty.

"Yes?" Irving asks.

"My impatience is not only in regards to the prisoners."

"I'm searching on my end as well," they say. She recruited an idiot half-elf to help.

"That's the opposite of my concern. You see, I have...time to consider things here. I have more time to consider your plans than you do, and even if the Fey is too far to speak clearly with me, I have time to see the many paths you've sketched."

Irving should put the fragments back, but they can't. It looks like the Blind Adder's reaching hand has spilled the Chalice into theirs. Can these little things make worlds? It still seems like a fairy tale.

"This will truly begin, quite soon. I do not think you have allies where you think you do. Not with your fellow rulers, and not with Sigyn Aphithea."

"What about him?"

"You hope for him to forget all that makes him mortal so he'll appeal to the Woven. So he will watch out for you. And I know how you hope to achieve this." Khidell asks, "Whose death will be as secret as mine?"

Khidell's face has morphed into something that's all his own in its cruelty, but so much like Sigyn in how it empties behind the eyes. He's trying to anticipate Irving's next moves—Vyriseh's. Unluckily for him and the Fey, Irving has no fucking clue what to do.

"You have traded me for your tower and your secrets," he says through his teeth like he's using all his restraint, "but do not forget, Sunmirren, I know more secrets than you."

He steps close enough that Irving backs into the sculpture. He smells like dust, like time.

"But you serve the Fey," Irving says hurriedly. It hits them how much power the Moonwardens have, for him to intimidate his captor, his queen, like this.

Khidell says, even and distant in a way far too much like Sigyn, "Precisely, I do. The Moonwarden does not serve the Sunmirren, and they certainly do not serve the Woven."

Light glints off a dagger he takes from his robes.

35

Irving

It isn't that Etreal didn't understand what Moonwarden Khidell meant to us. No, Ventaris didn't understand, and then they learned, and they refused to change. Vyriseh is inconsolable. Her grief is like the Archfey's. She will make something out of her pain, and so I will too. The Hawks will storm Ventaris to take back whatever broken thing is made of Khidell.

Adamantine to Scintia, letter, Age of Shields 200

If Khidell is set on killing Vyriseh, then there's one way to stop him. They rip off the disguise spell on their wrist, and fold into their true smaller shape, shielding their head on the way.

There's a wet, jagged crunch. Then a gasp. Irving blinks the scene back into clarity.

Khidell's stabbed himself.

When he takes in Irving's appearance, they expect him to be shocked, but a strange relief moves across his features. Maybe he knew he wasn't dealing with Vyriseh at all.

Irving takes a step towards him, but he staggers back and lurches the dagger further up his stomach. It forces out another gasp, but he keeps going.

They can't let him die in Etreal. His power will get stuck here, but worse than that, the Cypress in him will, too.

Something in both of us belongs in Cypress. Where do you think that piece of you should go, if not to Her?

"Cypress'll save you," they say, frantic. "If they know you're alive, they'll know Vyriseh's been—"

"I will find her myself." Blood spatters out with his words. His robes are turning shiny and black.

With clear effort, he yanks the knife up another few inches; Irving flinches at a soft crack. A cool, steely calm washes over Khidell's face. His grip relaxes; his hand is almost casual on the hilt, smeared in red. A light in his eyes snuffs out as the Fey pulls back.

Instinct clicks back into place, and Irving runs.

In the doorframe, something like ink in water shudders into Khidell's form, blocking their way. He's monochrome, the hall behind him swimming in his silhouette. He's centuries younger, scars gone.

"Help me to Cypress, Aphithea," he says dreamily, lifting a hand like he might touch their face.

He had his chance. Now Irving's bargaining on if they remember how to get back to the portal.

They don't know what the Archfey's echoes are like, not really. Not outside of stories. But they've got an unexpected faith in stories right now.

Khidell whispers, "Take me to Vyriseh."

To tear her apart, clearly. She must have trapped him here for decades, and if he ever wanted to move against her, she could shut that down with a spell.

But echoes only show up when an elf dies in Etreal, so they can kill in Etreal. He wants back to Cypress. Khidell's still in there—maybe Irving can reach him.

"You'll hurt Cypress, too," they say, inching to the doorway. "I know you don't want that. Or at least the Nelaeryn Fey doesn't."

"Nele," he whispers like he forgot about her. "I've missed being close to her. I will find her again in Cypress. Help me."

Irving's palms are sweaty and pinched by the Chalice fragments—in all the mess, they forgot they were holding them. Irving shoves the fragments into their pocket. It's idiotic to keep them, but they for sure can't leave them here.

Khidell tilts his head, like trying to remember something—then his apparition tears apart.

Irving ducks through the door and the space Khidell left behind. Whatever plan they had to get to the map room dissipates as that ink-in-water black spreads through the hall—behind them, above them, bleeding into every corner. It seems to be trying to pick a form; it solidifies, then melts again. Clawed hands gripping the wall. Spider-like limbs dragging it forward. Ink splashing on the floor, dissipating right back into the cloud. They fold around the displays of dragon parts that line the walls. It's too silent, like Khidell's inviting Irving to slow down, to listen.

They don't know if they want it to be Khidell or not. They don't know if they'd rather his mind be in there, or for it to be a mess of echoed desires and memories and instinct.

One of the limbs stabs down, a breath away from them. They dodge right into the trajectory of another that catches in the back of their shirt. It wrenches them back, momentum throwing them to the floor, and for a second, they're consumed in the black.

And then, as Khidell, it touches down near the end of the hallway. He's holding something, toying with it idly; his colours are so dulled that it seems fluorescent.

It's a flower.

A Dianthus flower, their key to get back through the portal and into the city.

And a bitter, betrayed little something in them snaps, *Why not let him go?*

Oh, shut the fuck up. There are a million reasons not to. For one, they're not Envai—they're not heartless. And they don't want to know what he's capable of.

They don't want to know what they'll be capable of.

They'll die in Etreal. They want to die in Etreal, leaving behind friends and a home and with something figured out for once. The Cypress in them will try to hurt the world they want to be a part of. The Archfey's rage and heartbreak made manifest.

Khidell vanishes. The ink stain on the walls and ceiling spreads towards the portal.

Swearing, Irving scrambles to their feet. They run past dragon skins and displays of bones and talons. When they catch up at the portal room doorway, the darkness expands to fill the whole hall, trapping them inside of it. It's like being plunged into freezing, pitch-black water. Their breath stalls in their lungs.

Sweat rolls down the back of their neck. They turn around blindly, trying to see Khidell's shape in the swirling black mass.

Instead, they find a spot of brightness. The flower, pressed in by the darkness. They lunge for it. Their shoulder strikes something as they spill out of the dark, and with them comes a ton of objects—they must have ran into some display of dragon bones.

But at least they've got that little flower crushed in their fist. They slam the key into the receptor, trip onto the platform, and the room wrenches away.

Irving tumbles through the thin space between the Ventaris tower and the Dianthus portal. They crash to the floor, smacking their head hard enough to see stars. The room explodes with noise—everything they knocked over came through with them.

They blink hard to get their bearings. The room clears. The portal worker has thrown herself back into the console, a hand over her mouth, as Irving pulls themselves up from the pile of Ventaris junk. There's no sign of Khidell.

Khidell had more than enough chances to rip them to shreds, but he didn't.

"Sorry about this," they say offhandedly. They pat their pockets, trying to ignore the way they're shaking. The fragments are still there—and not broken into three.

Khidell's words about Sigyn knock around in their head.

You hope for him to forget all that makes him mortal.

Despite everything, they want to give him one last chance to explain himself.

And, staggering out of the portal, they find their chance has raced up and met them. Halfway up the secluded cobblestone road from the portal to the Dawn Hall are Eirjatal, Kinthe, and Sigyn.

36

Rhoheme

Madainn takes Rhoheme to a temple.

As he ducks in the white stone doors, he reverts to the height of a normal male, then Rho is popped out of that bubble and walking alongside him like a date at a dance. She's got her feet under her and she can breathe, but her hair and clothing float like they're underwater.

Madainn grins at her, broad mouth full of serrated little teeth. "Thanks for coming along so quietly, tinkerer."

Rho clutches her flouncy skirts to hide the sphere belted around her waist.

The temple's sloping walls are crammed with stained glass murals and bone-white coral. The floor shimmers in the wavering way that light moves through water. While the Adder's space was empty except for the card table, Madainn's is a kaleidoscope of *stuff*. Everything's white and turquoise and gold, packed with furniture even more ornamented than the Dawn Hall's, and a giant crystal-like coral reef at the head is twisted into a tower, so complex that her eyes can't find anywhere to rest. Countless altars are piled with shining offerings.

And in the center is a decaying body of a sea dragon, somehow elegant, bright in its death. In its open mouth are three daggers buried to the hilt.

She wonders how it feels to be Staventa in this situation. No wonder the Woven argue all the time—they're always tripping on each other's feet. So much so that even *Rho's* become an obstacle.

Madainn circles her, his inspection crawling a shudder up her spine. If only she could make better sense of him; everything from his black hair to his clothing melts away into the breathable water around them. His hands end in long claws, and his face is so like the sirens' in its sharp, fine-boned beauty, glittering eyes, slit nostrils, and corners of his mouth that slit open into membranous fibres when he smiles too widely at her.

"You're not hard to take care of, are you? No one ever brings things like you here."

"What, elves?"

He lifts his eyebrows. "Mortals."

"Why take me from Staventa?" She turns with him so he never gets a good look at her back or the sphere strapped to her hip.

"I'm not taking you from *Staventa*. I'm taking you from the Adder. Speaking of." He sweeps a webbed hand and it comes up laced in those gold threads, their light playing off the subtle sheen of scales on his cheeks. "We need to talk, if she dares show her pretty porcelain face."

He tugs on the threads. Rho feels it like they're tied to her spine, and one goes taut.

He kicks off and swims to the peak of the temple.

"Wait!" Rho screams. "What do you need me for!?"

He slips out a panel in the ceiling and is gone. Standing beneath the towering ceiling and piles of offerings, Rho realizes her smallness, the way Eirjatal must have in the Ineiren Fort. She's a pawn. She's in the way.

They're telling her nothing.

But at least they left her alone.

She heads right for that dragon.

It's high up, but it's easy enough to climb a nearby pile of offerings. Inside the sea dragon's mouth are three knives, even longer than the polished fangs. They're beautiful, reflecting the swimming light with their own rainbows. The hilts are encrusted with multi-coloured jewels that twist into a mosaic of a wave.

And bizarrely, one's blade is rough with frost, the other with leaves, and the other with melting, shimmering words she can't read.

She should know better than to mess around in a world she doesn't understand. But her magic is drawn to them the same way they sensed the purity of Staventa's swords. These are pure power—all the human offerings seem filthy to her magic in comparison.

Careful to keep one of the rings of the sphere in a fist, Rho unwinds the gold from around her waist, turning it pliant once more. She draws it back like a whip and snaps it around the—well, first, around the fangs, but on her second try, she gets it fused around the three blades, anchored on hilts shaped like fluttery fins.

It takes a few yanks. She's even off the floor completely at a point, using all her body weight to pull, and then they jostle. The frost-covered one, bearing the full brunt of her weight, starts to slide free—

A force like a steam train throws Rho clear across the temple.

Her vision whites out. She's frantically blinking, stomach flipping with the fear of having lost her vision—when she realizes the room is so full of light that there's nothing but white to see. The shadows pull in, defining the storm of floating offerings and a male silhouette. Thick, snowy gales and clouds form and reform around him.

The dagger's slid across the floor to her. Rho lunges for it and doesn't yet lock it into her belt, just in case.

With black claws of ice, he wrenches out the two remaining daggers.

Rho shields her face from two more tornadoes of force, one full of music, one shaking the floor with wildly-growing sunflowers as big as Staventa's hands.

They all blast through the walls. Madainn's treasures cascade from shelves and piles and displays, the floor splits, the rubble caves in, the stained glass explodes with a sound like a scream. Keeping a tight hold on the sphere, Rho claws the gold whip into a thin shield over her head, but it's *gold*—it bends, as useless as paper within the collapsing temple.

The floor gives way beneath her.

The universe shutters open and closed around her—a black void, the golden atrium, a mountainside, a temple full of bowing worshipers, a tunnel packed with insects, a skyscape.

She falls into nothingness, fast and small as a pebble, twisting and clawing for anything that passes her like it'll break her fall.

A net, a cloud, a tree, come on, come on! Exist! Appear! Anything but ground or—

Rho's heart nearly flies out her throat as something wraps around her middle and swings her in the opposite direction of her death plummet.

Everything stops. She's in a nest of soft, satiny sunflowers and velvet-covered vines. And there's a goddess peering right into her face.

She's enormous like Staventa, but even so, Rho can tell this goddess is squat in stature, plump and soft. Her mossy hair spirals out in the shape of an unopened tulip bulb and the eyes fixed on Rho's are cotton candy pink.

Pique. The goddess of—

A crystal scythe plummets from the sky and nearly takes Pique's head with it, except she dodges by devolving into a mass of roots. Reforming, she cries, "Ilharel!"

Up above, a sheet of ice appears right before being pummeled by stained glass and crystal, gems and jewels, the sea dragon carcass and hunks of temple. The ocean turns into sharp splashes of ice. The first god Rho freed swoops to Pique's level. His face is obscured by an elk's skull mask and his silhouette flares out in curls of snow and shadow.

Rho's seen so many gods by now, but her heart still hammers from pure instinct. She blurts, "Thank you?"

"Thank *you*, little caterpillar." Pique's voice is high and gentle. Her eye still squirms with roots.

"That's Relyn's! How did she get here?" another voice joins in. This one's source, she can't find.

Ilharel says, "Perhaps for the same reason Madainn sealed us."

"Why seal *us*?" Pique asks. "We're an unlikely trio."

"Oh, I think I know." Even with the mask, Rho can tell that Ilharel's countenance has darkened. "I caught him taking a Chalice piece from the Glasswood."

"I saw him uprooting something in the Dvrasken Dawnfront, but didn't catch what it was…could it really be a…" Her cheeks pink.

"And as for me, he must've known I'd spread the word!" the disembodied voice drawls. It gets very close to Rho, and when she turns in the pile of greenery, she's facing Eirjatal.

Almost-Eirjatal. Enough-Eirjatal to make her both want to backpedal off this platform and for her heart to kick with hope.

Not-Eirjatal touches his lapel, his horns. "Someone important to you?"

"Oh, don't tease the thing, Mythmaker!" Pique sighs. "However she got here, she freed us, so let's try to free her."

Not-Eirjatal holds out his hand to her. Rho stares at it, mute, then she takes it—what does she have to lose?

"Wait," she says. "What Madainn's hunting for. Do you know where they are?"

Pique shakes her head. "They were all very well-hidden. Why?"

Because how can there be one in Dianthus? How can there be one in the Glasswood? Unless it's a cruel prank the Carrion Queen pulled on the Fey.

And if Madainn doesn't know yet if there *is* one in Dianthus, how was Scintia so sure that he'd be looking there?

Not these gods' business. Rho doesn't want to give away more about Cypress to the Woven than she has to.

"You need to put me back where you found me," she says instead.

"That temple's gone, love." The Mythmaker turns her hand over. His voice is exactly Eirjatal's, all the warm edges and even the jolt in his Etren accent. "And why should we—" He quirks an auburn eyebrow. "Well, well."

"What?" Rho stiffens.

"She's the Adder's. She's dead."

"I'm not dead!"

"Pretty much. They pumped you full of Adder magic, girl." The Mythmaker sweeps his hand and it comes up draped in those golden threads, all tethered to different spots on her and fading into the dark, like marionette strings meant to control her heart and lungs, not her limbs.

Ilharel scoffs. "Then there's nothing we can do. This is the Adder's business. Let us find Madainn—"

The sea god's voice booms, "And do what? You've already torn down my temple."

The Mythmaker groans. "You'd swear he does it on purpose."

At that, Pique unravels into a tornado of vines, a tempest of greenery. Ilharel is a thousand icy blades shooting towards Madainn. The Mythmaker has vanished.

Rho does the only thing she can think of to draw Madainn's attention back to her.

She jumps into the abyss.

37

Irving

It is our way and it is again my time, my love. We serve and we fade. I am unique in that I have things that can fade from me.
Please do not think of it as Her taking everything away from me. She is trying to give me too much but I am mortal and frail.
She will let me come back.
Would you take Irving into Etreal until I return?

Sigyn to Penelope Whitfore, letter, Age of Shields 238

Sigyn turns to Irving a second before the others.

They freeze a few steps away from him, heart still jumping like when Khidell turned on them. That's the unchanging, unwavering Sigyn they know. Somehow he seems as unfamiliar as the young male in the evocation.

"I have to talk to you," they say.

Surprise is shallow on his face.

Eirjatal's pulled them in by the sleeve. "Were you in that portal? Where did you—Fey watching, what happened to you?"

Eirjatal has always seemed one missing hour of sleep away from keeling over, and he looks especially bad now. Exactly like he was in that courtroom, fired up about getting Sigyn's half-human kid killed.

Revulsion washing over them, Irving wrenches out of Eirjatal's grip. Kinthe's backed up a step with the same preternatural stillness as Sigyn, but at least Irving can tell she's paying attention.

Eirjatal catches their arm again. This time his fingers are hot on their skin. "We can deal with this later."

"I'm not going to tell him about *that*," Irving says, realizing what's got Eirjatal up in arms. "This is about *my father*."

Kinthe exclaims, "Is that yours, Sigyn?"

Despite themselves, despite everything, still shame runs cold to Irving's toes. They wriggle free from Eirjatal and fall back, as Sigyn answers without looking at Kinthe, "Yes."

"How old is it? You were keeping this for how long?"

Eirjatal snaps, "This is not the time."

"We've only just lost Scintia, to add to all the other lost rulers and Moonwardens. I want to know *now* if we're about to lose another."

Vyriseh trapped Khidell. Ashvaren killed Spring's ruler, whoever that was. And Sigyn left Heatherwol without one for years. So maybe it's Cypress causing all of Cypress's problems.

They bite that back. However, what does spill out is a lot more caustic and childish, something that's been rolling in them for years. "I'm not an *it*, and fuck if I care if you lose him as a Moonwarden."

Kinthe lifts a hand to Eirjatal as if to block him, stepping closer to Irving. "His child or not, you're still—"

"A thief. A liar. I don't care. Sigyn, I'm here because I've been selling off Heartswain to humans."

"That is—"

"Kinthe, Eirjatal."

Sigyn's voice is a cold, sharp knife. His unwavering gaze pins down Irving.

"We will discuss this morning's events with the nobility. For now, give us privacy."

That's apparently good enough for the obedience Sigyn bred into everyone, though Irving can tell neither are happy about it.

Soon it's only Sigyn and Irving on the pathway. Like their last conversation before Irving was arrested, they're blocked in by flowers and the humid Dianthus air. This time Irving feels like they see Sigyn even less.

They wanted clarity from that evocation. They left it even foggier.

He's barely changed since the evocation—since the massacre—except the hollowness, one Irving recognized in Khidell.

In time he's going to forget about you, too, and it won't matter.

"Would Vyriseh have a reason to lie about you and Esme?"

Sigyn holds his breath. It's nearly impossible to notice, like hearing when the ticking of a clock stops: a deafening silence where you didn't think more silence was possible.

And he says quietly, "No. Not to you."

"Would you have ever told me?"

"If you were going to live as long as I did. Yes, I would have. But I can't explain it to you like this."

Like this, as if dying like a human is a bad mood they're making him endure. "It was two centuries ago, so I'll never get it, right?"

"You are young—"

"You were the same age as me."

For half a second, panic flits over his face. "I do not remember it well. Though there was an unbelievable hatred in me, Irving. I had lost my first child to fear. I was going to lose the woman I loved for the same reason. And I would soon lose myself to a goddess who justified all of them in hurting me."

They say quietly, "Vyriseh said you saved who you could."

"Did I? I know that I ran. Esme and I stayed in Kava with her cult. I should not have helped her. I am..." He draws back further, somehow by barely moving. "I am so sorry I hurt you. But I am glad you can recognize the hurt others do to you better than I could."

He's talking. He's explaining things, which should be what they wanted, and yet some part of them wants him to stop instead. "Why did you come back?"

"My connection to the Fey faded in Etreal, so I thought it belonged to someone else and she had, rightly, judged me unworthy. I do not think I was sorry. I do not think I was unhurt. I think I returned to do something worse."

"What's *worse*?"

"I do not remember, because when I returned, the power was waiting for me. And it..."

He doesn't have his mechanical arm, looking somehow off-balance, too mortal. As he speaks, there are flashes of feeling, like some emotion's trying to break through. Their whole life, he's never yelled at them, never scolded them; all his love is carefully balanced, and even the first time he saw them after he got the Blind Adder to save their life, his sympathy was remote, like he'd forgotten to practice.

"The transfer of the Fey's magic is not discussed much with the public. It is terrible. She is aware it is terrible. I forgot everything that happened to me. I forgot Esme and my child. I knew the war and my involvement, but not what I did, precisely. I knew my dearest friend in Cypress loathed me and I had betrayed him but I did not remember who that was. I felt as if I never existed, and was instead made of broken pieces from all the realms and times the Fey existed in."

"You remember now, though."

"It returned in pieces," he murmurs, reminding Irving of the Chalice tucked dangerously in their pocket. "I could choose what I wanted to keep or discard. I am still unsure if the pain of that night is something I feel, or something I only learned."

"Does mom know?"

"Which part?"

"All of it. Any of it."

"It was my telling and not Vyriseh's, so she may have understood it differently. But she knows. It was only fair."

Irving pushes their glasses onto their forehead, pressing their sleeves into their eyes. All this explains everything and absolutely nothing at the same time. And a frustrated part of them doesn't even want it.

Sigyn says, "Regardless of what this battle tries to make of me, I choose to strive to know love, and light, and power, and nothing that will let me harm another again."

"Battle?"

"If you know all this from Vyriseh, then I know what else you want to ask me."

"You could explain without me begging for once. It's what you warned me about, that night in the gardens. You warned me about you."

Sigyn faintly smiles. Irving wonders if he knows that he didn't recollect all of himself after all. "You do not have much reason to trust me anymore. But trust that it is my nature to serve the Fey."

"I picked that up."

"Vyriseh and I were once in agreement. We wanted to build a realm where She could be safe for once. Maybe we would not be able to join Her, but that was not of consequence. I quickly learned how foolish it was. To find one fragment of Karadenza's Chalice risked the Woven competing and collapsing Etreal. I also feared Karadenza catching on, as if she did, Karadenza would crush the Fey."

"Then why are you even trying?"

"My only weapon is keeping ahead of Vyriseh and knowing what she is doing. She has always trusted me." His grey eyes search Irving's. "I'll admit to you now what I was too scared to say before. After two centuries of this, it is difficult to remember that I am mortal still. I cannot ask gods to help my goddess, as if I have sway at that table. Vyriseh often tries to make me forget that. So I remember the mortal damage she has done to me, and I remember my very, very mortal family."

"Mortal damage?" Sigyn looks uncertain how to explain, but Irving jumps ahead to the biggest question they've always had, but now it seems so pathetic and small. "She's got something to do with what happened to your arm."

"She nearly had the Chalice fixed, and I stopped her." He recites like he's reading it off the back of a book, "She enchanted me to cut my arm off as a warning, and I did."

"And you're *still* working with her?" They run their hands through their hair. They don't expect the burn of sympathy that hits them. "Shit, never mind. She's done other damage. I went to the tower."

Sigyn's eyebrows draw together. "Alone?"

"Yeah. And Khidell is still alive."

"She must have bargained him for Esme's tower or Chalice fragment in the first place."

"There were dead humans." They nearly add there's a damned human priestess in the palace now, stealing the very evocations that led Irving to the first fragment. "Khidell killed himself to stop Vyriseh from using him later on, whatever that means. He implied she was going to do what you said—make you forget who you were. Do you still feel a step ahead of her?"

He doesn't answer.

Plotting and planning, the fucking Fey, always the fucking Nelaeryn Fey. They feel a touch unsteady, the anger making them tired rather than righteous.

"I don't know why I'm asking. I don't know who you are. I believe that to you, that massacre was a really long time ago, and I really want to believe you did all you could. But you still knew that all happened when you brought mom to Cypress. You could have lost me the same way."

Sigyn breathes out slowly. "Irving, I think I already have."

You haven't, not yet. "And now what? I'm screwed. I'm always told I need to pick a side but if neither wants me, then I don't want them, but I guess I better pick quickly if they all start fighting, and I want—I want to belong to something." This is ridiculous. They're supposed to be arguing with him about easy things. "Vyriseh's already killed people and those are just the ones I found. You don't get credit for the moral high ground. You don't get credit for telling mom and I to come to Cypress and wait out you deciding what you want to save. I didn't tell her, by the way."

Sigyn looks up.

"I never got home."

Sigyn approaches. Irving inches back a step and is glad for the distance of Sigyn's expressions because they don't want to bother seeing the hurt.

The fragment presses, accusing, against their side. They have no idea what to do with it. They have no idea what they're doing in general. Saving Johana and Noah is their only goal. Saving their father is too much.

Sigyn says, "I do not know my own parents. I know the shape of the bloodline but I do not know them. It was my choice. It is always a choice in Cypress."

He doesn't even say it in a pitying way. Just pragmatic, thin, like it's a mildly interesting fact he read in a book, only self-conscious that Irving won't find it half as interesting.

"I can't do that."

"I suppose that Etreal's custom—"

"Not because of Etreal or Cypress. I can't because you're my father. That's it." They swallow. They need to get out of here, away from the feeling threatening to take them over again. "You're not a Moonwarden or a god or mortal or anything else when you're dealing with me. But you do have a say in what happens."

Irving finds themselves in Dianthus proper. Even if they've got bigger issues than Johana, they know they're being a serious asshole. But they feel like they can't find solid ground.

There's always drink to get somewhere, so they snag a glass from an ostentatious fountain, the surface crowded with petals and pollen. They wander. They should find it worrying that all they want to do is move—all they've wanted to do since they were first arrested here is move. Since they left Cypress, even.

The city is weirdly quiet. It isn't that late, and it's not like that matters to the revelers anyways. Irving doesn't know if it's because they were chased by an echo and saw a male kill himself in the last hour, but there's a taut current of tension that feeds through the streets.

There's no music, they realize. There's no food, no laughter in the streets. It's like everyone is packing up. The people still wandering don't seem the same; they're too careful of keeping their voices down.

They spot Envai. She's sitting on a low fence around a topiary garden, showing some distinctly annoyed Summer elves some card tricks to distract them as they pack up their wagon. Envai meets Irving's eye, hands one of the elves a card for keeps, and then trots up to them.

She gets within a few steps and her expression folds into something trickier. It's like how the people at the theatre pretend to step into the role of a flirtatious rake. Irving thinks of telling her about the corpses in Vyriseh's tower.

She speaks before they can measure the pros and cons of another grim topic. "I didn't expect you. With your hair down, no less. Looking...playfully mussed, let's say. Long day?"

They give a noncommittal shrug and take too big of a swallow. They still can't handle it any better than they could on the balcony with Noah, and Envai laughs at them wrinkling up their nose at the bubbles. They can hardly drink soda. "I needed air."

"Well, good, because I need a friend." Envai toys with the cards in her hands. They're custom painted, the higher cards depicting old mythic heroes and monsters.

Irving picks one without her offering. They flip it. It's the towering, teetering monster that took down the Ineiren Fort way back when. Its many segmented limbs remind them of the echo, scrambling in the hall like a giant spider.

"Oh, that's no good," Envai says, peering at the card. Her hair smells like metal, like her booth was near the Heatherwol inventors today. "It means everything's about to flip on its head."

"These are playing cards, not oracle cards."

"And? That motherfucker means the same thing in cards or dreams or tea dregs. It could also mean you're like Madainn. Flirting with what you shouldn't."

They hand it back. Someone near them chuckles, a high nervous sound that Irving suddenly realizes sounds deafening. The street has drained like a wound. It's only them, the scraps of stalls, closed shutters, and the people not dressed for the weather.

Robes, they realize.

Robes and gold. Tokens.

Envai grabs their wrist. They're whirling to follow the path of the laughing person, but Envai pulls them to a halt.

She points. The sky is reddening. Not a natural dawn or dusk red from Eojhest, but a furious spill of curling carmine, zapping from scrap of cloud to scrap of cloud. The sky's setting on fire.

"For once," she whispers, "a good reason to smell human."

The Iron Phoenix has arrived in Dianthus.

38

Rhoheme

The instant Madainn catches Rho, she's right back in the temple where she started.

She leaps to her feet. "This was just—"

"Destroyed?" Madainn sighs, bubbles frothing around his mouth. "This temple's come with me from another universe, sweetheart. It'll take a lot more than my colleagues' tantrums to ruin it."

So she freed a few angry gods for nothing? At least she has one of the daggers that sealed them, tucked under her makeshift belt and concealed by the draping fabric. "Did you find the Adder?"

"No. You know, I shouldn't be surprised. The Adder loves to think she's above meddling, but what else would I call *this*? You, here, and her sneaking around about it? She pretends in front of Karadenza all the time."

"If you explain this, maybe I can help."

Keenly regarding her, he laces his fingers; they fade from a greenish pallor to black fingertips. He bends them behind his head. "Should we sit?

Let's sit."

The temple spins on an axis, and Rho's thrown with floaty gravity onto a divan. She snags the edge of it. Madainn, up above and close enough for her eye line to run up his legs, reclines on the decorated foot of a throne made of uncountable junk.

"Why did she bring *you*? What do you know?"

She wants to retort that all she did was get bit by a siren, but Staventa's accusation pricks her. She's the only Blind Adder patient in this dizzying realm.

Rho retorts, "I don't even know what this is about."

Madainn hits her with the full force of an eye roll. "Little Fey, it's about finding Karadenza's lost bits of power."

"You're going to have to explain more. I've never left Cypress."

"Chalice? You know. Slivers of her magic that the Carrion Queen stole and hid for laughs? You find 'em all, you make a world. We all want out from under her shadow."

"That's what you found in the Glasswood," Rho says carefully.

"Where?" He scrunches up his flat, slit-nostril nose. "Oh. The sapphire eye."

The offerings behind him clatter with something else spontaneously hitting the pile. He catches it: a little diadem plastered with emeralds. Her skin prickles, magic intrigued by its attributes.

"They were made dormant when they were hidden, so the hunt's easier if you have mortals to do it for you. Even mortal monsters, if that's your style. You creatures have games like this, you know—little wooden pieces hopping around a board, and even if you need the little pieces to play, you don't need them all to win? That's what this is like. Mortals are the pieces."

Rumours and whimsy and bedtime stories for gods.

Rho says, "Whatever you're doing, Staventa thinks Karadenza's going to end the world for it."

"Why do you all think I want the world destroyed?" Madainn snaps, turning the diadem into a cloud of bubbles. "I *like* this one. I had to fight to get what I wanted at the start of it, but now it's exactly my style, and I'm not about to throw that all away. I want to get these pieces *quietly.* That's why I shut those gods up by sealing parts of them. But apparently someone wants it to be even quieter, because she chose *you,* and Karadenza can't see *you.*"

While the Blind Adder and Staventa moved like unreal things, the Adder too slow and Staventa too sure, Madainn moves like a mortal. It sets Rho on edge. His tone rises and falls and loops as he speaks, and he's throwing her punctuated grins like he's riling up the crowd and she's the prettiest face.

"What do you mean, she can't see me?"

"Your Fey can't see us, and Karadenza can't see her." Is this why Moonwardens have blind spots related to the Woven? "You're so much like her that Karadenza can't sniff you out easily either."

Rainbow fish swim above his head, and he plucks a set of rings from their ranks.

"Having you would break the Carrion Queen's rules, bless her. You're a *tool*, not a real player. You can't claim anything for us like a priestess or a monster could." He flicks the rings one by one overhead, back to the fish. He stands and circles the pile of offerings.

When he's concealed, Rho lets herself release a shuddering breath—and a faceful of bubbles.

"But the Adder kept you for a reason. Those fragments will enhance your magic even more than being untethered, but that can't be all—you're hardly trained. You're close. You've *got* to be close. You've got to know where the next piece is hiding." He asks, cheerily flippant, "Where is it you said you were from?"

39

Irving

Attempts by new-age worshipers to re-characterize the Iron Phoenix as something more charitable (beginnings, breaking from hostile relationships, regrowth, to name a few) have been met with refusals by the goddess herself. She sees herself as chaos and ruination only, and this modest theologian believes we owe her the title she wants.

Mythos, published Age of Illumination 16

Envai pulls Irving down the street by the wrist, flanking the thin stream of robed elves. They think of how Sigyn tried to stop them—did he get a vision?

The Woven burn a huge blindspot in Moonwarden prophecies. The visions also waver depending on what decisions the subjects make; they can't predict anything accidental or random.

Not like it matters now.

The city is streaked with carmine. All the dampness in the air has burned off, making Irving's lungs ache. Windows open and shut, the sound rattling down the whole street; elves are setting out charms.

"Let's get to the Dawn Hall," Irving says. It's the only shelter they can think of. Did Sigyn make it back?

"They'll have shut it down already. I want you to see this. Elves love her. Isn't that weird? They just want to feel safe."

They certainly don't. Not with these damn fragments in their pocket.

They've done a lot of stupid shit lately—well, their whole life—but stealing those could, if this all goes sideways, be the worst.

More robed elves pass, with the odd gold glint. Which of those are trinkets that Irving brought in over the years?

The two of them spill into a main pavilion, where Envai's booth used to be set up. The red up above is going solid, making the sky seem like it's pressing down; the heat crashing up against Dianthus's cool night air is fogging up Irving's glasses. Envai's biting her lip but failing to quash the smile.

Irritation sparking, they whisper, "I know why you want the evocations. They lead to Karadenza's Chalice, or at least start you on the right path."

"Right you are. How'd you put it together?" She asks it like they're setting up a joke.

"I saw inside one. People have already died for this, you know. Are you guys really starting something so dangerous for a stupid myth?"

Ignoring them, she whistles, the sound shuddering in the dead-quiet street. "Five stories from five different Cypress rulers. Five pieces in a puzzle they didn't realize they were making. Isn't that twisted? Etreal's been looking for centuries. And the place with clues is *Cypress*."

Noah said that Ashvaren saw them all, then locked them up and stopped anyone else from trying. Are the other four as clear as the one they saw, or is Vyriseh the only one who knows enough about the myth to give Scintia the key details?

Envai yanks them into the shadow of a gazebo, half-hidden behind greenery. They're pressed so closely that they can feel her heartbeat against the arm she's holding.

The sky splits. Light, dense and slow like lava, pours into the shape of a giant woman's torso and head, reclining on her stomach and bisected by a wall of fire that cuts off the pavilion from the rest of the street. Her shoulders are higher than the roofs, and her flaming hair crackles around a headdress of black rock, all of it reaching up into the gathering, glowing clouds.

The Iron Phoenix folds her hands beneath her chin. Her face is so bright that it's nearly impossible to take in, but Irving feels like they have to fight for it. Witnessing her is both too terrifying and too incredible to miss the chance. She's smiling. They know that much. This close to her, it's something they feel rather than see.

Irving's spoken to the Blind Adder before. They've lived with a fraction of the Nelaeryn Fey. Staventa's workhorse, Suvor, can be spotted during winter as he carries her supplies into the mountains. But this—

Envai points at the corner of the street. More hooded elves are filing in, and these carry a palanquin of objects that throw around the Phoenix's light. Now the pavilion has twenty, thirty elves in it. No one speaks. No one's even close to each other.

Irving asks, "What do they expect from her?"

She whispers with her mouth on their ear, breath cool compared to the air, "The Fey's going to lose and they know it. They want something to save them."

The Woven don't seem to care much about particular humans unless they're some outstanding warrior or artist or thinker. But as the Phoenix daintily picks over the offerings, she's paying more attention to the elves themselves, like they're the real riches.

And the elves know it. They remove their hoods, some even taking off masks.

Ash and embers rain off the Phoenix's eyelashes as she focuses on one figure. Irving is too far to see what might have piqued her interest. Her intent shifts; Irving's flooded with the instinct to *run*.

A droplet of flame drips off her fingertip and into the waiting hands of the elf. They hold it without trouble, only a firm, squared-shoulders intensity. Then—because it's burned itself into their memory—Irving can tell immediately when the elf stabs themselves with whatever they were handed.

Envai watches through her fingers. The elf drops to their knees before the goddess. Head rolling back, arms falling limp to graze the glowing street. A thick, oily black smoke pours out of them. It curls before the Fey in calligraphy tendrils.

"Archfey's echo," Irving whispers.

"No," Envai replies. "Worse."

The smoke takes shape—a shape that steps out of the body, leaving it behind like shrugging off an old coat. It's the same size as the elf it left behind, naked and made of fire. It flickers from an elf to a floating fireball, unsteady in both forms, but with an encouraging little touch from its goddess, it firms up into its humanoid form. Four flaming wings rip out of its back.

Envai says, "Azfell."

The Phoenix reaches for another elf, this time using her dagger-point fingernail to shred them open. Then another, another, bodies hitting the stone and blooming open around the smoke crawling out of them.

When the Phoenix sets her chin back on her hand, all of their wings flare, and Envai yanks Irving back. "*Now* we run."

Fire roars up the street, ripping through the greenery they're standing in. The air churns with the Azfell taking flight, like fireworks shooting into the red sky.

Irving's vision is streaked and stained by all the light. They turn, expecting the buildings to be razed, but besides the shimmer of heat coming off their metal gates, they're unhurt. They spot what people were setting out.

Enchantments—little baubles of glass like Kinthe's scrying tools, on doorways and in windows. The waves of fire divert like streams or entirely fizzle out when they get too near.

A Moonwarden can cut any sorcery by touching it. Kinthe—and maybe other Moonwardens—must have infused these ages ago. Just in case.

Still, anything unprotected goes up in flames. Irving and Envai keep as close to the enchantments as possible, but the smoke fills Irving's lungs. Azfell wheel past them, sometimes on wings, sometimes as streaks of fire.

They catch their breath between two shops. Envai's grinning, but it's shivering. Sweat mats her Heartswain-red hair to her neck and face. They should get into one of these buildings—maybe there's a temple nearby. They try to peer around a corner to assess the burning street, squinting against all the light, but a violent yelp wrenches their attention up the road.

It's that massive lizard creature they first saw with Noah at the tracks, closing its jaws around an Azfell. It throws her in their direction, forcing Irving to duck back into the alley, but the creature's next attack ends with a burn to the face.

Discordant music starts up. A fountain statue twists to life, enclosing an Azfell as he tries to fly by. Glass traps the Azfell like nets when they get too close, bursting holes through their magical forms and choking out their fire. And still doors blast open, elves scream, and the air fills with thick smoke.

The Iron Phoenix lays in the road, immense as a tower, enjoying her chaos.

A lifetime of Cypress paranoia races through Irving and coalesces into one certainty. If there's anything they want, it'll be to hurt the Fey. It'll be Sigyn.

They instantly lose Envai when they race into the mayhem, and find their father nearly as quickly. He's what a Moonwarden should never be, and yet looks exactly the way he's meant to. He's standing tall with glass in his fists, singes already on his sleeves, and when he finds Irving, he reaches out his bare hand.

No hesitation. No warmth. Only certainty.

Right now, Irving will take it.

Sigyn hands them a glass blade and touches the top of their head, pulling them close, the smoke and fire pressing in on them both.

40

Eirjatal

I didn't know Yrena well. She was politically spirited, but surely she knew martyring herself would be stupid. The rebellion had their pick of martyrs, and it would be counterproductive to choose the Woven-bound one.
I do know the rumour that my mother's brother is my own father, because Yrena wanted to keep our magic. As if the curse would be crushed by something as pathetic as a pureblood father.

Eirjatal, interview with Adamantine about Yrena Ga'vrynn, Age of Shields 232

Fire destroyed most of the Ga'vrynns.

They died in nightmares or in arguments, died in ecstasy or wondrous panic. On the grounds of the Dawn Hall, Yrena lit up like a pyre that ate through whatever protection the Iron Phoenix's magic grants them, boiling her within, blazing through her without. Reports said that her hair lifted like the blue core of a candle flame, dancing as she turned to ash long after the screaming died. Whether it was purposeful or accidental, spurned by her arrest and inevitable banishment, no one knew.

Vyriseh meets with Cereus, Kinthe, and Eirjatal at Rho's workroom, holding her high heels and hair tumbling out of her bun.

"You couldn't find Sigyn?" Cereus asks, voice pitchy with panic. Ringal winds between his feet, wings and ears pinned.

"He's likely still in the city," Kinthe says.

"And this group," Vyriseh interjects, panting, "is the last…that should run after him. He has survived…*this* long." She starts writing on the doorframe with a ballpoint pen. "I've hidden the…staff apartments and lent them a few of my spies. Adamantine, Tavreah, and the others have the Hawks in the…third floor parlour."

She looks at Cereus. And then deliberately shifts her gaze to Eirjatal instead.

"How should *we* split?"

Eirjatal doesn't have the time to be caught off guard by her asking him. Besides, he thought it over when they were discussing Radiance's defences for the city. "Kinthe and I will stay here with Cereus. He's the only one who can't defend himself. Vyriseh, I entrust Rho and Johana to you."

"Lovely." She finishes her inscription and presses all four hands into the wall, whispering under her breath to infuse her spell. Right before her yellow eyes roll back in her head and she slumps.

Cereus catches her. Ringal paws her leg. Thankfully, after a few seconds, Vyriseh's eyes flutter open. She sucks a long inhale through her teeth and hisses, gripping the wall for balance, "This was…an ingenious idea, Eirjatal, really. But it's taking all I've got."

Cereus says, "Vyriseh, I owe you a life debt for this."

"You'd best stay alive…so I can cash that." She pats his shoulder and he hovers a hand behind her back. She returns to the spell.

The instant Kinthe had her premonition and the sky tinged orange, Eirjatal had asked if, with the twisting outer limits of her Mythmaker magic, she could conceal the rooms—make doors lead to nothing, hide the smell of blood and sound of voices, turn the Dawn Hall into enough of an illusion that if they were attacked, they could buy precious minutes.

Luckily, old defences still hold latent magic in the city from troubles passed, but if the Iron Phoenix means business at all, she will enter the Dawn Hall.

Cereus asks, "What is the goddess even coming for?"

"Responding to the call of her worshipers, most likely," Kinthe says. "Their movements are the only reason I saw this happening at all."

"So maybe she's collecting tithes."

"It's the Phoenix." Eirjatal is all too aware of the heat twitching in his veins. "She can't take without destroying."

Vyriseh swoons again, but not hard enough to prevent her from loudly cursing as the purple glow in her inscription gutters out.

At that, flame bursts from a lattice section of the ceiling. It races through the opposite wall, back out of the castle, leaving a crater of black behind.

Vyriseh groans, sounding as lightheaded as she looks, "Well. We've been breached."

Cereus squeezes her arm. "You can do it, Vyri. We'll watch your back."

Kinthe takes two knives made from her scrying glass from her belt. She'd fetched them while Vyriseh was hiding rooms and Eirjatal was collecting stray staff. She hands one to Cereus, who fumbles it.

Another streak of fire, this time so close that Eirjatal's magic senses it, like he can sense torchlight, bonfires, candles. It vanishes through the balcony door of the workroom and lands for a moment on the railing, barely long enough to coalesce into the shape of a humanoid creature with four wings that stretch the width of the room. She leaps into a ball of fire again, vanishing into the dawn.

Eirjatal snaps, "Go, Vyriseh."

"I'm trying!"

"Go protect Rho. Now." Every inch of him prickles with his magic's desperation to reach out for the fire. "Kinthe and I can handle this."

Cereus helps Vyriseh up the stairwell until she bats him off, leaving her shoes behind, and she disappears up the steps.

Eirjatal, Kinthe, and Cereus back into the workroom. It's far more spacious than the hallway. Cereus is white-knuckling the glass knife. Kinthe angles herself so Cereus is between her and Eirjatal; when Eirjatal catches her eye, she solemnly nods.

Cereus asks, "What was that thing?"

"I'm guessing an Azfell." Eirjatal scans the sky beyond the balcony, measuring his breath. The castle smells like sweltering metal.

Kinthe explains, "From the Age of Beasts. Human clerics to rival gods, transformed into her slaves."

"Elves," Eirjatal says. "That one was definitely an elf."

Cereus lets loose a shuddering half-laugh. When he looks at Eirjatal, red light draws patterns on his face. "We're okay. You've done this before."

As if the Ineiren Fort was a triumph.

The Azfell whirls out of the wall. She makes a grab for Eirjatal, but he pivots Cereus behind him and, with a gesture like ripping off a cloak, wrenches her fire away. She tumbles through the air, dim and almost elvish again. Cereus barely jolts out of the way before she kicks off the floor and rolls back into a fireball.

Kinthe lashes out with her dagger of glass; it cancels whatever spell keeps the Azfell together. Her leg turns solid, spraying ash like blood, but she still vanishes between Rho's display of tools.

Eirjatal's pulse pounds, deafening.

The sky is pure red. He feels pulled in a thousand different directions, all the fire calling for him.

And then he's pulled like a magnet to the floor under the worktable. He throws a hand out, sinking into the fire an instant before it appears, but still the Azfell crashes into the table, launching it towards them. He sends her fire right back out, burning the table into a cloud of ash. A simple cut across the phantom's midsection by Kinthe has her howling. The wings shred open, glowing along the tears like cracking lava rock. She hits the floor. A stream of burns sear behind her.

Eirjatal approaches her, both hands lifted. He can feel his sweaty hair sticking against his face, he knows the room is sweltering, but he's fully entrenched in her fire alone. He's holding it like glass he can shatter if he adds enough pressure.

She curls up on the floor. Shivering, seething. Eirjatal pulls back, like yanking out threads from a tapestry, until he's smothering tiny candle flames that desperately try to light themselves all over her body. She doesn't seem to know what to do, kicking and trembling like a confused animal on a tight leash. Black smoke pours off of her.

Did she pray for this? Is this why the Iron Phoenix came? Will the goddess report back to Madainn on all the holes of Dianthus?

Was it worth it?

Eirjatal holds a hand out blindly, the other still flicking in the air to stop her attempts to light up. "Cereus."

"What?"

"Give me a hammer."

The smoke burns his nose. Then he sees it's curling around his wrist, too solid, too controlled. He jerks away, but it's already covered his arm, and his vision fills with black as it pours, searing, into his mouth and nose.

Blood roars through his veins, nearly taking him off his feet. And his cursed blood sends fire erupting from his hands. It rages around him, and in seconds, the Azfell has stolen it and erupted into a fireball again.

She spreads like a swarm, completely uncontrolled. He can't pin down her magic versus his own. It's too oppressive, too much, like he's losing consciousness underwater, and his heart is seizing. The workshop rains with light.

And Kinthe says from behind him, very softly, "Nele. So you found me."

His reflexes understand that before his mind, but he's still too slow. He turns to see the Azfell, so nearly an elf again, swoop upon what was her Moonwarden, and burn a wide hole clear through her chest.

Cereus catches Kinthe. He slides to the floor. Kinthe's head falls back, and the Fey's light leaves after her own life does.

The room fills with fire, and Eirjatal cannot feel anything at all.

41

Irving

I wish I could explain more about what awaits you in Heatherwol and what is happening to me. You have made me appreciate that not knowing what is coming is a privilege, but this time, all I can sense is dread. From myself in the future to the past, or from myself now to the future. I miss you and need you in a way I cannot explain.

Letter from Sigyn to Penelope, Age of Shields 250

Sigyn collapses like someone's cut his strings.

Irving moves on instinct. They catch him against their shoulder and are nearly pulled down too, until they get a solid grip on him. He weighs nothing.

He's also not bleeding anywhere on those bright white robes.

Sigyn's head falls back, eyes sliding open. It's the look Irving saw in

Khidell, that draining away of light and presence.

His face empties, like snow covering up every footprint of his emotions.

"*Sigyn*," they snap, but don't get to say more.

A clawed fist closes on the back of their neck and throws Irving across the searing cobblestone. Their back crashes into the fountain wall. The pain explodes sense back in their head, and fear quickly with it. The impact scattered the glass knife and the two Chalice fragments across the stones.

They lunge for the closest fragment, narrowly missing the flaming feet that drop down before them.

One of them kicks Irving onto their back. It's a female Azfell. Somehow, even if corruption grew her wings and tapered her limbs into pure fire, she still has more elf in her than Khidell did as an echo, than Irving will.

"Half-blood," she sneers. "The Phoenix only wants the pure—"

Her flaming face brightens, going blue and white, as she spots the fragments. They're dim and dead, but maybe so close, the bit of the goddess in her knows their pull.

Scrambling to their knees, Irving makes another swipe on the cobblestones, but this time it's for the glass knife.

She sweeps up the fragments in her fiery hands and only clenches them tighter when Irving slashes the knife at her. Where it splits her thigh, she turns to ember, but it's not like Irving can grab her to snatch the pieces back.

She whirls on them. Fire consumes every one of their senses—blinding their eyes, choking their lungs, narrowing the chaos of the street to the crackle of flame. Wherever she's holding them, it doesn't matter. All of them is burning.

"Do you even know what you have? What god could *you* offer these to?" Her voice is a joyful shriek coming from every direction. So is the light.

It brightens, brightens, until it's white and ice cold through their eyelids. The Azfell screams.

They hit the ground. Scraps of embers and stone rain on them, searing. The Azfell is shattered into pieces in a heap, still faintly glowing. Relief gives Irving barely enough wherewithal to brush the embers off their skin before they whirl to find Sigyn.

He's back on his feet. White as a corona. And walking away.

Irving's struck with a sudden fear that he's got the fragments, but they find them in the pile of ash that was the Azfell.

Fear?

Watching him go, they realize why. He's moving through the chaos like Esme did, lofty and distant amongst her massacre.

"Sigyn. Sigyn!"

He glides into the madness of the Azfell. They spiral away from him like they're afraid, but Sigyn cuts through them, practically anticipating their patterns. The elves who were dragged into the street are too unashamed with relief to look away from him, and Irving scrambles to their feet at the border of this tableau: their father, High Priest, Moonwarden of two centuries, voice of Relyn, Nele, and the Archfey, heading straight for the Iron Phoenix.

"Sigyn!"

Irving stuffs the Chalice fragments into their pocket and sprint after him, but the smoke in their lungs drags them down. Their shouts dwindle out. They can only watch as their father and whatever's puppeteering him approach the goddess in the city square.

Blue light flushes her cheeks, and the edges of her grin flicker with endless rolling fire. She throws a few jets of fire his way and he's quick to dispatch them with the glass knife.

She slaps a hand on the ground, pushing herself up. A shockwave of heat cascades in a ring around it; Irving ducks behind a flipped vendor cart to avoid it, but Sigyn has, again, cut through it, continuing his path. She's toying with him. She must know who he is.

The longest-serving Moonwarden, though something's really wrong now, they think, right as the unnerving, musical voice of a goddess come to the earth sings, "Is this a new trick, Relyn?"

Despite all the heat, their blood goes icy.

Every Moonwarden is a fraction of their goddess, like human sorcerers. The Blind Adder wasn't alongside Irving, wasn't *in* Irving, but it was like they were a small, negotiable part of her, one strand of hair, one fragment of a nerve, enough for her to know if something was wrong. That's why Moonwardens forget. Why Sigyn could tell them all these strange, disjointed stories with the shadow-shapes of the Fey's old universe.

But Moonwardens aren't her. It isn't possession. It isn't…

The cart's on fire; they can feel it licking against their back, hear it crackling. The square's quiet except for the *whoosh* of the Phoenix's attacks, the last few Azfell whirling away, and the panicked calls for loved ones, too desperate to care about the goddess playing games in their midst.

Relyn.

Someone pushes Irving to their feet. Envai. There's a horrible burn on her shoulder, her clothes reduced to clinging ash. She steers them out of the square at a jolting run, and when they look over their shoulder, their father's silhouette is swallowed up by the Phoenix's overwhelming light.

42

Eirjatal

If you're bringing in Rhoheme, you may as well bring in Eirjatal. Find something for him. He'll follow Rho into the Amber Crawl. I know he wants to—he wants this kingdom, he wants Rho, he wants you—he wants it all under his watch.

Tavreah Ansett to the Cypress nobility, hiring interview, Age of Shields 245

Eirjatal feels himself, for the first time in a very long time, set completely on fire.

It's not like the usual slow, insistent heat that assures as it spreads under his skin. It's simply that he's cold with grief and fear, and then he's another being entirely, heartbeat outside his body, weightless, power striking so suddenly that he doesn't notice the flames coursing up his arms and face until they encompass him.

The Azfell launches herself into the hallway chandelier so it swings, raining diamonds and candles on the floor. She scrambles along the burning holes in the carpet, leaps, catches herself, and then she's tearing down the stairs.

She is half herself and half fire, twisting through the air like an otter, coalescing barely enough for him to see her thrilled and terrified smile. Her form flickers between splashes of fire and plumes of smoke and whatever pathetic, self-hating creature she was before she turned herself over.

Mirrors and glass frames explode around them from the heat; plants hanging in the lattice walls curl into ash; his realm of power expands as he sets parts of the hallway alight.

"Will you burn me?" she teases.

He's numb, swept along by instincts he can't name. He can't extinguish her, so he only swallows, ripping the fire from her like he's a wild animal digging into gore, flaying skin, breaking bones. Her magic tastes so much like his.

She's much more resilient than she was in the workroom. Maybe it's because she's frightened.

She kicks off the wall and whirls into a ball of flame, heading for the metal wall and the burning city beyond. He sends his magic out like a net, and it rips her down, but she slips through his fingers again.

Then the volcano of her goddess comes into clarity. Her head is in her hands like a girl smiling over a perfect arrangement of toys that she's ready to knock down.

He understands, with ringing clarity, how his mother was so furious that she burned herself alive.

The gates slam on their own. He burns through them without stopping. The melted metal sticks to his skin and smokes.

The ceiling buckles, like something's punched it from above; lattice unravels, scratching through his inferno and catching in his clothes, but he blows it aside. Gears rip out of their tracks in the walls, reaching out for him before withering inches from his skin.

He burns through everything Rhoheme puts down.

The Iron Phoenix looks up, like she's felt him. Her eyes are cold.

He hears his name.

But he's caught the Azfell; she spirals, falls, a candlelit female again in the staircase. She shakes, pathetic like in the workroom.

The gate at the top of the suspended stairwell slams shut. It breaks from its hinges and bends into him, like someone grabbing his arm and wrenching him back, like Rhoheme underwater, a desperate weight as he tried to swim through the bloody river to save them.

"Leave me," he snaps at Rho, burning through her.

He makes it a step. The stairwell crushes closed, like a ball of foil crumpled in a fist, trapping the Azfell inside it.

He can't take in the next breath.

His heartbeat slows, heavy in his chest.

The fire sucks back into his skin with an audible hiss—the pain comes too, making him scream through his teeth.

"Eirjatal?" It's Cereus, staggering to a stop a few feet behind him. His clothing is bloody. He stares at Eirjatal with nothing short of horror.

Eirjatal's skin is still hot enough to melt a track into the twisted metal as he slides down it to his knees. He can hardly keep himself up, can hardly breathe. *I'm fine. I'm fine.*

He must sit there long enough for the heat to dissipate, because when he comes back to himself, Cereus is delicately breaking thin metal off his shoulders. Eirjatal's leather sandals have melted to his feet and ankles, and his bracers with Cereus's sigil are slag, fused into his skin.

Cereus presses him close for a moment, and then he folds, forehead on Eirjatal's shoulder. Even after all of that, Cereus's tears are warm enough to sting.

The red light gutters out. Eirjatal looks out the lattice at the exact moment the silhouette of the Iron Phoenix is crushed like a candle flame by a net of greenery and a shining cage of ice.

"What on earth," Cereus breathes.

The sky clears, and dawn breaks through the smoke.

There are two gods before the Dawn Hall labyrinth gardens.

Pique masquerades as a heavyset, stout woman made of bark and roots and verdant leaves, and Ilharel as a tall, slender man beneath a cloak of shining black ice and an elk-skull mask. He's impassive; she's smiling.

Cereus, meanwhile, seems apt to vomit. Adamantine and Tavreah are heavily flanked by tense Hawks. So Vyriseh takes the lead.

She bows deeply. In Etren, she says, "We have no titles for you, no honours. Especially not anything that would reflect our thanks."

Pique dips her head back. Carnations grow from her temples, winding up to control her hair of moss and mushrooms. "I wouldn't ask you to slight your goddess like that. There are no words for what the Iron Phoenix has done. We are so sorry."

Words won't cut it, especially words from two of the Phoenix's fellow Woven.

Tavreah whispers to Eirjatal, "Why does this feel so…*awkward*?"

Pique's pink gaze lands on them. His chest tightens and every part of him wars on how to react, especially when she pokes Ilharel and points him out.

Especially when Ilharel nods Eirjatal over.

He doesn't budge, so Vyriseh gently pulls him by the arm. The walk to the gods seems to last forever, unhelped by his limp.

When he's close enough to see the shadows of Ilharel's face through the skull's eye, the god of snow and storms steps back. The labyrinth vanishes. They're standing on white ice, the air cold against his burns, completely alone.

"I know your face," Ilharel says.

"I survived a war in the lands you gave the Nelaeryn Fey."

"No. You were in this girl's mind." He flicks a clawed hand and between them, under the ice, is a sleeping Rho.

Unscarred, unscathed, strong again, the way he remembers her.

His hackles rise, but there's no magic to follow. "How do you know her?"

"Pique and I owed her a debt."

"A debt?" The fear bubbling up in him feels so pathetic without the promise of fire.

Ilharel peers at him under the mask. Then the skull disappears, revealing an earnest face that's pointed, stern, handsome, with iced-over eyes and a map of swimming blue veins. "She freed us."

Somehow this seems inherently true. He trusts Rho enough to believe it from even the Woven's mouth. "Where is she now?"

"The Adder is holding her tightly. Only a fragment of her freed us, like only a fragment of us needed to be freed. Protect her body, wherever it is." Ilharel replaces his mask. "She is strong enough to return to it, if she can find her way."

Rho has vanished, and in her place is a reflection of the labyrinth's greenery, growing brighter by the moment. Eirjatal says without thinking, "You reclaimed the Glasswood after the Age of Beasts, didn't you?"

Nodding, he removes the mask once more, and Eirjatal recognizes that as politeness.

"Madainn took something from there; a sapphire was all we knew it as." He's not so confident in this god that he'll say that Madainn might look in Dianthus next. "Why would Madainn want it?"

Ilharel watches him, eyes reminding him so much of Scintia's wide, fathomless stare. "What do you know of our Chalices?"

"I know of Madainn's. He uses it to capture ships in the Evertide and turn them into ghosts."

"Not Karadenza's? Not after all she's done to your Fey?"

"Madainn has done more to me personally."

"On the eve of this world's making, one of us broke Karadenza's Chalice into fragments and hid them all across the Tapestry. She does not know."

"And Madainn is looking for them."

"Madainn has *found* them."

And the next piece is in Dianthus. How did Scintia know that? Her magic is strange, but she's not prophetic; her Moonwarden sleeps like the other Winter elves.

But she did want him to destroy the evocations.

Sigyn can't know.

Ilharel says, "I tell you this only because that girl is dangerously close to this scheme, and there is some pity in me still for the small creatures. We do not play kindly."

A sting colder than the ice around them sinks into Eirjatal's bones.

"Now," Ilharel replaces the mask once more with a wave of his hand, and greenery fills the ice, air cloying and warm on Eirjatal's skin, "save this girl who loves you."

Eirjatal stands aside from the elaborate, enormous funeral in the pavilion before the Dawn Hall's gardens, eyes closed, feeling the warming air against his burns and listening to Sigyn speak.

The Moonwarden unceremoniously strode into the Dawn Hall while Cereus broke the news of all the death to the staff and the officials from other kingdoms. His robes were singed but otherwise he was entirely unharmed. His child was in the pack of staff, and Eirjatal was curious how they'd been split up, but Sigyn didn't react at all to Whitfore's unyielding stare.

Then Eirjatal had stood before Sigyn in this funeral, accepting his prayers, his promises, and knew this was not Sigyn.

"Do you remember," Eirjatal had whispered, feet away from the rest of the city, the air smelling of the Iron Phoenix's smoke, "the last time we spoke before the Fey took your memories?"

The grey of his eyes was so pale that it gleamed frosty white.

"Would you like me to fill in what you begged me to tell you last night?" He inched closer. Sigyn didn't flinch, those cold eyes tracking him down the line of his long nose. "It was after I killed your infant. You clamped a hand over my mouth and dragged me into some unused, reeking room. I heard the palace dying around me. And I thought, *there it is again*—" He exhales a single, dry beat of a laugh. "The feeling that being so afraid didn't seem real.

"And you whispered to me, *It would have happened without you. But I wish it wasn't you.*"

By then, the vengeance he'd felt about getting rid of that half-blood was already dead in him. It had seemed like Sigyn had abandoned him to Madainn, so he'd let Cypress abandon Sigyn in turn. But he was pulling everyone under with him.

I want my daughter back, Eirjatal. I want it all back. Though you will lose so much more. This is only the start of it. Archfey, know I love him.

Eirjatal had managed, *You sound like you think you'll die.*

"Do you know me at all?" he hissed, control over his voice slipping. "Are you there? Have you ever been?"

He shoved Sigyn's chest. The emptiness was infuriating, but it bolstered him; he couldn't have handled any shattering in the true Sigyn's face.

"Where are you?"

Fury that had dulled since the Iron Phoenix roared in his ears.

"Where *were you*?"

Tavreah dragged him away before it could escalate. Now, he listens to the rest of the funerary rites, but it's all so hollow. He has never felt further away from Her than now.

At least the Phoenix could prove she had the power to protect them.

Tavreah did a circuit of the temples, even the ones outside of the city, and came back with the news that no elves had manifested the Moonwarden's power. Elves had been showing flickers of it for years, as is typical, and had been folded into temples for training, but the full power had gone to no one.

Tavreah agreed with what Adamantine, Vyriseh, and the other inner circle elves guessed. The power had gone to Sigyn.

Now, Cereus comes to Eirjatal's side. His good looks are worn by grief, and he thumbs away stray tears.

They stand in silence for a while, watching the mass crowd in mourning. Eirjatal lets Cereus take his hand and sets it against his chest.

Finally, Cereus asks, "What are you going to do with the Blind Adder priestess?"

While they were in the Crystal Gardens, Johana was connected with the theft of the evocations. Of course—she was stolen from Ventaris, so why not return the favour? He doesn't know the exact terms of the deal Vyriseh made with that temple to take her. Perhaps Vyriseh used her sorcery to force them to give up Johana. Brute force seems to be the only way to get a leg up on Etreal.

"She'll die," Eirjatal says. "But I'll tell her she's fine, or else she'll withhold Rho."

Does Ventaris know what's in the evocations?

Cereus presses the heel of his hand to his eye before saying, "Can we...talk privately for a second?"

Eirjatal gives him a nod to go ahead. Cereus instead leads him deep into the ivy. He keeps looking over his shoulder until they're at the base of the gold tower in the middle of the labyrinth. The tower's made for grand proclamations, for the best views, and it was the pedestal Ashvaren was shot off five years ago.

"Sorry." Cereus leans against a pillar carved with bird wings. "I didn't want the Fey to listen for a moment."

Eirjatal has a headache, like his mind was scoured by all the fire. Still, he firmly wraps his arms around his king. Against all odds, something strung tight in Eirjatal releases when Cereus hugs him back. He feels so fantastically real when held against him, Cereus warm and strong, his hair soft against the burns in Eirjatal's wrists when he cards his fingers through it.

Eirjatal remembers Cereus in his first couple years on the throne, unashamed and unfrightened when facing down a kingdom that in turn feared him, put all their hopes into him, and hated him. For weeks, he went to elves' homes, leaving his guards on the stoops, to listen.

These are times for blood, and Cereus isn't made for them.

Yet Dianthus needs him. Eirjatal needs him; he can barely let him go.

Cereus is the one who manages it, then heaves a sigh. "I don't know what to do about any of this."

"You'll figure it out. You're good for this kingdom."

"Am I? They're terrified. We're all terrified and always have been. This is the kind of thing that drove Ashvaren to…to what he was."

Eirjatal braces a hand on Cereus's chest and says, "You are nothing like him," as Cereus interrupts, "I know why he died."

"We all do. He was a tyrant."

"I don't mean the motive. I mean why someone would betray the Fey like that."

Dianthus must have something in the water that makes elves doom themselves for a future they'll never see. Eirjatal nearly did it himself.

Cereus shoots a furtive glance behind them. "There was a…group that I was invited to join. The plan wasn't to kill him ourselves—it never was, we wouldn't hurt the Fey like that. But they were working to make the right conditions so when he was ousted—properly—there wouldn't be a spot for his supporters to hop back into."

If they were close enough to manage that, then these weren't vigilantes.

"Everyone was wondering back then how he could get away with all he did and not have Relyn turn on him. There was no way he was playing fair with Her. He was hiding something, somehow. Even with Kinthe around.

"One of us devised something. A ritual? It would..." He flexes his hands, looking for the right word. "Transpose, I guess, the weight of everything onto someone else. Make it real and visible in case he'd cloaked himself somehow. We'd make Relyn see and pass judgement on those sins, and then She'd see who they belonged to, and...do what She needed. It was never done before because we never *needed* to, and it looked really dangerous, so no one wanted to do it, except..."

"Except you. Who built the ritual?"

Cereus's smile is more a quirk of the mouth than anything. "Who does the Fey apparently trust the most?"

"Sigyn."

"Him and Adamantine and the Hawks. But the ritual...maybe it was for nothing. Or maybe it worked too well. Because we weren't even finished when Ashvaren was killed."

"Do you know who shot him?"

"I think maybe the Fey whispered to a Hawk, so fast they couldn't think before they did it. I don't know how *any* of Her aspects could feel the agony I was feeling and think of anything besides how much they wanted to...to rip him apart. He really hurt Her." Unlike Eirjatal, who tends to go hollow before he burns, Cereus's voice is full of unabashed, vulnerable emotion. "If Adamantine found out who actually shot him, she never told me. I don't think it matters."

"Do you think some of his darkness remained in you?"

"Sigyn took it all away. I mean, he pulled me out of Dianthus as soon as we heard the news, and I didn't leave a temple for a month. He was doing cleansing rituals every day."

The thought of Cereus in any acute pain brings an empty, defensive heat to his palms.

"I'm...I'm just scared. I'm scared of doing something wrong. Or stepping out of line like he did. What if She hasn't forgiven me yet? We were supposed to be appealing to Relyn, but it was the Archfey. She wanted to tear me into pieces. I tried to explain how it felt to Sigyn, but I really don't think I can. He didn't get it. I think you're the only person who might."

Eirjatal pulls him in. Cereus turns his face into Eirjatal's, palm skimming his burned and bandaged arm, releasing a single shaky breath.

"Madainn," Eirjatal whispers, "didn't hate me. He didn't see me. We were in his way. I know this when I think back on it, but every moment after that feels like he knew me and wanted me and still hunts me. I can't imagine knowing that fear was always real."

Cereus taking on Ashvaren's punishment is no surprise. Eirjatal thinks that somewhere under all of this, he does love Cereus in an uncomplicated way.

Vyriseh emerges from the shadows. She puts her hands up, smiling apologetically, and Eirjatal steps away.

"My apologies," Vyriseh says. "Cereus, love, may I steal Eirjatal for a word?"

"Of course." He squeezes Eirjatal's wrist. Vyriseh kisses his hand before he vanishes between the walls of ivy and flowers.

Once they're in private, Vyriseh asks, "How did it feel, your rage an inferno? Your claws in her?" She sets a hand on his throat. "Think of it."

He does. Or he tries. His mind snags on the moments around it—Kinthe whispering her goddess's name, Cereus gently removing the metal from his shoulders.

Vyriseh is singing under her breath. He's floating, losing track of where his hands and lungs are; he lets the memory unfurl before he drifts off entirely.

Every flicker of flame was like his nerves lifting out of his skin. He could feel the edges of the goddess's burning core, his power only a tiny winking star next to the sun.

Vyriseh pulls back. When he opens his eyes, she releases a soft breath on a shudder.

"I wanted to feel it for myself," she says. "Anger coming to *something*."

She adjusts her hold so it's tight around his jaw; this second song fights through her teeth. Memories fill his mind like a spool spilling thread. The glittering ice on the walls of the Ineiren Fort as he entered the courtyard, flanked with swords he barely knew how to use. Sunlight rolled down the snow and into the sea like tears, too bright, too clear, for all the death so far. When wandering the forest, the Fort stood immense and strong like a gift from the gods, promising shelter. He'd once seen it the same way.

It's like trying to swim through mud, but he scrambles away before she takes complete control. Vyriseh's song falters. "There's no triumph there."

Vyriseh strokes his jaw as she releases him. It's like she's being careful of the fragile corners on a prized object. "I'm sorry. Eventually, I will mourn Kinthe properly." She laughs. "For now I'm too angry. When I'm angry, I make plans. At times it seems like only my anger keeps Cypress moving forward at all. But, Eirjatal Ga'vrynn," she says, "you have fought a god."

"And he's won for longer than he's even had to try."

"Maybe so." Vyriseh sets two of her hands on his arm. "Still you fought. Still you lived. You've seen and done incredible things. Dianthus isn't here to protect you, nor is Cereus. You're the protector."

He thinks of Scintia, her ice creations from the Ineiren Fort, the dream she pulled him into, like it still lives so clearly in her head. No one deserves what they were both given. But he can't collapse like her; she hasn't done anything for her kingdom in a century.

"Eirjatal Ga'vrynn," Vyriseh says, "may I empty your city of Iron Phoenix worshipers?"

"Would you like help?"

She lifts her hand and out of the ivy flies a small black bat that alights on her shoulder. Even after everything, Radiance's presence inspires a small frisson through him.

As the pavilion is weighed down with Sigyn's mournful silence, the two of them head into the city.

43

Rhoheme

Madainn, disappearing and reappearing in the turquoise waters, has been searching for the Blind Adder. He keeps interrogating Rho.

Worse, he's explaining a whole lot of nothing for someone who was so chatty before. Maybe she has to piss him off again.

One thing's clear. He won't believe that Dianthus isn't tied into this.

Rho dares to wonder if it is. This whole game is ancient, but it was only when Cereus took the throne that Dianthus felt clear, knowable to her. Before that, she hated it like elves hated Etreal.

At least Madainn's accidentally giving her the time and the tools to craft. She can still seek out with her magic (folded into Cypress and it folded into her, like Staventa said) and tell that somewhere, somehow, the Dawn Hall is out there, but she's lost track of Eirjatal's fox sparrow and the wards and the walls.

One night (or, at least, the waters are blacker than usual) after Madainn was particularly short and annoying with her, Rho summons her playing cards. *The Dream. The Nightmare.* A seriously good hand, but she doesn't know what to use it for.

Instantly, the Adder crouches in the temple shadows with her like they're playing hide-and-seek. Her powder-pale skin swims with the gold light thrown around by the piles and piles of offerings.

Rho asks, "What am I here for?"

The Blind Adder arranges her cards perfectly equidistant in her mismatched hands. "It's not simple to explain."

"Yeah, well, maybe you can explain it to *him* better."

In a stream of froth, Madainn and his blue tail like a tattered sail swim through one of the skylights. The Blind Adder's cards are instantly gone and she's standing, unfazed when facing his wide, sharp-toothed grin.

"I've been looking for you." Madainn regains his legs as he lands on the floor, giving her a mocking bow. "Let's discuss."

The temple slides beneath Rho—it slides off her smug expression, too. She tumbles away from the gods, and away, and away, and *away*, until they're as giant as Staventa and the room rights itself. She scrambles to her feet, ensuring she's still got the sphere wrapped up in her skirts. Around Rho is something she swears is parchment.

"Let's start in Ventaris, hm?" Madainn says.

The world transforms around her. It *is* parchment—worn soft and inked by invisible pens as it tears, folds, and transforms into the silhouette of a life-size city.

Rho has never been here, but Hawks have drawn this city in detail unmatched by even Eirjatal. Here's Ventaris, a city chiselled out of obsidian, every surface a blade, from the gate spokes to the crowns of the buildings stabbing the sky. Rho stands on the paper stoop of an immense tower, elaborate rings folding around it like a ribcage and its shoulders flanked by dragon-shaped gargoyles.

"You were confident, I'll give you that. A Chalice fragment right in the Alastaric Academy. Well, part of a fragment."

"Broken before my time," the Adder says modestly.

"And powerless because of it. I kept an eye on it, in case you decided to fuse it or another one of us recognized what it secretly was."

The tower folds down, then rebuilds itself in whispery folds, into the interior of a library that rivals Heatherwol's. A splotchy-ink human circles a curio cabinet, so stuffed with knick-knacks made of inkblots and earring backs and watch gears, that Rho can't immediately see what he's focusing on until—

"One day, it disappears." Madainn opens his webbed hands, skimming them across the map. It all flattens around Rho into a sea of worn paper. "I waited for you to retaliate for the theft because you're so like the rest of us."

"In all but one thing," the Adder says. "I don't retaliate. I get revenge."

"Well, exactly. But your cultists didn't even start sniffing around, did they? So no one stole it. You moved it yourself. Maybe you knew I was looking, but either way, you were holding your cards under the table to risk none of us peeking a little too closely."

"On that you're wrong, Madainn. I don't know where it went."

"Sure. And then the Phoenix finds you in Chiroscuroi's temple."

A staircase springs up under Rho's feet, nearly knocking her on her ass. Staventene pours towards the sky, and a dome-shaped temple enfolds her. A sphere creates itself out of a crumpled ball of paper and the edges burst into orange flame. It starts eating itself with alarming speed.

"You sound paranoid. Chiroscuroi and I are fellows."

"You hate them. All of us do. Worst of all, you immediately knew what I was up to. You offered the Phoenix an alliance and gave her a task to quiet Faowist and Eojhest, and I had you pinned."

"Are you accusing me of being on the other side of the board than you?"

"No. I'm getting us up to speed, so you know *I'll* know when you're bullshitting me about that elf."

The flaming paper burns up the ceiling of the temple, all the tiny statues and watercolour walls, the two-dimensional worshipers sprung from the floor. Rho darts through the falling ash. She tumbles into Staventene's papercraft streets, horses with their joints made of flat tin rivets and road dust of puffs of paper dust. She finds a quiet spot in an alley to listen, hidden from them both.

"Rhoheme is mine, that's all."

"The Nelaeryn Fey can't play," Madainn says through his teeth. "We decided that when the Carrion Queen hid all the pieces. Something she made can't be a pawn on the board. You're no idiot, Adder."

"Thank you."

"So you're trying to be clever again. Last time you did that, you smuggled a goddess across universes."

"And Karadenza still hasn't found her, has she?" The Blind Adder's tone hasn't wavered once. "I'm not cheating. You've evolved from your usual strategy quite adeptly—I'll admit I had no inkling of the fragments you stole from right under Ilharel and Pique's noses. Sealing them was a stroke of genius, as well. You've evolved from rushing in with guns blazing and an eye for hostages, to sneaking into our locked windows with quiet knives."

Her hands expand, more and more of them fading in until they brush the tops of the paper buildings, casting shadows over Rho like clouds. "*I* am doing what I always do. To beat you, I never have to even step into your home."

Madainn scoffs. The Blind Adder flicks the map. Temples and brick buildings shift into farmhouses and shacks, prairies and rolling foothills, lighthouses and ships. An origami sea nearly swallows Rho's leg in its complex folds and then she's home.

The Dianthus tropics are blotted with foggy watercolour, the sand worn cotton-soft under her slippers. She whirls to the Dawn Hall. The lattice is cutting itself out of the paper as all eight levels of it unfold with the rifling of pages, the little pieces falling around her like petals.

And beyond it, the paper town is on fire.

Madainn says sharply, "That was the Iron Phoenix."

"She's yours."

Madainn says, "It was a test. Karadenza didn't come calling, did she? Not even the Fey showed her face! Looks like Cypress is still neutral ground."

She let this happen.

The Adder continues, "And yet you harangue me about the elf. What is it, Madainn? Are you angry you have competition?"

"Karadenza is my competition."

"Will you stab me, too? Will you use one of your spies in Ventaris to track down my Ciphers' leader and seal me through her?"

Her hands flutter in mockery, like silent laughs. For Rho, standing on the paper beach and beneath the paper trees, the air is dizzying and thick with grey smoke.

"I have worked for centuries to shield Ventaris against all of the Woven's mischief. Good luck."

"No, of course I won't seal you through one of those cultists."

The shadows over the Dawn Hall shift. He's suddenly gone from the table. There's a *shush* behind Rho and she whirls to find Madainn, her size once again, his face lit by the burning map.

"I'm sealing you through her."

Rho tries to block it, but the bone-handled knife is sharp enough to plunge straight through her hand and to the hilt in her chest.

The Adder lunges, all of her hands swatting and snatching, but Madainn pulls Rho through the map, and above, Rho sees the Adder fizzle out like a gutted candle flame, her face betraying the first instance of genuine shock Rho's ever seen.

44

Irving

The Age of Illumination gave us such famous stories about the elves as the theft of the Carrion Queen cultists in Kava and the tradition of setting out food and youths.
But today, one merely must turn to Staventene and Sirren for a living legend: Penelope Whitfore, the betrothed of an elf who reportedly saved her town from the starlight rains of a mourning Eojhest. She is the only human we have known of to be able to walk between the worlds.

Veils We Share, published Age of Shields 231

"Don't look at me like that," Irving snaps at the Eclipsed guard outside Johana's room. "I'm the only one who's meant to be here, aren't I?"

They flash the butterfly-bow key at the guard. Considering how not even Sigyn knows what's going on in the infirmary, Irving figures that acting confident is enough to sway them. Helps, too, that they're flanked by Tavreah.

It is. Irving locks the door behind them.

Johana bursts from her corner like someone set fire to her skirt. Noah immediately drops the illusion (and nearly a foot of height), hissing, "Shh! It's me!"

Johana regains some colour. "You're both alright!"

Irving says, "So are you." Except her hands are shiny with spider webs and she's shivering. "What did they do with Marie?"

Johana gives a hapless shrug. Irving's worry twinges for the snake.

Irving nods them into what once must've been a sensible storage nook, but is now crammed with everything that made this room what it was before an infirmary.

Irving whispers, "This whole thing with the wards? It has to end."

Johana and Noah trade a startled look. Probably the first time they've ever been on each other's wavelength.

Irving explains how the Ciphers intend to start the chase for the Chalices and Vyriseh's close on their heels. Vyriseh might even be ahead if Envai hasn't brought the evocation stories back to Ventaris. Even if the myth isn't real, everyone involved thinks it is, and Irving's already seen some of the blood that spills when people want something that powerful, that badly.

Noah tugs at the overgrown, shaved hair by her ear. "If Vyriseh's story was *that* obviously about the Chalices, she must know that's what they all lead to."

"And she knew we were collecting them. It would explain why her security spells didn't affect me, since I was wearing magic *she* gave me. I never understood why guards were missing on the night we did the Eclipsed puzzle, but she probably had something to do with that too."

Johana nibbles a nail. "Vyriseh was quite proficient at cloaking this room when the Iron Phoenix... She could have made all this very easy for you."

"She knows the House of Ciphers know *something*—explains why she went after me to help her so early." Irving tugs off their glasses, scrubbing at a spot with the end of their shirt. "It doesn't matter. I don't want to help the Ciphers *or* Vyriseh."

Johana shrinks deeper into the shadows. "We can't stop now," she squeaks.

Noah says, "Yeah, I don't get how this is a step too far for you, Irving. If you don't believe in the myth, then why not get through the evocations as quickly as possible, then hurry out with our payday?"

"I don't want to fuck with this at all, okay?"

Noah raises her eyebrows. How can they put their aversion into words without fumbling around what happened to Sigyn?

Johana saves them. "The Ciphers won't accept this. They'll never get this chance again. Even if you two stay behind, they won't—"

"Oh, no way," Noah says, right as Irving interjects, "We're all getting out, no matter what."

"Why even wait?" Noah hisses. "Let's leave now without her!"

Johana says, "Irving is Rhoheme's best chance. I will *not* let Rhoheme die. This has nothing to do with her." She sinks her head in her hands. "The Ciphers will do something. I know it."

"Do something to help us, or do something *to* you…?"

"I don't know! Either? Both? They'll do *something* to me either way. No one from Cypress was supposed to know about this!" Her voice increases in pitch like a boiling tea kettle. "You—you forced me into letting you help, and then you're going to drop me, after only two? You can't—" She curls into herself. "You can't *leave* me."

Irving cracks their knuckles as they think. They can quit stealing, help with Rhoheme, and then get out at top speed with Noah and Johana. But Johana's speaking as if there's nowhere for her to go if she fails.

And if they fail, there's nowhere for them, either.

But they keep seeing all that death in Ventaris. Anya Zarina, the Ciphers, whoever else got in Vyriseh and Khidell's way. Damn it, Khidell himself.

He knew Vyriseh was planning on giving all the Moonwardens' powers to Sigyn so he'd become this. So he killed himself in Etreal to stop the powers from transferring. Was Kinthe's murder a happy coincidence, or has Vyriseh tied herself that tightly into the Woven's machinations?

What would the Fey think of this mess?

Irving catches the thought and shoves it away.

"Johana. I know Cypress. Once Vyriseh gets more rulers on her side, *they won't stop.* What does Ventaris want a new world for? To say they did it first? Their motive doesn't hinge on centuries of being told that Cypress is falling apart and the goddess is hurting because of it. Ventaris will get over it."

Noah folds her arms. "If you stop helping Johana, that doesn't mean Vyriseh's search stops too."

"What am I supposed to do about her?"

"You just don't want your name attached to all this."

"I don't know, Noah," they groan.

Irving tries to channel the persona of the elf at the estates, not needing to spill all the information for people to listen and take their advice. But something about Cypress has whittled them down to the simplest, messiest version of themselves. How exactly do you put into words, *My dad's more magic than elf right now, and I've learned too much about him. And even if this never gets out, even if the gods don't care and the planet is safe and nothing falls into the sort of crap that history books get written about—*

My father is dangerous.

And I can't let him start something he can't stop.

Johana suddenly cries, "What do you know of Etreal? Nothing! You're a child. You believe the worst of Cypress, but can you even see the worst of Etreal, how the gods push us into everything—how much safer we would feel in a realm that is run by the ones we put faith in, not Karadenza who ends worlds, or Madainn who starts wars, or—or the Iron Phoenix, who ruins all she touches? You—you were *afraid* of your magic, and you still want its temple to listen to you?"

Noah gives Irving's sleeve a hard jerk when they try to respond. That's probably best—they have no idea what was going to come out of their mouth, but they'd probably regret it.

"Okay, okay, let's cool off," Noah says. "The guard's going to get suspicious. We'll come back. Sit tight."

Noah puts the illusion on and steers Irving out of the infirmary in a pretty convincing Tavreah impression. Once they're far enough for her to revert back, she hisses, "You know Johana's going to die, right? They caught her stealing for *Ventaris*. She's done. Not even Cereus can make excuses."

That's not a surprise, but it hits them like it is. "I'll get her out."

"Good luck." There's a new wall over her expression, worse than usual. It bugs them, but at least she gives them the next step with confidence they wish they felt. "Let's stop Envai."

45

Eirjatal

If you imagine the eventual clash between Karadenza and the Nelaeryn Fey, which aspect takes the helm? Does Relyn mete out even justice from a bloodless height? Does Nele swaddle Cypress in triumph or failure? I find it difficult to see this without the Archfey, resplendent in rage. She may frighten us, but I trust Her most to win.

Sigyn, sermon, Age of Shields 102

Eirjatal has clearly interrupted something. Cereus and Tavreah look noticeably ill and Vyriseh stands at the head of the table, welcoming him in with a sweep of her four arms.

Tavreah stands too, nearly knocking over her chair. "Tell him what you mean to do, Vyriseh."

Vyriseh gestures at Sigyn, who places something on the table. Adamantine leans subtly away from what looks to Eirjatal like broken pieces of a clay pot, carved with glimpses of an ornate design.

Eirjatal has a sinking feeling that Vyriseh only confirms. "It's time to go on the offensive against the Woven."

All he's learned in the last day weaves together until it does not seem so nonsensical for him to say, "And you'll use the Chalice to do that."

"Oh, thank goodness. I'd hate to explain it all again."

Sigyn stands next to her like a statue. A strange clicking picks at Eirjatal's ear, but he can't figure out where it's coming from; none of Rho's inventions are in the dining hall.

Tavreah says, "That's not only a Woven thing, it's a *Karadenza* thing."

Eirjatal keeps his focus on Vyriseh, though Sigyn and Cereus flanking her feel like two opposing forces pressing in on him. "We can't fight them."

"I don't intend to. I want to put us confidently in play for a new world. I'm quite serious. *Sigyn* is quite serious. And I want the Woven to see that."

Eirjatal trusts that he isn't the only one hearing the echo behind her use of *Sigyn*. If Moonwardens have always been connected to the Fey, then what does that mean for Sigyn now that Kinthe's power has been added to his own?

Adamantine is curiously quiet, but Eirjatal can practically see the gears turning in her head. Eirjatal, meanwhile, isn't sure what he feels. He wants to have someone else's voice in his head besides his own, someone else's feelings.

"They make everything into a war." Eirjatal addresses Sigyn, who is closely watching him. The irritating clicking scatters across his senses. "Or at least squabbles between them become wars for us."

"Eirjatal, Kinthe is dead and I need not remind you of everything else Cypress has been through in our lifetimes alone. War has already started."

That truth hooks under his ribcage, pulling him to her.

Tavreah scoffs. "Let him know how you're planning on *starting* all of this, how about?"

Vyriseh smiles like Tavreah's heat is an invitation for her to step onstage. "I will wake Rhoheme, in the way we already planned, Eirjatal. Yes, I told them." She sidesteps whatever expression he involuntarily made. "We all need total transparency, you see."

He expects himself to be angry. But it's as if a crushing weight has been taken off his chest.

"So I wake her, and Rhoheme can repair and therefore restore power to the Chalice piece."

"And *so*," Tavreah interjects, "Madainn can sense it and he comes out of the sea—"

"And Rhoheme and I use the fragment to build defences over Dianthus. It is a sort of…well, put simply, the fragments are pure power from the goddess of magic herself. There are certainly enough stories noting how it should amplify the magic around it. I can seal Dianthus into an invisible pocket like I hid the rooms of the Dawn Hall." She tilts her hand like she's conducting a song, wistfully smiling. "Give a rabbit a wolf's shadow, or hide a wolf in sunlight, so to speak."

Eirjatal hears his own voice at a distance, even quieter than that mad clicking. "But Madainn will come to Dianthus."

"Invariably, if Scintia, you, and I are right about what he wants."

Adamantine asks, "Why tempt fate? Why draw more attention?"

"How has sitting idly worked for us in the past?" Vyriseh folds one set of arms, the others ticking off examples on her fingers. "We waited for the Age of Beasts. We waited for the Carrion Queen to give Sigyn the Packmothers and then steal our future Moonwarden away. We *are* waiting for the curse to kill off all of Winter. We waited for Ventaris to discard Khidell." Her voice fractures on that one. "We *waited* for the Iron Phoenix to try to bring the city down, and waited for those other gods to save us.

"The Fey cannot save us, but She wants to. She's here and we must help Her."

Sigyn surveys them all in the following fragile, trembling silence. The fine clicking ticks on.

Cereus isn't loud, but it's unwavering when he says, "I don't want you to turn Dianthus into your sacrifice."

Adamantine adds, "Why not activate it outside of Cypress and pull his attention there?"

"And build my barrier over, what, Fain's Shadow? No. We start here."

"Then we empty the city." Adamantine straightens, seeming to regain confidence now that she has logistics she can handle. "Everyone must be moved to Heatherwol immediately. My Hawks will not participate in this. You would do good to remove your spies as well. Sigyn is too valuable—"

"I will stay in Dianthus." Sigyn's voice is as cold and solid as ice.

Tavreah knots her fingers in her hair. "No way! You're the only Moonwarden we've got left!"

"And this will be my first act as that Moonwarden."

Tavreah groans, dropping into her chair and burying her face into fistfuls of her black hair.

Cereus nods at Adamantine. "Thank you. We'll get everyone off the island, and I'll—"

"You're leaving too," Eirjatal says without thinking.

Vyriseh says, "I agree. Cereus, you'd only be a risk if you stayed."

Eirjatal's ruled by emotion—that order spilled out of him—but Vyriseh has thought all of this through. She was meticulous and passionless in her blinding of the rebels, and the collecting and banishment of the Iron Phoenix worshipers this morning.

Cereus is rubbing his tattooed arm, the way he does when nervous. For a flash, all Eirjatal can see is Cereus in his wildest imaginings of that ritual, crushed under the Archfey's fury. "…I know. I was going to say that. I'm better off if I can have my people with me and explain everything to them myself."

Relieved, Eirjatal refocuses on Vyriseh. "And Rho chooses if she participates. Rho chooses for herself."

Vyriseh bows her head. "I swear it."

Did Scintia hold onto this for years? Did she know that if Sigyn was involved, it would fall in line and begin? Was this something she was so terrified of that she told no one—and chose to pass to him without all of the information, so she wouldn't have to face it?

Eirjatal realizes what the clicking noise is. Sigyn's arm is malfunctioning again. He doesn't even feel it.

Vyriseh says, "Thank you for your trust, my friends. I am going to make Cypress a new world if the Fey doesn't yet have the strength for it." Vyriseh treats them all to a steady glare, and when she reaches Eirjatal, she holds it with such confidence that he can't help but believe her. "*We* are going to make Cypress a new world."

Vyriseh has proven herself. Though Johana was duplicitous, still, Vyriseh dared reach out to Ventaris. Without her, there would be no chance of reviving Rho. It was Vyriseh who caught the rebels, Vyriseh who killed Corsair, Vyriseh who protected so many of them in the Azfell attack, even if she couldn't protect the key piece.

With her holding the worst of all of this, he can step out of the Ineiren Fort's shadow. Maybe soon he can once again take up the sword.

For now, he can let her wield it.

46

Irving

You can talk to this Cypress Queen like a human, right? Humans make deals, and so do I. My offer requires an introduction: I know the restrictions you put on your sorcerers with Mythmaker magic like mine, how you tie them up in laws and surveillance and tethers.
I have none of that.
But I have a very impressive imagination.

Vyriseh to Alastaric Academy, recording bird, Age of Shields 200

"Fey watching, the city feels so weird." Noah shudders. The streets are still stained with ash and the gardens that weren't protected are burned to heaps of black refuse, like storm clouds spread all over the ground. There are displays for funerary rites but they're incomplete. "No one's around."

The ballroom and lower levels of the palace have instead taken on most of the crowds. "Sure not a great end to Lightbringing," Irving mumbles.

Noah points at a small home tucked behind a destroyed gazebo. "I think I met her in that one."

The two change streets, crossing through a group of Relyn, Archfey, and Nele statues. They all have scuffed glass pieces around their necks so they each stand, flawless, but the grass around them crunches like autumn leaves under Noah and Irving's feet.

Noah grabs their sleeve. "Wait."

"Something wrong?"

"No, I—I want to tell you something."

"What's up?"

"This is—this is all fucking weird. Really. I mean, we started out like, messing around, and this," she gestures at the street, "*this* happened, and I was a part of it. I took elves' money, I joked about them to you, but…I don't understand."

"You weren't a part of this."

"I mean, kick around the ash a bit and you'll find elves who weren't supposed to be here at all but I let them. Maybe our tokens summoned her."

"They thought they were on the losing side. That's not a feeling that goes away whether they got a trinket or not."

Noah looks away. She doesn't let them go. "I know. Almost no one wants to say it, and we keep doing the same song and dance, like Lightbringing and prayer and all that, but… Dianthus, especially, is like living somewhere already dead. It's not only the big stuff, like Winter and Khidell and whatever. It's the stuff that would happen to me every day in that fucking castle. The fact that people couldn't stop fighting about the nuances of everything, like what was happening was normal or justified if you found the right argument for it. We feel abandoned. I've always felt abandoned. Do you get that?"

Do you think she'll accept your apology?

"Yeah," they say, and it's so honest that it comes out brittle. "Maybe not like you, but I do."

Noah squeezes their wrist. "Let's try to work a bit more honestly from now on."

"Deal. We'll pick a nice, safe money laundering job next time, eh?"

Deflated as she may be, Noah does laugh, and that sound's a glimmer of sunlight in this ash-covered mess.

"And I meant it." Irving digs a hand into the pocket of their vest. "I'm getting all of us out."

They take out a compass on a chain. Noah snatches it and frowns.

"This is Eirjatal's."

"It's also Staventene's. I know the brand."

"You're stealing from the castle again. So much for money laundering." Noah blows her bangs out of her eyes. She's holding the compass tightly. "You're leaving Rhoheme?"

"I'll try to convince Johana to let it go. If she won't budge, I'll figure it out. I'm going to run. I'm good at that. So be ready." They take the compass back and tuck it away.

They reach the house at the end of the street, and Irving recognizes it much better from here. There's a shard of glass swinging precariously from a burned thread on the front stoop. The house is pretty intact—it must have worked. For all her cockiness, Envai still wanted to protect something.

They ring the bell-pull. They wait for a bit, but there's no reaction. They call through the door, "Envai. I know it's a weird time, but…it's Irving and Noah."

Still, only silence from inside the house. Noah whispers, "Crap. You were with her when the whole Phoenix thing happened, right? Maybe she's helping clean up the city?" They exchange a look. "Yeah, stupid idea."

Irving has a bad feeling, certainly not helped by the grim feeling of the street. Maybe the bell's muffled, so they knock hard with the side of their fist.

The door swings inwards. The bad feeling triples. Noah elbows around them and peeks into the house. There are lit candles along the kitchen counter and table to fight back the dark of the smog-filled sky. It bears the hallmarks of a rental, from an untouched, nearly-empty bookshelf to the open, bare pantries.

Irving follows Noah in. She takes a cursory glance at the kitchen before moving into the next move. Would it be possible to find the other pendants here? Could they get rid of them or try to empty the power they're holding before Envai can carry them off to Ventaris, and solve half their issues without even leaving Dianthus?

Noah shrieks.

Irving rushes into the room she's in, and she backs up into them. Envai is spilled on the floor, her wash of red hair matted in a pool of the same colour.

Maybe it's all the time around Rhoheme's unnerving corpse or how clean Envai is next to the horror they saw in Ventaris, but Irving only takes a second to brace themselves before approaching her. They crouch beside her, staying as far out of the blood as possible. When they delicately turn her head to see her face and check if she's breathing, they find her eyes open and glassy and two jagged punctures in her throat.

Noah grabs their shoulder. They whirl to see a stunning human woman in a long, almost funerary robe, stepping down the staircase. She tilts her head at two of them. Two pendants swing from her long fingers like a metronome.

Her eyes light up. A slow, lazy smile spreads on her bright red lips. "I was about to go looking for you, Irving. I'm Radiance. Vyriseh wants to have a chat."

47

Irving

I want Khidell back. Extend me a hand, a meeting (I'm not so frightening), and we can discuss. If you throw in a little something extra, I'll let you tell them you killed him so no one has to fear revenge. We both need to keep up appearances, after all.

Vyriseh to Alastaric Academy, recording bird, Age of Shields 200 (cont.)

Irving backs towards the door, shifting Noah behind them. Radiance follows, one step for two of theirs, like she isn't intending on ending this with a chase.

Irving. She only wants them.

Radiance lifts the two pendants swaying from her fist. "You were very helpful, and Vyriseh always pays her debts."

Irving tries not to look at Envai, but it isn't as easy to block them out of their mind as the Blind Adder clerics were. Barely a day ago, she was pulling them through the street like the danger of the Azfell was a ton of fun.

They've gotten into the front room. Radiance veers in a side-step to see Noah behind them, first one direction, then the other, playful.

Noah whispers, "Irving, come *on*."

They put a hand behind their back, as if they're only releasing her grip on their shirt. Instead, they fish out the chain of Eirjatal's compass from their back pocket and suspend it on a finger for her to take.

And the instant they feel her take it, they want it back.

The betraying thought's broken by Radiance flashing into the shape of a small bat, zipping over their heads, and alighting as a woman behind them with Noah's wrist clasped and held aloft. Noah utters a short scream.

"What's this?" Radiance asks.

Irving looks at Noah more than Radiance. "The way into Etreal."

Noah shoots them a panicked look. Her fist closes harder over the chain and in response, Radiance's nails dig into her skin.

They continue in a rush, trying to outpace the pinch of regret in their chest from seeing it in Noah's hand, "Get to the Duchall theatre. You know what Leila looks like; she's the manager there, and she has my spare apartment keys. She knows where to take you. I'll follow you."

"Irving, you'll get more than burned for this—"

They recover some of that old Etreal authority and tell Radiance, steady and sure, "Let her go. Vyriseh already protected her once for me."

"She can still speak," Radiance says, baring her teeth, observing the now-squirming Noah with clear interest. Her fangs are bright white in her red mouth, corners of her lips still scabbed with Envai's blood. "I don't like loose ends. Why would Vyriseh protect her again? No more dresses for you to fix, tailor."

"Because I'm trading this." They take out the Chalice fragments from their pocket.

The vampire's eyes brighten. Her hand goes briefly tight, making Noah gasp, then relaxes enough for Noah to squirm away. Her back hits the doorway.

Panic blares in their head. Don't offer those when Vyriseh will know you tried to steal them. She already took Sigyn's—Sigyn's!—arm for this!

Irving cuts half a glance at Noah. This is something that would get her to warn them to not be stupid, to not get in their own way, but instead she looks terrified. "Go. Stay in Staventene, and I'll find you."

Noah clutches the compass to her chest. She nods, mouth set in a hard line, and whispers, in a soft tone they've never heard from her, "Thank you."

Radiance lets Noah go and grabs the back of Irving's neck. She flashes them a grin, teeth a searing red at the roots, and leads them away from Envai.

※

Vyriseh is delighted when she invites Irving into her repaired apartment. She leads them with a hand on the back of the shoulder to the sofa, Radiance taking post at the door. When Radiance had told her Irving had the fragments, her second set of eyes flashed open with a menacing, sour light.

She alights daintily on a loveseat across from them, folding one set of arms in her lap. "I assume that I don't need to threaten to erase the *idea* of escaping from your mind?"

"No."

"Lovely. Now, if you'd be so kind."

She extends a hand. Her tone is uncannily like someone scolding a dog who's gone on the run with a slipper.

Irving cards through their options. Bargains, questions, another trade that gets them stuck in Vyriseh's web. Could they get anything for telling her Khidell's an echo? They feel intensely small, sitting on the queen of Silvershale's couch like a misbehaving child when she's gamed Ventaris, Sigyn, and who knows what else.

They should consider themselves lucky she's only got a hand out for the fragments, instead of letting Radiance have dessert. But Cypress wants Rhoheme—so, Vyriseh wants them. Rhoheme doesn't wake up without them and Johana. That gives them a little relief.

So they place the fragments in her hand.

Vyriseh's fingers snap shut like a rabbit trap.

"How long did you know it was me?"

"Stealing the evocations?" Vyriseh tilts her head. "As soon as you began. Radiance is quite easy to hide, and I had been watching that room for Rhoheme's sake since she was first brought back with that Ventaris sorcerer. One can never trust those sorts."

"You always knew what they were?"

"I had a guess. A poor one, might I add. Knowing Ventaris wanted them cleared up all my questions. Ventaris wants so little from Cypress except that which can break the two of us apart." She leans back in her seat, fixing her skirts. "I didn't care for your method, but I thank you for your efficiency. Except, of course, for the last two."

"What happened to those?"

"Oh, Eirjatal forced the wards a little, so I could take what I wanted of the evocations. You know his magic. Not even Rhoheme is any match for it."

Eirjatal? They feel like they haven't thought of him in months, but it seems right, considering what they saw in that evocation, that he'd side with Vyriseh.

Could they ask to be let go after Rhoheme wakes up? Maybe they can catch Noah before she leaves, and they can escape together, and all of this craziness can happen in Cypress, away from them. But they think over and over of Sigyn's warning in the gardens. About him, about Irving, about their mother, about everything.

How can they get out of this without abandoning everyone?

There's a careful knock on the door. Radiance's nostrils flare as she sniffs out whoever's on the other side. "Sigyn."

Vyriseh brightens. "Delightful. Let him in."

Irving feels like throwing up. Radiance opens the door and Sigyn glides through, right to the open balcony windows facing the sea. He's a ghost, in the room with them but interacting with a time, people, long gone.

His gaze lands on Irving. Everything in them tenses, like he's about to slap them and they're ready for it. Sigyn's never raised a hand to Irving, but the way he's looking at them gives them some idea of the heat and pain and shame.

Their father, or whatever's inside him, studies them.

Vyriseh says, "Are you ready, half-blood, to usher in a new age, a new era, quite like your father?"

"It could kill me," they say, but they aren't directing the words at Vyriseh.

The Sunmirren glances between Irving and Sigyn. Sigyn is watching them, but with no understanding, no fondness, no concern. He's Sigyn, the strongest Moonwarden in two centuries, untouchable, unquestionable, the end of all things. He could stop her if he'd bother to say anything.

But he turns to the door.

She grins. "Oh, yes. It's perfect."

48

Rhoheme

Madainn wrenches Rho through a flipbook of worlds.

With each dizzy plane that flashes by—ocean, skies, grimy river floors, cups and fangs and sweltering fires, all of it, exactly as Staventa said—the bone dagger sinks deeper and deeper into her chest, unyielding to her scrabbling hands, until it vanishes beneath the skin.

Madainn throws her across black sand on the bottom of a dark sea. She catches in those threads that connect her to the Adder like a discarded marionette, tangled in her own strings. Now they're as solid and bright as slats of sunlight through the Dawn Hall's walls.

"There." Madainn shakes out his clawed hands. "I've lost her. And if you're as important as she threatened" —he pins her with a sharp-toothed grin— "I've locked away a key enough part of her to slow you both down."

Rho doesn't understand much in this world, but she understands that. If he sealed the Adder through her, then there's a good chance Rho's stuck here.

She drags herself to her feet. Her hair floats around her face in these false currents. She rips the gold belt from her hips, the sphere and the blade that once sealed Ilharel swinging free.

It reacts to her to such a fine degree that everything slows. Rho controls every separation, peeling the spheres apart from each other. The metal is made by the goddess who invented it, and that purity sings a crescendo with the magic that invented *her*.

The rings seal, one by one, around Madainn's throat. They interlock and the dagger locks between them and against his throat.

Madainn's mouth twists in sardonic disbelief.

Her hands reach out into the grimy water, bones pressing against her skin like gears straining against each other. Each nerve only feels the delicate makeup of the metal.

"Let me go," she snarls through her teeth.

The moment where his arrogance splinters coincides with her *deciding* to tighten the garrote, and it does, every interlocked sphere clicking and shimmering as they slide into each other.

"What do you expect to—" He makes the mistake of stopping for a laughing breath, and she spots when he realizes it's not so easy to inhale.

"Let me go."

She *feels* every scale the rings press into, the cool flush of the deep sea water, the hum of unbearable power in that dagger's point shuddering so near his heart.

The collar tightens again.

And the plane around them shudders.

Black sand, dying coral, sunken ships. The corners of it all bend inwards.

Another twist. The world crushes as easily as a fistful of foil. The horizon goes jagged; the water weighs heavy upon them.

Madainn has caught on. His eyes go panicked as he insists, "You can't *kill* me."

Rho has no idea what she's doing or how she's doing it, but any fear from him is encouragement.

The ship cracks in half. A current of water bursts off it and lifts her black hair like a flag.

The rings click closed, notch by notch. Her hands tremble, muscle twitching in her jaw from how she's clenching her teeth. Madainn is shifting shape, turning less human-like in a juddering way that keeps snapping him back to his recognizable face. Maybe the metal is stopping that too.

For a flash, the part-planes and half-realms peek open around her. The Dawn Hall becomes a limb, a collection of nerves and muscle and blood, and she sees—no, again she *feels* herself closing it around a demon, feels herself reaching out to Eirjatal's fury.

She feels the sun warm in its walls, gears wrapped with plants that even seemed to grow better without Ashvaren. She feels the thrum of music playing off Eirjatal's phonograph, feels her face tucked comfortably against his shoulder. The ring of Tavreah's wild laughter and the smell of her perfumes. The glow of Kinthe's scrying room, a rainfall of glass. The soft weight of Cereus's footsteps winding between hers when he taught her how to dance. The tremor of applause on his coronation, the thunder of unspoken grief after they caught their first would-be assassin. The way the metal folded around her, folded around all of them, warm and wonderful and hers, the castle was hers, this city was hers, these people were hers, her life was hers.

Sure, she can't kill him, but she's never felt so powerful in her life, and Madainn looks terrified.

She nearly loses her breath as the dagger pulls against her sternum.

The world crumples. It's bending her down, too, forcing her and Madainn into a tiny space.

The hilt frees itself from her bones. Rho slides her consciousness into the dagger and dissolves it into shards of silver.

Only a few more notches, then the other dagger will be buried in Madainn. He'll be sealed, lost to this small, miserable little plane, and he'll be out of her world, her head, Eirjatal's head, for good.

Only a few—

The magic slips just enough for her to lose her grip, and again the world opens beneath her. The water doesn't spill in. Not even the shadows do. It's a blank space trying to suck her in.

Rho digs in her nails, clawing towards Madainn, but he's got the final word. A smile unfurls on his face as a bead of blackish blood curls into the water from the point of the dagger, barely grazing his chest.

Rho falls back into the atrium. She's holding her playing cards.

She screams and slaps the cards aside and storms to her feet. She tries to throw her mind into bursting apart the table, but whatever magic came with Staventa's metals and creations is entirely gone.

"I almost—"

"What, almost *had* him?" The Adder fans her cards in front of her face, hiding her mouth and nose, only her bizarre eyes staring out at Rho. "We're due one more round."

49

Irving

...the strangest sight. Directly beneath Hyacinthus. If we hadn't taken the palace, would we have never found it? I worry so...

Ashvaren's evocation

For the entire walk to the center of the labyrinth gardens, Irving can't ignore the smell of blood.

Everyone's unharmed: Vyriseh, Sigyn, Johana, even technically Rhoheme, carried by Irving and Eirjatal. So it's got to be coming from the decorated chest Vyriseh has under two arms.

Despite how they didn't last speak on the best terms, Johana sticks to Irving's side. Her hands are wrapped in spider webs so thick that her skin shimmers in the evening light, she's given up on hiding and wears her Blind Adder tokens around her neck, and Marie clutches her shoulders like a vice, lunging at anyone who gets too close—except Irving.

Overnight and through the morning, everyone in the palace and city were moved to Heatherwol.

At the top of the spiral tower that oversees the labyrinth (the only way out is a steep stairwell they'll never descend fast enough), Vyriseh sets down the chest. Irving and Eirjatal lay Rhoheme on a bench. Eirjatal stands sentry near her head, pivoting to shield her whenever someone moves around them.

Sigyn stands near the balcony railing, surveying the sea behind the Dawn Hall, silent and still. His hair is bleached by the low light. He's got the broken arm back on and it's ticking like the Dawn Hall.

Irving asks Eirjatal, "How long did it take for him to come back the first time?"

He says tightly, "He never did."

Maybe that's a good thing, considering the Sigyn in the evocation. But there was a flash of someone better in that conversation they had before the Iron Phoenix. Someone Irving actually could trust.

Vyriseh smiles at them all, carding her fingers together. "Let's bring Rhoheme into the story, shall we?"

Vyriseh flips the clasps on the chest and opens it. The stench of gore billows out; Irving smacks their hand over their mouth and nose and Eirjatal neatly clears his throat. Inside is a pile of innards and neat little jars of orange blood and violet venom. Johana gravitates towards it all, like it's the only familiar thing in the room.

Irving and Johana set up for the ritual. Johana cuts open organs with a miraculously steady hand, and she at least *sounds* certain about what herbs and metals from her bag that Irving should measure out. Irving tries to keep their head on their shoulders, but they lose their grip on the materials more than once.

Irving trusts Johana, sure. But they don't trust magic. They don't trust any of this.

Eventually, they're set up. Eirjatal kneels near Rhoheme's head, a hand protectively under it, like she's at risk of thrashing, the other hand on her chest. Bracketing it are green-grey strips of dead coral and ridges of gold—what with all that's been occupying Irving and Johana the last couple days, her condition's gotten worse.

Does she *want* to come back? Is she done what she thought she needed to do? They don't want to know what it'll feel like if she fights back.

Irving and Rhoheme are all tangled in sinew and silk. Johana cuts Irving's fingers, then her own, like she did when curing Eirjatal to share her power. "The Adder's on your side," she whispers, locking their bloody hands together.

The ritual's the same process as for Eirjatal, but now the tiny ritual space is coloured with strips of gore. As Johana works, the blood freshens, seeming to pump anew through the organs in the shifting light. It runs through Irving's hands, slick and hot.

Irving anchors their attention on Eirjatal as the magic scrapes its way through them. He's bowed his head near Rhoheme's, whispering frantic prayers under his breath. He's covering his bases. Irving catches *Nele—* warding her off, maybe. He also asks for the Archfey, who fights viciously for survival.

Irving feels bizarrely lonely.

There's a whisper through the room and between one hazy blink and the next, the Blind Adder is sitting with them all.

Maybe she's using the same power that cooled their head when they were dying the first time, or maybe they're *that* lost in Johana's magic, but Irving doesn't have the energy to be surprised. No one else notices.

Her hands are Johana's—thin, scarred, and pale. In them are playing cards that she folds together and apart like moth wings folding open and shut.

Suddenly there's a matching set in Irving's hand. The Adder sets down one of her cards, with art whose starburst yellows and sunbeams remind

Irving of Faowist.

Irving asks, "What do you want? For me to swear to live a better life or something?"

"She wants to see your cards," Rhoheme says.

Irving jumps. Rhoheme sits across from them, two cards gripped in a tight hand, her gaze pointedly averted from her own body.

There's no text on the cards. "I don't know what this game is."

"Doesn't matter. We're in the last round." Rhoheme flicks a wrist at the ritual gore all around her. She laughs bitterly, firing a glare at the Adder. "You really don't care what happens to me."

"I wouldn't say that. Both options are interesting."

"Huh." Rhoheme leans to see the card the goddess put down. "Makes me think of Lightbringing. I've missed it all by now, haven't I?"

One of Irving's cards is a painting of a wyvern, and the other's a grizzled old man in a cave with a rusted sword. Another's a one-eyed pirate spattered in blood on the bow of her ship. Great. They're all grim.

Rhoheme continues idly, "Relyn bought bits of the world from all those gods, promising to pay them back once her powers returned. I wonder how long the Woven plan to wait."

The Adder's gaze is like a knife against the back of their neck. Everything Irving's learned about her from Etreal funnels together, and they realize what's happening.

Life for life, pieces for pieces. The ritual's costing them their life for Rhoheme's. Unless this game turns in their favour.

If they had their magic, would they be able to bargain?

Rhoheme shrugs. She starts to present her cards.

Another card takes her spot, slapped down by spider web-wrapped, pockmarked hands.

Johana's card shows a glowing white thread tethered slantwise across the art.

"You told me *The Thread* was in your hand," the Adder says to Rhoheme.

"Oops."

Johana is breathing unevenly, entirely focused on her goddess. "Karadenza's thread. I sacrifice all the playing power of my hand."

Rhoheme says, "That'll make you lose."

Irving reaches for Johana's wrist but they phase right through her. Before they can say anything to her, she gasps, "I'm first out. That's all you need, right?"

The Adder folds her hand. "It is. Would you like to choose, Priestess?"

"Let me come back home."

The room flashes back to life. Rhoheme's eyes snap open.

The goddess is gone. The cards are gone.

Eirjatal is immediately on Rhoheme, helping her up. Irving holds themselves against the edge of the bench. The room shifts, unsteady like a ship.

Marie slides across their shoulders and the weight of her grounds them as Johana takes apart the apparatus of the ritual, her breath coming fast. She looks at Irving and seems to stumble over what she wants to say next, but there's nothing in her expression that hints she'd done this under the threat of punishment in a kingdom that hates her. Despite everything's that's happened, despite how Irving failed her, she succeeded at saving someone.

"I'm sorry if she makes it scary," she says, "but I wasn't going to leave Cypress anyways."

Marie strikes from Irving's shoulders, fangs unsheathed, and bites Johana in the throat.

The suddenness of it even has Vyriseh flinching. Marie strikes again, again, until she drops off Irving's shoulders and tangles around the furniture and equipment, seeming bigger than ever, hissing and snapping.

Irving lunges for Johana. They should hold her head, lift her, anything, but their hands flutter uselessly over her, blood pooling around their knees. Her eyes are wild and she grasps at their sleeves. Her gasps for air swallow up all the other sounds in the room.

When Marie snaps at Vyriseh, the queen stomps hard on her head. Finally, Rhoheme screams, and the room is too clear, too bright, too noisy again.

There's a crash of colour in the pool of Johana's blood. Shale-black, verdant green, like plants, like vitaea. It crackles like lightning.

Magic. Without Marie, it's like Irving's own blood, years ago, frantic with untethered magic. But Johana lent them a bit of her abilities. Maybe there's something left.

Irving presses on the punctures in Johana's throat, willing it to heal with the confused desperation they tried to persuade their own magic with for years.

They hiss, "She devoted her life to you; come the fuck *on*."

Their hands are hot with her blood. Frantic, they check her throat, but the wound is still deep and black and bubbling. Their human side had healers. They're hollow now.

I hated you and you came for me. Please.

Johana's hands slip off their arms. A horrible spasming under their palms stops, and yet Irving keeps their hands pressed there, half sure it'll start up again.

It takes another moment before they rock back onto their heels. They're cold to their fingertips. The blood is now deep red.

In the corner of their eye, Marie fades into a crushed skeleton, like years of decomposition in a breath. Johana follows, suddenly little more than a skeleton strewn in linens. Irving can't help scrambling back.

Approaching Rhoheme, Vyriseh steps over Marie and pushes Johana out of the way with a slide of her shoe. When she reveals the broken fragments from her skirt pocket and holds them out, Rhoheme says, "I'm not repairing the Chalice fragment. I'm not pulling Cypress into this."

"What do you know about such things?"

"Where do you think I've been this whole time?" Rhoheme bites back.

Vyriseh touches one of the gold pieces breaking out of Rhoheme's chest. "This is much bigger than a bargain for your life, Rhoheme. And I'm afraid you have little choice."

"You won't kill me."

"Correct; I need you too much. You're immensely powerful. I've seen as much, and if Madainn comes, you can prove it. I know you can."

Rhoheme's gaze flicks to the necklace around Vyriseh's neck. Irving didn't notice it before, but it's a huge silver thing with sapphire lilies. The flowers are moving in the same seamless way as the wards.

Rhoheme says, "You'll call Madainn here. And then every god will be watching Cypress."

"My dear, you've been dead, so I'll excuse your ignorance. But I've already had this discussion many times. With your own king and most importantly, with the Fey." She gestures to Sigyn, who has swept into the room, soundless. "Without you, Dianthus doesn't stand a chance, and I'll merely be the megalomaniac fool who doomed us all. I would rather a kinder reputation." She tilts her head. "You're also the only sorcerer of your ilk that I have leverage over. Sigyn?"

The space feels impossibly small as Sigyn crosses it. It's with a calm gesture that he slides a hand across Eirjatal's bare collar and holds a blade of glass against his bare throat.

"Eirjatal had to pay up eventually. So, Rhoheme?

50

Rhoheme

...as if the dragon wanted us to know it. I would wake up every morning to it on the crest of the Avinian, but I wouldn't let anyone trap it...

Firewe's evocation

Rho takes the fragments. They look...well, they look like nothing, really.

She imagines a goblet in Staventa and Madainn's hands. It must be huge. This must be such a small part of it.

It must be a very, very long game.

Rho turns to Eirjatal. Sigyn is still holding him close, no doubt stopping him from setting on fire. He gives her a half-smile, breath shivering through his teeth.

"I'm your only chance?" she asks.

"It's still your choice," Eirjatal says. There's such a weird vacancy to Sigyn that she believes the threat of that knife on Eirjatal's throat. Still, Rho figures that Vyriseh could never threaten Eirjatal with anything worse than Madainn. "Please."

She could shatter the fragments. And then what, be chased forever by Vyriseh? What choice is Cypress ever afforded in the matters of the Woven? They already a step behind.

Rho traces the fragments' edges with her fingertips, closing her eyes to really focus. A thrill runs into her heart. She was a ghost for so long, and finally, even considering the collar, here's something she can hold. Madainn admitted that this would augment her magic. This could let her defend Dianthus against anything.

She casts her power through every divot and every piece of dust. Every vein of old, dried, mystical wine, every fingerprint from mystical hands.

She dreams of it being repaired. She dreams of pulling secrets together with metal and glass, building a thousand little hearts in Dianthus, first to protect herself, then to make a palace that will survive anything in its new world.

New world echoes in her mind, and it sounds like the tiniest plea.

Protect this one, she pushes back. *Let me protect this one.*

Rho opens her eyes. The fragments are in one piece, curving in her hand like a long, flat fang. Now it hums. Now there's something in it that feels vicious, wrong.

The sea roars.

Beyond the Dawn Hall, the froth turns bright white and thick, wrapped around the shoreline like the gauzy silk of her dress in the other world. The rest of the water's black.

Sigyn tries to pull a shockingly pale Eirjatal back, his grip still smothering against his bare skin—Rhoheme doesn't have the time for this. She gets up and closes her hand over the metal arm she once made for him. Similar to like she said to Madainn, she snaps, "Let him go."

Sigyn regards her, impassive.

If everyone's going to be threatening each other, she can join in. After giving him another second to reconsider, she digs her magic through the arm and crushes it. The heart of it twists and stalls. If there's anything living in him at all, he'll feel it.

He doesn't flinch or wince. He just releases Eirjatal in a slow, considering way, like she's a whining child demanding him for something inconsequential. She pulls Eirjatal a step away, fighting a shudder. What happened to him?

"Listen," she says to Eirjatal. "We always knew this would happen. We started this. I'll try to make the most of every advantage. And I'll look out for you."

He hugs her. Through the back of her thin shirt, his hands are cold, somehow worse than his usual anxious heat. "I'm sorry," he whispers, "I kept them from you."

"No one needed to see me like this anyways," she says with a shallow laugh, pulling back and showing off the strange, uncomfortable stabs of gold in her arms.

Vyriseh interrupts, "Rhoheme. This will augment both of our power enough that we can defend the island."

"Until what?"

"Until I make it known to Madainn that this Chalice piece has an owner, and it is the Nelaeryn Fey." She presses her mouth into a firm line. "I know the rules. They cannot steal the pieces from each other. A claim is a claim is a claim."

"And what about the kid?"

Vyriseh lifts an eyebrow. "I'm tired of bloodshed. I don't care."

The water has flooded what they can see of the beach.

"Screw that," Irving hisses and steers for the door with a passing, conflicted look at what remains of the priestess. They're stopped by Rhoheme grabbing their arm.

"Where will you run?"

"I'm not a part of this anymore." They yank away. "I'm not here for the Fey. I'm—"

Eirjatal notices before Rhoheme does. He tugs both Irving and Rhoheme into the back wall—the latticed window they were near is suddenly filled with a black, writhing shape. Long, scaled claws grab the metal, the creature holding itself like an insect against the tower. Rhoheme can't make sense of its shape before Eirjatal has hit it with a jet of flame so powerful that its claws leaves deep scars in the heat-softened metal.

Metal.

Rhoheme rushes for the still-hot wall and presses her hands to it. Instantly, the lattice melts and closes the opening.

Vyriseh catches her attention with a sharp call of her name. She unlatches a violin case and, taking out the ebony instrument, she says, "Let's begin."

Rho joins the queen on the balcony. Beneath them, the grounds flood fast with frothy water, creatures roiling inside. They climb the walls of the gardens and scurry across the beach. Most look like insects from dark tide pools.

Vyriseh has the Chalice in her palm, and, showing an intense amount of faith, she hands it to Rho. Of course if Rho tries to discard the thing, she may as well throw herself off the tower too and save Madainn the trouble.

The sound of Vyriseh playing her violin shivers across Rho's bones, imbued with a spell from the very first note. The Chalice shudders too until, scale by scale, it glows, a silvery film covering it like the dead priestess's hands.

It hovers above Rho's palm. And the music quickens, expands, into a full song that fills Rho from her toes to the tips of her horns. It bends the air like ripples in water.

Vyriseh gets her first piece of resistance from a giant eel-like monster swimming hard against the new wall, and she staggers.

It's as if Rho's in Madainn's underwater half-plane again, in that she can feel everything around her. Her mind whispers the scratch of claws on the walls she repaired, the sea consuming the sculptures she built. The creatures are closing in on their tower.

She flings out her magic. The structure lurches violently, forcing her to clutch the rail, and Irving calls, "Unconventional, but you got it!"

Vyriseh keeps playing madly, but everywhere that her slowly-expanding wall doesn't protect them, Rho bends the metal to her whim. Barriers. Cages. Crushing coils like a massive gold python protecting the base of their tower.

Irving's swearing, frantically and creatively, Etren things that tempt her to smirk. They move from one side of the tower to the other, calling out directions to Rho. Vyriseh's barrier expands over the island shores, turning the outside world into a haze.

The Chalice spreads her magic through the palace grounds, like it's blood and Rho's the heart. A twist of her wrist pulls the sculpted walls from the earth. A flick of her finger twists the lattice into a rabbit trap. She feels like Staventa, the world her forge.

But the monsters keep coming. They're heading right for Vyriseh and Rho, ploughing under and over and around the Dawn Hall and Vyriseh's barrier to get there. Rho spots a sea dragon like the dead one in Madainn's temple, twisting out of the water; it alights on the top of the sculpture of the Fey atop the Dawn Hall, claws digging into Her back as it presides over the flood.

There's sweat rolling down her back. And yet she's like a perfectly-wound clock, ticking to a time she was always meant to.

All the while, Vyriseh sheds her fingertips on the violin.

"The Heartswain gardens!" Irving yells. Rho swings her focus. A herd of great kelp-haired horses rear out of the water, and she catches a few through the chests when she brings down some labyrinth walls. The black water has swallowed up the garden of the red flowers.

"Eirjatal!" she calls.

He tears his gaze away from the water. She has never seen him so terrified. This isn't a dream she can help him out of. And if they don't do anything, they're all going to be caught in nightmares.

Eirjatal meets her at the balcony. "I can burn it all."

The red magic waves off the water like steam. It wraps around everything, like it's trying to drink fears from plants or the water itself—or the monsters, their silhouettes skittering and writhing.

Rho says, "The whole garden's underwater. Anything I do will only damage them further. I don't—"

"I can burn it," he insists. "I have to try. I don't want to see what terrifies a god."

Even after those words, he hesitates. He looks to the palace, the sea, to her. She reads it all over him—*I lost you once.* It's not like he's wrong; if this goes sideways, the Adder's not letting her come back again.

She says, "Bring them down with you if you have to. But bring them down."

Resolve sneaks onto his face. He goes, firing back only a certain, almost angry, "I love you."

She nods. He visibly inhales before stepping into the steep stairwell, like how he prepared himself before the river with the sirens. She watches him go for a moment too long.

Then Sigyn says, quiet and even and shockingly cool, "Madainn is here."

They don't get the chance to react. Rho watches the sea rise, then split, over that immense frilled head.

Vyriseh grits her teeth. "Keep him from us. All you can."

Rho takes a huge breath. He's closer to the Dawn Hall than he is to the tower. What in the Dawn Hall can she pull apart? She casts herself through the metal—Madainn's torso rises from the water—the walls of the Dawn Hall's lower floors break open like a lotus, turning the lower level into a collar of thorns, forcing him back. His hands splay across the beach and crush the forests. But he's behind Vyriseh's wall. If she can close it completely, finish the spell, then maybe...

She wants the Dawn Hall to move. The walls, the clockwork, the stairs, the elevators, all of it.

Madainn rolls his shoulders like he's waking after a very long sleep.

Around his throat is the gold collar she built.

She flings out her magic to that, to choke him, to drag him back where he came from, anything—

All the magic is sucked out of her like she's punctured a lung. She drops to a knee, scuffing her hands on the sandy tower. Vyriseh collapses and so does her barrier with a roar like thunder. The violin skids and nearly spins off the tower before Rho narrowly catches it.

Sigyn lifts his hands from Rho and Vyriseh's shoulders. He steps between them and towards Madainn.

The Chalice is only faintly glowing as Sigyn blindly steps over it. Vyriseh slaps a weak hand on it, but doesn't have the strength to do more than pull it to herself as she tries to sit up. Irving runs to the balcony doors, then freezes.

Again, Rho reaches for that collar. But there's no whisper of that perfect connection she had with it in the other world.

Madainn's glare is bright and alive and taking up the whole world. "So you've finally decided to show yourself, Nelaeryn Fey."

51

Irving

…here in Etreal, I feel drawn to these stories…so drawn that I wonder if they are the Fey's, calling me home…

Sunmirren Nia's evocation

Seeing Sigyn now, framed by the massive spectre that is Madainn, Irving understands a little more of what Vyriseh saw in him. No wonder it made his own mortality difficult to remember.

Madainn says, "Here you are, still a parasite after all. Karadenza's our villain, not yours, especially not if you're going to be cheating in that form."

"We are in agreement, then," Sigyn says softly. "Whatever happens, however I am involved, we play against Karadenza in the end."

Madainn grins, the effect unnerving at such a scale. Even from so far away, he still towers over the Dawn Hall. He's made of water and light and stone, colours shifting in his skin like how light plays on the ocean floor. "Oh, don't get grandiose. Right now it's just you and me, and I'd advise you to not make another move, alright?"

Irving is behind Rhoheme and Vyriseh, so they see them get their bearings back from Sigyn choking out their power. Rhoheme pushes herself up to sitting and Vyriseh clutches the Chalice piece to her chest. She's glowering at Sigyn, teeth bared.

Vyriseh heaves a breath and right as Irving realizes she's about to sing, her sapphire necklace twists and tightens, choking her. The surprise forces her to drop the Chalice fragment to the tower floor.

Rhoheme throws Irving a look, her casting hand extended and shaking, and they don't need an order. They lunge for the Chalice. The momentum carries them past the females until their back smacks into Sigyn's. The piece digs into their palm. Before, it felt like pottery, like something easy to not believe in. Now, they feel Sigyn and Madainn's attentions shift onto them like a cannon changing targets.

Rhoheme hisses, "They'll never accept you claiming it for the Fey, Vyriseh. You'll mark yourself for dead as they try to get it back." Her magic finally falters, leaving Vyriseh gasping for breath. She addresses Irving. "They'll only accept the claim of someone who's theirs."

"The Adder resurrected you—"

"I was resurrected by you and the priestess. I wasn't born under the Woven."

They hate the taste of the words. "I was."

Their skin crawls. Johana's skeleton seems to shift in the wavering dark and Marie is rot and moss on the floor. Their hands are covered in blood. The space beneath their missing rib stabs at them, the dregs of whatever happened to the Heartswain curling over the edge of the tower, reminding them of all the magic in the world ruining them from the inside and begging for another chance.

Sigyn catches Irving's upper arm, turning them to him. Sigyn or Relyn or—does it even matter? Sigyn and the Fey have always been the same, always at the same distance, and now closer to Irving than ever.

I think I am going to ruin something and I cannot have either of you suffer for it.

If they claim the piece, they'll be giving up the Fey, turning themselves into an agent in a game she's losing. A game she was born to lose anyways.

But they can't give up on Sigyn and let him do this to himself. They aren't letting him be taken away again.

Irving backs up a step, pulling out of his touch. They don't even need to speak to give in. They know and so do the Woven.

A shadow steps between Vyriseh pulling herself up with fury in her eyes and Sigyn's attempt, again, to snatch them and the way he says, sharp and desperate, "*Irving.*" The Blind Adder takes her place between Irving and the rest of the world.

The Blind Adder smiles first at them, then at the rush of water they can hear coming. "You name yourself as my game piece?"

"I do," they say, and the Fey feels more distant than ever.

They feel ridiculously small between the goddess that saved their life, the god who felled a kingdom, and their father, claiming to be a part of them.

The Adder takes the piece from their hand. She announces, voice not rising above a conversational tone, "Thank you for a fortuitous start, Madainn. I think your work here is done."

Madainn snarls, the sound shivering through the tower and rattling against their heart. "Cypress still wasted my time. That won't be solved by a half-breed becoming your pet."

The Blind Adder sighs. "You've lost this round, Madainn. I'm willing to keep your involvement quiet if you are, and willing to sabotage it all if you're not. We wouldn't want Karadenza to stop us before we've really gotten started. Would we?"

Madainn still looks furious, but Irving feels the air shift as he backs down.

The Adder inclines her head pleasantly to Sigyn. "I personally believe the more, the merrier. I hope to see you at the table again soon."

52

Eirjatal

…I stole from the Woven, and they have never stopped stealing from me…

Sunmirren Scintia's evocation

The instant he steps into the thigh-deep water, Eirjatal knows the Heartswain has found him.

The chaos around him is real—he burns down and suffocates water-logged creatures when he can—and the water dragging his steps is real and the magic razing through him is real. Still, he's well-versed in the flirtations of unreality when it tries to pull him in.

Red snowdrifts whip past his bare skin, that illusory cold still biting. He keeps his chin up to ignore the fragmented bodies strewn around him.

During the worst of the Ineiren, the storms had closed off the sky, turning the white landscape into steel and shale and casting the inside of the Fort in grimy shadow. They called the last night the Ineiren Dusk, because it never fell into full black, never dared to promise that this was the worst it would get and eventually there would be a dawn. He'd pressed his back to the wall and waited, caught between fighting to the last breath and simply spending a last moment in the quiet with himself before he lost him.

Now, half his steps are against rising water, and the others are against the snow of the Fort.

Heartswain, he repeats. It's all a spell. It's all a dream conjured by old magic from Relyn. Not so long ago, it conjured Rho in the street, gone when he shut his eyes, and this is just as simple, just as frail.

Find the Heartswain gardens, he reminds himself. *Don't wonder what a god fears. It's not so different than what you fear.*

The cold takes him over, sealing his limbs and choking the magic in his veins.

He can't die here again.

Fire won't ignite in his hands. His teeth are chattering. Above him, the Fort streams into the sky, impossibly high. The illusion shouldn't be a tower. It should be Madainn turning on him.

Unless his nightmare is dying here. Dying without a second chance, or that second chance that She gave him coming to nothing.

Wake up.

You cannot stop a god. But you can stop this.

He feels snow on his cheeks.

There's no water, he realizes. The tower walls force the sea away to make space for themselves.

It's only made of Heartswain and still the stone is so real against his fingers. It's freezing and glass-smooth with ice the way he remembers it.

Another step; the walls fall, reform, letting in one wave of freezing water but blocking out the next before the scrabbling creatures can follow.

He keeps moving. Even if everything is hazy, he knows this damn castle, this damn city, better than anything. Maybe he knows it even better than the memory.

With every step, the red walls wash up, break, tumble forth with him. They grow tighter, higher until he can't see the sky at all.

A male, limned in red, turns to him in the mayhem. Ashvaren, eyes alight, teeth bared with a delighted grimace.

The walls barrel through him and break him apart into smoke.

His mother, a pyre—destroyed into embers.

Corsair's blood on his hands—only freezing water.

Tundras of dead—they sink back into the dark.

Red appears under his feet. The Heartswain is soaked with the acrid water Madainn's pushed into Dianthus. His tower gives them another gasp of clean air. Unfortunately, they're already rotting, curling up and blackening before his very eyes, as much in a panic as his heart beneath the layers and layers of ice and cold.

A shadow falls over them. Madainn is closer than he expected. The tower walls blocked him out the entire time, and now Eirjatal is entranced.

It's the first time it feels as if he's seen Madainn, and Madainn cannot look back.

He doesn't fly into a million pieces. He feels as blind and bolstered as he did walking into that river with Rho, knowing the inevitable could never be as bad as his anticipation. That knowledge is built into the walls, into the cold, and suddenly the Heartswain isn't very frightening at all.

After what may be moments of watching Madainn or may be an eternity, the walls break down enough to let him see through them. The world is filled with red. Monsters and mayhem, yes, but more than that, this rising flood, this endless suffocation, unending and unspecific. A fear lives in the ground of the island, expecting to suffocate alone with no one to save it.

He knows how the Fort ends. This time it will fall with him inside, and the Heartswain twists inside him until that seems like a mercy.

Eirjatal, wake up.

Warm across his face, like the sun breaking across the snow. There was so little sun there.

He opens his eyes.

Rho's in front of him, her hands on his chest.

"You're home in Dianthus," she whispers. "Come back."

Awareness slides in. The world is his again and he's in the middle of the drowned Heartswain gardens, Rho with him, Dianthus under threat from its own scars. And under threat from this moment of his pain too, that feels both so small compared to it all and also feels like everything he's made of.

He lets go of his magic like a long-held breath. Fire ploughs against the walls of the tower. It shines through the cloak of suffocating red, bright as sunlight, and within the borders of the tower that hold back the water, it burns the garden to ash.

The tower breaks away, not into red shadows and smoke, but into gravel and dust. The water washes back into the sea.

Rho wraps her arms around him. He feels her breathing hitch against his chest.

The garden, the labyrinth around it—everywhere he can see is burnt to black, gone.

They can try again, he knows with sudden clarity.

They will try again, and again, and again, for this island, for Cypress, for the Fey, wherever She is. They will always regrow.

53

Rhoheme

Write me whenever you can get around Ashvaren. I'll come if you need me. I'll come at any instant, for anything, for everything.

Eirjatal to Rhoheme, recording bird, undated

Three days later

Rhoheme must be the last person Irving expected to see at their bedroom door. They even look scared before the confusion takes over.

"Can we talk?"

"I guess."

Rhoheme shuts the door behind her. She's wrapped up in a sweater to keep out Heatherwol's brisk wind, and Irving has the manners her Dianthus cohorts don't. They don't look at her scars that poke out the collar.

Irving's been packing. They fight with the clasps on an embroidered leather trunk, more likely because the trunk is old, not because it's overstuffed. From the way they move it, it seems pretty empty.

Cereus knows Irving was in the thick of everything. Evocations, thefts, whatever. But Sigyn demanded no recourse. Whatever Sigyn says, goes, but Cereus, Rho sensed, was already tired of blood on his sand.

Rhoheme asks, "Has Vyriseh spoken to you?"

She's been asking everyone that. Cereus, Irving multiple times already, Tavreah, Adamantine, fuck propriety.

"Nope. My mind's totally intact. I've been locking myself up here. I don't want to run into anybody, you know?"

Rhoheme folds her arms. This is the bedroom of a much younger person who was wary of putting down roots. Should she know this kid better? "Thank you. For saving me."

Irving leans a knee on the trunk to get another clasp shut. "I didn't have much of a choice."

"Yes, you did. You could have left me at any point. *Thank you*." She scuffs the floor with her shoe. She can't think of an appropriate transition, so she jumps right in. "When I was in that other...when I was gone, I was with the Blind Adder."

"Playing cards, I gathered."

She reaches into her pocket and hands them two cards. "I realized after that whole mess that I came back with these. Weird, huh? They're *The Dream* and *The Nightmare*."

Irving takes them, screwing up their mouth. "I don't even know what this game is."

"I bet they'll change into something you recognize. You never know." She stuffs her hands into the back pockets of her trousers. "If the priestess didn't step in...that hand would have killed you."

Irving gives her a little hapless smile as they slot the cards into an open corner of their trunk. They're such a…such a kid. She can't stand it all of a sudden.

Rho turns for the door, but she's halted in her tracks by them saying, "I don't know what to do." There's a brittle quality in their voice, like she's the first and last person they'll admit that to.

"Neither do I. Still, if we have to play, then this puts us on opposite sides, you realize? So be careful." She adds with a shrug, slipping out the door, "If you don't win, I will. Think hard about which is the better option."

Rho doesn't know how long she's been on the balcony, staring at this Relyn statue half-melted into slag, but she knows it sure isn't making her feel any better.

From the top of the ladder, she fiddles with her goggles, sliding the glass panels in and out of place as if one of them will zoom in close enough for her to see what she's missing. She already knows.

She thought it was a fluke when she could barely recover after Sigyn cut her powers off. When she twisted Vyriseh's necklace, everything seemed fixed. And yet, now…

She presses her fingers into Relyn's face and tries to sculpt it back the way it was. It bends. No more easily or more significantly than she's seen Tavreah do to necklace clasps she's forcing.

Someone knocks on the balcony doorframe. Eirjatal gives her half a wave.

"Yeah, come in."

He holds the ladder frame, as if he's trying to help her, as if she's even *doing* something. "Seems as if no one's been leaving you alone."

"What, did someone say I'm cranky?"

"No. They're only reporting back to me like I'm your keeper."

"Funny. Everyone's reporting back to me about *you*."

"Is there any room for me up there?"

Rho scoots aside on the top rung of the ladder. Eirjatal climbs up. It's not the roomiest, but they've managed worse.

"No one's expecting you to fix this," he says, gesturing at the statue.

"I want to."

"But you're not."

Rho wraps her arm around the handrail and flicks a few more glass lenses in front of her goggles. She's seeing a whole lot of nothing, besides more burns, more scratches on the poor thing. Can she not even see what she used to see? Feel what she used to feel?

What if it never comes back?

Eirjatal says softly, "I brought a new assortment of nightmares and you brought a five-hundred-pound statue carved into pieces."

She shrugs. Even if she doesn't think she can manage words right now, there's something about his presence that inspires her, like it'd be a waste if she doesn't say anything at all. "Everything feels so weird. Heavy. I can always feel my heartbeat in my ears and everything's so solid and in the way… I don't know. Everything's off."

"Is your magic off, too?"

She narrows her eyes at him over her shoulder. Whether he can see her expression behind the goggles or not, he gives her a little smile. "We've been through enough shit. I know."

"It'll be back. I'm just…tapped, I think."

He nods, massaging his hands between his knees. He looks off the balcony, taking in that orange and yellow and red city beneath them. Heatherwol's low and dense, all brick and stone that cuts the constant wind, though you're lucky if you can manage a stroll without getting a ton of leaves stuck in your hair. Stone's never been what she liked to work with, so the echoing absence doesn't seem so…echoey out there.

Eirjatal says suddenly, "We're not on opposite sides in this, Rho."

Oh, this. Rho counts busted rivets where Relyn's chest meets Her neckline. Who made this? Hammering it all together like ship parts… "You and Vyriseh, huh?"

"It's hardly me and Vyriseh. It's me, Vyriseh, Cereus, Sigyn, Adamantine—"

"Persuaded under duress—"

"—and the future."

She sits up, budging him over a little in their tight squeeze on the ladder rung. "What future? You're setting us up to repeat your own past."

"Rho, what do you want to do, then? Right now." He's sharp, but not angry; they know exactly how to rile each other up and if they both go in, guns blazing, they'll overstep the line. He's clearly decided she'll be the angry one and he'll be the pragmatist in this discussion. "Would you like to give summoning a god a try again? You can't ask them to put everything down and give up. It's already started. It started before Vyriseh and Sigyn."

His expression softens enough that she reflexively swallows her argument. "If we want this done, we help Vyriseh finish this as quickly as possible. The only way out is through, Rho."

Rho pushes up her goggles. He helps her when they catch in her hair and settles them on the roots of her horns. He's filled in with colour and detail. She wonders if the problem's that she's unable to match his total faith in the Fey—or his total lack of it.

"I might have to learn to trust you again," she says.

"Deserved, I'd say."

She touches his shoulder. With the goggles off, she can spot thin, delicate tracks of half-healed burns. "What's this from?"

"You," he says, and exhales a humourless laugh. He shows her more on his other arm, even under his hair on his neck.

"What? When?"

"You don't know?" She shakes her head. "When the Iron Phoenix attacked. The Dawn Hall practically came alive."

She's folded into it, it's folded into her.

"I hurt you?"

"You saved me."

54

Irving

Staventa priestesses are alerting citizens that communication from the divine has greatly increased in hostility. Remain on the alert for notice of evacuation, lockdown, or restrictions on air or land travel.

Staventene announcement, Age of Shields 250

The next day, Irving's at a train station. A real one in Etreal, not a portal—the air smells like acrid steam and metal, and they're back to their usual habit of hiding their ears under their blonde hair and a pageboy cap.

Plus a scarf. It's chilly in Sirren even if it's summer. In Heatherwol, Irving found a little carving of a dog made of wood from their mother's hometown, a childhood gift. So at this station they bought a real train ticket to Staventene and are now waiting with dozens of humans.

They feel more dangerous than they ever have in their life, like out of nowhere, a god will pop out and make a move against them, or worse, ask *them* to make a move.

Breathing into their scarf is fogging up their glasses, so they contend with the chill wind on their chin and mouth instead.

Sigyn let them leave Heatherwol. Sigyn, *actual* Sigyn from the start of Lightbringing, told them to look out for Penelope.

How can they?

They want their choice to be unmade and they want the Fey's acceptance and they want their father back. They want it with the selfish anger of a kid, and with the hopeless, regretful ache of an adult. Like all they can do is want and want for things they'll never have, and they still think there's a chance if they apologize enough.

The train pulls up, gusting hot steam into Irving's face. They keep their head down as they slip into the line, handing off their trunk to the station master, and smiling like they've been given a compliment when the man notes how the design on the Cypress trunk looks extremely old...and extremely expensive. *Cypress palace brat. I'm a fairy tale here, twice over.*

How's Noah handling this? Humans feel, as Leila's explained, like Irving is impossible, a thing out the corner of their eye that they think, over and over, they didn't see right the first time.

Irving's perspective is as skewed as when they first moved to Etreal. Humans are jerky, bizarre. They're clumsy and scattered. They smell so powerfully like their acrid emotions—Irving forgot they could sense that when in a whole pack of them.

They slide into a booth and lock the door. They pile their coat and luggage on the opposite seat instead of the racks overhead so it looks to anyone who glances at the frosted glass that the booth is full. Over the crackly loudspeaker, the conductor assures the passengers that the serving and service automatons are from Staventene, though their models are a little older.

Irving pulls a paperback from their luggage. And a white snake crawls out too.

Irving leaps back. Marie slides onto the seat, tasting the air, black dart on her white forehead and everything.

The Blind Adder is suddenly sitting across from them. She's wearing a smart black and white suit, starched and stiff right up to her chin.

She says, "I understand that you don't want to be the hero."

"Or the villain," they snap back. They're fixed on Marie, the safer of the two ridiculous things. She's even casting a shadow on the seats and reflected in the frosted glass partition. She slithers onto the Adder's lap and accepts her pets like a smug cat.

"You want to save people, but not save everyone."

"Why are you a part of this? You're not like Madainn." They know they sound a little petulant. "I didn't think you were one to piss off Karadenza."

"I don't want to win or lose. It's not in my nature. I only want to play." She studies them, so perfectly still, not even jostled by the rumbling train. "We can keep this all quiet."

"That whole thing at the Dawn Hall was not quiet."

She reaches into her suit jacket and pulls out an envelope. She hands it over like she's popped in for a chat about her new business in radio and moving pictures.

Inside the envelope is an airship ticket to Ventaris. There's a date (a few days away) printed on the face.

"Recover what you need in Staventene. Then find Temeraire Pryce in Ventaris, and she will help you begin your search."

On the envelope is an address they can't parse. *Temeraire Pryce* is written beneath, like she's very concerned Irving will forget the bizarre name given to them by a literal goddess.

The Blind Adder eases Marie onto the seat. The snake curls up in the warm, secretive mass of Irving's coat and luggage. When the goddess has gotten up and rested one of her floating sets of hands on the door, she says, "Find help. I believe you have some say with the House of Ciphers?"

The hand she uses to unlatch the door is their own. She slips out, taking care not to bump the frame or the door.

Irving studies the note. They fold it back up and bite the inside of their cheek. They scoff. Well, if they wanted an in with the Ciphers again, this is it.

They lean across the booth. Marie lets them pet her. The dart still glistens on her forehead, indicating that whatever magic Johana left behind, it's still inside her.

Irving asks, "Do you want to come with?"

Epilogue
Madainn

The god of oceans and monsters of the depths heaves his exhausted body onto the beach, coughing up seawater.

That's new. There've been many new things these days. Drowning, being cheated by the Adder, getting a rare glimpse of the Nelaeryn Fey shining through that mortal body. Worst of all was Karadenza not bothering to ask Madainn's side of the story once the Adder scurried to her skirts.

Insults screw up between his teeth, but none are venomous enough. He slams a hand into the sand for some catharsis. Not even that kicks up a satisfying-enough wave.

What did that silver-tongue Adder tell Karadenza? How did she even *find* Karadenza? If she's lured her permanently back to this galaxy...

Madainn drags himself to his feet. He looks at his grimy hands. One of the rocks he scrabbled on in his journey here sliced his palm, and red blood trickles through the sand. He sits in these grievances, enjoying the sour taste of their pettiness, because the anger beneath it all is poison even in his own mouth.

Maybe he's not mortal, but he's able to bleed.

Maybe he's not mortal, but he feels too much like one.

Maybe he's not mortal, but the Adder thought she could trick him like one.

And maybe he's not mortal, but—

He wraps a hand around his throat.

He's still got that damn *collar*.

She's somewhere, that elf who locked him in it. Only she can get him out—that's usually how these things work. When he reworks his sealing spells, he's tying that clause in the riddles.

Madainn heads up the beach, circling the lighthouse that bears down on him. He doesn't want Eojhest's irritating pity, so he rolls his eyes when he feels the pressure of a god peeling itself out of that tower.

Yet it's the Iron Phoenix who alights before him. She's peering at the collar, grinning mouth full of white light. The lighthouse has gone dark.

"How are things, love?" she lilts.

"Been better."

"You bleed now!"

"No matter." Everyone will be too pleased if he reveals his annoyance.

"Well, chin up! What's next?"

He can't keep his hand off the collar, palm gritty with bloody sand against the metal. No sense being angry. No sense glowering. He straightens up. "You know, the Adder had a point. What better way to get a new start on this than with allies?"

The Phoenix flutters into a fireball, darting around him as he scales the beach.

"The Adder thinks she's put the elf and I out of play." The collar presses against his throat as he talks. What gills he has left gasp beneath it; at least he's been afforded a mortal's lungs. "Lucky we didn't kill her. I need that tinkerer one last time."

DEEP ROOTS

Acknowledgements

Here are all the magical forces that supported me in writing this book and the challenge writing became in the last few years:

Lydia and Jals, undeniably two dedicated and celebrated acolytes of the Mythmaker. You both welcomed me into the world of indie publishing and are such positive forces with your unwavering work ethic, endless enthusiasm, and inspiring creative passion.

My beta readers, who must have Staventa as their patron because of how they helped me hone my craft: Ros, Mercy, Kelsey, Meg, Stormy, Mirina, (Lydia and Jals again), and everyone else who lent a hand. Forging a story can be hard, grueling work, so thank you to Ros, Chelsea, and the rest of the Discord pals for making all these long editing and writing sessions much less lonely.

Steph, Fer, and Nadine are definitely followers of Pique, helping my creative endeavours grow from a silly little sprout to a weed-filled garden to whatever this is. Thank you for creating with me. It was perfect, unabashed, joyful, and so fantastically amateur.

There were times where I felt like Karadenza, about to destroy Etreal and Cypress because they were being unruly and ticked me off. But thankfully I had Marielle, who must have a little blessing from all the members of the pantheon. After all, Karadenza and her creations would be nothing without them lending her their cleverness, support, and magic. I'd follow you from world to world to world.

Printed in the USA
CPSIA information can be obtained
at www.ICGtesting.com
LVHW091239100224
771442LV00002B/254